HAUNTINGS
ELLEN DATLOW, EDITOR
TACHYON • SAN FRANCISCO

ALSO EDITED BY ELLEN DATLOW

A Whisper of Blood

A Wolf at the Door (with Terri Windling)

After: Nineteen Stories of Apocalypse and Dystopia (with Terri Windling)

Alien Sex

Black Heart, Ivory Bones (with Terri Windling)

Black Swan, White Raven (with Terri Windling)

Black Thorn, White Rose (with Terri Windling)

Blood and Other Cravings

Blood Is Not Enough: 17 Stories of Vampirism

Darkness: Two Decades of Modern Horror

Digital Domains: A Decade of Science Fiction and Fantasy

Haunted Legends (with Nick Mamatas)

Inferno: New Tales of Terror and the Supernatural

Lethal Kisses

Little Deaths

Lovecraft Unbound

Naked City: Tales of Urban Fantasy

Nebula Awards Showcase 2009

Off Limits: Tales of Alien Sex

Omni Best Science Fiction: Volumes One through Three

Omni Books of Science Fiction: Volumes One through Seven

OmniVisions One and Two

Poe: 19 New Tales Inspired by Edgar Allan Poe

Ruby Slippers, Golden Tears (with Terri Windling)

Salon Fantastique: Fifteen Original Tales of Fantasy (with Terri Windling)

Silver Birch, Blood Moon (with Terri Windling)

Sirens and Other Daemon Lovers (with Terri Windling)

Snow White, Blood Red (with Terri Windling)

Supernatural Noir

Swan Sister (with Terri Windling)

Tails of Wonder and Imagination: Cat Stories

Teeth: Vampire Tales (with Terri Windling)

The Beastly Bride and Other Tales of the Animal People (with Terri Windling)

The Best Horror of the Year: Volumes One through Four

The Coyote Road: Trickster Tales (with Terri Windling)

The Dark: New Ghost Stories

The Del Rey Book of Science Fiction and Fantasy

The Faery Reel: Tales from the Twilight Realm (with Terri Windling)

The Green Man: Tales of the Mythic Forest (with Terri Windling)

Troll's Eye View: A Book of Villainous Tales (with Terri Windling)

Twists of the Tale

Vanishing Acts

The Year's Best Fantasy and Horror: Volumes One through Twenty-one (with Terri Windling, Gavin J. Grant, and Kelly Link)

Wild Justice (e-book of *Lethal Kisses*)

Hauntings

Pages 421–422 constitute an extension of this copyright page.

Interior and cover design by Elizabeth Story
Cover art "Voice of Shades" © 2010 by Valentina Brostean
Author photo by Gregory Frost

Tachyon Publications
1459 18th Street #139
San Francisco, CA 94107
(415) 285-5615
www.tachyonpublications.com
tachyon@tachyonpublications.com

Series Editor: Jacob Weisman
Project Editor: Jill Roberts

ISBN 13: 978-1-61696-088-9

Printed in the United States of America by Worzalla

First Edition: 2013

9 8 7 6 5 4 3 2 1

Hauntings

edited by ELLEN DATLOW

Contents

ACKNOWLEDGMENTS

Thanks to E. Michael Lewis, Jenny Blackford, Anna Tambour, Adam Golaski, and other friends on the web for their suggestions, whether I used them or not.

Thank you, Veronica Schanoes, for your gracious help with the introduction. And a big thank you to Jacob Weisman and Jill Roberts of Tachyon Publications.

Last but not least, in addition to thanking Stefan Dziemianowicz, whose library is vast and who supplied all the necessary photocopies, I would like to dedicate *Hauntings* to Stefan, and the library in his head.

Introduction

ELLEN DATLOW

Death and dying haunts us. We are obsessed with the question of what happens after death, whether we can leave a part of ourselves in this world, the only one we know well. This obsession is manifested in the popularity of ghosts and hauntings in fiction over the centuries from Homer, William Shakespeare, Oscar Wilde, Henry James, William Faulkner, and Edith Wharton, through Shirley Jackson and Robert Aickman, and up to contemporary writers such as Peter Straub, Joyce Carol Oates, David Morrell, Kelly Link, and the twenty other contributors to this volume. Despite the barrenness of death, the genre of the ghost story is fertile with possibility, blooming with life.

Ghosts are not like the other revenants that haunt our imaginations. Unlike zombies, vampires, and werewolves, the ghost can almost never be fought physically. They seek the society of the living, but not to consume us, like vampires and zombies, or to walk among us unsuspected, like werewolves, but to communicate with us, to bring the past into the present. Ghosts are persistent memories, refusing to let us forget the people and things that we had thought gone, the people and things whose loss had grieved us, and especially the people and things whose loss had brought us relief.

Ghosts haunt, and so do we—how many of us have "old haunts" we can remember with nostalgia and perhaps also a bit of distress? And of course that is because ghosts *are* us. Becoming a vampire, a zombie, a werewolf, these are all fates that are inflicted from something outside us, outside our own lives. But ghosts stay with us because of something in their own lives—a need for familiar comforts, a desire for revenge, a powerful love. The emotions that drive us also create ghosts.

While the desire for revenge is one of the most persistent motives for a haunting, it is perhaps love that is the most poignant, for the very notion of ghosts is one way of expressing the fantasy that those we love are not really dead, that we can still communicate with and care for them just as we did when they were alive, and that they can still care for us, as well. Ghosts in this anthology are parents hoping to protect their children, are witnesses or perpetrators of terrible events hoping to make up for their misdeeds.

As I put together this anthology, I noticed again and again how so many of the stories involve children. These come in several varieties: a memory of a childhood experience of trauma, a story of a dangerous or cruel child, or a story in which a terrible fate befalls a child. Why might this be? There are several possibilities. First of all, children are deeply vulnerable, and so often experience an intensity of emotion—particularly fear—that greater experience of life dulls. I have never experienced any terror as an adult that can compare to how I felt about entering the pitch-black room I shared with my already-sleeping sister. Dark is harmless...but dark *was* terrifying. Second, we in the first world live in a fortunate age our ancestors could scarcely dream of, one in which a parent can usually be sure that all of his or her children will live to grow up. Childhood mortality has metamorphosed from an ever-present fear to an almost unimaginable obscenity, and what is horror but the bringing to life the unimaginable? Finally we come to the dangerous child, the evil child, in this volume, the ghost child who has the power to reach across the division between living and dead and threaten those she or he has left behind. Perhaps this child is the manifestation of the creeping adult knowledge that given how helpless children so often are in this world, and how much cruelty is so often inflicted on them, the powerful child really is someone we should fear.

Hauntings reprints some of the most disturbing and chilling tales of ghosts and other hauntings published between 1983 and 2012. This is by no means a definitive survey of recent ghostly tales, but a sampling of different types of hauntings, and as I do with every theme I address, I've chosen stories that will broaden our understanding of what a haunting can be.

Eenie, Meenie, Ipsateenie

PAT CADIGAN

Pat Cadigan has twice won the Arthur C. Clarke Award, for her novels *Synners* and *Fools*, and been nominated many times for just about every other award. Although primarily known as a science fiction writer (and as one of the original cyberpunks), she also writes fantasy and horror, which can be found in her collections *Patterns*, *Dirty Work*, and *Home by the Sea*. The author of fifteen books, including two nonfiction and one young adult novel, she currently has two new novels in progress.

She lives in North London with her husband, the Original Chris Fowler, and her son Rob.

In the long, late summer afternoons in the alley behind the tenement where Milo Sinclair had lived, the pavement smelled baked and children's voices carried all over the neighborhood. The sky, cracked by TV aerials, was *blue*, the way it never is after you're nine years old and in the parking lot of La Conco D'Oro Restaurant the garlic-rich aroma of Sicilian cooking was always heavy in the air.

It had never been that way for the boy walking down the alley beside Milo. La Conco D'Oro didn't exist anymore; the cool, coral-tinted interior Milo had glimpsed when he'd been a kid now held a country-western bar, ludicrous in a small industrial New England town. He smiled down at the boy a little sadly. The boy grinned back. He was much smaller than Milo remembered being at the same age. He also remembered the world being bigger. The fence around Mr. Parillo's garden had been several inches higher than his head. He paused at the spot where the garden had been, picturing it in front of the brown and tan Parillo house where the irascible old gardener had been landlord to eleven other families. The Parillo house was worse than just gone—the city was erecting a smacking new apartment house on the spot. The new building was huge, its half-finished shell spreading over to the old parking lot where the bigger boys had sometimes played football. He looked at the new building with distaste. It had a nice clean brick facade and would probably hold a hundred families in plasterboard box rooms. Several yards back up the alley, his old tenement stood, empty now, awaiting the wrecking ball. No doubt another erstwhile hundred-family dwelling would rise there, too.

Beside Milo, the boy was fidgeting in an innocent, patient way. Some things never changed. Kids never held still, never had, never would. They'd always fumble in their pants pockets and shift their weight from one foot to the other, just the way the boy was doing. Milo gazed thoughtfully at the top of the white-blond head. His own sandy hair had darkened a good deal, though new grey was starting to lighten it again.

Carelessly, the boy kicked at a pebble. His sneaker laces flailed the air. "Hey," said Milo. "Your shoelaces came untied."

The boy was unconcerned. "Yeah, they always do."

"You could trip on 'em, knock your front teeth out. That wouldn't thrill your mom too much. Here." Milo crouched on one knee in front of the boy. "I'll tie 'em for you so they'll stay tied."

The boy put one sneaker forward obligingly, almost touching Milo's shoe. It was a white sneaker with a thick rubber toe. And Milo remembered again how it had been that last long late summer afternoon before he and his mother had moved away.

There in the alley behind Water Street, in Water St. Lane, when the sun hung low and the shadows stretched long, they had all put their feet in, making a dirty canvas rosette, Milo and Sammy and Stevie, Angie, Kathy, Flora and Bonnie, for Rhonda to count out. Rhonda always did the counting because she was the oldest. She tapped each foot with a strong index finger, chanting the formula that would determine who would be IT for a game of hide-'n-seek.

Eenie, meenie, ipsateenie
Goo, gah, gahgoleenie
Ahchee, pahchee, Liberace
Out goes Y-O-U!

Stevie pulled his foot back. He was thin like Milo but taller and freckled all over. Protestant. His mother was living with someone who wasn't his father. The Sicilian tongues wagged and wagged. Stevie didn't care. At least he didn't have an oddball name like Milo and he never had to get up for church on Sunday. His black high-top sneakers were P.F. Flyers for running faster and jumping higher.

Eenie, meenie, ipsateenie...

Nobody said anything while Rhonda chanted. When she counted you, you stayed counted and you kept quiet. Had Rhonda been the first to say *Let's play hide-'n-seek?* Milo didn't know. Suddenly all of them had been clamoring to play, all except him. He hated hide-'n-seek, especially just before dark, which was when they all wanted to play most. It was the only time for hide-'n-seek, Rhonda always said. It was more fun if it was getting dark. He hated it, but if you didn't play you might as well go home, and it was too early for that. Besides, the moving van was coming tomorrow. Aunt Syl would be driving him and his mother to the airport. He might not play anything again for months. But why did they have to play hide-'n-seek?

Out goes Y-O-U!

Kathy slid her foot out of the circle. She was never IT. She was Rhonda's sister, almost too young to play. She always cried if she lost a game. Everyone let her tag the goal so she wouldn't cry and go home to complain Rhonda's friends were picking on her, bringing the wrath of her mother down on them. Her mother would bust up the game. Milo wished she'd do that now, appear on the street drunk in her housedress and slippers, the way she did sometimes, and scream Rhonda and Kathy home. Then they'd have to play something else. He didn't like any of them when they were playing hide-'n-seek. Something happened to them when they were hiding, something not very nice. Just by hiding, they became *different*, in a way Milo could never understand or duplicate. All of them hid better than he could, so he always ended up being found last, which meant that he had to be IT. He had to go look for them, then; he was the hunter. But not really. Searching for them in all the dark places, the deep places where they crouched breathing like animals, waiting to jump out at him, he knew they were all the hunters and he was the prey. It was just another way for them to hunt him. And when he found them, when they exploded from their hiding places lunging at him, all pretense of his being the hunter dropped away and he ran, ran like hell and hoped it was fast enough, back to the goal to tag it ahead of them. Otherwise he'd have to be IT all over again and the things he found squatting under stairs and behind fences became a little worse than before, a little more powerful.

Out goes Y-O-U!

Sammy's sneaker scraped the pavement as he dragged it out of the circle. Sammy was plump around the edges, the baby fat he had carried all his life melting away. He wore Keds, at war with Stevie's P.F. Flyers to see who could *really* run faster and jump higher. Sammy could break your arm. Milo didn't want to have to look for him. He'd never be able to outrun Sammy. He stared at Rhonda's fuzzy brown head bent over their feet with the intentness of a jeweler counting diamonds. He tried to will her to count him out next. If he could just make it through one game without having to be IT, then it might be too late to play another. They would all have to go home when the streetlights came on. Tomorrow he would leave and never have to find any of them again.

Out goes Y-O-U!

Bonnie. Then Flora. They came and went together in white sneakers and blue Bermuda shorts, Bonnie the follower and Flora the leader. You could tell that right away by Flora's blue cat's-eye glasses. Bonnie was chubby, ate a lot of pasta, smelled like sauce. Flora was wiry from fighting with her five brothers. She was the one who was always saying you could hear Milo coming a mile away because of his housekeys. They were pinned inside his pocket on a Good Luck key chain from Pleasure Island, and they jingled when he ran. He put his hand down deep in his pocket and clutched the keys in his sweaty fist.

Out goes Y-O-Me!

Rhonda was safe. Now it was just Milo and Angie, like a duel between them with Rhonda's finger pulling the trigger. Angie's dark eyes stared out of her pointy little face. She was a thin girl, all sharp angles and sharp teeth. Her dark brown hair was caught up in a confident ponytail. If he were IT, she would be waiting for him more than any of the others, small but never frightened. Milo gripped his keys tighter. None of them were ever frightened. It wasn't fair.

Out goes Y-O-U!

Milo backed away, his breath exploding out of him in relief. Angie pushed her face against the wall of the tenement, closing her eyes and throwing her arms around her head to show she wasn't peeking. She began counting toward one hundred by fives, loud, so everyone could hear. You couldn't stop it now. Milo turned and fled, pounding down the alley until he caught up with Stevie and Sammy.

"Don't follow us!""Your keys are jingling!""Milo, you always get caught, bug off!" Stevie and Sammy ran faster, but he kept up with them all the way across the parking lot down to Middle Street, where they ducked into a narrow space between two buildings. Milo slipped past them so Stevie was closest to the outside. They stood with their backs to the wall like little urban guerrillas, listening to the tanky echoes of their panting.

"She coming?" Milo whispered after a minute.

"How the hell should we know, think we got X-ray vision?"

"Why'd you have to come with us, go hide by yourself, sissy-piss!"

Milo didn't move. If he stayed with them, maybe they wouldn't change into the nasty things. Maybe they'd just want to hurry back and tag the goal fast so they could get rid of him.

Far away Angie shouted, "Ready or not, here I come, last one found is IT!" Milo pressed himself hard against the wall, wishing he could melt into it like Casper the Friendly Ghost. They'd never find him if he could walk through walls. But he'd always be able to see them, no matter where they hid. They wouldn't make fun of him then. He wouldn't need his housekeys anymore, either, so they'd never know when he was coming up behind them. They'd be scared instead of him.

"My goal one-two-three!" Kathy's voice was loud and mocking. She'd just stuck near the goal again so she could tag it the minute Angie turned her back. Angie wouldn't care. She was looking for everyone else and saving Milo for last.

"She coming?" Milo asked again.

Sammy's eyes flickered under half-closed lids. Suddenly his hand clamped onto Milo's arm, yanking him around to Stevie, who shoved him out onto the sidewalk. Milo stumbled, doing a horrified little dance as he tried to scramble back into hiding. Sammy and Stevie blocked his way.

"Guess she isn't. Coming." Sammy smiled. Milo retreated, bumping into a car parked at the curb as they came out and walked past him. He followed, keeping a careful distance. They went up the street past the back of Mr. Parillo's to the yard behind the rented cottage with the grapevine. Sammy and Stevie stopped at the driveway. Milo waited behind them.

The sunlight was redder, hot over the cool wind springing up from the east. The day was dying. Sammy nodded. He and Stevie headed silently up the driveway to a set of cool stone steps by the side door of the cottage. The steps led to a skinny passage between the cottage and Bonnie's father's garage that opened at the alley directly across from the goal. They squatted at the foot of the steps, listening. Up ahead, two pairs of sneakers pattered on asphalt.

"My goal one-two-three!" "My goal one-two-three!" Flora and Bonnie together. Where was Angie? Sammy crawled halfway up the steps and peeked over the top.

"See her?" Milo asked.

Sammy reached down and hauled him up by his shirt collar, holding him so the top step jammed into his stomach.

"*You* see her, Milo? Huh? She there?" Sammy snickered as Milo struggled out of his grasp and slid down the steps, landing on Stevie, who pushed him away.

"Rhonda's goal one-two-three!" Angie's voice made Sammy duck down quickly.

"Shit!" Rhonda yelled.

"Don't swear! I'm tellin'!"

"Oh, shut up, you say it, too, who're you gonna tell anyway?"

"Your mother!"

"She says it, too, tattletale!"

"Swearer!"

Milo crept closer to Stevie again. If he could just avoid Angie till the streetlights came on, everything would be all right. "She still there?" he asked.

Stevie crawled up the steps and had a look. After a few seconds he beckoned to Sammy. "Let's go."

Sammy gave Stevie a few moments headstart and then followed.

Milo stood up. "Sammy?"

Sammy paused to turn, plant one of his Keds on Milo's chest, and shove. Milo jumped backward, lost his balance, and sat down hard in the dirt. Sammy grinned at him as though this were part of a prank they were playing on everyone else. When he was sure Milo wouldn't try to get up, he turned and went down the passage. Milo heard him and Stevie tag their goals together. He closed his eyes.

The air was becoming deeper, cooler, clearer. Sounds carried better now. Someone wished on the first star.

"That's an airplane, stupid!"

"Is not, it's the first star!"

And then Angie's voice, not sounding the least bit out of breath, as though she'd been waiting quietly for Milo to appear after Sammy. "Where's Milo?"

He sprang up and ran. Sammy would tell where they'd been hiding and she'd come right for him. He sprinted across Middle Street, cut between the nurse's house and the two-family place where the crazy man beat his wife every Thursday to Middle St. Lane. Then down to Fourth Street and up to the corner where it met Middle a block away from the Fifth Street bridge.

They were calling him. He could hear them shouting his name, trying to fool him into thinking the game was over, and he kept out of sight behind the house on the corner. Two boys went by on bikes, coasting leisurely. Milo waited until they were well up the street before dashing across to the unpaved parking area in front of the apartment house where the fattest woman in town sat on her porch and drank a quart of Coke straight from the bottle every afternoon. There was a garbage shed next to the house. The Board of Health had found rats there once, come up from the polluted river running under the bridge. Milo crouched behind the shed and looked cautiously up the alley.

They were running back and forth, looking, listening for the jingle of his keys. "He *was* back there with us!" "Spread out, we'll find him!" "Maybe he sneaked home." "Nah, he couldn't." "Everybody look for him!" They all scattered except for Kathy, bored and playing a lazy game of hopscotch under a streetlight that hadn't come on yet.

Impulsively Milo snatched open the door of the shed and squeezed in between two overflowing trash barrels. The door flapped shut by itself, closing him in with a ripe garbagey smell and the keening of flies. He stood very still, eyes clenched tightly, and his arms crossed over his chest. They'd never think he was in here. Not after the rats.

Thick footsteps approached and stopped. Milo felt the presence almost directly in front of the shed. Lighter steps came from another direction and there was the scrape of sand against rubber as someone turned around and around, searching.

"He's gotta be somewhere." Sammy. "I didn't think the little bastard could run *that* fast." Milo could sense the movement of Sammy's head disturb the air. The flies sang louder. "We'll get him. He's gonna be IT."

"Call 'olly, olly, out-free.'" Stevie.

"Nah. Then he won't have to be IT."

"Call it and then say we had our fingers crossed so it doesn't count."

"Let's look some more. If we still can't find him, then we'll call it."

"He's a sissy-piss."

They went away. When the footsteps faded, Milo came out cautiously, choking from the smell in the shed. He stood listening to the sound of the neighborhood growing quieter. Darkness flowed up from the east more quickly now, reaching for the zenith, eager to spill itself down into the west and blot out the last bit of sunlight. Above the houses a star sparkled and winked, brightening. Milo gazed up at it, wishing as hard as he could.

Star light, star bright
First star I see tonight
I wish I may, I wish I might
Have this wish...
Eenie, meenie, ipsateenie...
Don't let me be IT

He stood straining up at the star. Just this once. If he wouldn't have to be IT. If he could be safe. Just this once—

"Angie! Angie! Down here, quick!"

He whirled and found Flora pointing at him, jumping up and down as she shouted. *No!* he wanted to scream. But Flora kept yelling for Angie to hurry, *hurry,* she could still get him before the streetlights came on. He fled to Middle Street, across Fourth to the next block, going toward the playground. There was nowhere to hide there among the swings and seesaws, but there was an empty house next to it. Without much hope, Milo ran up the back steps and pushed at the door.

He found himself sprawling belly-down on the cracking kitchen linoleum. Blinking, he got to his feet. There was no furniture, no curtains in the windows. He tried to remember who had lived there last, the woman with the funny-looking dogs or the two queer guys? He went to one of the windows and then ducked back. Angie was coming down the sidewalk alone, smiling to herself. She passed the house, her ponytail bobbing along behind her. Milo tiptoed into the living room, keeping close to the wall. Shadows spread from the corners, unpenetrated by the last of the daylight coming through the windows and the three tiny panes over the front door.

He ran to the door and pulled at it desperately, yanking himself back and forth like a yo-yo going sideways.

"Milo?"

He clung to the door, holding his breath. He had left the back door open and she was in the kitchen. The floor groaned as she took one step and then another. "I know you're hiding in here, Milo." She laughed.

Behind him were stairs leading to the second floor. He moved to them silently and began to crawl upward, feeling years of grit in the carpet runner scraping his hands and knees.

"You're gonna be IT now, Milo." He heard her walk as far as the entrance to the living room and then stop.

Milo kept crawling. If the streetlights went on now, it wouldn't make any difference. You couldn't see them in here. But maybe she'd give up and go away, if he could stay in the dark where she couldn't see him. She had to see him, actually lay eyes on him, before she could run back and tag his goal.

"Come on, Milo. Come on out. I know you're here. We're not supposed to be in here. If you come out now, I'll race you to the goal. You might even win."

He knew he wouldn't. She'd have Sammy waiting for him, ready to tackle him and hold him down so Angie could get to the goal first. Sammy would tackle him and Stevie would sit on him while everyone else stood and laughed and laughed and laughed. Because then he'd have to be IT forever. No matter where he went, they'd always be hiding, waiting to jump out at him, forcing him to find them again and again and again and he'd never get away from them. Every time he turned a corner, one of them would be there yelling. *You're IT, you're IT!*

"What are you afraid of, Milo? Are you afraid of a girl? Milo's a fraidycat! 'Fraid of a girl, 'fraid of a girl!" She giggled. He realized she was in the middle of the living room now. All she had to do was look up to see him between the bars of the staircase railing. He put his hand on the top step and pulled himself up very slowly, praying the stairs wouldn't creak. His pants rubbed the dirty runner with a sandpapery sound.

"Wait till I tell everyone you're scared of a *girl*. And you'll still be IT, and everyone will know." Milo drew back into the deep shadows on the second-floor landing. He heard her move to the bottom of the stairs and put her foot on the first step. "No matter where you go, everyone will know," she singsonged. "No matter where you go, everyone will know. Milo's IT, Milo's IT."

He wrapped his arms around his knees, pulling himself into a tight ball. In his pocket the housekeys dug into the fold between his hip and thigh.

"You'll have to take your turn sometime, Milo. Even if you move away everyone will know you're IT. They'll all hide from you. No one will play with you. You'll always be IT. Always and always."

He dug in his heels and pushed himself around to the doorway of one of the bedrooms. Maybe she wouldn't be able to see him in the darkness and she'd go away. Then he could go home.

"I heard you. I heard you move. Now I know where you are. I'm gonna find you, Milo." She came up the last steps, groping in the murky shadows. He could just make out the shape of her head and her ponytail.

"Got you!" She sprang at him like a trap. "You're IT!"

"No!"

Milo kicked out. The darkness spun around him. For several seconds he felt her grabbing his arms and legs, trying to pull him out of hiding before her clutching hands fell away and her laughter was replaced by a series of thudding, crashing noises.

On hands and knees, panting like a dog, he crept to the edge of the top step and looked down. Angie's small form was just visible where it lay at the foot of the stairs. Her legs were still on the steps. The rest of her was spread on the floor with her head tilted at a questioning angle. Milo waited for her to get up crying, *You pushed me, I'm telling!* but she never moved. Slowly he went halfway down the stairs, clinging to the rickety bannister.

"Angie?"

She didn't answer. He descended the rest of the way, careful to avoid her legs in case she suddenly came to life and tried to kick him.

"Angie?"

He knelt beside her. Her eyes were open, staring through him at nothing. He waited for her to blink or twitch, but she remained perfectly still. Milo didn't touch her. *She'd have done it to me,* he thought. She would have, too. She'd have pushed him down the stairs to get to the goal first. After all, Sammy had kicked him off the other stairs so he couldn't touch goal with him and Stevie. Now they were even. Sort of. Sammy had been on her side, after all. Milo stood up. She wouldn't chase him anymore and she'd never touch his goal on him.

He found his way to the back door, remembering to close it as he left. For a few moments he stood in the yard, trying to find the star he had wished on. Others were beginning to come out now. But the streetlights—something must be wrong with them, he thought. The city had forgotten about them. Or maybe there was a power failure. He should have wished for them to come on. That would have sent everyone home.

While he stood there, the streetlights did come on, like eyes opening everywhere all over the neighborhood. Milo's shoulders slumped with relief. Now he really had won. Everyone had to go home now. The game was over. It was over and he wouldn't have to be IT.

He ran through the playground, across Water St. Lane and up Water, getting home just as the final pink glow in the west died.

"There." Milo finished tying a double bow in the boy's shoelaces. "Now they won't come undone."

The boy frowned at his feet critically. "How'm I gonna get 'em off?"

"Like this." Milo demonstrated for him. "See?" He retied the bow. "It's easy when you get the hang of it."

"Maybe I'll just leave 'em on when I go to bed."

"And when you take a bath, too?" Milo laughed. "Sneakers in the tub'll go over real well with your mom."

"I won't take baths. Just wipe off with a washcloth."

Milo restrained himself from looking behind the kid's ears. Instead, he stood up and began walking again. The boy stayed beside him, trying to whistle between his teeth and only making a rhythmic hissing noise. Milo could have sympathized. He'd never learned to whistle very well himself. Even today his whistle had more air than tune in it. Sammy had been a pretty good whistler. He'd even been able to whistle between his fingers like the bigger boys. Stevie hadn't been able to, but Sammy hadn't made fun of him the way he'd made fun of Milo.

Milo half-expected to see Sammy and Stevie as he and the boy approached the spot where the garbage shed had been. Now there was a modern dumpster there, but Milo imagined that the rats could get into that easily enough if any cared to leave the river. Aunt Syl had written his mother that environmentalists had forced the city to clean up the pollution, making it more livable for the rats under the bridge.

But the dumpster was big enough for someone Sammy's size to hide behind. Or in. Milo shook his head. Sammy's size? Sammy was all grown up now, just like he was. All of them were all grown up now. Except Angie. Angie was still the same age she'd been on that last day, he knew that for a fact. Because she'd never stopped chasing him.

It took her a long, long time to find him because he had broken the rule about leaving the neighborhood. You weren't supposed to leave the neighborhood to hide. You weren't supposed to go home, either, and he had done that, too.

But then he'd thought the game was really over. He'd thought it had ended at the bottom of the stairs in the vacant house with the daylight's going and the streetlights' coming on. Rhonda had been the last one found, the *only* one found, so she should have been IT, not Milo. The next game should have gone on without him. Without him and Angie, of course. He thought it had. All through the long, dull ride to the airport and the longer, duller flight from New England to the Midwest, through the settling in at the first of the new apartments and the settling down to passable if lackluster years in the new school, he thought the game had continued without him and Angie.

But the night came when he found himself back in that darkening empty house, halfway up the stairs to the second floor. He froze in the act of reaching for the next step, feeling the dirt and fear and approach of IT.

When the floor creaked, he screamed and woke himself up before he could hear the sound of her childish, taunting voice. He was flat on his back in bed, gripping the covers in a stranglehold. After a few moments he sat up and wiped his hands over his face.

The room was quiet and dark, much darker than the house had been that last day. He got up without turning on the light and went to the only window. This was the fourth apartment they'd had since coming to the Midwest, but they'd all been the same. Small, much smaller than the one in the tenement, done in plaster ticky-tacky with too few windows. Modern housing in old buildings remodeled for modern living with the woodwork painted white. At least the apartment was on the eighth floor. Milo preferred living high up. You could see everything from high up. Almost.

The street that ran past the building gleamed wetly under the streetlights. It had rained. He boosted the window up and knelt before the sill, listening to the moist sighing of occasional passing cars. A damp breeze puffed through the screen.

Across the street something moved just out of the bright circle the streetlight threw on the sidewalk.

When the streetlights came on, it was time to go home.

A stray dog. It was probably just a stray dog over there. In the distance, a police siren wailed and then cut off sharply. Milo's mouth was dry as he squinted through the screen. It was too late for kids to be out.

But if you didn't get home after the streetlights came on, did that mean you never had to go home ever?

The movement came again, but he still couldn't see it clearly. A shadow was skirting the patch of light on the pavement, dipping and weaving, but awkwardly, stiffly. It wanted to play, but there was no one awake to play with, except for Milo.

He spread his fingers on the windowsill and lowered his head. It was too late for kids to be out. Any kids. The streetlights—

Something flashed briefly in the light and then retreated into the darkness. Milo's sweaty fingers slipped on the sill. The game was over. He wasn't IT. He wasn't. She'd found him but she hadn't tagged his goal and all the streetlights had come on. The game was over, had been over for years. It wasn't fair.

The figure made another jerky movement. He didn't have to see it clearly now to know about the funny position of its head, its neck still crooked in that questioning angle, the lopsided but still confident bobbing of the ponytail, the dirty-white sneakers. Another police siren was howling through the streets a few blocks away, but it didn't quite cover up the sound of a little girl's voice, singing softly because it was so late.

Eenie, meenie, ipsateenie
Goo, Gah, gahgoleenie
Ahchee, pahchee, Liberace
Out goes Y-O-U!
Eenie, meenie, ipsateenie
Goo, gah, gahgoleenie...

He covered his ears against it, but he could still hear it mocking him. No one was being counted out, no one would ever be counted out again because he was IT and he had missed his turn.

Come out, Milo. Come out, come out, come out You're IT.

He pressed his hands tighter against his ears, but it only shut the sound of her voice up in his head and made it louder. Then he was clawing at the screen, yelling, "I'm not! I'm not! I'm not IT, the game's over and *I'm not IT!*"

His words hung in the air, spiraling down around him. There was a soft pounding on the wall behind the bed. "Milo!" came his mother's muffled, sleepy voice. "It's four in the morning, what are you screaming for?"

He sank down onto the floor, leaning his head hopelessly against the windowsill. "A, a dream, Mom," he said, his voice hoarse and thick in his tight throat. "Just a bad dream."

The wind poured through his hair, chilling the sweat that dripped down to his neck. Laughter came in with the wind, light, careless, jeering laughter. He knew Angie was looking up at his window, her sharp little teeth bared in a grin.

"'Fraid of a girl," the laughter said. "'Fraid of a girl..."

The boy was staring at Milo's pants pocket and Milo realized he'd been jingling his loose change without thinking as they walked. He thought about giving the kid a quarter, but his mother had probably warned him not to take candy or money from strangers. Most likely he wasn't even supposed to talk to strangers. But most kids were too curious not to. They were programmed to answer questions from adults anyway, so all you had to do was ask them something and pretty soon you were carrying on a regular conversation. As long as you didn't make the mistake of offering them any money or candy, the kids figured they were safe.

"Housekeys," Milo lied, jingling the change some more. "When I was your age, my mother pinned them inside my pocket and they jingled whenever I ran."

"How come she did that?"

"She worked. My father was dead. I had to let myself in and out when she wasn't home and she didn't want me to lose my keys."

The boy accepted that without comment. Absent fathers were more common now anyway. The boy probably knew a lot of kids who carried housekeys, if he wasn't carrying any himself.

"She pin 'em in there today?"

"What?" Milo blinked at him.

"Your housekeys." The boy grinned insolently.

Milo gave him half a smile. Some things never changed. Kids still thought a joke at someone else's expense was funny. He glanced down at the double bows he'd tied in the boy's laces. Yeah, he could picture one of those sneakers on some other kid's chest, kicking him off some steps. The boy looked more like Stevie than Sammy, but that didn't matter. Stevie would have done it if he'd had the chance. Milo was sure this boy would have been great friends with Angie.

They were past the dumpster, almost to the corner where Water St. Lane crossed Fourth. The house where the fattest woman in town had consumed her daily quart of Coke straight from the bottle was still inhabited. Somewhere inside, a radio was boasting that it had the hits, all the hits and nothing but the hits. Milo didn't think it would be long before this house stood as empty as his old tenement, condemned and waiting to fall. It wasn't about to collapse by itself. These old houses had been built to stay up, no matter how tired and shabby they became. Endurance, that was what it was. But anything could reach the end of its endurance eventually—a neighborhood, a building, a person. Neighborhoods and buildings had to be taken care of but people could take things into their own hands. You didn't have to endure something past the point when it should have ended. Not if you knew what to do.

Milo hadn't known what to do at first though. He found himself helpless again, as helpless as he'd been on those old stairs so many years ago. In the dream or wide-awake, crouched at his bedroom window while the little-girl thing that hadn't made it home before dark played on the sidewalk and called him, he was helpless. Angie didn't care that Rhonda should have been IT. Rhonda and the others had gone home after the streetlights had come on, but he and Angie hadn't. The game wasn't done even though it was just the two of them now.

Slowly he began to realize it was the other kids. One of the bigger boys with the bikes must have seen him climb into the car with his mother and Aunt Syl the next day and passed it on to another kid who passed it on to another kid in a long, long game of "Gossip" that stretched over hundreds and hundreds of miles, with Angie following, free to leave the neighborhood because he had, free to stay out late because she had never gone home. Angie, following him all the way to the Midwest to the new neighborhood, to the new apartment because of the new kids at the new school who had been happy to tell her where he was because everyone loved a good hunt. The new kids, they were all just Sammys and Stevies and Floras and Bonnies with different names and faces anyway. They all knew he was IT and had missed his turn. Even his mother knew something; she looked at him strangely sometimes when she thought he didn't know, and he could feel her waiting for him to tell her, explain. But he couldn't possibly. She had taken her turn a long time ago, just like all the adults, and when you took your turn, you forgot. She couldn't have understood if he had explained until the day he died.

So he'd held out for a long, long time and they moved to new apartments, but Angie always found him. Kids were everywhere and they always told on him. And then one day he looked at himself and found Milo staring out at him from a grown-up face, a new hiding place for the little boy with the same old fear. And he thought, *Okay; okay. We'll end it now, for you and for Angie.* He was big now, and he hadn't forgotten. He would help little Milo still helpless inside of him, still hiding from Angie.

He went back. Back to the old neighborhood, taking Angie up on her offer of a race to the goal at last.

Deep summer. The feel of it had hit him the moment he'd walked down to the alley from the bus stop at Third and Water, where most of the old buildings were still standing all the way down to St. Bernard's Church. In the alley, things had changed, but he wouldn't look until he had walked deliberately down to the tenement.

He knew then she must have won. He put his face close to the wall and closed his eyes. The smell of hot baked stone was there, three-quarters of a century of hot summer afternoons and children's faces pressed against the wall, leaving a faint scent of bubble gum and candy and kid sweat. The building had stood through the exodus of middle-class white families and the influx of poor white families and minorities and the onslaught of urban renewal, waiting for Angie to come back and touch it one more time, touch it and make him really and truly IT. And now he was here, too, Milo was here, but grown big and not very afraid anymore, now that it was done. If he had to be IT, if he had no choice—and he'd never had, really—he would be a real IT, the biggest, the scariest, and no one would know until it was too late.

Counting to one hundred by fives hadn't taken very long at all—not nearly as long as he had remembered. When he'd opened his eyes, he'd found the boy hanging around in front of the rented cottage.

"Hi," he'd said to the boy. "Know what I'm doing?"

"No, what?" the boy had asked.

"I'm looking for some friends." Milo had smiled. "I used to live here."

Now they stood at the end of the alley together and Milo smiled again to see that the house was still there. But then, he'd known that it would be. He walked slowly down Fourth to stand directly across the street from it, staring at the stubborn front door. It probably still wouldn't open. The red paint had long flaked away and been replaced by something colorless. What grass had surrounded the place had died off. Overhead the sky, almost as blue as it had been that day, was beginning to deepen. He listened for children's voices and the sound of the bigger boys' English bikes ticking by on the street. If he strained, he could almost hear them. It was awfully quiet today, but some days were like that, he remembered.

"Who lives there?" he asked the boy. "Who lives in that house now?"

"Nobody."

"Nobody? Nobody at all?"

"It's a dump." The boy bounced the heel of his right sneaker against the toe of his left. "I been in there," he added, with only a little bit of pride.

"Have you."

"Yeah. It's real stinky and dirty. Joey says it's haunted, but *I* never seen nothin'."

Milo pressed his index finger along his mouth, stifling the laugh that wanted to burst out of him. *Haunted? Of course it's haunted, you little monster—I've been haunting it myself!* "Must be fun to play in, huh?"

The boy looked up at him as though he were trying to decide whether he could trust Milo with that information. "Well, nobody's supposed to go in there anymore, but you can still get in."

Milo nodded. "I know. Say, did you ever play a game where you have to put your feet in and somebody counts everybody out and the last one left is IT?"

The boy shrugged. "Like 'eenie, meenie, miney, mo'?"

"Something like that. Only we used to say it differently. I'll show you." Milo knelt again, putting the toe of his shoe opposite the boy's sneaker, ignoring the boy's bored sigh. Oh, yes, he'd show the boy. It wouldn't be nearly as boring as the boy would think, either. The boy was a Stevie. That meant that pretty soon there'd be a Sammy coming along and then maybe a Flora and a Bonnie and all the rest of the ones who had helped look for him and who had told Angie where to find him. But he'd give all of them a better chance than they'd given him. He'd do the chant for them, the way he was doing now for the boy, starting with the boy's foot first.

Eenie, meenie, ipsateenie
Goo, gah, gahgoleenie
Ahchee, pahchee, Liberace
Out goes Y-O-U!

Milo grinned. "Looks like I'm IT." He stood up. Still IT, he should have said. They hadn't let him quit; they hadn't let him miss his turn. All right. He would take it now and keep taking it, because he was IT and it was his game now.

"C'mon," he said to the boy as he stepped off the curb to cross the street "Let's see if that old house is still fun to play in."

Hunger: A Confession

DALE BAILEY

Dale Bailey lives in North Carolina with has family, and has published three novels, *The Fallen, House of Bones,* and *Sleeping Policemen* (with Jack Slay, Jr.). His short fiction, collected in *The Resurrection Man's Legacy and Other Stories,* has won the International Horror Guild Award and has been twice nominated for the Nebula Award. His website and blog are at www.dalebailey.com.

Me, I was never afraid of the dark.

It was Jeremy who bothered me—Jeremy with his black rubber spiders in my lunchbox, Jeremy with his guttural demon whisper (*I'm coming to get you, Simon*) just as I was drifting off to sleep, Jeremy with his stupid Vincent Price laugh (*Mwah-ha-ha-ha-ha*), like some cheesy mad scientist, when he figured the joke had gone far enough. By the time I was walking, I was already shell-shocked, flinching every time I came around a corner.

I remember this time, I was five years old and I had fallen asleep on the sofa. I woke up to see Jeremy looming over me in this crazy Halloween mask he'd bought: horns and pebbled skin and a big leering grin, the works. Only I didn't realize it was Jeremy, not until he cut loose with that crazy laugh of his, and by then it was too late.

Things got worse when we left Starkville. The new house was smaller and we had to share a bedroom. That was fine with me. I was seven by then, and I had the kind of crazy love for my big brother that only little kids can feel. The thing was, when he wasn't tormenting me, Jeremy was a great brother—like this one time he got a Chuck Foreman card in a package of Topps and he just handed it over to me because he knew the Vikings were my favorite team that year.

The room thing was hard on Jeremy, though. He'd reached that stage of adolescence when your voice has these alarming cracks and you spend a lot of time locked in the bathroom tracking hair growth and...well, you know, you were a kid once, right? So the nights got worse. I couldn't even turn to Mom for help. She was sick at that time, and she had this frayed, wounded look. Plus, she and Dad were always talking in these strained whispers. You didn't want to bother either one of them if you could help it.

Which left me and Jeremy alone in our bedroom. It wasn't much to look at, just this high narrow room with twin beds and an old milk crate with a lamp on it. Out the window you could see one half-dead crab-apple tree—a crap-apple, Jeremy called it—and a hundred feet of crumbling pavement and a rusting 1974 El Camino which our neighbor had up on blocks back where the woods began. There weren't any street lights that close to the edge of town, so it was always dark in there at night.

That's when Jeremy would start up with some crap he'd seen in a movie or something. "I heard they found a whole shitload of bones when they dug the foundation of this house," he'd say, and he'd launch into some nutty tale about how it turned out to be an Indian burial ground, just crazy stuff like that. After a while, it would get so I could hardly breathe. Then Jeremy would unleash that crazy laugh of his. "C'mon, Si," he'd say, "you know I'm only kidding."

He was always sorry—genuinely sorry, you could tell by the look on his face—but it never made any difference the next night. It was like he forgot all about it. Besides, he always drifted off to sleep, leaving me alone in the dark to ponder open portals to Hell or parallel worlds or whatever crazy stuff he'd dreamed up that night.

The days weren't much better. The house was on this old winding road with woods on one side and there weren't but a few neighbors, and none of them had any kids. It was like somebody had set off a bomb that just flattened everybody under twenty—like one of those neutron bombs, only age-specific.

So that was my life—interminable days of boredom, torturous insomniac nights. It was the worst summer of my life, with nothing to look forward to but a brand-new school come the fall. That's why I found myself poking around in the basement about a week after we moved in. Nobody had bothered to unpack—nobody had bothered to do much of anything all summer—and I was hoping to find my old teddy bear in one of the boxes.

Mr. Fuzzy had seen better days—after six years of hard use, he *literally* had no hair, not a single solitary tuft—and I'd only recently broken the habit of dragging him around with me everywhere I went. I knew there'd be a price to pay for backsliding—Jeremy had been riding me about Mr. Fuzzy for a year—but desperate times call for desperate measures.

I'd just finished rescuing him from a box of loose Legos and Jeremy's old *Star Wars* action figures when I noticed a bundle of rags stuffed under the furnace. I wasn't inclined to spend any more time than necessary in the basement—it smelled funny and the light slanting through the high dirty windows had a hazy greenish quality, like a pond you wouldn't want to swim in—but I found myself dragging Mr. Fuzzy over toward the furnace all the same.

Somebody had jammed the bundle in there good, and when it came loose, clicking metallically, it toppled me back on my butt. I stood, brushing my seat off with one hand, Mr. Fuzzy momentarily forgotten. I squatted to examine the bundle, a mass of grease-stained rags tied off with brown twine. The whole thing was only a couple feet long.

I loosened the knot and pulled one end of the twine. The bundle unwrapped itself, spilling a handful of rusty foot-long skewers across the floor. There were half a dozen of them, all of them with these big metal caps. I shook the rag. A scalpel tumbled out, and then a bunch of other crap, every bit of it as rusty as the skewers. A big old hammer with a wooden head and a wicked-looking carving knife and one of those tapered metal rods butchers use to sharpen knives. Last of all a set of ivory-handled flatware.

I reached down and picked up the fork.

That's when I heard the stairs creak behind me.

"Mom's gonna kill you," Jeremy said.

I jumped a little and stole a glance over my shoulder. He was standing at the foot of the stairs, a rickety tier of backless risers. That's when I remembered Mom's warning that I wasn't to fool around down here. The floor was just dirt, packed hard as concrete, and Mom always worried about getting our clothes dirty.

"Not if you don't tell her," I said.

"Besides, you're messing around with the furnace," Jeremy said.

"No, I'm not."

"Sure you are." He crossed the room and hunkered down at my side. I glanced over at him. Let me be honest here: I was nobody's ideal boy next door. I was a scrawny, unlovely kid, forever peering out at the world through a pair of lenses so thick that Jeremy had once spent a sunny afternoon trying to ignite ants with them. The changeling, my mother sometimes called me, since I seemed to have surfaced out of somebody else's gene pool.

Jeremy, though, was blond and handsome and already broad-shouldered. He was the kind of kid everybody wants to sit with in the lunchroom, quick and friendly and capable of glamorous strokes of kindness. He made such a gesture now, clapping me on the shoulder. "Geez, Si, that's some weird-looking shit. Wonder how long it's been here?"

"I dunno," I said, but I remembered the landlord telling Dad the house was nearly a hundred and fifty years old. *And hasn't had a lick of work since,* I'd heard Dad mutter under his breath.

Jeremy reached for one of the skewers and I felt a little bubble of emotion press against the bottom of my throat. He turned the thing over in his hands and let it drop to the floor. "Beats the hell out of me," he said.

"You're not gonna tell Mom, are you?"

"Nah." He seemed to think a moment. "Course I might use that scalpel to dissect Mr. Fuzzy." He gazed at me balefully, and then he slapped my shoulder again. "Better treat me right, kid."

A moment later I heard the basement door slam behind me.

I'd been clutching the fork so tightly that it had turned hot in my hand. My knuckles grinned up at me, four bloodless white crescents. I felt so strange that I just let it tumble to the floor. Then I rewrapped the bundle, and shoved it back under the furnace.

By the time I'd gotten upstairs, I'd put the whole thing out of my mind. Except I hadn't, not really. I wasn't thinking about it, not consciously, but it was there all the same, the way all the furniture in a room is still there when you turn out the lights, and you can sense it there in the dark. Or the way pain is always there. Even when they give you something to smooth it out a little, it's always there, a deep-down ache like jagged rocks under a swift-moving current. It never goes away, pain. It's like a stone in your pocket.

The bundle weighed on me in the same way, through the long night after Jeremy finally fell asleep, and the next day, and the night after that as well. So I guess I wasn't surprised, not really, when I found myself creeping down the basement stairs the next afternoon. Nobody saw me steal up to my room with the bundle. Nobody saw me tuck it under my bed. Mom had cried herself to sleep in front of the TV (she pretended she wasn't crying, but I knew better) and Dad was already at work. Who knew where Jeremy was?

Then school started and Mom didn't cry as often, or she did it when we weren't around. But neither one of them talked very much, except at dinner Dad always asked Jeremy how freshman football was going. And most nights, just as a joke, Jeremy would start up with one of those crazy stories of his, the minute we turned out the light. He'd pretend there was a vampire in the room or something and he'd thrash around so that I could hear him over the narrow space between our beds. "Ahhh," he'd say, "Arrggh," and, in a strangled gasp, "When it finishes with me, Si, it's coming for you." I'd hug Mr. Fuzzy tight and tell him not to be afraid, and then Jeremy would unleash that nutty mad scientist laugh.

"C'mon, Si, you know I'm only kidding."

One night, he said, "Do you believe in ghosts, Si? Because as old as this house is, I bet a whole shitload of people have died in it."

I didn't answer, but I thought about it a lot over the next few days. We'd been in school a couple of weeks at this point. Jeremy had already made a lot of friends. He talked to them on the phone at night. I had a lot of time to think.

I even asked Dad about it. "Try not to be dense, Si," he told me. "There's no such thing as ghosts, everybody knows that. Now chill out, will you, I'm trying to explain something to your brother."

So the answer was, no, I didn't believe in ghosts. But I also thought it might be more complicated than that, that maybe they were like characters in a good book. You aren't going to run into them at the Wal-Mart, but they seem real all the same. I figured ghosts might be something like that. The way I figured it, they had to be really desperate for something they hadn't gotten enough of while they were alive, like they were jealous or hungry or something. Otherwise why would they stick around some crummy old cemetery when they could go on to Heaven or whatever? So that's what I ended up telling Jeremy a few nights later, after I'd finished sorting it all out inside my head.

"*Hungry?*" he said. "Christ, Si, that's the stupidest thing I've ever heard." He started thrashing around in his bed and making these dumb ghost noises. "Ooooooooh," he said, and, "Ooooooooh, I'm a ghost, give me a steak. Ooooooooh, I want a bowl of Cheerios."

I tried to explain that that wasn't what I meant, but I couldn't find the words. I was just a kid, after all.

"Christ, Si," Jeremy said, "don't tell anybody anything that stupid. It's like that stupid bear you drag around everywhere, it makes me ashamed to be your brother."

I knew he didn't mean anything by that—Jeremy was always joking around—but it hurt Mr. Fuzzy's feelings all the same. "Don't cry, Mr. Fuzzy," I whispered. "He didn't mean anything by it."

A few days later, Jeremy came home looking troubled. I didn't think anything about it at first because it hadn't been a very good day from the start. When Jeremy and I went down to breakfast, we overheard Day saying he was taking Mom's car in that afternoon, the way they had planned. Mom said something so low that neither one of us could make it out, and then Dad said, "For Christ's sake, Mariam, there's plenty of one-car families in the world." He slammed his way out of the house, and a few seconds later we heard Mom shut the bedroom door with a click. Neither one of us said anything after that except when Jeremy snapped at me because I was so slow getting my lunch. So I knew he was upset and it didn't surprise me when he came home from football practice that day looking a bit down in the mouth.

It turned out to be something totally different, though, because as soon as we turned out the light that night, and he knew we were really alone, Jeremy said, "What happened to that bundle of tools, Si?"

"What bundle of tools?" I asked.

"That weird-looking shit you found in the basement last summer," he said.

That's when I remembered that I'd put the bundle under my bed. What a crazy thing to do, I thought, and I was about to say *I'd* taken them—but Mr. Fuzzy kind of punched me. He was so sensitive, I don't think he'd really forgiven Jeremy yet.

I thought it over, and then I said, "Beats me."

"Well, I went down the basement this afternoon," Jeremy said, "and they were gone."

"So?"

"It makes me uncomfortable, that's all."

"Why?"

Jeremy didn't say anything for a long time. A car went by outside, and the headlights lit everything up for a minute. The shadow of the crap-apple danced on the ceiling like a man made out of bones, and then the night swallowed him up. That one little moment of light made it seem darker than ever.

"I met this kid at school today," Jeremy said, "and when I told him where I lived he said, 'No way, Mad Dog Mueller's house?' 'Mad Dog who?' I said. 'Mueller,' he said. 'Everyone knows who Mad Dog Mueller is.'"

"I don't," I said.

"Well, neither did I," Jeremy said, "but this kid, he told me the whole story. 'You ever notice there aren't any kids that live out that end of town?' he asked, and the more I thought about it, Si, the more right he seemed. There *aren't* any kids."

The thing was, he was right. That's when I figured it out, the thing about the kids. It was like one of those puzzles with a picture hidden inside all these little blots of color and you stare at it and you stare at it and you don't see a thing, and then you happen to catch it from just the right angle and—

Bang!—there the hidden picture is. And once you've seen it, you can never unsee it. I thought about the neighbors, this scrawny guy who was always tinkering with the dead El Camino and his fat wife—neither one of them really old, but neither one of them a day under thirty, either. I remember how they stood out front watching us move in, and Mom asking them if they had any kids, her voice kind of hopeful. But they'd just laughed, like who would bring kids to a place like this?

They hadn't offered to pitch in, either—and people *always* offer to lend a hand when you're moving stuff inside. I *know*, because we've moved lots of times. I could see Dad getting hotter and hotter with every trip, until finally he turned and said in a voice just dripping with sarcasm, "See anything that strikes your fancy, folks?" You could tell by the look on Mom's face that she didn't like that one bit. When we got inside she hissed at him like some kind of animal she was so mad. "Why can't you ever keep your mouth shut, Frank?" she said. "If you kept your mouth shut we wouldn't *be* in this situation."

All of which was beside the point, of course. The point was, Jeremy was right. There wasn't a single kid in any of the nearby houses.

"See," Jeremy said, "I told you. And the reason is, this guy Mad Dog Mueller."

"But it was some old lady that used to live here," I said. "We saw her the first day, they were moving her to a nursing home."

"I'm not talking about her, stupid. I'm talking like a hundred years ago, when this was all farm land, and the nearest neighbors were half a mile away."

"Oh."

I didn't like the direction this was going, I have to say. Plus, it seemed even darker. Most places, you turn out the light and your eyes adjust and everything turns this smoky blue color, so it hardly seems dark at all. But here the night seemed denser somehow, weightier. Your eyes just never got used to it, not unless there was a moon, which this particular night there wasn't.

"Anyway," Jeremy said, "I guess he lived here with his mother for a while and then she died and he lived here alone after that. He was a pretty old guy, I guess, like forty. He was a blacksmith."

"What's a blacksmith?"

"God you can be dense, Si. Blacksmiths make horseshoes and shit."

"Then why do they call them *black*smiths?"

"I don't know. I guess they were black or something, like back in slavery days."

"Was *this* guy black?"

"No! The point is, he makes things out of metal. That's the point, okay? And so I told this kid about those tools I found."

"*I'm* the one who found them," I said.

"Whatever, Si. The point is, when I mentioned the tools, the kid who was telling me this stuff, his eyes bugged out. 'No way,' he says to me, and I'm like, 'No, really, cross my heart. What gives?'"

Jeremy paused to take a deep breath, and in the silence I heard a faint click, like two pieces of metal rubbing up against each other. That's when I understood what Jeremy was doing. He was "acting out," which is a term I learned when I forgot Mr. Fuzzy at Dr. Bainbridge's one day, back at the clinic in Starkville, after I got suspended from school. When I slipped inside to get him, Dr. Bainbridge was saying, "You have to understand, Mariam, with all these pressures at home, it's only natural that he's acting out."

I asked Dr. Bainbridge about it the next week, and he told me that sometimes people say and do things they don't mean just because they're upset about something else. And now I figured Jeremy was doing it because he was so upset about Mom and stuff. He was trying to scare me, that's all. He'd even found the little bundle of tools under my bed and he was over there clicking them together. I'd have been mad if I hadn't understood. If I hadn't understood, I might have even been afraid—Mr. Fuzzy was, I could feel him shivering against my chest.

"Did you hear that?" Jeremy said.

"I didn't hear anything," I said, because I wasn't going to play along with his game.

Jeremy didn't answer right away. So we lay there, both of us listening, and this time I really *didn't* hear anything. But it seemed even darker somehow, darker than I'd ever seen our little bedroom. I wiggled my fingers in front of my face and I couldn't see a thing.

"I thought I heard something." This time you could hear the faintest tremor in his voice. It was a really fine job, he was doing. I couldn't help admiring it. "And that would be bad," Jeremy added, "because this Mueller, he was crazy as a shithouse rat."

I hugged Mr. Fuzzy close. "Crazy?" I said.

"Crazy," Jeremy said solemnly. "This kid, he told me that all the farms around there, the farmers had about a zillion kids. Everybody had a ton of kids in those days. And one of them turned up missing. No one thought anything about it at first—kids were always running off—but about a week later *another* kid disappears. This time everybody got worried. It was this little girl and nobody could figure out why *she* would run off. She was only like seven years old."

"She was my age?"

"That's right, Si. She was just your age."

Then I heard it again: this odd little clicking like Grandma's knitting needles used to make. Jeremy must have really given that bundle a shake.

"*Shit,*" Jeremy said, and now he sounded really scared. Somebody ought to have given him an Oscar or something.

He switched on the light. It was a touch of genius, that—his way of saying, *Hey, I'm not doing anything!*, which of course meant he was. I stared, but the bundle was nowhere in sight. I figured he must have tucked it under the covers, but it was hard to tell without my glasses on. Everything looked all blurry, even Jeremy's face, blinking at me over the gap between the beds. I scooched down under the covers, holding Mr. Fuzzy tight.

"It was coming from over there," he said. "Over there by your bed."

"I didn't hear anything," I said.

"No, I'm serious, Si. I heard it, didn't you?"

"You better turn out the light," I said, just to prove I wasn't afraid. "Mom'll be mad."

"Right," Jeremy said, and the way he said it, you could tell he knew it was an empty threat. Mom had told me she was sick when I'd knocked on her bedroom door after school. I opened the door, but it was dark inside and she told me to go away. The room smelled funny, too, like the stinging stuff she put on my knee the time Jeremy accidentally knocked me down in the driveway. I just need to sleep, she said. I've taken some medicine to help me sleep.

And then Jeremy came home and made us some TV dinners. "She must have passed out in there," he said, and that scared me. But when I said maybe we should call the doctor, he just laughed. "Try not to be so dense all the time, okay, Si?"

We just waited around for Dad after that. But Jeremy said he wouldn't be surprised if Dad *never* came home again, the way Mom had been so bitchy lately. Maybe he was right, too, because by the time we went up to bed, Dad still hadn't shown up.

So Jeremy was right. Nobody was going to mind the light.

We both had a look around. The room looked pretty much the way it always did. Jeremy's trophies gleamed on the little shelf Dad had built for them. A bug smacked the window screen a few times, like it really wanted to get inside.

"You sure you didn't hear anything?"

"Yeah."

Jeremy looked at me for a minute. "All right, then," he said, and turned out the light. Another car passed and the crap-apple man did his little jig on the ceiling. The house was so quiet I could hear Jeremy breathing these long even breaths. I sang a song to Mr. Fuzzy while I waited for him to start up again. It was this song Mom used to sing when I was a baby, the one about all the pretty little horses.

And then Jeremy started talking again.

"Nobody got suspicious," he said, "until the third kid disappeared—a little boy, he was about your age too, Si. And then someone happened to remember that all these kids had to walk by this Mueller guy's house on their way to school. So a few of the parents got together that night and went down there to see if he had seen anything."

It had gotten colder. I wished Jeremy would shut the window and I was going to say something, but he just plowed on with his stupid story. "Soon as he answered the door," Jeremy said, "they could tell something was wrong. It was all dark inside—there wasn't a fire or anything—and it smelled bad, like pigs or something. They could hardly see him, too, just his eyes, all hollow and shiny in the shadows. They asked if he'd seen the kids and that's when things got really weird. He said he hadn't seen anything, but he was acting all nervous, and he tried to close the door. One of the men held up his lantern then, and they could see his face. He hadn't shaved and he looked real thin and there was this stuff smeared over his face. It looked black in the light, like paint, only it wasn't paint. You know what it was, Si?"

I'd heard enough of Jeremy's stories to be able to make a pretty good guess, but I couldn't seem to make my mouth say the word. Mr. Fuzzy was shaking he was so scared. He was shaking real hard, and he was mad, too. He was mad at Jeremy for trying to scare me like that.

"It was blood, Si," Jeremy said.

That's when I heard it again, a whisper of metal against metal like the sound the butcher makes at the grocery store when he's putting the edge on a knife.

Jeremy gasped. "Did you hear that?"

And just like that the sound died away.

"No," I said.

We were silent, listening.

"What happened?" I whispered, because I wanted him to finish it. If he finished he could do his dumb little mad scientist laugh and admit he made it all up.

"He ran," Jeremy said. "He ran through the house and it was all dark and he went down the basement, down where you found those rusty old tools. Only it wasn't rust, Si. It was blood. Because you know what else they found down there?"

I heard the whisper of metal again—*shir shir shir,* that sound the butcher makes when he's putting the edge on a knife and his hands are moving so fast the blade is just a blur of light. But Jeremy had already started talking again.

"They found the missing kids," he said, but it sounded so far away. All I could hear was that sound in my head, *shir shir shir.* "They were dead," Jeremy was saying, "and pretty soon he was dead, too. They killed the guy right on the spot, he didn't even get a trial. They put him down the same way he'd killed those kids."

I swallowed. "How was that?"

"He used those long nails on them, those skewer things. He knocked them on the head or something and then, while they were out, he just hammered those things right through them—*wham wham wham*—so they were pinned to the floor, they couldn't get up. And then you know what he did?"

Only he didn't wait for me to answer, he couldn't wait, he just rolled on. He said, "Mueller used the scalpel on them, then. He just ripped them open and then—" Jeremy's voice broke. It was a masterful touch. "And then he started eating, Si. He started eating before they were even dead—"

Jeremy broke off suddenly, and now the sound was so loud it seemed to shake the walls—*SHIR SHIR SHIR*—and the room was so cold I could see my breath fogging up the dark.

"Christ, what's that sound?" Jeremy whimpered, and then he started making moaning sounds way down in his throat, the way he always did, like he wanted to scream but he was too afraid.

Mr. Fuzzy was shaking, just shaking so hard, and I have to admit it, right then I hated Jeremy with a hatred so pure I could taste it, like an old penny under my tongue. The darkness seemed heavy suddenly, an iron weight pinning me to my bed. It was cold, too. It was so cold. I've never been so cold in my life.

"Christ, Si," Jeremy shrieked. "Stop it! *Stop it! STOP IT!*"

Mr. Fuzzy was still shaking in my arms, and I hated Jeremy for that, I couldn't help it, but I tried to make myself get up anyway, I really tried. Only the dark was too thick and heavy. It seemed to flow over me, like concrete that hadn't quite formed up, binding me to my mattress with Mr. Fuzzy cowering in my arms.

Jeremy's whole bed was shaking now. He was grunting and wrestling around. I heard a *pop*, like a piece of taut rubber giving way, and a metallic *wham wham wham*. There was this liquidy gurgle and Jeremy actually screamed, this long desperate scream from the bottom of his lungs. I really had to admire the job he was doing, as much as I couldn't help being mad. He'd never taken it this far. It was like watching a master at the very peak of his form. There was another one of those liquidy thumps and then the sound of the hammer and then the whole thing happened again and again. It happened so many times I lost track. All I knew was that Jeremy had stopped screaming, but I couldn't remember when. The only sound in the room was this muffled thrashing sound, and that went on for a little while longer and then it stopped, too. Everything just stopped.

It was so still. There wasn't any sound at all.

The dark lay heavy on my skin, pinning me down. It was all I could do to open my mouth, to force the word out—

"Jeremy?"

I waited then. I waited for the longest time to hear that stupid Vincent Price laugh of his, to hear Jeremy telling me he'd gotten me this time, he was only joking, *Mwah-ha-ha-ha-ha.*

But the laugh never came.

What came instead was the sound of someone chewing, the sound of someone who hadn't had a meal in ages just tucking right in and having at it, smacking his lips and slurping and everything, and it went on and on and on. The whole time I just lay there. I couldn't move at all.

It must have gone on for hours. I don't know how long it went on. All I know is that suddenly I realized it was silent, I couldn't hear a thing.

I waited some more for Jeremy to make that stupid laugh of his. And then a funny thing happened. I wasn't lying in my bed after all. I was standing up between the beds, by the milk crate we used for a night stand, and I was tired. I was so tired. My legs ached like I'd been standing there for hours. My arms ached, too. Every part of me ached. I ached all over.

I kept having these crazy thoughts, too. About ghosts and hunger and how hungry Mad Dog Mueller must have been, after all those years down in the basement. About how maybe he'd spent all that time waiting down there, waiting for the right person to come along, someone who was just as hungry as he was.

They were the craziest thoughts, but I couldn't seem to stop thinking them. I just stood there between the beds. My face was wet, too, my whole face, my mouth and everything. I must have been crying.

I just stood there waiting for Jeremy to laugh that stupid mad scientist laugh of his and tell me it was all a game. And I have to admit something: I was scared, too. I was so scared.

But it wasn't the dark I was scared of.

God help me, I didn't want to turn on the light.

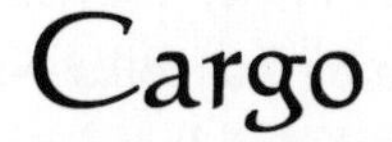

E. MICHAEL LEWIS

E. Michael Lewis studied creative writing at the University of Puget Sound. He loves to write ghost stories. His story "Lost and Found" premiered as an e-book from Samhain Publications this year. Other stories can be found in *Exotic Gothic 4*, *The Horror Anthology of Horror Anthologies*, *All Hallows*, and on various websites. He's also on Facebook. Mr. Lewis is a lifelong native of the Pacific Northwest, where he lives with his two sons.

Of "Cargo," he writes: "Of the nine hundred people who died in the Jonestown Massacre, nearly a third of them were under the age of eighteen. This story is dedicated to the families who lost loved ones at Jonestown, and to the servicemen and -women who brought them home." He is currently under contract to write a screenplay based on this story.

November 1978

I dreamt of cargo. Thousands of crates filled the airplane's hold, all made of unfinished pine, the kind that drives slivers through work gloves. They were stamped with unknowable numbers and bizarre acronyms that glowed fiercely with dim red light. They were supposed to be jeep tires, but some were as large as a house, others as small as a spark plug, all of them secured to pallets with binding like straitjacket straps. I tried to check them all, but there were too many. There was a low shuffling as the boxes shifted, then the cargo fell on me. I couldn't reach the interphone to warn the pilot. The cargo pressed down on me with a thousand sharp little fingers as the plane rolled, crushing the life out of me even as we dived, even as we crashed, the interphone ringing now like a scream. But there was another sound too, from inside the crate next to my ear. Something struggled inside the box, something sodden and defiled, something that I didn't want to see, something that wanted *out*.

It changed into the sound of a clipboard being rapped on the metal frame of my crew house bunk. My eyes shot open. The airman—new in-country, by the sweat lining his collar—stood over me, holding the clipboard between us, trying to decide if I was the type to rip his head off just for doing his job. "Tech Sergeant Davis," he said, "they need you on the flight line right away."

I sat up and stretched. He handed me the clipboard and attached manifest: a knocked-down HU-53 with flight crew, mechanics, and medical support personnel bound for...somewhere new.

"Timehri Airport?"

"It's outside Georgetown, Guyana." When I looked blank, he went on, "It's a former British colony. Timehri used to be Atkinson Air Force Base."

"What's the mission?"

"It's some kind of mass med-evac of ex-pats from somewhere called Jonestown."

Americans in trouble. I'd spent a good part of my Air Force career flying Americans out of trouble. That being said, flying Americans out of trouble was a hell of a lot more satisfying than hauling jeep tires. I thanked him and hurried into a clean flight suit.

I was looking forward to another Panamanian Thanksgiving at Howard Air Force Base—eighty-five degrees, turkey and stuffing from the mess hall, football on Armed Forces Radio, and enough time out of flight rotation to get good and drunk. The in-bound hop from the Philippines went by the numbers and both the passengers and cargo were free and easy. Now this.

Interruption was something you grew accustomed to as a Loadmaster. The C-141 StarLifter was the largest freighter and troop carrier in the Military Air Command, capable of carrying seventy thousand pounds of cargo or two hundred battle-ready troops and flying them anywhere in the world. Half as long as a football field, the high-set, swept-back wings drooped batlike over the tarmac. With an upswept T-tail, petal-doors, and a built-in cargo ramp, the StarLifter was unmatched when it came to moving cargo. Part stewardess and part moving man, my job as a Loadmaster was to pack it as tight and as safe as possible.

With everything onboard and my weight and balance sheets complete, the same airman found me cussing up the Panamanian ground crew for leaving a scuffmark on the airframe.

"Sergeant Davis! Change in plans," he yelled over the whine of the forklift. He handed me another manifest.

"More passengers?"

"New passengers. Med crew is staying here." He said something unintelligible about a change of mission.

"Who are these people?"

Again, I strained to hear him. Or maybe I heard him fine and with the sinking in my gut, I wanted him to repeat it. I wanted to hear him wrong.

"Graves registration," he cried.

That's what I'd thought he'd said.

Timehri was your typical third world airport—large enough to squeeze down a 747, but strewn with potholes and sprawling with rusted Quonset huts. The low line of jungle surrounding the field looked as if it had been beaten back only an hour before. Helicopters buzzed up and down and US servicemen swarmed the tarmac. I knew then that things must be bad.

Outside the bird, the heat rising from the asphalt threatened to melt the soles of my boots even before I had the wheel chocks in place. A ground crew of American GIs approached, anxious to unload and assemble the chopper. One of them, bare chested with his shirt tied around his waist, handed me a manifest.

"Don't get comfy," he said. "As soon as the chopper's clear, we're loading you up." He nodded over his shoulder.

I looked out over the shimmering taxiway. Coffins. Rows and rows of dull aluminum funerary boxes gleamed in the unforgiving tropical sun. I recognized them from my flights out of Saigon six years ago, my first as Loadmaster. Maybe my insides did a little flip because I'd had no rest, or maybe because I hadn't carried a stiff in a few years. Still, I swallowed hard. I looked at the destination: Dover, Delaware.

• • •

The ground crew loaded a fresh comfort pallet when I learned we'd have two passengers on the outbound flight.

The first was a kid, right out of high school by the look of it, with bristle-black hair, and too-large jungle fatigues that were starched, clean, and showed the rank of Airman First Class. I told him, "Welcome aboard," and went to help him through the crew door, but he jerked away, nearly hitting his head against the low entrance. I think he would have leapt back if there had been room. His scent hit me, strong and medicinal—Vicks VapoRub.

Behind him a flight nurse, crisp and professional in step, dress, and gesture, also boarded without assistance. I regarded her evenly. I recognized her as one of a batch I had flown regularly from Clark in the Philippines to Da Nang and back again in my early days. A steel-eyed, silver-haired lieutenant. She had been very specific—more than once—in pointing out how any numbskull high school dropout could do my job better. The name on her uniform read Pembry. She touched the kid on his back and guided him to the seats, but if she recognized me, she said nothing.

"Take a seat anywhere," I told them. "I'm Tech Sergeant Davis. We'll be wheels up in less than a half an hour so make yourself comfortable."

The kid stopped short. "You didn't tell me," he said to the nurse.

The hold of a StarLifter is most like the inside of a boiler room, with all the heat, cooling, and pressure ducts exposed rather than hidden away like on an airliner. The coffins formed two rows down the length of the hold, leaving a center aisle clear. Stacked four high, there were one hundred and sixty of them. Yellow cargo nets held them in place. Looking past them, we watched the sunlight disappear as the cargo hatch closed, leaving us in an awkward semidarkness.

"It's the fastest way to get you home," she said to him, her voice neutral. "You want to go home, don't you?"

His voice dripped with fearful outrage. "I don't want to see them. I want a forward facing seat."

If the kid would have looked around, he could have seen that there were no forward facing seats.

"It's okay," she said, tugging on his arm again. "They're going home, too."

"I don't want to look at them," he said as she pushed him to a seat nearest one of the small windows. When he didn't move to strap himself in, Pembry bent and did it for him. He gripped the handrails like the oh-shit bar on a roller coaster. "I don't want to think about them."

"I got it." I went forward and shut down the cabin lights. Now only the twin red jump lights illuminated the long metal containers. When I returned, I brought him a pillow.

The ID label on the kid's loose jacket read "Hernandez." He said, "Thank you," but did not let go of the armrests.

Pembry strapped herself in next to him. I stowed their gear and went through my final checklist.

Once in the air, I brewed coffee on the electric stove in the comfort pallet. Nurse Pembry declined, but Hernandez took some. The plastic cup shook in his hands.

"Afraid of flying?" I asked. It wasn't so unusual for the Air Force. "I have some Dramamine..."

"I'm not afraid of flying," he said through clenched teeth. All the while he looked past me, to the boxes lining the hold.

Next the crew. No one bird was assigned the same crew, like in the old days. The MAC took great pride in having men be so interchangeable that a flight crew who had never met before could assemble at a flight line and fly any StarLifter to the ends of the Earth. Each man knew my job, like I knew theirs, inside and out.

I went to the cockpit and found everyone on stations. The second engineer sat closest to the cockpit door, hunched over instrumentation. "Four is evening out now, keep the throttle low," he said. I recognized his hangdog face and his Arkansas drawl, but I could not tell from where. I figured after seven years of flying StarLifters, I had flown with just about everybody at one time or another. He thanked me as I set the black coffee on his table. His flight suit named him Hadley.

The first engineer sat in the bitchseat, the one usually reserved for a

"Black Hatter"—mission inspectors were the bane of all MAC aircrews. He asked for two lumps and then stood and looked out the navigator's dome at the blue rushing past.

"Throttle low on four, got it," replied the pilot. He was the designated Aircraft Commander, but both he and the co-pilot were such typical flight jocks that they could have been the same person. They took their coffee with two creams each. "We're trying to outfly some clear air turbulence, but it won't be easy. Tell your passengers to expect some weather."

"Will do, sir. Anything else?"

"Thank you, Load Davis, that's all."

"Yes, sir."

Finally time to relax. As I went to have a horizontal moment in the crew berth, I saw Pembry snooping around the comfort pallet. "Anything I can help you find?"

"An extra blanket?"

I pulled one from the storage cabinet between the cooking station and the latrine and gritted my teeth. "Anything else?"

"No," she said, pulling a piece of imaginary lint from the wool. "We've flown together before, you know."

"Have we?"

She raised an eyebrow. "I probably ought to apologize."

"No need, ma'am," I said. I dodged around her and opened the fridge. "I could serve an in-flight meal later if you are..."

She placed her hand on my shoulder, like she had on Hernandez, and it commanded my attention. "You do remember me."

"Yes, ma'am."

"I was pretty hard on you during those evac flights."

I wished she'd stop being so direct. "You were speaking your mind, ma'am. It made me a better Loadmaster."

"Still..."

"Ma'am, there's no need." Why can't women figure out that apologies only make things worse?

"Very well." The hardness of her face melted into sincerity, and suddenly it occurred to me that she wanted to talk.

"How's your patient?"

"Resting." Pembry tried to act casual, but I knew she wanted to say more.

"What's his problem?"

"He was one of the first to arrive," she said, "and the first to leave."

"Jonestown? Was it that bad?"

Flashback to our earlier evac flights. The old look, hard and cool, returned instantly. "We flew out of Dover on White House orders five hours after they got the call. He's a Medical Records Specialist, six months in the service, he's never been anywhere before, never saw a day of trauma in his life. Next thing he knows, he's in a South American jungle with a thousand dead bodies."

"A thousand?"

"Count's not in yet, but it's headed that way." She brushed the back of her hand against her cheek. "So many kids."

"Kids?"

"Whole families. They all drank poison. Some kind of cult, they said. Someone told me the parents killed their children first. I don't know what could make a person do that to their own family." She shook her head. "I stayed at Timehri to organize triage. Hernandez said the smell was unimaginable. They had to spray the bodies with insecticide and defend them from hungry giant rats. He said they made him bayonet the bodies to release the pressure. He burned his uniform." She shuffled to keep her balance as the bird jolted.

Something nasty crept down the back of my throat as I tried not to visualize what she said. I struggled not to grimace. "The AC says it may get rough. You better strap in." I walked her back to her seat. Hernandez's mouth gaped as he sprawled across his seat, looking for all the world like he'd lost a bar fight—bad. Then I went to my bunk and fell asleep.

Ask any Loadmaster: after so much time in the air, the roar of engines is something you ignore. You find you can sleep through just about anything. Still, your mind tunes in and wakes up at the sound of anything unusual, like the flight from Yakota to Elmendorf when a jeep came loose and rolled into a crate of MREs. Chipped beef everywhere. You can bet the ground crew heard from me on that one. So it should not come as a shock that I started at the sound of a scream.

On my feet, out of the bunk, past the comfort pallet before I could think. Then I saw Pembry. She was out of her seat and in front of Hernandez, dodging his flailing arms, speaking calmly and below the engine noise. Not him, though.

"I heard them! I heard them! They're in there! All those kids! All those kids!"

I put my hand on him—hard. "Calm down!"

He stopped flailing. A shamed expression came over him. His eyes riveted mine. "I heard them singing."

"Who?"

"The children! All the..." He gave a helpless gesture to the unlighted coffins.

"You had a dream," Pembry said. Her voice shook a little. "I was with you the whole time. You were asleep. You couldn't have heard anything."

"All the children are dead," he said. "All of them. They didn't know. How could they have known they were drinking poison? Who would give their own child poison to drink?" I let go of his arm and he looked at me. "Do you have kids?"

"No," I said.

"My daughter," he said, "is a year-and-a-half old. My son is three months. You have to be careful with them, patient with them. My wife is really good at it, y'know?" I noticed for the first time how sweat crawled across his forehead, the backs of his hands. "But I'm okay too, I mean, I don't really know what the fuck I'm doing, but I wouldn't hurt them. I hold them and I sing to them and—and if anyone else tried to hurt them..." He grabbed me on the arm that had held him. "Who would give their child poison?"

"It isn't your fault," I told him.

"They didn't know it was poison. They still don't." He pulled me closer and said into my ear, "I heard them singing." I'll be damned if the words he spoke didn't make my spine shiver.

"I'll go check it out," I told him as I grabbed a flashlight off the wall and started down the center aisle.

There was a practical reason for checking out the noise. As a Loadmaster, I knew that an unusual sound meant trouble. I had heard a story about how an aircrew kept hearing the sound of a cat meowing from somewhere in the hold. The loadmaster couldn't find it, but figured it'd turn up when they off-loaded the cargo. Turns out the "meowing" was a weakened load brace that buckled when the wheels touched runway, freeing three tons of explosive ordnance and making the landing very interesting. Strange noises meant trouble, and I'd have been a fool not to look into it.

I checked all the buckles and netting as I went, stooping and listening, checking for signs of shifting, fraying straps, anything out of the ordinary. I went up one side and down the other, even checking the cargo doors. Nothing. Everything was sound, my usual best work.

I walked up the aisle to face them. Hernandez wept, head in his hands. Pembry rubbed his back with one hand as she sat next to him, like my mother had done to me.

"All clear, Hernandez." I put the flashlight back on the wall.

"Thanks," Pembry replied for him, then said to me, "I gave him a Valium, he should quiet down now."

"Just a safety check," I told her. "Now, both of you get some rest."

I went back to my bunk to find it occupied by Hadley, the second engineer. I took the one below him but couldn't fall asleep right away. I tried to keep my mind far away from the reason that the coffins were in my bird in the first place.

Cargo was the euphemism. From blood plasma to high explosives to secret service limousines to gold bullion, you packed it and hauled it because it was your job, that was all, and anything that could be done to speed you on your way was important.

Just cargo, I thought. But whole families that killed themselves...I was glad to get them the hell out of the jungle, back home to their families—but the medics who got there first, all those guys on the ground, even my crew, we were too late to do any more than that. I was interested in having kids in a vague, unsettled sort of way, and it pissed me off to hear about anyone harming them. But these parents did it willingly, didn't they?

I couldn't relax. I found an old copy of the *New York Times* folded into the bunk. Peace in the Middle East in our lifetimes, it read. Next to the article was a picture of President Carter and Anwar Sadat shaking hands. I was just about to drift off when I thought I heard Hernandez cry out again.

I dragged my ass up. Pembry stood with her hands clutched over her mouth. I thought Hernandez had hit her, so I went to her and peeled her hands away, looking for damage.

There was none. Looking over her shoulder, I could see Hernandez riveted to his seat, eyes glued to the darkness like a reverse color television.

"What happened? Did he hit you?"

"He—he heard it again," she stammered as one hand rose to her face again. 'You—you ought to go check again. You ought to go check..."

The pitch of the plane shifted and she fell into me a little, and as I steadied myself by grabbing her elbow she collapsed against me. I met her gaze matter-of-factly. She looked away. "What happened?" I asked again.

"I heard it too," Pembry said.

My eyes went to the aisle of shadow. "Just now?"

"Yes."

"Was it like he said? Children singing?" I realized I was on the verge of shaking her. Were they both going crazy?

"Children playing," she said. "Like—playground noise, y'know? Kids playing."

I wracked my brain for some object, or some collection of objects, that when stuffed into a C-141 StarLifter and flown thirty-nine thousand feet over the Caribbean, would make a sound like children playing.

Hernandez shifted his position and we both brought our attention to bear on him. He smiled a defeated smile and said to us, "I told you."

"I'll go check it out," I told them.

"Let them play," said Hernandez. "They just want to play. Isn't that what you wanted to do as a kid?"

I remembered my childhood like a jolt, endless summers and bike rides and skinned knees and coming home at dusk to my mother saying, "Look how dirty you are." I wondered if the recovery crews washed the bodies before they put them in the coffins.

"I'll find out what it is," I told them. I went and got the flashlight again. "Stay put."

I used the darkness to close off my sight, give me more to hear. The turbulence had subsided by then, and I used my flashlight only to avoid tripping on the cargo netting. I listened for anything new or unusual. It wasn't one thing—it had to be a combination—noises like that just don't stop and start again. Fuel leak? Stowaway? The thought of a snake or some other jungle beast lurking inside those metal boxes heightened my whole state of being and brought back my dream.

Near the cargo doors, I shut off my light and listened. Pressurized air. Four Pratt and Whitney turbofan engines. Fracture rattles. Cargo straps flapping.

And then, something. Something came in sharp after a moment, at first dull and sweeping, like noise from the back of a cave, but then pure and unbidden, like sounds to a surprised eavesdropper.

Children. Laughter. Like recess at grade school.

I opened my eyes and flashed my light around the silver crates. I found them waiting, huddled with me, almost expectant.

Children, I thought, just children.

I ran past Hernandez and Pembry to the comfort pallet. I can't tell you what they saw in my face, but if it was anything like what I saw in the little mirror above the latrine sink, I would have been at once terrified and redeemed.

I looked from the mirror to the interphone. Any problem with the cargo should be reported immediately—procedure demanded it—but what could I tell the AC? I had an urge to drop it all, just eject the coffins and call it a day. If I told him there was a fire in the hold, we would drop below ten thousand feet so I could blow the bolts and send the whole load to the bottom of the Gulf of Mexico, no questions asked.

I stopped then, straightened up, tried to think. *Children,* I thought. *Not monsters, not demons, just the sounds of children playing. Nothing that will get you. Nothing that* can *get you.* I tossed off the shiver that ran through my body and decided to get some help.

At the bunk, I found Hadley still asleep. A dog-eared copy of a paperback showing two women locked in a passionate embrace lay like a tent on his chest. I shook his arm and he sat up. Neither of us said anything for a moment. He rubbed his face with one hand and yawned.

Then he looked right at me and I watched his face arch into worry. His next action was to grab his portable oxygen. He recovered his game face in an instant. "What is it, Davis?"

I groped for something. "The cargo." I said. "There's a...possible shift in the cargo. I need a hand, sir."

His worry snapped into annoyance. "Have you told the AC?"

"No sir," I said. "I—I don't want to trouble him yet. It may be nothing."

His face screwed into something unpleasant and I thought I'd have words from him, but he let me lead the way aft. Just his presence was enough to revive my doubt, my professionalism. My walk sharpened, my eyes widened, my stomach returned to its place in my gut.

I found Pembry sitting next to Hernandez now, both together in a feigned indifference. Hadley gave them a disinterested look and followed me down the aisle between the coffins.

"What about the main lights?" he asked.

"They don't help," I said. "Here." I handed him the flashlight and asked him, "Do you hear it?"

"Hear what?"

"Just listen."

Again, only engines and the jetstream. "I don't..."

"Shhh! Listen."

His mouth opened and stayed there for a minute, then shut. The engines quieted and the sounds came, dripping over us like water vapor, the fog of sound around us. I didn't realize how cold I was until I noticed my hands shaking.

"What in the hell is that?" Hadley asked. "It sounds like—"

"Don't," I interrupted. "That can't be it." I nodded at the metal boxes. "You know what's in these coffins, don't you?"

He didn't say anything. The sound seemed to filter around us for a moment, at once close, then far away. He tried to follow the sound with his light. "Can you tell where it's coming from?"

"No. I'm just glad you hear it too, sir."

The engineer scratched his head, his face drawn, like he swallowed something foul and couldn't lose the aftertaste. "I'll be damned," he drawled.

All at once, as before, the sound stopped, and the roar of the jets filled our ears.

"I'll hit the lights." I moved away hesitantly. "I'm not going to call the AC."

His silence was conspiratorial. As I rejoined him, I found him examining a particular row of coffins through the netting.

"You need to conduct a search," he said dully.

I didn't respond. I'd done midair cargo searches before, but never like this, not even on bodies of servicemen. If everything Pembry said was true, I couldn't think of anything worse than opening one of these caskets.

We both started at the next sound. Imagine a wet tennis ball. Now imagine the sound a wet tennis ball makes when it hits the court—a sort of dull THWAK—like a bird striking the fuselage. It sounded again, and this time I could hear it inside the hold. Then, after a buffet of turbulence, the thump sounded again. It came clearly from a coffin at Hadley's feet.

Not a serious problem, his face tried to say. We just imagined it. *A noise from one coffin can't bring a plane down,* his face said. *There are no such things as ghosts.*

"Sir?"

"We need to see," he said.

Blood pooled in my stomach again. *See,* he had said. *I didn't want to see.*

"Get on the horn and tell the AC to avoid the chop," he said. I knew at that moment he was going to help me. He didn't want to, but he was going to do it anyway.

"What are you doing?" Pembry asked. She stood by as I removed the cargo netting from the row of caskets while the engineer undid the individual straps around that one certain row. Hernandez slept head bowed, the downers having finally taken effect.

"We have to examine the cargo," I stated matter-of-factly. "The flight may have caused the load to become unbalanced."

She grabbed my arm as I went by. "Was that all it was? A shifting load?"

There was a touch of desperation in her question. *Tell me I imagined it,* the look on her face said. *Tell me and I'll believe you, and I'll go get some sleep.*

"We think so," I nodded.

Her shoulders dropped and her face peeled into a smile too broad to be real. "Thank God. I thought I was going crazy."

I patted her shoulder. "Strap in and get some rest," I told her. She did.

Finally, I was doing something. As Loadmaster, I could put an end to this nonsense. So I did the work. I unstrapped the straps, climbed the other caskets, shoved the top one out of place, carried it, secured it, removed the next one, carried it, secured it, and again. The joy of easy repetition.

It wasn't until we got to the bottom one, the noisy one, that Hadley stopped. He stood there watching me as I pulled it out of place enough to examine it. His stance was level, but even so it spoke of revulsion, something that, among swaggering Air Force veterans and over beers, he could conceal. Not now, not to me.

I did a cursory examination of the deck where it had sat, of the caskets next to it, and saw no damage or obvious flaws.

A noise sounded—a moist "thunk." From inside. We flinched in unison. The engineer's cool loathing was impossible to conceal. I suppressed a tremble.

"We have to open it," I said.

The engineer didn't disagree, but like me, his body was slow to move. He squatted down and, with one hand firmly planted on the casket lid, unlatched the clasps on his end. I undid mine, finding my fingers slick on the cold metal, and shaking a little as I pulled them away and braced my hand on the lid. Our eyes met in one moment that held the last of our resolve. Together, we opened the casket.

First, the smell: a mash of rotten fruit, antiseptic, and formaldehyde, wrapped in plastic with dung and sulfur. It stung our nostrils as it filled the hold. The overhead lights illuminated two shiny black body bags, slick with condensation and waste. I knew these would be the bodies of children, but it awed me, hurt me. One bag lay unevenly concealing the other, and I understood at once that there was more than one child in it. My eyes skimmed the juice-soaked plastic, picking out the contour of an arm, the trace of a profile. A shape coiled near the bottom seam, away from the rest. It was the size of a baby.

Then the plane shivered like a frightened pony and the top bag slid away to reveal a young girl, eight or nine at the most, half in and half out of the bag. Wedged like a mad contortionist into the corner, her swollen belly, showing stab wounds from bayonets, had bloated again, and her twisted limbs were now as thick as tree limbs. The pigment-bearing skin had peeled away everywhere but her face, which was as pure and as innocent as any cherub in heaven.

Her face was really what drove it home, what really hurt me. Her sweet face.

My hand fixed itself to the casket edge in painful whiteness, but I dared not remove it. Something caught in my throat and I forced it back down.

A lone fly, fat and glistening, crawled from inside the bag and flew lazily towards Hadley. He slowly rose to his feet and braced himself, as if against a body blow. He watched it rise and flit a clumsy path through the air. Then he broke the moment by stepping back, his hands flailing and hitting it—I heard the slap of his hand—and letting a nauseous sound escape his lips.

When I stood up, my temples throbbed and my legs weakened. I held onto a nearby casket, my throat filled with something rancid.

"Close it," he said like a man with his mouth full. "Close it."

My arms went rubbery. After bracing myself, I lifted one leg and kicked the lid. It rang out like an artillery shot. Pressure pounded into my ears like during a rapid descent.

Hadley put his hands on his haunches and lowered his head, taking deep breaths through his mouth. "Jesus," he croaked.

I saw movement. Pembry stood next to the line of coffins, her face pulled up in sour disgust. "What—is—that—smell?"

"It's okay." I found I could work one arm and tried what I hoped looked like an off-handed gesture. "Found the problem. Had to open it up though. Go sit down."

Pembry brought her hands up around herself and went back to her seat.

I found that with a few more deep breaths, the smell dissipated enough to act. "We have to secure it," I told Hadley.

He looked up from the floor and I saw his eyes as narrow slits. His hands were in fists and his broad torso stood fierce and straight. At the corner of his eyes, wetness glinted. He said nothing.

It became cargo again as I fastened the latches. We strained to fit it back into place. In a matter of minutes, the other caskets were stowed, the exterior straps were in place, the cargo netting draped and secure.

Hadley waited for me to finish up, then walked forwards with me. "I'm going to tell the AC you solved the problem," he said, "and to get us back to speed."

I nodded.

"One more thing," he said. "If you see that fly, kill it."

"Didn't you..."

"No."

I didn't know what else to say, so I said, "Yes, sir."

Pembry sat in her seat, nose wriggled up, feigning sleep. Hernandez sat upright, eyelids half open. He gestured for me to come closer, bend down.

"Did you let them out to play?" he asked.

I stood over him and said nothing. In my heart, I felt that same pang I did as a child, when summer was over.

When we landed in Dover, a funeral detail in full dress offloaded every coffin, affording full funeral rights to each person. I'm told as more bodies flew in, the formality was scrapped and only a solitary Air Force chaplain met the planes. By week's end I was back in Panama with a stomach full of turkey and cheap rum. Then it was off to the Marshall Islands, delivering supplies to the guided missile base there. In the Military Air Command, there is no shortage of cargo.

Delta Sly Honey

LUCIUS SHEPARD

Lucius Shepard's short fiction has won the Nebula Award, the Hugo Award, the International Horror Guild Award, the National Magazine Award, the Locus Award, the Theodore Sturgeon Award, and the World Fantasy Award.

Shepard's most recent book is *The Dragon Griaule*, which brings together five previously published stories and one new short novel about a 6,000 foot dragon.

Forthcoming is another short fiction collection, *Five Autobiographies*, and two novels, tentatively titled *The Piercefields* and *The End of Life As We Know It.*

There was this guy I knew at Noc Linh, worked the corpse detail, guy name of Randall J. Willingham, a skinny red-haired Southern boy with a plague of freckles and eyes blue as poker chips, and sometimes when he got high, he'd wander up to the operations bunker and start spouting all kinds of shit over the radio, telling about his hometown and his dog, his opinion of the war (he was against it), and what it was like making love to his girlfriend, talking real pretty and wistful about her ways, the things she'd whisper and how she'd draw her knees up tight to her chest to let him go in deep. There was something pure and peaceful in his voice, his phrasing, and listening to him, you could feel the war draining out of you, and soon you'd be remembering your own girl, your own dog and hometown, not with heartsick longing but with joy in knowing you'd had at least that much sweetness of life. For many of us, his voice came to be the oracle of our luck, our survival, and even the brass who tried to stop his broadcasts finally realized he was doing a damn sight more good than any morale officer, and it got to where anytime the war was going slow and there was some free air, they'd call Randall up and ask if he felt in the mood to do a little talking.

The funny thing was that except for when he had a mike in his hand, you could hardly drag a word out of Randall. He had been a loner from day one of his tour, limiting his conversation to "Hey" and "How you?" and such, and his celebrity status caused him to become even less talkative. This was best explained by what he told us once over the air: "You meet ol' Randall J. on the street, and you gonna say, 'Why, that can't be Randall J.! That dumb-lookin' hillbilly couldn't recite the swearin'-in-oath, let alone be the hottest damn radio personality in South Vietnam!' And you'd be right on the money, 'cause Randall J. don't go more'n double figures for IQ, and he ain't got the imagination of a stump, and if you stopped him to say 'Howdy,' chances are he'd be stuck for a response. But lemme tell ya, when he puts his voice into a mike, ol' Randall J. becomes one with the airwaves, and the light that's been dark inside him goes bright, and his spirit streams out along Thunder Road and past the Napalm Coast, mixin' with the ozone and changin' into Randall J. Willingham, the High Priest of the Soulful Truth and the Holy Ghost of the Sixty-Cycle Hum."

The base was situated on a gently inclined hill set among other hills, all of which had once been part of the Michelin rubber plantation, but now were almost completely defoliated, transformed into dusty brown lumps. Nearly seven thousand men were stationed there, living in bunkers and tents dotting the slopes, and the only building with any degree of permanence was an outsized Quonset hut that housed the PX; it stood just inside the wire at the base of the hill. I was part of the MP contingent, and I guess I was the closest thing Randall had to a friend. We weren't really tight, but being from a small Southern town myself, the son of gentry, I was familiar with his type—fey, quiet farmboys whose vulnerabilities run deep—and I felt both sympathy and responsibility for him. My sympathy wasn't misplaced: nobody could have had a worse job, especially when you took into account the fact that his top sergeant, a beady-eyed, brush-cut, tackle-sized Army lifer named Andrew Moon, had chosen him for his whipping boy. Every morning I'd pass the tin-roofed shed where the corpses were off-loaded (it, too, was just inside the wire, but on the opposite side of the hill from the PX), and there Randall would be, laboring among body bags that were piled around like huge black fruit, with Moon hovering in the background and scowling. I always made it a point to stop and talk to Randall in order to give him a break from Moon's tyranny, and though he never expressed his gratitude or said very much about anything, soon he began to call me by my Christian name, Curt, instead of by my rank. Each time I made to leave, I would see the strain come back into his face, and before I had gone beyond earshot, I would hear Moon reviling him. I believe it was those days of staring into stomach cavities, into charred hearts and brains, and Moon all the while screaming at him... I believe that was what had squeezed the poetry out of Randall and birthed his radio soul.

I tried to get Moon to lighten up. One afternoon I bearded him in his tent and asked why he was mistreating Randall. Of course I knew the answer. Men like Moon, men who have secured a little power and grown bloated from its use, they don't need an excuse for brutality; there's so much meanness inside them, it's bound to slop over onto somebody. But—thinking I could handle him better than Randall—I planned to divert his meanness, set myself up as his target, and this seemed a good way to open.

He didn't bite, however; he just lay on his cot, squinting up at me and nodding sagely, as if he saw through my charade. His jowls were speckled with a few days' growth of stubble, hairs sparse and black as pig bristles. "Y'know," he said, "I couldn't figure why you were buddyin' up to that fool, so I had a look at your records." He grunted laughter. "Now I got it."

"Oh?" I said, maintaining my cool.

"You got quite a heritage, son! All that noble Southern blood, all them dead generals and senators. When I seen that, I said to myself, 'Don't get on this boy's case too heavy, Andy. He's just tryin' to be like his great-grandaddy, doin' a kindness now and then for the darkies and the poor white trash.' Ain't that right?"

I couldn't deny that a shadow of the truth attached to what he had said, but I refused to let him rankle me. "My motives aren't in question here," I told him.

"Well, neither are mine...'least not by anyone who counts." He swung his legs off the cot and sat up, glowering at me. "You got some nice duty here, son. But you go fuckin' with me, I'll have your ass walkin' point in Quanh Tri 'fore you can blink. Understand?"

I felt as if I had been dipped in ice water. I knew he could do as he threatened—any man who's made top sergeant has also made some powerful friends—and I wanted no part of Quanh Tri.

He saw my fear and laughed. "Go on, get out!" he said, and as I stepped through the door, he added, "Come 'round the shed anytime, son. I ain't got nothin' against *noblesse oblige*. Fact is, I love to watch."

And I walked away, knowing that Randall was lost.

In retrospect, it's clear that Randall had broken under Moon's whip early on, that his drifty radio spiels were symptomatic of his dissolution. In another time and place, someone might have noticed his condition; but in Vietnam everything he did seemed a normal reaction to the craziness of the war, perhaps even a bit more restrained than normal, and we would have thought him really nuts if he hadn't acted weird. As it was, we considered him a flake, but not wrapped so tight that you couldn't poke fun at him, and I believe it was this misconception that brought matters to a head....

Yet I'm not absolutely certain of that.

Several nights after my talk with Moon, I was on duty in the operations bunker when Randall did his broadcast. He always signed off in the same distinctive fashion, trying to contact the patrols of ghosts he claimed were haunting the free-fire zones. Instead of using ordinary call signs like Charlie Baker Able, he would invent others that suited the country lyricism of his style, names such as Lobo Angel Silver and Prairie Dawn Omega.

"Delta Sly Honey," he said that night. "Do you read? Over."

He sat a moment, listening to static filling in from nowhere.

"I know you're out there, Delta Sly Honey," he went on. "I can see you clear, walkin' the high country near Black Virgin Mountain, movin' through twists of fog like battle smoke and feelin' a little afraid, 'cause though you gone from the world, there's a world of fear 'tween here and the hereafter. Come back at me, Delta Sly Honey, and tell me how it's goin'." He stopped sending for a bit, and when he received no reply, he spoke again. "Maybe you don't think I'd understand your troubles, brothers. But I truly do. I know your hopes and fears, and how the spell of too much poison and fire and flyin' steel warped the chemistry of fate and made you wander off into the wars of the spirit 'stead of findin' rest beyond the grave. My soul's trackin' you as you move higher and higher toward the peace at the end of everything, passin' through mortar bursts throwin' up thick gouts of silence, with angels like tracers leadin' you on, listenin' to the cold white song of incoming stars.... Come on back at me, Delta Sly Honey. This here's your good buddy Randall J., earthbound at Noc Linh. Do you read?"

There was a wild burst of static, and then a voice answered, saying, "Randall J., Randall J.! This is Delta Sly Honey. Readin' you loud and clear."

I let out a laugh, and the officers sitting at the far end of the bunker turned their heads, grinning. But Randall stared in horror at the radio, as if it were leaking blood, not static. He thumbed the switch and said shakily, "What's your position, Delta Sly Honey? I repeat. What's your position?"

"Guess you might say our position's kinda relative," came the reply. "But far as you concerned, man, we just down the road. There's a place for you with us, Randall J. We waitin' for you."

Randall's Adam's apple worked, and he wetted his lips. Under the hot bunker lights, his freckles stood out sharply.

"Y'know how it is when you're pinned down by fire?" the voice continued. "Lyin' flat with the flow of bullets passin' inches over your head? And you start thinkin' how easy it'd be just to raise up and get it over with.... You ever feel like that, Randall J.? Most times you keep flat, 'cause things ain't bad enough to make you go that route. But the way things been goin' for you, man, what with stickin' your hands into dead meat night and day—"

"Shut up," said Randall, his voice tight and small.

"—and that asshole Moon fuckin' with your mind, maybe it's time to consider your options."

"Shut up!" Randall screamed it, and I grabbed him by the shoulders. "Take it easy," I told him. "It's just some jerkoff puttin' you on." He shook me off; the vein in his temple was throbbing.

"I ain't tryin' to mess with you, man," said the voice. "I'm just layin' it out, showin' you there ain't no real options here. I know all them crazy thoughts that been flappin' 'round in your head, and I know how hard you been tryin' to control 'em. Ain't no point in controllin' 'em anymore, Randall J. You belong to us now. All you gotta do is to take a little walk down the road, and we be waitin'. We got some serious humpin' ahead of us, man. Out past the Napalm Coast, up beyond the high country..."

Randall bolted for the door, but I caught him and spun him around. He was breathing rapidly through his mouth, and his eyes seemed to be shining too brightly—like the way an old light bulb will flare up right before it goes dark for good. "Lemme go!" he said. "I gotta find 'em! I gotta tell 'em it ain't my time!"

"It's just someone playin' a goddamn joke," I said, and then it dawned on me. "It's Moon, Randall! You know it's him puttin' somebody up to this."

"I gotta find 'em!" he repeated, and with more strength than I would have given him credit for, he pushed me away and ran off into the dark.

He didn't return, not that night, not the next morning, and we reported him AWOL. We searched the base and the nearby villes to no avail, and since the countryside was rife with NLF patrols and VC, it was logical to assume he had been killed or captured. Over the next couple of days, Moon made frequent public denials of his complicity in the joke, but no one bought it. He took to walking around with his holster unlatched, a wary expression on his face. Though Randall hadn't had any real friends, many of us had been devoted to his broadcasts, and among those devotees were a number of men who...well, a civilian psychiatrist might have called them unstable, but in truth they were men who had chosen to exalt instability, to ritualize insanity as a means of maintaining their equilibrium in an unstable medium: it was likely some of them would attempt reprisals. Moon's best hope was that something would divert their attention, but three days after Randall's disappearance, a peculiar transmission came into operations; like all Randall's broadcasts, it was piped over the PA, and thus Moon's fate was sealed.

"Howdy, Noc Linh," said Randall or someone who sounded identical to him. "This here's Randall J. Willingham on patrol with Delta Sly

Honey, speakin' to you from beyond the Napalm Coast. We been humpin' through rain and fog most of the day, with no sign of the enemy, just a few demons twistin' up from the gray and fadin' when we come near, and now we all hunkered down by the radio, restin' for tomorrow. Y'know, brothers, I used to be scared shitless of wakin' up here in the big nothin', but now it's gone and happened, I'm findin' it ain't so bad. 'Least I got the feelin' I'm headed someplace, whereas back at Noc Linh I was just spinnin' round and round, and close to losin' my mind. I hated ol' Sergeant Moon, and I hated him worse after he put someone up to hasslin' me on the radio. But now, though I reckon he's still pretty hateful, I can see he was actin' under the influence of a higher agency, one who was tryin' to help me get clear of Noc Linh...which was somethin' that had to be, no matter if I had to die to do it. Seems to me that's the nature of war, that all the violence has the effect of lettin' a little magic seep into the world by way of compensation...."

To most of us, this broadcast signaled that Randall was alive, but we also knew what it portended for Moon. And therefore I wasn't terribly surprised when he summoned me to his tent the next morning. At first he tried to play sergeant, ordering me to ally myself with him; but seeing that this didn't work, he begged for my help. He was a mess: red-eyed, unshaven, an eyelid twitching.

"I can't do a thing," I told him.

"You're his friend!" he said. "If you tell 'em I didn't have nothin' to do with it, they'll believe you."

"The hell they will! They'll think I helped you." I studied him a second, enjoying his anxiety. "Who did help you?"

"I didn't do it, goddammit!" His voice had risen to a shout, and he had to struggle to keep calm. "I swear! It wasn't me!"

It was strange, my mental set at that moment. I found I believed him—I didn't think him capable of manufacturing sincerity—and yet I suddenly believed everything: that Randall was somehow both dead and alive, that Delta Sly Honey both did and did not exist, that whatever was happening was an event in which all possibility was manifest, in which truth and falsity had the same valence, in which the real and the illusory were undifferentiated. And at the center of this complex circumstance—a bulky, sweating monster—stood Moon. Innocent, perhaps. But guilty of a seminal crime.

"I can make it good for you," he said. "Hawaii...you want duty in Hawaii, I can arrange it. Hell, I can get you shipped Stateside."

He struck me then as a hideous genie offering three wishes, and the fact that he had the power to make this offer infuriated me. "If you can do all that," I said, "you ain't got a worry in the world." And I strode off, feeling righteous in my judgment.

Two nights later while returning to my hooch, I spotted a couple of men wearing tiger shorts dragging a large and apparently unconscious someone toward the barrier of concertina wire beside the PX—I knew it had to be Moon. I drew my pistol, sneaked along the back wall of the PX, and when they came abreast I stepped out and told them to put their burden down. They stopped but didn't turn loose of Moon. Both had blackened their faces with greasepaint, and to this had added fanciful designs in crimson, blue, and yellow that gave them the look of savages. They carried combat knives, and their eyes were pointed with the reflected brilliance of the perimeter lights. It was a hot night, but it seemed hotter there beside them, as if their craziness had a radiant value. "This ain't none of your affair, Curt," said the taller of the two; despite his bad grammar, he had a soft, well-modulated voice, and I thought I heard a trace of amusement in it.

I peered at him, but was unable to recognize him beneath the paint. Again I told them to put Moon down.

"Sorry," said the tall guy. "Man's gotta pay for his crimes."

"He didn't do anything," I said. "You know damn well Randall's just AWOL."

The tall guy chuckled, and the other guy said, "Naw, we don't know that a-tall."

Moon groaned, tried to lift his head, then slumped back.

"No matter what he did or didn't do," said the tall guy, "the man deserves what's comin'."

"Yeah," said his pal. "And if it ain't us what does it, it'll be somebody else."

I knew he was right, and the idea of killing two men to save a third who was doomed in any event just didn't stack up. But though my sense of duty was weak where Moon was concerned, it hadn't entirely dissipated. "Let him go," I said.

The tall guy grinned, and the other one shook his head as if dismayed by my stubbornness. They appeared wholly untroubled by the pistol, possessed of an irrational confidence. "Be reasonable, Curt," said the tall guy. "This ain't gettin' you nowhere."

I couldn't believe his foolhardiness. "You see this?" I said, flourishing the pistol. "Gun, y'know? I'm gonna fuckin' shoot you with it, you don't let him go."

Moon let out another groan, and the tall guy rapped him hard on the back of the head with the hilt of his knife.

"Hey!" I said, training the pistol on his chest.

"Look here, Curt..." he began.

"Who the hell are you?" I stepped closer, but was still unable to identify him. "I don't know you."

"Randall told us 'bout you, Curt. He's a buddy of ours, ol' Randall is. We're with Delta Sly Honey."

I believed him for that first split second. My mouth grew cottony, and my hand trembled. But then I essayed a laugh. "Sure you are! Now put his ass down!"

"That's what you really want, huh?"

"Damn right!" I said. "Now!"

"Okay," he said. "You got it." And with a fluid stroke, he cut Moon's throat.

Moon's eyes popped open as the knife sliced through his tissues, and that—not the blood spilling onto the dust—was the thing that froze me: those bugged eyes in which an awful realization dawned and faded. They let him fall facedownward. His legs spasmed, his right hand jittered. For a long moment, stunned, I stared at him, at the blood puddling beneath his head, and when I looked up I found that the two men were sprinting away, about to round the curve of the hill. I couldn't bring myself to fire. Mixed in my thoughts were the knowledge that killing them served no purpose and the fear that my bullets would have no effect. I glanced left and right, behind me, making sure that no one was watching, and then ran up the slope to my hooch.

Under my cot was a bottle of sour mash. I pulled it out and had a couple of drinks to steady myself; but steadiness was beyond me. I switched on a battery lamp and sat cross-legged, listening to the snores of my bunkmate. Lying on my duffel bag was an unfinished letter home, one I had begun nearly two weeks before; I doubted now I'd ever finish it. What would I tell my folks? That I had more or less sanctioned an execution? That I was losing my fucking mind? Usually I told them everything was fine, but after the scene I had just witnessed, I felt I was forever past that sort of blithe invention. I switched off the lamp and lay in the dark, the bottle resting on my chest. I had a third drink, a fourth, and gradually lost both count and consciousness.

I had a week's R & R coming and I took it, hoping debauch would shore me up. But I spent much of that week attempting to justify my inaction in terms of the inevitable and the supernatural, and failing in that attempt. You see, now as then, if pressed for an opinion, I would tell you that what happened at Noc Linh was the sad consequence of a joke gone sour, of a war twisted into a demonic exercise. Everything was explicable in that wise. And yet it's conceivable that the supernatural was involved, that—as Randall had suggested—a little magic had seeped into the world. In Vietnam, with all its horror and strangeness, it was difficult to distinguish between the magical and the mundane, and it's possible that thousands of supernatural events went unnoticed as such, obscured by the poignancies of death and fear, becoming quirky memories that years later might pass through your mind while you were washing the dishes or walking the dog, and give you a moment's pause, an eerie feeling that would almost instantly be ground away by the mills of the ordinary. But I'm certain that my qualification is due to the fact that I want there to have been some magic involved, anything to lessen my culpability, to shed a less damning light on the perversity and viciousness of my brothers-in-arms.

On returning to Noc Linh, I found that Randall had also returned. He claimed to be suffering from amnesia and would not admit to having made the broadcast that had triggered Moon's murder. The shrinks had decided that he was bucking for a Section Eight, had ordered him put back on the corpse detail, and as before, Randall could be seen laboring beneath the tin-roofed shed, transferring the contents of body bags into aluminum coffins. On the surface, little appeared to have changed. But Randall had become a pariah. He was insulted and whispered about and shunned. Whenever he came near, necks would stiffen and conversations die. If he had offed Moon himself, he would have been cheered; but the notion that he had used his influence to have his dirty work jobbed out didn't accord with the prevailing concept of honorable vengeance. Though I tried not to, I couldn't help feeling badly toward him myself. It was weird. I would approach with the best of intentions, but by the time I reached him, my hackles would have risen and I would walk on in hostile silence, as if he were exuding a chemical that had evoked my contempt. I did get close enough to him, however, to see that the mad brightness was missing from his eyes; I had the feeling that all his brightness was missing, that whatever quality had enabled him to do his broadcasts had been sucked dry.

One morning as I was passing the PX, whose shiny surfaces reflected a dynamited white glare of sun, I noticed a crowd of men pressing through the front door, apparently trying to catch sight of something inside. I pushed through them and found one of the canteen clerks—a lean kid with black hair and a wolfish face—engaged in beating Randall to a pulp. I pulled him off, threw him into a table, and kneeled beside Randall, who had collapsed to the floor. His cheekbones were lumped and discolored; blood poured from his nose, trickled from his mouth. His eyes met mine, and I felt nothing from him: he seemed muffled, vibeless, as if heavily sedated.

"They out to get me, Curt," he mumbled.

All my sympathy for him was suddenly resurrected. "It's okay, man," I said. "Sooner or later, it'll blow over." I handed him my bandanna, and he dabbed ineffectually at the flow from his nose. Watching him, I recalled Moon's categorization of my motives for befriending him, and I understood now that my true motives had less to do with our relative social status than with my belief that he could be saved, that—after months of standing by helplessly while the unsalvageable marched to their fates—I thought I might be able to effect some small good work. This may seem altruistic to the point of naïveté, and perhaps it was, perhaps the brimstone oppressiveness of the war had from the residue of old sermons heard and disregarded provoked some vain Christian reflex; but the need was strong in me, nonetheless, and I realized that I had fixed on it as a prerequisite to my own salvation.

Randall handed back the bandanna. "Ain't gonna blow over," he said. "Not with these guys."

I grabbed his elbow and hauled him to his feet. "What guys?"

He looked around as if afraid of eavesdroppers. "Delta Sly Honey!"

"Christ, Randall! Come on." I tried to guide him toward the door, but he wrenched free.

"They out to get me! They say I crossed over and they took care of Moon for me...and then I got away from 'em." He dug his fingers into my arm. "But I can't remember, Curt! I can't remember nothin'!"

My first impulse was to tell him to drop the amnesia act, but then I thought about the painted men who had scragged Moon: if they were after Randall, he was in big trouble. "Let's get you patched up," I said. "We'll talk about this later."

He gazed at me, dull and uncomprehending. "You gonna help me?" he asked in a tone of disbelief.

I doubted anyone could help him now, and maybe, I thought, that was also part of my motivation—the desire to know the good sin of honest failure. "Sure," I told him. "We'll figure out somethin'."

We started for the door, but on seeing the men gathered there, Randall balked. "What you want from me?" he shouted, giving a flailing, awkward wave with his left arm as if to make them vanish. "What the fuck you want?"

They stared coldly at him, and those stares were like bad answers. He hung his head and kept it hung all the way to the infirmary.

That night I set out to visit Randall, intending to advise him to confess, a tactic I perceived as his one hope of survival. I'd planned to see him early in the evening, but was called back on duty and didn't get clear until well after midnight. The base was quiet and deserted-feeling. Only a few lights picked out the darkened slopes, and had it not been for the heat and stench, it would have been easy to believe that the hill with its illuminated caves was a place of mild enchantment, inhabited by elves and not frightened men. The moon was almost full, and beneath it the PX shone like an immense silver lozenge. Though it had closed an hour before, its windows were lit, and—MP instincts engaged—I peered inside. Randall was backed against the bar, holding a knife to the neck of the wolfish clerk who had beaten him, and ranged in a loose circle around him, standing among the tables, were five men wearing tiger shorts, their faces painted with savage designs. I drew my pistol, eased around to the front, and—wanting my entrance to have shock value—kicked the door open.

The five men turned their heads to me, but appeared not at all disconcerted. "How's she goin', Curt?" said one, and by his soft voice I recognized the tall guy who had slit Moon's throat.

"Tell 'em to leave me be!" Randall shrilled.

I fixed my gaze on the tall guy and with gunslinger menace said, "I'm not messin' with you tonight. Get out now or I'll take you down."

"You can't hurt me, Curt," he said.

"Don't gimme that ghost shit! Fuck with me, and you'll be humpin' with Delta Sly Honey for real."

"Even if you were right 'bout me, Curt, I wouldn't be scared of dyin'. I was dead where it counts halfway through my tour."

A scuttling at the bar, and I saw that Randall had wrestled the clerk to the floor. He wrapped his legs around the clerk's waist in a scissors and yanked his head back by the hair to expose his throat. "Leave me be," he said. Every nerve in his face was jumping.

"Let him go, Randall," said the tall guy. "We ain't after no innocent blood. We just want you to take a little walk...to cross back over."

"Get out!" I told him.

"You're workin' yourself in real deep, man," he said.

"This ain't no bullshit!" I said. "I *will* shoot."

"Look here, Curt," he said. "S'pose we're just plain ol' ordinary grunts. You gonna shoot us all? And if you do, don't you think we'd have friends who'd take it hard? Any way you slice it, you bookin' yourself a silver box and air freight home."

He came a step toward me, and I said, "Watch it, man!" He came another step, his devil mask split by a fierce grin. My heart felt hot and solid in my chest, no beats, and I thought, He's a ghost, his flesh is smoke, the paint a color in my eye. "Keep back!" I warned.

"Gonna kill me?" Again he grinned. "Go ahead." He lunged, a feint only, and I squeezed the trigger.

The gun jammed.

When I think now how this astounded me, I wonder at my idiocy. The gun jammed frequently. It was an absolute piece of shit, that weapon. But at the time its failure seemed a magical coincidence, a denial of the laws of chance. And adding to my astonishment was the reaction of the other men: they made no move toward Randall, as if no opportunity had been provided, no danger passed. Yet the tall guy looked somewhat shaken to me.

Randall let out a mewling noise, and that sound enlisted my competence. I edged between the tables and took a stand next to him. "Let me get the knife from him," I said. "No point in both of 'em dyin'."

The tall guy drew a deep breath as if to settle himself. "You reckon you can do that, Curt?"

"Maybe. If you guys wait outside, he won't be as scared and maybe I can get it."

They stared at me, unreadable.

"Gimme a chance."

"We ain't after no innocent blood." The tall guy's tone was firm, as if this were policy. "But..."

"Just a coupla minutes," I said. "That's all I'm askin'."

I could almost hear the tick of the tall guy's judgment. "Okay," he said at last. "But don't you go tryin' nothin' hinkey, Curt." Then, to Randall. "We be waitin', Randall J."

As soon as they were out the door, I kneeled beside Randall. Spittle flecked the clerk's lips, and when Randall shifted the knife a tad, his eyes rolled up into heaven. "Leave me be," said Randall. He might have been talking to the air, the walls, the world.

"Give it up," I said.

He just blinked.

"Let him go and I'll help you," I said. "But if you cut him, you on your own. That how you want it?"

"Un-unh."

"Well, turn him loose."

"I can't," he said, a catch in his voice. "I'm all froze up. If I move, I'll cut him." Sweat dripped into his eyes, and he blinked some more.

"How 'bout I take it from you? If you keep real still, if you lemme ease it outta your hand, maybe we can work it that way."

"I don't know.... I might mess up."

The clerk gave a long shuddery sigh and squeezed his eyes shut.

"You gonna be fine," I said to Randall. "Just keep your eyes on me, and you gonna be fine."

I stretched out my hand. The clerk was trembling, Randall was trembling, and when I touched the blade it was so full of vibration, it felt alive, as if all the energy in the room had been concentrated there. I tried pulling it away from the clerk's neck, but it wouldn't budge.

"You gotta loosen up, Randall," I said.

I tried again and, gripping the blade between my forefinger and thumb, managed to pry it an inch or so away from the line of blood it had drawn. My fingers were sweaty, the metal slick, and the blade felt like it was connected to a spring, that any second it would snap back and bite deep.

"My fingers are slippin'," I said, and the clerk whimpered.

"Ain't my fault if they do." Randall said this pleadingly, as if testing the waters, the potentials of his guilt and innocence, and I realized he was setting me up the way he had Moon's killers. It was a childlike attempt compared to the other, but I knew to his mind it would work out the same.

"The hell it ain't!" I said. "Don't do it, man!"

"It ain't my fault!" he insisted.

"Randall!"

I could feel his intent in the quiver of the blade. With my free hand, I grabbed the clerk's upper arm, and as the knife slipped, I jerked him to the side. The blade sliced his jaw, and he screeched; but the wound wasn't mortal.

I plucked the knife from Randall's hand, wanting to kill him myself. But I had invested too much in his salvation. I hauled him erect and over to the window; I smashed out the glass with a chair and pushed him through. Then I jumped after him. As I came to my feet, I saw the painted men closing in from the front of the PX and—still towing Randall along—I sprinted around the corner of the building and up the slope, calling for help. Lights flicked on, and heads popped from tent flaps. But when they spotted Randall, they ducked back inside.

I was afraid, but Randall's abject helplessness—his eyes rolling like a freaked calf's, his hands clawing at me for support—helped to steady me. The painted men seemed to be everywhere. They would materialize from behind tents, out of bunker mouths, grinning madly and waving moonstruck knives, and send us veering off in another direction, back and forth across the hill. Time and again, I thought they had us, and on several occasions, it was only by a hairsbreadth that I eluded the slash of a blade that looked to be bearing a charge of winking silver energy on its tip. I was wearing down, stumbling, gasping, and I was certain we couldn't last much longer. But we continued to evade them, and I began to sense that they were in no hurry to conclude the hunt; their pursuit had less an air of frenzy than of a ritual harassment, and eventually, as we staggered up to the mouth of the operations bunker and—I believed—safety, I realized that they had been herding us. I pushed Randall inside and glanced back from the sandbagged entrance. The five men stood motionless a second, perhaps fifty feet away, then melted into the darkness.

I explained what had happened to the MP on duty in the bunker—a heavyset guy named Cousins—and though he had no love for Randall, he was a dutiful sort and gave us permission to wait out the night inside. Randall slumped down against the wall, resting his head on his knees, the picture of despair. But I believed that his survival was assured. With the testimony of the clerk, I thought the shrinks would have no choice but to send him elsewhere for examination and possible institutionalization. I felt good, accomplished, and passed the night chain-smoking, bullshitting with Cousins.

Then, toward dawn, a voice issued from the radio. It was greatly distorted, but it sounded very much like Randall's.

"Randall J.," it said. "This here's Delta Sly Honey. Do you read? Over."

Randall looked up, hearkening to the spit and fizzle of the static.

"I know you out there, Randall J.," the voice went on. "I can see you clear, sitting with the shadows of the bars upon your soul and blood on your hands. Ain't no virtuous blood, that's true. But it stains you alla same. Come back at me, Randall J. We gotta talk, you and me."

Randall let his head fall; with a finger, he traced a line in the dust.

"What's the point in keepin' this up, Randall J.?" said the voice. "You left the best part of you over here, the soulful part, and you can't go on much longer without it. Time to take that little walk for real, man. Time to get clear of what you done and pass on to what must be. We waitin' for you just north of base, Randall J. Don't make us come for you."

It was in my mind to say something to Randall, to break the disconsolate spell the voice appeared to be casting over him; but I found I had nothing left to give him, that I had spent my fund of altruism and was mostly weary of the whole business...as he must have been.

"Ain't nothin' to be 'fraid of out here," said the voice. "Only the wind and the gray whispers of phantom Charlie and the trail leadin' away from the world. There's good company for you, Randall J. Gotta man here used to be a poet, and he'll tell you stories 'bout the Wild North King and the Woman of Crystal. Got another fella, guy used to live in Indonesia, and he's fulla tales 'bout watchin' tigers come out on the highways to shit and cities of men dressed like women and islands where dragons still live. Then there's this kid from Opelika, claims to know some of your people down that way, and when he talks, you can just see that ol' farmboy moon heavin' up big and yellow over the barns, shinin' the blacktop so it looks like polished jet, and you can hear crazy music leakin' from the Dixieland Café and smell the perfumed heat steamin' off the young girls' breasts. Don't make us wait no more, Randall J. We got work to do. Maybe it ain't much, just breakin' trail and walkin' point and keepin' a sharp eye out for demons...but it sure as hell beats shepherdin' the dead, now, don't it?" A long pause. "You come on and take that walk, Randall J. We'll make you welcome, I promise. This here's Delta Sly Honey. Over and out."

Randall pulled himself to his feet and took a faltering few steps toward the mouth of the bunker. I blocked his path and he said, "Lemme go, Curt."

"Look here, Randall," I said. "I might can get you home if you just hang on."

"Home." The concept seemed to amuse him, as if it were something with the dubious reality of heaven or hell. "Lemme go."

In his eyes, then, I thought I could see all his broken parts, a disjointed shifting of lights and darks, and when I spoke I felt I was giving tongue to a vast consensus, one arrived at without either ballots or reasonable discourse. "If I let you go," I said, "be best you don't come back this time."

He stared at me, his face gone slack, and nodded.

Hardly anybody was outside, yet I had the idea everyone was watching us as we walked down the hill; under a leaden overcast, the base had a tense, muted atmosphere such as must have attended rainy dawns beneath the guillotine. The sentries at the main gate passed Randall through without question. He went a few paces along the road, then turned back, his face pale as a star in the half-light, and I wondered if he thought we were driving him off or if he believed he was being called to a better world. In my heart I knew which was the case. At last he set out again, quickly becoming a shadow, then the rumor of a shadow, then gone.

Walking back up the hill, I tried to sort out my thoughts, to determine what I was feeling, and it may be a testament to how crazy I was, how crazy we all were, that I felt less regret for a man lost than satisfaction in knowing that some perverted justice had been served, that the world of the war—tipped off-center by this unmilitary engagement and our focus upon it—could now go back to spinning true.

That night there was fried chicken in the mess, and vanilla ice cream, and afterward a movie about a more reasonable war, full of villainous Germans with Dracula accents and heroic grunts who took nothing but flesh wounds. When it was done, I walked back to my hooch and stood out front and had a smoke. In the northern sky was a flickering orange glow, one accompanied by the rumble of artillery. It was, I realized, just about this time of night that Randall had customarily begun his broadcasts. Somebody else must have realized this, because at that moment the PA was switched on. I half expected to hear Randall giving the news of Delta Sly Honey, but there was only static, sounding like the crackling of enormous flames. Listening to it, I felt disoriented, completely vulnerable, as if some huge black presence were on the verge of swallowing me up. And then a voice did speak. It wasn't Randall's, yet it had a similar countrified accent, and though the words weren't quite as fluent, they were redolent of his old raps, lending a folksy comprehensibility to the vastness of the cosmos, the strangeness of the war. I had no idea whether or not it was the voice that had summoned Randall to take his walk, no longer affecting an imitation, yet I thought I recognized its soft well-modulated tones. But none of that mattered. I was so grateful, so relieved by this end to silence, that I went into my hooch and—armed with lies—sat down to finish my interrupted letter home.

Nothing Will Hurt You

DAVID MORRELL

David Morrell is the critically acclaimed author of *First Blood*, the novel in which Rambo was created. He holds a Ph.D. in American literature from Penn State and was a professor in the English department at the University of Iowa. His numerous *New York Times* bestsellers include the classic spy trilogy *The Brotherhood of the Rose* (the basis for the only television mini-series to premiere after a Super Bowl), *The Fraternity of the Stone*, and *The League of Night and Fog*. An Edgar, Anthony, and Macavity nominee, Morrell is the recipient of three Bram Stoker Awards from the Horror Writers Association as well as the prestigious lifetime Thriller Master Award from the International Thriller Writers' organization. He was also nominated for two World Fantasy Awards. His writing book, *The Successful Novelist*, discusses what he has learned in his four decades as an author.

You can find out more about David and his work at: http://www.davidmorrell.net/.

Later the song would have agonizing significance for him. "I can't stop hearing it," Chad would tell his psychiatrist and fight to control his rapid breathing. His eyes would ache. "It doesn't matter what I'm doing, meeting a client, talking to a publisher, reading a manuscript, walking through Central Park, even going to the bathroom, I hear that song! I've tried my damnedest not to. I hardly sleep, but when I manage to, I wake up, feeling I've been humming it all night."

Chad vividly remembered the first time he'd heard it. He could date it exactly: Wednesday, April 20, 1979. He could give the time precisely: 9:46 p.m., because although he'd found the song poignant and the singer's performance outstanding, he'd felt an odd compulsion to glance at his watch. It must have been a tougher day than I realized, he'd thought. So tired. Nine forty-six. Is that all?

Sweeney Todd: The Demon Barber of Fleet Street. Stephen Sondheim's musical had opened on Broadway in March, a critical success, tickets impossible to get, except that Chad had a playwright client with contacts in the production company. When Chad's wife, Linda, broke one of their marriage's rules and gave Chad a surprise birthday party, the client (pretending to be a magician) pulled two tickets from behind Chad's ear. "Happy forty-second, old buddy."

But Chad remembered the precise date he saw the musical not because it had anything to do with his birthday. Instead, he had a deeper reason. The demon barber of Fleet Street. Come in for a shave and a haircut, have your throat slit, get dumped down a chute, ground up into hamburger, and baked into Mrs. Lovett's renowned, ever-popular, scrumptious, how-do-you-get-that-distinctive-taste meat pies.

Can't eat enough of them. To startle the audience, a deafening whistle shrilled each time Sweeney slashed a throat. Blood spurted. And one of Mrs. Lovett's waiters was an idiot kid who hadn't the faintest idea of what was going on, but he had misgivings that *something* was wrong. He confessed his fears to Mrs. Lovett, who thought of him fondly as her son. She promised that she'd protect him. She sang that nothing would hurt him—a magnificent performance by Angela Lansbury of a tune that forever after would torture Chad, its title: "Not While I'm Around." A lilting heartbreaking song in the midst of multiple murders and cannibalism.

After the show, Chad and Linda had trouble finding a taxi and didn't get back to their Upper East Side apartment until almost midnight. They felt so disturbed by the plot yet elated by the music that they decided to have some brandy and discuss their reactions to the show, and that's when the phone rang. Scowling, Chad wondered who in hell would be calling at such an hour. Immediately he suspected one of his nervous, not to mention important, authors with whom he'd been having tense conversations all week because of a publisher's unfavorable reaction to the author's new manuscript. Chad tried to ignore the phone's persistent jangle. Let the answering machine take it, he thought. At once, he angrily picked up the phone.

A man's gravelly voice, made faint by the hiss of a long-distance line, sounded tense. "This is Lieutenant Raymond MacKenzie. I'm with the New Haven police force. I know it's late. I apologize if I woke you, but... There's been an emergency, I'm afraid."

What Chad heard next made him quiver. In response, he insisted, "No. You're wrong. There's got to be some mistake."

"Don't I wish." The lieutenant's voice became more gravelly. "You have my deepest sympathy. Times like this, I hate my job." The lieutenant gave instructions.

Chad murmured compliance and set down the phone.

Linda, who'd been staring, demanded to know why Chad was so pale.

When Chad explained, Linda blurted, "No! Dear God, it can't be!"

Urgency canceled numbness. They each threw clothes into a suitcase, hurried from their apartment to the rental garage three blocks away where they stored their two-year-old Ford (they'd bought the car at the same time they'd bought their cottage in Connecticut, so they could spend weekends near their daughter), and sped with absolutely no memory of the drive (except that they kept repeating, "No, it's impossible!") to New Haven and Lieutenant MacKenzie, whose husky voice, it turned out, didn't match his short, thin frame.

Denial was reflexive, insistent, stubborn. Even when the lieutenant sympathetically repeated and re-repeated that there had *not* been a mistake, when he regretfully showed them Stephanie's purse, her wallet, her driver's license, when he showed them a statement from Stephanie's roommate that she hadn't come back to the dormitory last night...even when Chad and Linda went down to the morgue and identified the body, or what was left of the body, although it hadn't been Stephanie's *face* that was mutilated...they still kept insisting, no, this had to be someone who looked like Stephanie, someone who stole Stephanie's purse, someone who...some mistake!

Nothing would hurt him, Angela Lansbury had sung to the boy her character thought of as a son in *Sweeney Todd*, and the night before when Chad had listened to the lilting near-lullaby, he had been briefly reminded of his own and only child, dear sweet Stephanie, when she was a tot and he had read to her at bedtime, had sung nursery rhymes to her, and had taught her to pray.

"Now I lay me down to sleep," his beloved daughter had obediently repeated. "I pray the Lord my soul to keep. If I should die before I wake, I pray the Lord my soul to take.... Daddy, is there a bogeyman?"

"No, dear. It's just your imagination. Go to sleep. Don't worry. Daddy's here. Nothing will hurt you."

"Not While I'm Around," the song had been called. But two years earlier Stephanie had gone to New Haven, for a B.A. in English at Yale, and last night there *had* been a bogeyman, and despite Chad's long-ago promise, he had *not* been around when the bogeyman very definitely hurt Stephanie.

"When did it..." Chad struggled to breathe as he stared at Lieutenant MacKenzie. "What time did she..."

"The body was discovered at just before eleven last night. Based on heat loss from the brain, the medical examiner estimates the time of death between nine-thirty and ten p.m."

"Nine forty-six."

The lieutenant frowned. "More or less. It's difficult to be that precise."

"Sure." Chad bit his lip, tasting tears. "Nine forty-six."

He remembered the odd compulsion he'd felt to glance at his watch the previous night when Angela Lansbury had sung that nothing would hurt her friend.

While the bogeyman killed Stephanie.

Chad knew. He was absolutely certain. Nine forty-six. That was when Stephanie had died. He'd felt the tug of her death as if a little girl had jerked at the sleeve of his suit coat.

"Daddy, is there a bogeyman?"

"Not while I can help it."

Chad must have said that out loud.

Because the lieutenant frowned, asking, "What? I'm sorry, sir. I didn't quite hear what you just said."

"Nothing." Sobbing uncontrollably, holding Linda whose features were raw-red, dripping with tears, contorted with grief, Chad felt the terrible urge to ask the lieutenant to take him down to the morgue again—just so he could see Stephanie one more time, even if she looked like, even if her...

All he wanted was to *see* her again! Stephanie! No, it couldn't be! Jesus, not Stephanie!

Numbness. Denial. Confusion. Chad later tried to reconstruct the conversations, remembering them through a haze. No matter how often he was given details, he needed more and more clarification. "I don't understand. What the hell happened? Have you any clues? Witnesses? Have you found the son of a bitch who did this?"

The lieutenant looked bleak as he explained. Stephanie had gone to the university library the previous afternoon. A friend had seen her leave the library at six. On her way back to the dormitory, someone must have offered her a ride or asked her to help him carry something into a building or somehow grabbed her without attracting attention. The usual method was to appeal to the victim's sympathy by pretending to be disabled. However it was done, she had disappeared.

Afterward, the killer had stopped his car at the side of a road outside New Haven and dumped Stephanie's body into a ditch. The absence of blood at the scene indicated that the murder had occurred at another location. The road was far from a highway. At night, all the killer had to do was drive along the road until there weren't any headlights before or behind him, then stop and rush to open the trunk and get rid of the body. Twenty seconds later, he'd have been back on his way.

The lieutenant sighed. "It's only coincidence that a car on that road last night happened to have a flat tire where the killer left your daughter. The driver's a farmer who lives in the area. He switched on his flashlight, walked around the car to check his tire, and his light picked up your daughter. Pure coincidence, but clues, yes, because of that coincidence, this time we've got some. Tire tracks at the side of the road. It rained yesterday afternoon. Any tracks in the dirt would have to be fresh. Forensics got a *very* clear set of impressions."

"Tire tracks? But *they* won't identify the killer."

"What can I say, Mr. Dolan? At the moment, those tire tracks are all we've got—and believe me, they're more than any other police force involved in these killings has managed to get, except of course for the consistent marks on the victims."

Plural. On that point, at least, Chad didn't need an explanation. One look at Stephanie's body, at what the bastard had *done* to her body, and Chad had known who the killer was. Not the bastard's name, of course. But *everybody* knew his nickname. One of those cheap tabloids at the supermarket checkout counter had given it to him. The Biter. And reputable newspapers had stooped to the tabloid's level by repeating it. Because in addition to raping and strangling his victims (eighteen so far, all Caucasian females, attractive, blond, in their late teens, in college), the killer left bite marks on them, police reports revealed.

The published details were sketchy. Chad had grimly imagined teeth impressions on a neck, an arm, a shoulder. But nothing had prepared him for the horrors done to his daughter's corpse, for the killer didn't merely bite his victims. He *chewed* on them. He gnawed huge pieces from their arms and legs. He chomped holes in their stomachs, bit off their nipples, nipped off their labia. The son of a bitch was a cannibal! Multiple murders and...

Sweeney Todd.

Nothing will hurt you.

Imagining Stephanie's lonely panic, Chad moaned until he screamed.

In a stupor, he and Linda struggled through the nightmare of arranging for a funeral, waiting for the police to release the body, and collecting their daughter's things from her dormitory room. On her desk, they found a half-finished essay about Shakespeare's sonnets, a page still in the typewriter, a quotation never completed: "Shall I compare thee to a summer's..." On a shelf beside her bed, they picked up textbooks, sections of them underlined in red, that Stephanie had been studying for final exams she would never take. Clothes, keepsakes, her radio, her Winnie-the-Pooh bear. Everything filled a suitcase and three boxes. So little. So easily removed. Now you're here, now you aren't, Chad bitterly thought. Oh, Jesus.

"I'm sorry, Mr. and Mrs. Dolan," Stephanie's roommate said. She had freckles and wore glasses. Her long red hair hung in a ponytail. She looked devastated. "I really am. Stephanie was kind and smart and funny. I liked her. I'm going to miss her. She was special. It just isn't fair. Gosh, I'm so confused. I wish I knew what to say. I've never known anyone close to me who died before."

"I understand," Chad said bleakly. His father had died from a heart attack at the age of seventy, but that death hadn't struck Chad with the overwhelming shock of *this* death. After all, his father had battled heart disease for several years, and the massive coronary had been inevitable. He'd passed away, succumbed, joined his Maker, whatever euphemism hid the fact best and gave the most comfort. But what had happened to Stephanie was cruelly, starkly, brutally that she'd been *murdered*.

Dear God, it couldn't be!

Chad and Linda carried Stephanie's things to the car, returned to the police station, and badgered Lieutenant MacKenzie until he finally gave them directions to the road and the ditch where Stephanie had been found.

"Don't torture yourselves," the lieutenant tried to tell them, but Chad and Linda were already out the door.

Chad didn't know what he expected to find or feel or achieve by seeing the spot where the killer had parked and dumped Stephanie's body like a sack of garbage. As it turned out, he and Linda weren't able to get close anyhow—a police officer was standing watch over a section of the side of the road and a portion of the ditch, both enclosed by a makeshift fence of stakes linking yellow tape labeled POLICE CRIME SCENE: DO NOT ENTER. On the grass at the bottom of the ditch, the outline of Stephanie's twisted body had been drawn with white spray paint.

Linda wept.

Chad felt sick and hollow. At the same time, his heart and profoundly his *soul* swelled with rage. The bastard. The...Whoever did this, when they find him...Chad imagined punching him, stabbing him, choking him until his tongue bulged, and at once remembered that *Stephanie* had been choked. He leaned against the car and couldn't stop sobbing.

Finally, after seemingly endless bureaucratic delays, they were given their daughter. Following a hearse, they made the solemn drive back to New York for the funeral. Although Stephanie's face had not been mutilated, Chad and Linda refused to allow a public viewing of her remains. Granted, mourning friends and relatives wouldn't be able to see the obscene marks on her body beneath her burial clothes, but Chad and Linda *would* see those marks—in their minds—as if the burial clothes were transparent. More, Chad and Linda couldn't tolerate inflicting upon Stephanie the indignity of being forced to lie in her grave for all eternity with that monster's filthy marks on her. She had to be cremated. Purified. Made innocent again. Ashes to ashes. Cleansed with fire.

Each day, Chad and Linda drove out to the cemetery to visit her. The trip became the event around which they scheduled their other activities. Not that they *had* many other activities. Chad had no interest in reading manuscripts, meeting authors, and dealing with publishers, although his friends said that the thing to do was get back on track, distract himself, immerse himself in his literary agency. But his work didn't matter, and he spent more and more of each day taking long walks through Central Park. He had dizzy spells. He drank too much. For her part, Linda quit teaching piano, sequestered herself in the apartment, studied photographs of Stephanie, stared into space, and slept a great deal. They sold the cottage in Connecticut, which they'd bought and gone to each weekend only so they could be close to Stephanie in New Haven if she had wanted to visit. They sold their Ford, which they'd needed only to get to the cottage.

Nothing will hurt you. The bittersweet song constantly, faintly, echoed in the darkest chambers of Chad's mind. He thought he'd go crazy as he trembled from stress and obeyed the compulsion to visit places he associated with Stephanie: the playground of the grade school she'd attended, her high school, the zoo at Central Park, the jogging track around the lake. He conjured images of her—different ages, different heights, different hair and clothes styles—ghostly mental photographs, eerie double exposures in which then and now coexisted. A little girl, she giggled on a swing in a neighborhood park that had long ago become an apartment building. I can't stand this! Chad thought in mental rage and imagined the blessed release that he would feel if he hurled himself in front of a speeding subway train.

What helped him was that Stephanie told him not to. Oh, he knew that her voice was only in his mind. But she sounded so real, and her tender voice made him feel less tormented. He heard her so clearly.

"Dad, think of Mother. If you kill yourself, you'll cause her twice the pain she has now. She needs you. For my sake, help her."

Chad's legs felt unsteady. He slumped on a chair in the kitchen, where at three a.m. he'd been pacing.

Nothing will hurt you.

"Oh, baby, I'm sorry."

"You couldn't have saved me, Dad. It's not your fault. You couldn't watch over me *all* the time. It could have happened differently. I could have been killed in a traffic accident a block from our apartment. There aren't any guarantees."

"It's just that I miss you so damned much."

"And I miss *you*, Dad. I love you. But I'm not really gone. I'm talking to you, aren't I?"

"Yes...At least I think so."

"I'm far away, but I'm also inside you, and whenever you want to talk, we can. All you have to do is think of me, and I'll be there."

"But it's not the same!"

"It's the best we can do, Dad. Where I am is...bright! I'm soaring! I'm ecstatic! You mustn't feel sorry for me. You've got to accept that I'm gone. You've got to accept that your life is different now. You've got to become involved once more. Stop drinking. Stop skipping meals. *Start* reading manuscripts again. Answer your clients' phone calls. Get in touch with publishers. Work."

"But I don't care!"

"You've *got* to! Don't throw your life away just because I lost mine! I'll never forgive you if..."

"No, please, sweetheart. Please don't get angry. I'll try. I promise. I will. I'll try."

"For *my* sake."

Sobbing, Chad nodded as the speck of light faded.

But Angela Lansbury's voice continued echoing faintly. Nothing will hurt you. No matter how hard he tried, Chad couldn't get the song from his mind. The more he heard it, the more a lurking implication in the lyrics began to trouble him, a half-sensed deeper meaning, dark and disturbing, felt but not understood, a further horror.

The Biter's next victim was found by a hiker on the bank of a stream near Princeton. That was three months later. Although the victim, a co-ed who worked for the university's library during the summer, had been missing for two weeks and exposed to scavenging animals and the blistering sun, her remains were sufficiently intact for the medical examiner to establish the cause of death as strangulation and to distinguish between animal and human bite marks. That information was all the police revealed to the press, but Chad now knew what "bite marks" meant, and he shuddered, remembering the chunks that the killer had gnawed from Stephanie's body.

By then, Linda had started taking students again. Chad—true to his promise to Stephanie—had forced himself to pay attention to his authors and their publishers. But now the news of the Biter's latest victim threatened to tear away the fragile control that he and Linda had managed to impose on their lives. Compulsively, he wrote a letter to the murdered girl's parents.

> We mourn for your daughter as we mourn for our
> own. We pray that they're at peace and beg God for
> justice. May this monster be caught before he kills
> again. May he be punished to the limits of hell.

In truth, Chad didn't need to pray that Stephanie was at peace. He knew she was. She told him so whenever he stumbled sleeplessly into the kitchen at two or three a.m. and found her speck of light hovering, waiting for him. Nonetheless Chad's rage intensified. Each morning he mustered a motive to get out of bed, hoping that today would be the day when the authorities caught the monster.

What they found instead, in September, soon after the start of the fall semester, was the Biter's next victim, maggot-ridden, in a storm drain near Vassar College. Chad urgently phoned Lieutenant MacKenzie, demanding to know if the Vassar police had found any clues.

"Yes." MacKenzie's voice sounded even more gravelly. "It rained again. The Vassar police found the same tire marks." He exhaled wearily. "Mr. Dolan, I understand your despair. Your anger. Your need for revenge. But you have to let go. You have to get on with your life, while we do our job. Every police department involved in these killings has formed a network.

I promise you, we're doing everything we can to compare information and—"

Chad slammed down the phone and scribbled a letter to the parents of the Biter's latest victim.

> We share your loss. We weep as you do. If there's a
> God in heaven—as opposed to this Devil out of hell—
> our beautiful children will not have died unatoned.
> Their brilliantly speeding souls will be granted justice.
> The desecrations inflicted upon their innocent bodies
> will be avenged.

Chad never received responses from those other parents. It didn't matter. He didn't care. He'd done his best to console them, but if they were too overwhelmed by sorrow to muster the strength to comfort *him* as he strained to comfort *them*, well, that was all right. He understood. The main thing was, he'd assured them that he wouldn't rest until the monster was punished.

Each day, he made phone calls to all the police departments in the areas where the Biter had disposed of his victims. Canceling lunches with publishers, postponing meetings with authors, leaving manuscripts unread, Chad concentrated on questioning homicide detectives. He demanded to know why they weren't trying harder, why they hadn't achieved results, why they hadn't tracked down the bastard, allowing his victims to rest with the knowledge that their abuser would be punished, at the same time preventing other potential victims from suffering his brutality.

Just before Thanksgiving, the Biter's next target—the same profile: female, late teens, Caucasian, blond—was discovered in a Dumpster bin behind a restaurant a mile from Wellesley College. Sure, Chad thought. A Dumpster bin. The monster treated her the same way he did Stephanie and all his other victims. Like garbage.

He wrote another letter, but again he didn't receive an answer. The parents must be too stunned to react, he concluded. Whatever, it doesn't matter. I did my duty. I shared my grief. I let them realize they're not alone. I'm their and my daughter's advocate.

New Year's Eve. Another victim. Dartmouth College. More phone calls to detectives. More letters to parents. More visions in Chad's kitchen at three a.m. A speck of brilliant light. A tender voice.

"You're out of control, Dad! Please! I'm begging you. Get on with your life. Shave! Take a bath! Change your clothes! Most of your authors have left you! *Mother's* left you! I'm afraid for you."

Chad shook his head. "Your mother...What? She *left* me?"

With a shudder, Chad realized that Linda had packed several suitcases and...Dear God. He remembered now. Linda had shouted, "It's been too long! It's bad enough to grieve for Stephanie! But to watch you do this to yourself? It's too damned much! Don't destroy *my* life while you destroy *yours*."

Ah.

Of course.

So be it, Chad dismally thought. She needs a comfort I can't give her. God willing, she'll find it with someone else.

Vengeance. Retribution. With greater fury, Chad pursued his mission. More phone calls, more frantic letters.

And then a breakthrough. What the detectives hadn't told Chad—but what he now learned—was that the tire tracks left by his daughter's desecrater had been identified last year, back in April, as standard equipment on a particular model of American van. Not only Stephanie's corpse near Yale but the later victim near Vassar had been linked with the tire tracks on that year and model of van. Because the Biter's numerous targets had all been students at colleges and universities in New England, the authorities had concentrated their search in that area.

When a blond, attractive, female student narrowly escaped being dragged inside a van as she strolled toward her dormitory at Brown University, the local police—braced for the threat—ordered roadblocks around the area and stopped the type of van that they'd been seeking.

The handsome, ingratiating, male driver complied too calmly. His responses were too respectful, not at all curious. On a hunch, an officer asked the driver to open the back of the van.

The driver's eyes narrowed.

Chilled by the intensity of his gaze, the policeman grasped his revolver and repeated his request. What he and his team discovered...after the driver hesitated, after they took his keys...were stacks of boxes in the rear of the van.

And behind the boxes, a bound, gagged, unconscious co-ed.

That night, the police announced the suspected Biter's arrest, and Chad shouted in triumph.

Finally! A textbook salesman. The bastard's district was New England colleges. He stalked each campus. He studied his variety of quarry, reduced his choices, selected his final target, and...

Chad imagined the Biter's enticement. "These boxes of books. They're too heavy. I've sprained my left wrist. Would you mind? Could you help me? I'd really appreciate...Thank you. By the way, what's your major? No kidding? English? What a coincidence. That's *my* major. Here. In the back. Help me with this final box. You won't believe the first editions I've got in there."

Rape, torture, cannibalism, and murder were what he had in there.

Step in farther. Nothing's going to hurt you.

But now the bastard had finally been caught. His name was Richard Putnam. The *alleged* Biter, the media carefully called him, although Chad had no doubt of Putnam's guilt as he studied the television images of the monster. The unafraid expression. The unemotional eyes. The handsome suspect should have been sweating with fear, blustering with indignation, but instead he gazed directly at the cameras, disturbingly confident. A sociopath.

Chad phoned policemen and district attorneys to warn them not to be fooled by Putnam's calm manner. He wrote letters to the parents of every victim, urging them to make similar calls. Each night at three a.m. as he wandered through his cluttered apartment, he always found Stephanie's brilliant light hovering in the kitchen.

"At last they found him," she said. "At last you can give up your anger. Sleep. Eat. Rest. Distract yourself. Work. It's over."

"No, it won't be over until the son of a bitch is punished! I want him to suffer! To feel the terror *you* did!"

"But he *can't* feel terror. He can't feel *anything*. Except when he kills."

"Believe me, sweetheart, when the court finds him guilty, when the judge pronounces his sentence, that sociopath will suddenly find he can definitely feel emotion!"

"That's what I'm afraid of!"

"I don't understand! Don't you want revenge?"

"I'm speeding so brilliantly. I don't have time to...I'm afraid."

"Afraid about what?"

Stephanie's radiant light faded.

"What are you afraid of?"

Nothing will hurt you. The song kept echoing in Chad's mind. While he hadn't been able to protect his daughter as he had promised when she was a child, he could do his utmost to guarantee he was there to make sure that the monster suffered. Calls to police departments revealed that the various states in which the murders had occurred were each demanding to put the Biter on trial. The result was bureaucratic chaos, arguments about which city would have the first chance to prosecute.

As the authorities persisted in quarreling, Chad's frustration compelled him to visit the parents of each victim, to convince them to form a group, to conduct news conferences, to insist that jurisdictional egos be ignored in favor of the strongest evidence in any one city, to plead for justice.

It gave Chad intense satisfaction to believe that his efforts produced results—and even greater satisfaction that New Haven was selected as the site of the trial, that Stephanie's murder would be the crime against which the Biter was initially prosecuted. By then, a year had passed. As part of his divorce settlement, Chad had sold his co-op apartment in Manhattan, splitting the proceeds with Linda. He moved to cheaper lodgings in New Haven, relying on the income he received from his ten percent of royalties that his former authors were required to pay him for contracts that he'd negotiated.

Successful

Sure.

Before Stephanie was...

Nothing will hurt you?

Wrong! It hurts like hell!

Each day at the trial, Chad sat in the front row, far to the side so he could have a direct view of Putnam's unemotional, this-is-all-a-mistake, confident profile. Damn you, show fear, show remorse, show anything, Chad thought. But even when the district attorney presented photographs of the horrors done to Stephanie, the monster did not react. Chad wanted to leap across the courtroom's railing and claw Putnam's eyes out. It took all his self-control not to scream his litany of mental curses.

The jury deliberated for ten days.

Why did they need so long?

They finally declared him guilty

And yet again the monster showed no reaction.

Nor did he react when the judge pronounced the maximum punishment Connecticut allowed: life in prison.

But *Chad* reacted. He shrieked, "*Life in prison?* Change the law! That son of a bitch deserves to be executed!"

Chad was removed from the courtroom. Outside, Putnam's lawyer made a speech about a miscarriage of justice, vowing to demand a new trial, to appeal to a higher court.

Thus began a different kind of horror, the complexities and loopholes in the legal system. Another year passed. The monster remained in prison, yes, but what if a judge decided that a further trial was necessary, that Putnam was obviously insane and should have pleaded accordingly? A year in prison for what he'd done to Stephanie? If he was released on a technicality or sent to a mental institution where he would pretend to respond to treatment and perhaps eventually be pronounced "cured"...

He'd kill again!

At three a.m., in Chad's gloomy New Haven apartment, he raised his haggard face from where he'd been dozing at the kitchen table. He smiled toward Stephanie's speck of light.

"Hi, dear. It's wonderful to see you. Where have you been? How I've missed you."

"You've got to stop doing this!"

"I'm getting even for you."

"You're making me scared!"

"For me. Of course. I understand. But as soon as I know that he's punished, I'll put my life in order. I promise I'll clean up my act."

"That's not what I mean! I don't have time to explain! I'm soaring so fast! So brilliantly! Stop what you're doing!"

"I *can't*. How can you rest in peace if he isn't—"

"I'm afraid!"

Putnam's appeal was denied. But that was another year later. In the meantime, Chad's former wife, Linda, had married someone else, and Chad's percentage of royalties from his past authors dwindled. He was forced to move to more shabby lodgings. He began to withdraw money—with tax penalties—from his pension. He now had a beard. Less trouble. No necessity to shave. So what if his unwashed hair drooped over his ears? There was no one to impress. No authors. No publishers. No one.

Except Stephanie.

Where in God's name *was* she?

She'd abandoned him. *Why?*

While Stephanie's murder had officially been solved, others attributed to the Biter had not. Putnam refused to admit that he'd killed anyone, and the authorities—furious about Putnam's stubbornness—decided to put pressure on him to close the books on those other crimes, to force him to confess. Before he'd been a book salesman in New England, he'd worked in Florida. A blond, attractive co-ed had been murdered years before at Florida's state university. The killer had used a knife instead of his teeth to mutilate the victim. There wasn't any obvious reason to link the Biter with that killing. But a search of that Florida city's records revealed that Putnam had received a parking ticket near where the victim had disappeared as she left the university's library. Further, Putnam's rare blood type matched the type derived from the semen that the killer had left within the victim, just as the semen that the monster had left within Stephanie contained Putnam's blood type. Years ago, that evidence could not have been used in court because of limitations in forensic technology. But now...

Putnam was arrested for the co-ed's murder. His lawyer had insisted on another trial. Well, the monster would get one. In Florida. Where the maximum penalty wasn't life in prison. It was death.

Chad moved to the outskirts of Florida State University. His pension and his portion of royalties from contracts he'd negotiated increasingly declined. His clothes became more shabby, his appearance more unkempt, his frame more gaunt. At some hazy point in the intervening years, his former wife, Linda, died from breast cancer. He mourned for her but not as he mourned for Stephanie.

The Florida trial seemed to take forever. Again Chad came to stare at the monster. Again he endured the complexities of the legal system. Again the evidence presented at the trial made him shudder.

But finally Putnam was found guilty, and *this* time the judge—Chad cheered and had to be evicted from the courtroom again—sentenced the monster to death in the electric chair.

Anti-death-penalty groups raised a furor. They petitioned Florida's Supreme Court and the state's governor to reduce the sentence. For his part, Chad barraged the media and the parents of the Biter's victims with phone calls and letters, urging them to use all their influence to insist that the judge's sentence be obeyed.

Richard Putnam finally showed a reaction. Apparently now convinced that his life was in danger, he tried to make a deal. He hinted about other homicides he'd committed, offering to reveal specifics and solve murders in other states in exchange for a reduced sentence.

Detectives from numerous states came to question Putnam about unsolved disappearances of co-eds. In the end, after they listened in disgust to his explicit descriptions of torture and cannibalism, they refused to ask the judge to reduce the sentence. There were four stays of execution, but finally Putnam was shaved, placed in an electric chair, and exterminated with two thousand volts through his brain.

Chad was with the pro-death-sentence advocates in the darkness of a midnight rain outside the prison. Along with them, he held up a sign: BURN, PUTMAN BURN. I HOPE OLD SPARKY MAKES YOU SUFFER AS MUCH AS STEPHANIE DID. The execution occurred on schedule. At last, after so many years, Chad felt triumphant. Vindicated. At peace.

But when he returned to his cockroach-infested, one-room apartment, when at three a.m. he drank cheap red wine in victory, he blinked in further triumph. Because Stephanie's light again appeared to him.

Chad's heart thundered. He hadn't seen or spoken to her in so many years. Despite his efforts on her behalf, he had thought that she had abandoned him. He had never understood why. After all, she had promised that she would be there whenever he needed to talk to her. At the same time, she had also demanded that he stop his efforts to punish the monster. He had never understood that, either.

But now, in horror, he did.

"I warned you, Dad! I tried to stop you! *Why didn't you listen?* I'm so afraid!"

"I got even for you! You can finally rest in peace!"

"No! Now it starts again!"

"What do you mean?"

"He's free! He's coming for me! *Don't you remember?* I told you he doesn't feel emotion except when he kills! And now that he's been released, he can't wait to do it again! He's coming for me!"

"But you said you're soaring so brilliantly! *How can he catch up to you?*"

"Two thousand volts! He's like a rocket! He's grinning! He's reaching out his arms! Help me, Daddy! You promised!"

Based on the note Chad left, his psychiatrist concluded that Chad's final act made perfect, irrational sense. Chad bled profusely as he struggled over the barbed-wire fence. His hands were mangled. That didn't matter. Nor did his fear of heights matter as he climbed the high tower while guards shouted for him to stop. All that mattered was that Stephanie was in danger. What choice did he have? Except to grasp the high-voltage lines.

To be struck by twenty thousand volts. Ten times the power that had launched the Biter toward Stephanie. Chad's body burst into flames, but his agony meant nothing. The impetus of his soul meant *everything*.

Keep speeding, sweetheart! As fast as you can!

But I'll speed faster! The monster won't catch you! Nothing will hurt you!

Not while I can help it.

The Ammonite Violin (Murder Ballad No. 4)

CAITLÍN R. KIERNAN

Caitlín R. Kiernan is the author of several novels, including *Low Red Moon*, *Daughter of Hounds*, and *The Red Tree*, which was nominated for both the Shirley Jackson and World Fantasy awards. Her latest novel, *The Drowning Girl: A Memoir*, was published in 2012. Since 2000, her shorter tales of the weird, fantastic, and macabre have been collected in several volumes, including *Tales of Pain and Wonder*; *From Weird and Distant Shores*; *To Charles Fort, With Love*; *Alabaster*; *A is for Alien*; and *The Ammonite Violin & Others*. A retrospective of Kiernan's early writing, *Two Worlds and In Between: The Best of Caitlín R. Kiernan (Volume One)* was published in 2012 by Subterranean Press.

She lives in Providence, Rhode Island, with her partner Kathryn. She is currently working on her next two novels, *Blood Oranges* and *Blue Canary*. Caitlín blogs at: http://greygirlbeast.livejournal.com/.

If he were ever to try to write this story, he would not know where to begin. It's that sort of a story, so fraught with unlikely things, so perfectly turned and filled with such wicked artifice and contrivances that readers would look away, unable to suspend their disbelief even for a page. But he will never try to write it, because he is not a poet or a novelist or a man who writes short stories for the newsstand pulp magazines. He is a collector. Or, as he thinks of himself, a Collector. He has never dared to think of himself as *The* Collector, as he is not without an ounce or two of modesty, and there must surely be those out there who are far better than he, shadow men, and maybe shadow women, too, haunting a busy, forgetful world that is only aware of its phantoms when one or another of them slips up and is exposed to flashing cameras and prison cells. Then people will stare, and maybe, for a time, there is horror and fear in their dull, wet eyes, but they soon enough forget again. They are busy people, after all, and they have lives to live, and jobs to show up for five days a week, and bills to pay, and secret nightmares all their own, and in their world there is very little *time* for phantoms.

He lives in a small house in a small town near the sea, for the only time the Collector is ever truly at peace is when he is in the presence of the sea. Even collecting has never brought him to that complete and utter peace, the quiet which finally fills him whenever there is only the crash of waves against a granite jetty and the saltwater mists to breathe in and hold in his lungs like opium fumes. He would love the sea, were she a woman. And sometimes he imagines her so, a wild and beautiful woman clothed all in blue and green, trailing sand and mussels in her wake. Her grey eyes would contain hurricanes, and her voice would be the lonely toll of bell buoys and the cries of gulls and a December wind scraping itself raw against the shore. But, he thinks, were the sea but a woman, and were she his lover, then he would *have* her, as he is a Collector and *must* have all those things he loves, so that no one else might ever have them. He must draw them to him and keep them safe from a blind and busy world that cannot even comprehend its phantoms. And having her, he would lose her, and he would never again know the peace which only she can bring.

He has two specialties, this Collector. There are some who are perfectly content with only one, and he has never thought any less of them for it. But he has two, because, so long as he can recall, there has been this twin fascination, and he never saw the point in forsaking one for the other. Not if he might have them both and yet be a richer man for sharing his devotion between the two. They are his two mistresses, and neither has ever condemned his polyamorous heart. Like the sea, who is *not* his mistress but only his constant savior, they understand who and what and *why* he is, and that he would be somehow diminished, perhaps even undone, were he forced to devote himself wholly to the one or the other. The first of the two is his vast collection of fossilized ammonites, gathered up from the quarries and ocean-side cliffs and the stony, barren places of half the globe's nations. The second are all the young women he has murdered by suffocation, *always* by suffocation, for that is how the sea would kill, how the sea *does* kill, usually, and in taking life he would ever pay tribute and honor to that first mother of the world.

That first Collector.

He has never had to explain his collecting of suffocations, of the deaths of suffocated girls, as it is such a commonplace thing and a secret collection, besides. But he has frequently found it necessary to explain to some acquaintance or another, someone who thinks that she or he *knows* the Collector, about the ammonites. The ammonites are not a secret and, it would seem, neither are they commonplace. It is simple enough to say that they are mollusks, a subdivision of the Cephalopoda, kin to the octopus and cuttlefish and squid, but possessing exquisite shells, not unlike another living cousin, the chambered nautilus. It is less easy to say that they became extinct at the end of the Cretaceous, along with most dinosaurs, or that they first appear in the fossil record in early Devonian times, as this only leads to the need to explain the Cretaceous and Devonian. Often, when asked that question, *What is an ammonite?*, he will change the subject. Or he will sidestep the truth of his collection, talking only of mathematics and the geometry of the ancient Greeks and how one arrives at the Golden Curve. Ammonites, he knows, are one of the sea's many exquisite expressions of the Golden Curve, but he does not bother to explain that part, keeping it back for himself. And sometimes he talks about the horns of Ammon, an Egyptian god of the air, or, if he is feeling especially impatient and annoyed by the question, he limits his response to a description of the Ammonites from the *Book of Mormon* and how they embraced the god of the Nephites and so came to know peace. He is not a Mormon, of course, as he has use of only a singly deity, who is the sea and who kindly grants him peace when he can no longer bear the clamor in his head or the far more terrible clamor of mankind.

On this hazy winter day, he has returned to his small house from a very long walk along a favorite beach, as there was a great need to clear his head. He has made a steaming cup of Red Zinger tea with a few drops of honey and sits now in the room which has become the gallery for the best of his ammonites, oak shelves and glass display cases filled with their graceful planispiral or heteromorph curves, a thousand fragile aragonite bodies transformed by time and geochemistry into mere silica or pyrite or some other permineralization. He sits at his desk, sipping his tea and glancing occasionally at some beloved specimen or another—*this* one from South Dakota or *that* one from the banks of the Volga River in Russia or one of the *many* that have come from Whitby, England. And then he looks back to the desktop and the violin case lying open in front of him, crimson silk to cradle this newest and perhaps most precious of all the items which he has yet collected in his lifetime, the single miraculous piece which belongs strictly in neither one gallery nor the other. The piece which will at last form a bridge, he believes, allowing his two collections to remain distinct, but also affording a tangible transition between them.

The keystone, he thinks. *Yes, you will be my keystone.* But he knows, too, that the violin will be something more than that, that he has devised it to serve as something far grander than a token unification of the two halves of his delight. It will be a *tool,* a mediator or go-between in an act which may, he hopes, transcend collecting in its simplest sense. It has only just arrived today, special delivery, from the Belgian luthier to whom the Collector had hesitantly entrusted its birth.

"It must be done *precisely* as I have said," he told the violin-maker, four months ago, when he flew to Hotton to hand-deliver a substantial portion of the materials from which the instrument would be constructed. "You may not deviate in any significant way from these instructions."

"Yes," the luthier replied, "I understand. I understand completely." A man who appreciates discretion, the Belgian violin-maker, so there were no inconvenient questions asked, no prying inquiries as to *why,* and what's more, he'd even known something about ammonites beforehand.

"No substitutions," the Collector said firmly, just in case it needed to be stated one last time.

"No substitutions of any sort," replied the luthier.

"And the back must be carved—"

"I understand," the violin-maker assured him. "I have the sketches, and I will follow them exactly."

"And the pegs—"

"Will be precisely as we have discussed."

And so the Collector paid the luthier half the price of the commission, the other half due upon delivery, and he took a six a.m. flight back across the wide Atlantic to New England and his small house in the small town near the sea. And he has waited, hardly daring to *half*-believe that the violin-maker would, in fact, get it all right. Indeed—for men are ever at war with their hearts and minds and innermost demons—some infinitesimal scrap of the Collector has even *hoped* that there *would* be a mistake, the most trifling portion of his plan ignored or the violin finished and perfect but then lost in transit and so the whole plot ruined. For it is no small thing, what the Collector has set in motion, and having always considered himself a very wise and sober man, he suspects that he understands fully the consequences he would suffer should he be discovered by lesser men who have no regard for the ocean and her needs. Men who cannot see the flesh and blood phantoms walking among them in broad daylight, much less be bothered to pay tithes which are long overdue to a goddess who has cradled them all, each and every one, through the innumerable twists and turns of evolution's crucible, for three and a half thousand million years.

But there has been no mistake, and, if anything, the violin-maker can be faulted only in the complete sublimation of his craft to the will of his customer. In every way, this is the instrument the Collector asked him to make, and the varnish gleams faintly in the light from the display cases. The top is carved from spruce, and four small ammonites have been set into the wood—*Xipheroceras* from Jurassic rocks exposed along the Dorset Coast at Lyme Regis—two inlaid on the upper bout, two on the lower. He found the fossils himself, many years ago, and they are as perfectly preserved an example of their genus as he has yet seen anywhere, for any price. The violin's neck has been fashioned from maple, as is so often the tradition, and, likewise, the fingerboard is the customary ebony. However, the scroll has been formed from a fifth ammonite, and the Collector knows it is a far more perfect logarithmic spiral than any volute that could have ever been hacked out from a block of wood. In his mind, the five ammonites form the points of a pentacle. The luthier used maple for the back and ribs, and when the Collector turns the violin over, he's greeted by the intricate bas-relief he requested, faithfully reproduced from his own drawings—a great octopus, the ravenous devilfish of so many sea legends, and the maze of its eight tentacles makes a looping, tangled interweave.

As for the pegs and bridge, the chinrest and tailpiece, all these have been carved from the bits of bone he provided the luthier. They seem no more than antique ivory, the stolen tusks of an elephant or a walrus or the tooth of a sperm whale, perhaps. The Collector also provided the dried gut for the five strings, and when the violin-maker pointed out that they would not be nearly so durable as good stranded steel, that they would be much more likely to break and harder to keep in tune, the Collector told him that the instrument would be played only once and so these matters were of very little concern. For the bow, the luthier was given strands of hair which the Collector told him had come from the tail of a gelding, a fine grey horse from Kentucky thoroughbred stock. He'd even ordered a special rosin, and so the sap of an Aleppo Pine was supplemented with a vial of oil he'd left in the care of the violin-maker.

And now, four long months later, the Collector is rewarded for all his painstaking designs, rewarded or damned, if indeed there is some distinction between the two, and the instrument he holds is more beautiful than he'd ever dared to imagine it could be.

The Collector finishes his tea, pausing for a moment to lick the commingled flavors of hibiscus and rosehips, honey and lemon grass from his thin, chapped lips. Then he closes the violin case and locks it, before writing a second, final check to the Belgian luthier. He slips it into an envelope bearing the violin-maker's name and the address of the shop on the rue de Centre in Hotton; the check will go out in the morning's mail, along with other checks for the gas, telephone, and electric bills, and a handwritten letter on lilac-scented stationery, addressed to a Brooklyn violinist. When he is done with these chores, the Collector sits there at the desk in his gallery, one hand resting lightly on the violin case, his face marred by an unaccustomed smile and his eyes filling up with the gluttonous wonder of so many precious things brought together in one room, content in the certain knowledge that they belong to him and will never belong to anyone else.

✦ ✦ ✦

The violinist would never write this story, either. Words have never come easily for her. Sometimes, it seems she does not even think in words, but only in notes of music. When the lilac-scented letter arrives, she reads it several times, then does what it asks of her, because she can't imagine what else she would do. She buys a ticket and the next day she takes the train through Connecticut and Rhode Island and Massachusetts until, finally, she comes to a small town on a rocky spit of land very near the sea. She has never cared for the sea, as it has seemed always to her some awful, insoluble mystery, not so very different from the awful, insoluble mystery of death. Even before the loss of her sister, the violinist avoided the sea when possible. She loathes the taste of fish and lobster and of clams, and the smell of the ocean, too, which reminds her of raw sewage. She has often dreamt of drowning, and of slimy things with bulging black eyes, eyes as empty as night, that have slithered up from abyssal depths to drag her back down with them to lightless plains of silt and diatomaceous ooze or to the ruins of haunted, sunken cities. But those are *only* dreams, and they do her only the bloodless harm that comes from dreams, and she has lived long enough to understand that she has worse things than the sea to fear.

She takes a taxi from the train depot, and it ferries her through the town and over a murky river winding between empty warehouses and rotting docks, a few fishing boats stranded at low tide, and then to a small house painted the color of sunflowers or canary feathers. The address on the mailbox matches the address on the lilac-scented letter, so she pays the driver and he leaves her there. Then she stands in the driveway, watching the yellow house, which has begun to seem a disquieting shade of yellow, or a shade of yellow made disquieting because there is so much of it all in one place. It's almost twilight, and she shivers, wishing she'd thought to wear a cardigan under her coat, and then a porch light comes on and there's a man waving to her.

He's the man who wrote the letter, she thinks. *The man who wants me to play for him,* and for some reason she had expected him to be a lot younger and not so fat. He looks a bit like Captain Kangaroo, this man, and he waves and calls her name and smiles. And the violinist wishes that the taxi were still waiting there to take her back to the station, that she didn't need the money the fat man in the yellow house had offered her, that she'd had the good sense to stay in the city where she belongs. *You could still turn and walk away*, she reminds herself. *There's nothing at all stopping you from just turning right around and walking away and never once looking back, and you could still forget about this whole ridiculous affair.*

And maybe that's true, and maybe it isn't, but there's more than a month's rent on the line, and the way work's been lately, a few students and catch-as-catch-can, she can't afford to find out. She nods and waves back at the smiling man on the porch, the man who told her not to bring her own instrument because he'd prefer to hear her play a particular one that he'd just brought back from a trip to Europe.

"Come on inside. You must be freezing out there," he calls from the porch, and the violinist tries not to think about the sea all around her or that shade of yellow, like a pool of melted butter, and goes to meet the man who sent her the lilac-scented letter.

The Collector makes a steaming-hot pot of Red Zinger, which the violinist takes without honey, and they each have a poppy-seed muffin, which he bought fresh that morning at a bakery in the town. They sit across from one another at his desk, surrounded by the display cases and the best of his ammonites, and she sips her tea and picks at her muffin and pretends to be interested while be explains the importance of recognizing sexual dimorphism when distinguishing one species of ammonite from another. The shells of females, he says, are often the larger and so are called macroconchs by paleontologists. The males may have much smaller shells, called microconchs, and one must always be careful not to mistake the microconchs and macroconchs for two distinct species. He also talks about extinction rates and the utility of ammonites as index fossils and *Parapuzosia bradyi*, a giant among ammonites and the largest specimen in his collection, with a shell measuring slightly more than four and a half feet in diameter.

"They're all quite beautiful," she says, and the violinist doesn't tell him how much she hates the sea and everything that comes from the sea or that the thought of all the fleshy, tentacled creatures that once lived stuffed inside those pretty spiral shells makes her skin crawl. She sips her tea and smiles and nods her head whenever it seems appropriate to do so, and when he asks if he can call her Ellen, she says yes, of course.

"You won't think me too familiar?"

"Don't be silly," she replies, half-charmed at his manners and wondering if he's gay or just a lonely old man whose grown a bit peculiar because he has nothing but his rocks and the yellow house for company. "That's my name. My name is Ellen."

"I wouldn't want to make you uncomfortable or take liberties that are not mine to take," the Collector says and clears away their china cups and saucers, the crumpled paper napkins and a few uneaten crumbs, and then he asks if she's ready to see the violin.

"If you're ready to show it to me," she tells him.

"It's just that I don't want to rush you," he says. "We could always talk some more, if you'd like."

And so the violinist explains to him that she's never felt comfortable with conversation, or with language in general, and that she's always suspected she was much better suited to speaking through her music. "Sometimes, I think it speaks for me," she tells him and apologizes, because she often apologizes when she's actually done nothing wrong. The Collector grins and laughs softly and taps the side of his nose with his left index finger.

"The way I see it, language is language is language," he says. "Words or music, bird songs or all the fancy, flashing colors made by chemoluminescent squid, what's the difference? I'll take conversation however I can wrangle it." And then he unlocks one of the desk drawers with a tiny brass-colored key and takes out the case containing the Belgian violin.

"If words don't come when you call them, then, by all means, please, talk to me with this," and he flips up the latches on the side of the case and opens it so she can see the instrument cradled inside.

"Oh my," she says, all her awkwardness and unease forgotten at the sight of the ammonite violin. "I've never seen anything like it. Never. It's lovely. No, it's much, *much* more than lovely."

"Then you will play it for me?"

"May I touch it?" she asks, and he laughs again.

"I can't imagine how you'll play it otherwise."

Ellen gently lifts the violin from its case, the way that some people might lift a newborn child or a Minoan vase or a stoppered bottle of nitroglycerine, the way the Collector would lift a particularly fragile ammonite from its bed of excelsior. It's heavier than any violin she's held before, and she guesses that the unexpected weight must be from the five fossil shells set into the instrument. She wonders how it will affect the sound, those five ancient stones, how they might warp and alter this violin's voice.

"It's never been played, except by the man who made it, and that hardly seems to count. You, my dear, will be the very first."

And she almost asks him why *her*, because surely, for what he's paying, he could have lured some other, more talented player out here to his little yellow house. Surely someone a bit more celebrated, more accomplished, someone who doesn't have to take in students to make the rent, but would still be flattered and intrigued enough by the offer to come all the way to this squalid little town by the sea and play the fat man's violin for him. But then she thinks it would be rude, and she almost apologizes for a question she hasn't even asked.

And then, as if he might have read her mind, and so maybe she should have apologized after all, the Collector shrugs his shoulders and dabs at the corners of his mouth with a white linen handkerchief he's pulled from a shirt pocket. "The universe is a marvelously complex bit of craftsmanship," he says. "And sometimes one must look very closely to even begin to understand how one thing connects with another. Your late sister, for instance—"

"My *sister?*" she asks and looks up, surprised and looking away from the ammonite violin and into the friendly, smiling eyes of the Collector. A cold knot deep in her belly and an unpleasant pricking sensation along her forearms and the back of her neck, goosebumps and histrionic ghost-story clichés, and all at once the violin feels unclean and dangerous, and she wants to return it to its case. "What do you know about my sister?"

The Collector blushes and glances down at his hands, folded there in front of him on the desk. He begins to speak and stammers, as if, possibly, he's really no better with words than she.

"What do *you* know about my sister?" Ellen asks again. "*How* do you know about her?"

The Collector frowns and licks nervously at his chapped lips. "I'm sorry," he says. "That was terribly tactless of me. I should not have brought it up."

"How do you know about my sister?"

"It's not exactly a secret, is it?" the Collector asks, letting his eyes drift by slow, calculated degrees from his hands and the desktop to her face. "I do read the newspapers. I don't usually watch television, but I imagine it was there, as well. She was murdered—"

"They don't know that. No one knows that for sure. She is *missing*," the violinist says, hissing the last word between clenched teeth.

"She's been missing for quite some time," the Collector replies, feeling the smallest bit braver now and beginning to suspect he hasn't quite overplayed his hand.

"But they do not know that she's been murdered. They don't *know* that. No one ever found her body," and then Ellen decides that she's said far too much and stares down at the fat man's violin. She can't imagine how she ever thought it a lovely thing, only a moment or two before, this grotesque *parody* of a violin resting in her lap. It's more like a gargoyle, she thinks, or a sideshow freak, a malformed parody or a sick, sick joke, and suddenly she wants very badly to wash her hands.

"Please forgive me," the Collector says, sounding as sincere and contrite as any lonely man in a yellow house by the sea has ever sounded. "I live alone. I forget myself and say things I shouldn't. Please, Ellen. Play it for me. You've come all this way, and I would so love to hear you play. It would be such a pity if I've gone and spoiled it all with a few inconsiderate words. I so admire your work—"

"No one *admires* my work," she replies, wondering how long it would take the taxi to show up and carry her back over the muddy, murky river, past the rows of empty warehouses to the depot, and how long she'd have to wait for the next train to New York. "I still don't even understand how you found me?"

And at this opportunity to redeem himself, the Collector's face brightens, and he leans towards her across the desk. "Then I will tell you, if that will put your mind at ease. I saw you play at an art opening in Manhattan, you and your sister, a year or so back. At a gallery on Mercer Street. It was called...damn, it's right on the tip of my tongue—"

"Eyecon," Ellen says, almost whispering. "The name of the gallery is Eyecon."

"Yes, yes, that's it. Thank you. I thought it was such a very silly name for a gallery, but then I've never cared for puns and wordplay. It was at a reception for a French painter, Albert Perrault, and I confess I found him quite completely hideous, and his paintings were dreadful, but I loved listening to the two of you play. I called the gallery, and they were nice enough to tell me how I could contact you."

"I didn't like his paintings either. That was the last time we played together, my sister and I," Ellen says and presses a thumb to the ammonite shell that forms the violin's scroll.

"I didn't know that. I'm sorry, Ellen. I wasn't trying to dredge up bad memories."

"It's not a *bad* memory," she says, wishing it were all that simple and that were exactly the truth, and then she reaches for the violin's bow, which is still lying in the case lined with silk dyed the color of ripe pomegranates.

"I'm sorry," the Collector says again, certain now that he hasn't frightened her away, that everything is going precisely as planned. "Please, I only want to hear you play again."

"I'll need to tune it," Ellen tells him, because she's come this far, and she needs the money, and there's nothing the fat man has said that doesn't add up.

"Naturally," he replies. "I'll go to the kitchen and make us another pot of tea, and you can call me whenever you're ready."

"I'll need a tuning fork," she says, because she hasn't seen any sign of a piano in the yellow house. "Or if you have a metronome that has a tuner, that would work."

The Collector promptly produces a steel tuning fork from another of the drawers and slides it across the desk to the violinist. She thanks him, and when he's left the room and she's alone with the ammonite violin and all the tall cases filled with fossils and the amber wash of incandescent bulbs, she glances at a window and sees that it's already dark outside. *I will play for him,* she thinks. *I'll play on his violin, and drink his tea, and smile, and then he'll pay me for my time and trouble. I'll go back to the city, and tomorrow or the next day, I'll be glad that I didn't back out. Tomorrow or the next day, it'll all seem silly, that I was afraid of a sad old man who lives in an ugly yellow house and collects rocks.*

"I will," she says out loud. "That's exactly how it will go," and then Ellen begins to tune the ammonite violin.

And after he brings her a rickety old music stand, something that looks like it has survived half a century of high-school marching bands, he sits behind his desk, sipping a fresh cup of tea, and she sits in the overlapping pools of light from the display cases. He asked for Paganini; specifically, he asked for Paganini's Violin Concerto No. 3 in E. She would have preferred something contemporary—Górecki, maybe, or Philip Glass, a little something she knows from memory—but he had the sheet music for Paganini, and it's his violin, and he's the one who's writing the check.

"Now?" she asks, and he nods his head.

"Yes, please," he replies and raises his tea cup as if to toast her.

So Ellen lifts the violin, supporting it with her left shoulder, bracing it firmly with her chin, and studies the sheet music a moment or two more before she begins. *Introduzione, allegro marziale,* and she wonders if he expects to hear all three movements, start to finish, or if he'll stop her when he's heard enough. She takes a deep breath and begins to play.

From his seat at the desk, the Collector closes his eyes as the lilting voice of the ammonite violin fills the room. He closes his eyes tightly and remembers another winter night, almost an entire year come and gone since then, but it might only have been yesterday, so clear are his memories. His collection of suffocations may indeed be more commonplace, as he has been led to conclude, but it is also the less frequently indulged of his two passions. He could never name the date and place of each and every ammonite acquisition, but in his brain the Collector carries a faultless accounting of all the suffocations. There have been sixteen, sixteen in twenty-one years, and now it has been almost one year to the night since the most recent. Perhaps, he thinks, he should have waited for the anniversary, but when the package arrived from Belgium, his enthusiasm and impatience got the better of him. When he wrote the violinist his lilac-scented note, he wrote "at your earliest possible convenience" and underlined "earliest" twice.

And here she is, and Paganini flows from out the ammonite violin just as it flowed from his car stereo that freezing night, one year ago, and his heart is beating so fast, so hard, racing itself and all his bright and breathless memories.

Don't let it end, he prays to the sea, whom he has faith can hear the prayers of all her supplicants and will answer those she deems worthy. *Let it go on and on and on. Let it never end.*

He clenches his fists, digging his short nails deep into the skin of his palms, and bites his lip so hard that he tastes blood. And the taste of those few drops of his own life is not so very different from holding the sea inside his mouth.

At last, I have done a perfect thing, he tells himself, himself and the sea and the ammonites and the lingering souls of all his suffocations. *So many years, so much time, so much work and money, but finally I have done this one perfect thing.* And then he opens his eyes again, and also opens the top middle drawer of his desk and takes out the revolver that once belonged to his father, who was a Gloucester fisherman who somehow managed never to collect anything at all.

Her fingers and the bow dance wild across the strings, and in only a few minutes Ellen has lost herself inside the giddy tangle of harmonics and drones and double stops, and if ever she has felt magic—*true* magic—in her art, then she feels it now. She lets her eyes drift from the music stand and the printed pages, because it is all right there behind her eyes and burning on her fingertips. She might well have written these lines herself and then spent half her life playing at nothing else, they rush through her with such ease and confidence. This is ecstasy and this is abandon and this is the tumble and roar of a thousand other emotions she seems never to have felt before this night. The strange violin no longer seems unusually heavy; in fact, it hardly seems to have any weight at all.

Perhaps there is no violin, she thinks. *Perhaps there never was a violin, only my hands and empty air and that's all it takes to make music like this.*

Language is language is language, the fat man said, and so these chords have become her words. No, *not* words, but something so much less indirect than the clumsy interplay of her tongue and teeth, larynx and palate. They have become, simply, her *language*, as they ever have been. Her soul speaking to the world, and all the world need do is *listen.*

She shuts her eyes, no longer needing them to grasp the progression from one note to the next, and at first there is only the comfortable darkness there behind her lids, which seems better matched to the music than all the distractions of her eyes.

Don't let it stop, she thinks, not praying, unless this is a prayer to herself, for the violinist has never seen the need for gods. *Please, let it be like this forever. Let this moment never end, and I will never have to stop playing and there will never again be silence or the noise of human thoughts and conversation.*

"It can't be that way, Ellen," her sister whispers, not whispering in her ear but from somewhere within the Paganini concerto or the ammonite violin or both at once. "I wish I could give you that. I would give you that if it were mine to give."

And then Ellen sees, or hears, or simply *understands* in this language which is *her* language, as language is language is language, the fat man's hands about her sister's throat. Her sister dying somewhere cold near the sea, dying all alone except for the company of her murderer, and there is half an instant when she almost stops playing.

No, her sister whispers, and that one word comes like a blazing gash across the concerto's whirl, and Ellen doesn't stop playing, and she doesn't open her eyes, and she watches as her lost sister slowly dies.

The music is a typhoon gale flaying rocky shores to gravel and sand, and the violinist lets it spin and rage and she watches as the fat man takes four of her sister's fingers and part of a thighbone, strands of her ash-blonde hair, a vial of oil boiled and distilled from the fat of her breasts, a pink-white section of small intestine—all these things and the five fossils from off an English beach to make the instrument he wooed her here to play for him. And now there are tears streaming hot down her cheeks, but still Ellen plays the violin that was her sister and still she doesn't open her eyes.

The single gunshot is very loud in the room, and the display cases rattle and a few of the ammonites slip off their Lucite stands and clatter against wood or glass or other spiraled shells.

And finally she opens her eyes.

And the music ends as the bow slides from her fingers and falls to the floor at her feet.

"No," she says, "please don't let it stop, please," but the echo of the revolver and the memory of the concerto are so loud in her ears that her own words are almost lost to her.

That's all, her sister whispers, louder than any suicide's gun, soft as a midwinter night coming on, gentle as one unnoticed second bleeding into the next. *I've shown you, and now there isn't anymore.*

Across the room, the Collector still sits at his desk, but now he's slumped a bit in his chair and his head is thrown back so that he seems to be staring at something on the ceiling. Blood spills from the black cavern of his open mouth and drips to the floor.

There isn't anymore.

And when she's stopped crying and is quite certain that her sister will not speak to her again, that all the secrets she has any business seeing have been revealed, the violinist retrieves the dropped bow and stands, then walks to the desk and returns the ammonite violin to its case. She will not give it to the police when they arrive, after she has gone to the kitchen to call them, and she will not tell them that it was the fat man who gave it to her. She will take it back to Brooklyn, and they will find other things in another room in the yellow house and have no need of the violin and these stolen shreds of her sister. The Collector has kindly written everything down in three books bound in red leather, all the names and dates and places, and there are other souvenirs, besides. And she will never try to put this story into words, for words have never come easily to her, and like the violin, the story has become hers and hers alone.

Haunted

JOYCE CAROL OATES

Joyce Carol Oates is one of the most prolific and respected writers in the United States today. Oates has written fiction in almost every genre and medium. Her keen interest in the Gothic and psychological horror has spurred her to write dark suspense novels under the name Rosamond Smith, to write enough stories in the genre to have published five collections of dark fiction, the most recent being *The Museum of Dr. Moses: Tales of Mystery and Suspense* and *The Corn Maiden*, and to edit *American Gothic Tales*. Oates's short novel *Zombie* and her short story collection *The Corn Maiden*, won the Bram Stoker Award, and she has been honored with a Life Achievement Award by the Horror Writers Association.

Oates's most recent novels are *The Gravedigger's Daughter*, *My Sister, My Love: The Intimate Story of Skyler Rampike*, and *Little Bird of Heaven*.

She teaches creative writing at Princeton and with her late husband, Raymond J. Smith, ran the small press and literary magazine *The Ontario Review* for many years.

Haunted houses, forbidden houses. The old Medlock farm. The Erlich farm. The Minton farm on Elk Creek. *No Trespassing* the signs said, but we trespassed at will. *No Trespassing No Hunting No Fishing Under Penalty of Law* but we did what we pleased because who was there to stop us?

Our parents warned us against exploring these abandoned properties: the old houses and barns were dangerous, they said. We could get hurt, they said. I asked my mother if the houses were haunted and she said, Of course not, there aren't such things as ghosts, you know that. She was irritated with me; she guessed how I pretended to believe things I didn't believe, things I'd grown out of years before. It was a habit of childhood—pretending I was younger, more childish, than in fact I was. Opening my eyes wide and looking puzzled, worried. Girls are prone to such trickery; it's a form of camouflage when every other thought you think is a forbidden thought and with your eyes open staring sightless you can sink into dreams that leave your skin clammy and your heart pounding—dreams that don't seem to belong to you that must have come to you from somewhere else from someone you don't know who knows *you*.

There weren't such things as ghosts, they told us. That was just superstition. But we could injure ourselves tramping around where we weren't wanted—the floorboards and the staircases in old houses were likely to be rotted, the roofs ready to collapse, we could cut ourselves on nails and broken glass, we could fall into uncovered wells—and you never knew who you might meet up with, in an old house or barn that's supposed to be empty. "You mean a bum?—like somebody hitch-hiking along the road?" I asked. "It could be a bum, or it could be somebody you know," Mother told me evasively. "A man, or a boy—somebody you know—" Her voice trailed off in embarrassment and I knew enough not to ask another question.

There were things you didn't talk about, back then. I never talked about them with my own children; there weren't the words to say them.

We listened to what our parents said, we nearly always agreed with what they said, but we went off on the sly and did what we wanted to do. When we were little girls: my neighbor Mary Lou Siskin and me. And when we were older, ten, eleven years old, tomboys, roughhouses our mothers called us. We liked to hike in the woods and along the creek for miles; we'd cut through farmers' fields, spy on their houses—on people we knew, kids we knew from school—most of all we liked to explore abandoned houses, boarded-up houses if we could break in; we'd scare ourselves thinking the houses might be haunted though really we knew they weren't haunted, there weren't such things as ghosts. Except—

• • •

I am writing in a dime-store notebook with lined pages and a speckled cover, a notebook of the sort we used in grade school. *Once upon a time* as I used to tell my children when they were tucked safely into bed and drifting off to sleep. *Once upon a time* I'd begin, reading from a book because it was safest so: the several times I told them my own stories they were frightened by my voice and couldn't sleep and afterward I couldn't sleep either and my husband would ask what was wrong and I'd say, Nothing, hiding my face from him so he wouldn't see my look of contempt.

I write in pencil, so that I can erase easily, and I find that I am constantly erasing, wearing holes in the paper. Mrs. Harding, our fifth grade teacher, disciplined us for handing in messy notebooks: she was a heavy, toad-faced woman, her voice was deep and husky and gleeful when she said, "You, Melissa, what have you to say for yourself?" and I stood there mute, my knees trembling. My friend Mary Lou laughed behind her hand, wriggled in her seat she thought I was so funny. Tell the old witch to go to hell, she'd say, she'll respect you then, but of course no one would ever say such a thing to Mrs. Harding. Not even Mary Lou. "What have you to say for yourself, Melissa? Handing in a notebook with a ripped page?" My grade for the homework assignment was lowered from A to B, Mrs. Harding grunted with satisfaction as she made the mark, a big swooping B in red ink, creasing the page. "More is expected of you, Melissa, so you disappoint me more," Mrs. Harding always said. So many years ago and I remember those words more clearly than words I have heard the other day.

One morning there was a pretty substitute teacher in Mrs. Harding's classroom. "Mrs. Harding is unwell, I'll be taking her place today," she said, and we saw the nervousness in her face; we guessed there was a secret she wouldn't tell and we waited and a few days later the principal himself came to tell us that Mrs. Harding would not be back, she had died of a stroke. He spoke carefully as if we were much younger children and might be upset and Mary Lou caught my eye and winked and I sat there at my desk feeling the strangest sensation, something flowing into the top of my head, honey-rich and warm making its way down my spine. *Our Father who art in Heaven* I whispered in the prayer with the others my head bowed and my hands clasped tight together but my thoughts were somewhere else leaping wild and crazy somewhere else and I knew Mary Lou's were too.

On the school bus going home she whispered in my ear, "That was because of us, wasn't it!—what happened to that old bag Harding. But we won't tell anybody."

Once upon a time there were two sisters, and one was very pretty and one was very ugly.... Though Mary Lou Siskin wasn't my sister. And I wasn't ugly, really: just sallow-skinned, with a small pinched ferrety face. With dark almost lashless eyes that were set too close together and a nose that didn't look right. A look of yearning, and disappointment.

But Mary Lou was pretty, even rough and clumsy as she sometimes behaved. That long silky blond hair everybody remembered her for afterward, years afterward.... How, when she had to be identified, it was the long silky white-blond hair that was unmistakable....

Sleepless nights, but I love them. I write during the nighttime hours and sleep during the day, I am of an age when you don't require more than a few hours sleep. My husband has been dead for nearly a year and my children are scattered and busily absorbed in their own selfish lives like all children and there is no one to interrupt me no one to pry into my business no one in the neighborhood who dares come knocking at my door to see if I am all right. Sometimes out of a mirror floats an unexpected face, a strange face, lined, ravaged, with deep-socketed eyes always damp, always blinking in shock or dismay or simple bewilderment—but I adroitly look away. I have no need to stare.

It's true, all you have heard of the vanity of the old. Believing ourselves young, still, behind our aged faces—mere children, and so very innocent!

Once when I was a young bride and almost pretty my color up when I was happy and my eyes shining we drove out into the country for a Sunday's excursion and he wanted to make love I knew, he was shy and fumbling as I but he wanted to make love and I ran into a cornfield in my stockings and high heels, I was playing at being a woman I never could be, Mary Lou

Siskin maybe, Mary Lou whom my husband never knew, but I got out of breath and frightened, it was the wind in the cornstalks, that dry rustling sound, that dry terrible rustling sound like whispering like voices you can't quite identify and he caught me and tried to hold me and I pushed him away sobbing and he said, What's wrong? My God what's wrong? as if he really loved me as if his life was focused on me and I knew I could never be equal to it, that love, that importance, I knew I was only Melissa the ugly one the one the boys wouldn't give a second glance, and one day he'd understand and know how he'd been cheated. I pushed him away, I said, Leave me alone! don't touch me! You disgust me! I said.

He backed off and I hid my face, sobbing.

But later on I got pregnant just the same. Only a few weeks later.

Always there were stories behind the abandoned houses and always the stories were sad. Because farmers went bankrupt and had to move away, Because somebody died and the farm couldn't be kept up and nobody wanted to buy it—like the Medlock farm across the creek. Mr. Medlock died aged seventy-nine and Mrs. Medlock refused to sell the farm and lived there alone until someone from the country health agency came to get her. Isn't it a shame, my parents said. The poor woman, they said. They told us never, never to poke around in the Medlocks' barns or house—the buildings were ready to cave in, they'd been in terrible repair even when the Medlocks were living.

It was said that Mrs. Medlock had gone off her head after she'd found her husband dead in one of the barns, lying flat on his back his eyes open and bulging, his mouth open, tongue protruding, she'd gone to look for him and found him like that and she'd never gotten over it they said, never got over the shock. They had to commit her to the state hospital for her own good (they said) and the house and the barns were boarded up, everywhere tall grass and thistles grew wild, dandelions in the spring, tiger lilies in the summer, and when we drove by I stared and stared narrowing my eyes so I wouldn't see someone looking out one of the windows—a face there, pale and quick—or a dark figure scrambling up the roof to hide behind the chimney—Mary Lou and I wondered was the house haunted, was the barn haunted where the old man had died, we crept around to spy, we couldn't stay away, coming closer and closer each time until something scared us and we ran away back through the woods clutching and pushing at each other until one day finally we went right up to the house to the back door and peeked in one of the windows. Mary Lou led the way, Mary Lou said not to be afraid, nobody lived there any more and nobody would catch us, it didn't matter that the land was posted, the police didn't arrest kids our ages.

We explored the barns, we dragged the wooden cover off the well and dropped stones inside. We called the cats but they wouldn't come close enough to be petted. They were barn cats, skinny and diseased-looking, they'd said at the country bureau that Mrs. Medlock had let a dozen cats live in the house with her so that the house was filthy from their messes. When the cats wouldn't come we got mad and threw stones at them and they ran away hissing—nasty dirty things, Mary Lou said. Once we crawled up on the tar-paper roof over the Medlocks' kitchen, just for fun, Mary Lou wanted to climb up the big roof too to the very top but I got frightened and said, No, no please don't, no Mary Lou please, and I sounded so strange Mary Lou looked at me and didn't tease or mock as she usually did. The roof was so steep, I'd known she would hurt herself. I could see her losing her footing and slipping, falling, I could see her astonished face and her flying hair as she fell, knowing nothing could save her. You're no fun, Mary Lou said, giving me a hard little pinch. But she didn't go climbing up the big roof.

Later we ran through the barns screaming at the top of our lungs just for fun for the hell of it as Mary Lou said, we tossed things in a heap, broken-off parts of farm implements, leather things from the horses' gear, handfuls of straw. The farm animals had been gone for years but their smell was still strong. Dried horse and cow droppings that looked like mud. Mary Lou said, "You know what—I'd like to burn this place down." And she looked at me and I said, "Okay—go on and do it, burn it down." And Mary Lou said, "You think I wouldn't? Just give me a match." And I said, "You know I don't have any match." And a look passed between us. And I felt something flooding at the top of my head, my throat tickled as if I didn't know would I laugh or cry and I said, "You're crazy—" and Mary Lou said with a sneering little laugh, "*You're* crazy, dumbbell. I was just testing you."

By the time Mary Lou was twelve years old Mother had got to hate her, was always trying to turn me against her so I'd make friends with other girls. Mary Lou had a fresh mouth, she said. Mary Lou didn't respect her elders—not even her own parents. Mother guessed that Mary Lou laughed at her behind her back, said things about all of us. She was mean and snippy and a smart-ass, rough sometimes as her brothers. Why didn't I make other friends? Why did I always go running when she stood out in the yard and called me? The Siskins weren't a whole lot better than white trash, the way Mr. Siskin worked that land of his.

In town, in school, Mary Lou sometimes ignored me when other girls were around, girls who lived in town, whose fathers weren't farmers like ours. But when it was time to ride home on the bus she'd sit with me as if nothing was wrong and I'd help her with her homework if she needed help, I hated her sometimes but then I'd forgive her as soon as she smiled at me, she'd say, "Hey 'Lissa are you mad at me?" and I'd make a face and say no as if it was an insult, being asked. Mary Lou was my sister I sometimes pretended, I told myself a story about us being sisters and looking alike, and Mary Lou said sometimes she'd like to leave her family her goddamned family and come live with me. Then the next day or the next hour she'd get moody and be nasty to me and get me almost crying. All the Siskins had mean streaks, had tempers, she'd tell people. As if she was proud.

Her hair was a light blond, almost white in the sunshine, and when I first knew her she had to wear it braided tight around her head—her grandmother braided it for her, and she hated it. Like Gretel or Snow White in one of those damn dumb picture books for children, Mary Lou said. When she was older she wore it down and let it grow long so that it fell almost to her hips. It was very beautiful—silky and shimmering. I dreamt of Mary Lou's hair sometimes but the dreams were confused and I couldn't remember when I woke up whether I was the one with the long blond silky hair, or someone else. It took me a while to get my thoughts clear lying there in bed and then I'd remember Mary Lou, who was my best friend.

She was ten months older than I was, and an inch or so taller, a bit heavier, not fat but fleshy, solid and fleshy, with hard little muscles in her upper arms like a boy. Her eyes were blue like washed glass, her eyebrows and lashes were almost white, she had a snubbed nose and Slavic cheekbones and a mouth that could be sweet or twisty and smirky depending upon her mood. But she didn't like her face because it was round—a moon face she called it, staring at herself in the mirror though she knew damned well she was pretty—didn't older boys whistle at her, didn't the bus driver flirt with her?—calling her "Blondie" while he never called me anything at all.

Mother didn't like Mary Lou visiting with me when no one else was home in our house: she didn't trust her, she said. Thought she might steal something, or poke her nose into parts of the house where she wasn't welcome. That girl is a bad influence on you, she said. But it was all the same old crap I heard again and again so I didn't even listen. I'd have told her she was crazy except that would only make things worse.

Mary Lou said, "Don't you just hate them?—your mother, and mine? Sometimes I wish—"

I put my hands over my ears and didn't hear.

The Siskins lived two miles away from us, farther back the road where the road got narrower. Those days, it was unpaved, and never got plowed in the winter. I remember their barn with the yellow silo, I remember the muddy pond where the dairy cows came to drink, the muck they churned up in the spring. I remember Mary Lou saying she wished all the cows would die—they were always sick with something—so her father would give up and sell the farm and they could live in town in a nice house. I was hurt, her saying those things as if she'd forgotten about me and would leave me behind. Damn you to hell, I whispered under my breath.

I remember smoke rising from the Siskins' kitchen chimney, from their wood-burning stove, straight up into the winter sky like a breath you draw inside you deeper and deeper until you begin to feel faint.

Later on, that house was empty too. But boarded up only for a few months—the bank sold it at auction. (It turned out the bank owned most of the Siskin farm, even the dairy cows. So Mary Lou had been wrong about that all along and never knew.)

As I write I can hear the sound of glass breaking, I can feel glass underfoot. *Once upon a time there were two little princesses, two sisters, who did forbidden things.* That brittle terrible sensation under my shoes—slippery like water—"Anybody home? Hey—anybody home?" and there's an old calendar tacked to a kitchen wall, a faded picture of Jesus Christ in a long white gown stained with scarlet, thorns fitted to His bowed head. Mary Lou is going to scare me in another minute making me think that someone is in the house and the two of us will scream with laughter and run outside where it's safe. Wild frightened laughter and I never knew afterward what was funny or why we did these things. Smashing what remained of windows, wrenching at stairway railings to break them loose, running with our heads ducked so we wouldn't get cobwebs in our faces.

One of us found a dead bird, a starling, in what had been the parlor of the house. Turned it over with a foot—there's the open eye looking right up calm and matter-of-fact. *Melissa,* that eye tells me, silent and terrible, *I see you.*

That was the old Minton place, the stone house with the caved-in roof and the broken steps, like something in a picture book from long ago. From the road the house looked as if it might be big, but when we explored it we were disappointed to see that it wasn't much bigger than my own house, just four narrow rooms downstairs, another four upstairs, an attic with a steep ceiling, the roof partly caved in. The barns had collapsed in upon themselves; only their stone foundations remained solid. The land had been sold off over the years to other farmers, nobody had lived in the house for a long time. The old Minton house, people called it. On Elk Creek where Mary Lou's body was eventually found.

⁂

In seventh grade Mary Lou had a boyfriend she wasn't supposed to have and no one knew about it but me—an older boy who'd dropped out of school and worked as a farmhand. I thought he was a little slow—not in his speech which was fast enough, normal enough, but in his way of thinking. He was sixteen or seventeen years old. His name was Hans; he had crisp blond hair like the bristles of a brush, a coarse blemished face, derisive eyes. Mary Lou was crazy for him she said, aping the older girls in town who said they were "crazy for" certain boys or young men. Hans and Mary Lou kissed when they didn't think I was watching, in an old ruin of a cemetery behind the Minton house, on the creek bank, in the tall marsh grass by the end of the Siskins' driveway. Hans had a car borrowed from one of his brothers, a battered old Ford, the front bumper held up by wire, the running board scraping the ground. We'd be out walking on the road and Hans would come along tapping the horn and stop and Mary Lou would climb in but I'd hang back knowing they didn't want me and the hell with them: I preferred to be alone.

"You're just jealous of Hans and me," Mary Lou said, unforgivably, and I hadn't any reply. "Hans is sweet. Hans is nice. He isn't like people say," Mary Lou said in a quick bright false voice she'd picked up from one of the older, popular girls in town. "He's..." And she stared at me blinking and smiling not knowing what to say as if in fact she didn't know Hans at all. "He isn't *simple*," she said angrily, "he just doesn't like to talk a whole lot."

When I try to remember Hans Meunzer after so many decades I can see only a muscular boy with short-trimmed blond hair and protuberant ears, blemished skin, the shadow of a moustache on his upper lip—he's looking at me, eyes narrowed, crinkled, as if he understands how I fear him, how I wish him dead and gone, and he'd hate me too if he took me that seriously. But he doesn't take me that seriously, his gaze just slides right through me as if nobody's standing where I stand.

There were stories about all the abandoned houses but the worst story was about the Minton house over on the Elk Creek Road about three miles from where we lived. For no reason anybody ever discovered Mr. Minton had beaten his wife to death and afterward killed himself with a .12-gauge shotgun. He hadn't even been drinking, people said. And his farm hadn't been doing at all badly, considering how others were doing.

Looking at the ruin from the outside, overgrown with trumpet vine and wild rose, it seemed hard to believe that anything like that had happened. Things in the world even those things built by man are so quiet left to themselves...

The house had been deserted for years, as long as I could remember. Most of the land had been sold off but the heirs didn't want to deal with the house. They didn't want to sell it and they didn't want to raze it and they certainly didn't want to live in it so it stood empty. The property was posted with *No Trespassing* signs layered one atop another but nobody took them seriously. Vandals had broken into the house and caused damage, the McFarlane boys had tried to burn down the old hay barn one Halloween night. The summer Mary Lou started seeing Hans she and I climbed in the house through a rear window—the boards guarding it had long since been yanked away—and walked through the rooms slow as sleepwalkers our arms around each other's waists our eyes staring waiting to see Mr. Minton's ghost as we turned each corner. The inside smelled of mouse droppings, mildew, rot, old sorrow. Strips of wallpaper torn from the walls, plasterboard exposed, old furniture overturned and smashed, old yellowed sheets of newspaper underfoot, and broken glass, everywhere broken glass. Through the ravaged windows sunlight spilled in tremulous quivering bands. The air was afloat, alive: dancing dust atoms. "I'm afraid," Mary Lou whispered. She squeezed my waist and I felt my mouth go dry for hadn't I been hearing something upstairs, a low persistent murmuring like quarreling like one person trying to convince another going on and on and on but when I stood very still to listen the sound vanished and there were only the comforting summer sounds of birds, crickets, cicadas; birds, crickets, cicadas.

I knew how Mr. Minton had died: he'd placed the barrel of the shotgun beneath his chin and pulled the trigger with his big toe. They found him in the bedroom upstairs, most of his head blown off. They found his wife's body in the cistern in the cellar where he'd tried to hide her. "Do you think we should go upstairs?" Mary Lou asked, worried. Her fingers felt cold; but I could see tiny sweat beads on her forehead. Her mother had braided her hair in one thick clumsy braid, the way she wore it most of the summer, but the bands of hair were loosening. "No," I said, frightened. "I don't know." We hesitated at the bottom of the stairs—just stood there for a long time. "Maybe not," Mary Lou said. "Damn stairs'd fall in on us."

In the parlor there were bloodstains on the floor and on the wall—I could see them. Mary Lou said in derision, "They're just waterstains, dummy."

I could hear the voices overhead, or was it a single droning persistent voice. I waited for Mary Lou to hear it but she never did.

Now we were safe, now we were retreating, Mary Lou said as if repentant, "Yeah—this house *is* special."

We looked through the debris in the kitchen hoping to find something of value but there wasn't anything—just smashed chinaware, old battered pots and pans, more old yellowed newspaper. But through the window we saw a garter snake sunning itself on a rusted water tank, stretched out to a length of two feet. It was a lovely coppery color, the scales gleaming like perspiration on a man's arm; it seemed to be asleep. Neither one of us screamed, or wanted to throw something—we just stood there watching it for the longest time.

Mary Lou didn't have a boyfriend any longer; Hans had stopped coming around. We saw him driving the old Ford now and then but he didn't seem to see us. Mr. Siskin had found out about him and Mary Lou and he'd been upset—acting like a damn crazy man Mary Lou said, asking her every kind of nasty question then interrupting her and not believing her anyway, then he'd put her to terrible shame by going over to see Hans and carrying on with him. "I hate them all," Mary Lou said, her face darkening with blood. "I wish—"

We rode our bicycles over to the Minton farm, or tramped through the fields to get there. It was the place we liked best. Sometimes we brought things to eat, cookies, bananas, candy bars; sitting on the broken stone steps out front, as if we lived in the house really, we were sisters who lived here having a picnic lunch out front. There were bees, flies, mosquitoes, but we brushed them away. We had to sit in the shade because the sun was so fierce and direct, a whitish heat pouring down from overhead.

"Would you ever like to run away from home?" Mary Lou said. "I don't know," I said uneasily. Mary Lou wiped at her mouth and gave me a mean narrow look. "'I don't know,'" she said in a falsetto voice, mimicking me. At an upstairs window someone was watching us—was it a man or was it a woman—someone stood there listening hard and I couldn't move feeling so slow and dreamy in the heat like a fly caught on a sticky petal that's going to fold in on itself and swallow him up. Mary Lou crumpled up some wax paper and threw it into the weeds. She was dreamy too, slow and yawning. She said, "Shit—they'd just find me. Then everything would be worse."

I was covered in a thin film of sweat but I'd begun to shiver. Goose bumps were raised on my arms. I could see us sitting on the stone steps the way we'd look from the second floor of the house, Mary Lou sprawled with her legs apart, her braided hair slung over her shoulder, me sitting with my arms hugging my knees my backbone tight and straight knowing I was being watched. Mary Lou said, lowering her voice, "Did you ever touch yourself in a certain place, Melissa?" "No," I said, pretending I didn't know what she meant. "Hans wanted to do that," Mary Lou said. She sounded disgusted. Then she started to giggle. "I wouldn't let him, then he wanted to do something else—started unbuttoning his pants—wanted me to touch *him*. And..."

I wanted to hush her, to clap my hand over her mouth. But she just went on and I never said a word until we both started giggling together and couldn't stop. Afterward I didn't remember most of it or why I'd been so excited my face burning and my eyes seared as if I'd been staring into the sun.

• • •

On the way home Mary Lou said, "Some things are so sad you can't say them." But I pretended not to hear.

A few days later I came back to myself. Through the ravaged cornfield: the stalks dried and broken, the tassels burnt, that rustling whispering sound of the wind I can hear now if I listen closely. My head was aching with excitement. I was telling myself a story that we'd made plans to run away and live in the Minton house. I was carrying a willow switch I'd found on the ground, fallen from a tree but still green and springy, slapping at things with it as if it were a whip. Talking to myself. Laughing aloud. Wondering was I being watched.

I climbed in the house through the back window and brushed my hands on my jeans. My hair was sticking to the back of my neck.

At the foot of the stairs I called up, "Who's here?" in a voice meant to show it was all play; I knew I was alone.

My heart was beating hard and quick, like a bird caught in the hand. It was lonely without Mary Lou so I walked heavy to let them know I was there and wasn't afraid. I started singing, I started whistling. Talking to myself and slapping at things with the willow switch. Laughing aloud, a little angry. Why was I angry, well I didn't know, someone was whispering telling me to come upstairs, to walk on the inside of the stairs so the steps wouldn't collapse.

The house was beautiful inside if you had the right eyes to see it. If you didn't mind the smell. Glass underfoot, broken plaster, stained wallpaper hanging in shreds. Tall narrow windows looking out onto wild weedy patches of green. I heard something in one of the rooms but when I looked I saw nothing much more than an easy chair lying on its side. Vandals had ripped stuffing out of it and tried to set it afire. The material was filthy but I could see that it had been pretty once—a floral design—tiny yellow flowers and green ivy. A woman used to sit in the chair, a big woman with sly staring eyes. Knitting in her lap but she wasn't knitting just staring out the window watching to see who might be coming to visit.

Upstairs the rooms were airless and so hot I felt my skin prickle like shivering. I wasn't afraid!—I slapped at the walls with my springy willow switch. In one of the rooms high in a corner wasps buzzed around a fat wasp's nest. In another room I looked out the window leaning out the window to breathe thinking this was my window, I'd come to live here. She was telling me I had better lie down and rest because I was in danger of heatstroke and I pretended not to know what heatstroke was but she knew I knew because hadn't a cousin of mine collapsed haying just last summer, they said his face had gone blotched and red and he'd begun breathing faster and faster not getting enough oxygen until he collapsed. I was looking out at the overgrown apple orchard, I could smell the rot, a sweet winey smell, the sky was hazy like something you can't get clear in your vision, pressing in close and warm. A half mile away Elk Creek glittered through a screen of willow trees moving slow glittering with scales like winking.

Come away from that window, someone told me sternly.

But I took my time obeying.

In the biggest of the rooms was an old mattress pulled off rusty bedsprings and dumped on the floor. They'd torn some of the stuffing out of this too, there were scorch marks on it from cigarettes. The fabric was stained with something like rust and I didn't want to look at it but I had to. Once at Mary Lou's when I'd gone home with her after school there was a mattress lying out in the yard in the sun and Mary Lou told me in disgust that it was her youngest brother's mattress—he'd wet his bed again and the mattress had to be aired out. As if the stink would ever go away, Mary Lou said.

Something moved inside the mattress, a black glittering thing, it was a cockroach but I wasn't allowed to jump back. Suppose you have to lie down on that mattress and sleep, I was told. Suppose you can't go home until you do. My eyelids were heavy, my head was pounding with blood. A mosquito buzzed around me but I was too tired to brush it away. Lie down on that mattress, Melissa, she told me. You know you must be punished.

I knelt down, not on the mattress, but on the floor beside it. The smells in the room were close and rank but I didn't mind, my head was nodding with sleep. Rivulets of sweat ran down my face and sides, under my arms, but I didn't mind. I saw my hand move out slowly like a stranger's hand to touch the mattress and a shiny black cockroach scuttled away in fright, and a second cockroach, and a third—but I couldn't jump up and scream.

Lie down on that mattress and take your punishment.

I looked over my shoulder and there was a woman standing in the doorway—a woman I'd never seen before.

She was staring at me. Her eyes were shiny and dark. She licked her lips and said in a jeering voice, "What are you doing here in this house, miss?"

I was terrified. I tried to answer but I couldn't speak.

"Have you come to see me?" the woman asked.

She was no age I could guess. Older than my mother but not old-seeming. She wore men's clothes and she was tall as any man, with wide shoulders, and long legs, and big sagging breasts like cows' udders loose inside her shirt not harnessed in a brassiere like other women's. Her thick wiry gray hair was cut short as a man's and stuck up in tufts that looked greasy. Her eyes were small, and black, and set back deep in their sockets; the flesh around them looked bruised. I had never seen anyone like her before—her thighs were enormous, big as my body. There was a ring of loose soft flesh at the waistband of her trousers but she wasn't fat.

"I asked you a question, miss. Why are you here?"

I was so frightened I could feel my bladder contract. I stared at her, cowering by the mattress, and couldn't speak.

It seemed to please her that I was so frightened. She approached me, stooping a little to get through the doorway. She said, in a mock-kindly voice, "You've come to visit with me—is that it?"

"No," I said.

"No!" she said, laughing. "Why, of course you have."

"No. I don't know you."

She leaned over me, touched my forehead with her fingers. I shut my eyes waiting to be hurt but her touch was cool. She brushed my hair off my forehead where it was sticky with sweat. "I've seen you here before, you and that other one," she said. "What is her name? The blond one. The two of you, trespassing."

I couldn't move, my legs were paralyzed. Quick and darting and buzzing my thoughts bounded in every which direction but didn't take hold. "Melissa is *your* name, isn't it," the woman said. And what is your sister's name?"

"She isn't my sister," I whispered.

"What is her name?"

"I don't know."

"You don't know!"

"—don't know," I said, cowering.

The woman drew back half sighing half grunting. She looked at me pityingly. "You'll have to be punished, then."

I could smell ashes about her, something cold. I started to whimper started to say I hadn't done anything wrong, hadn't hurt anything in the house, I had only been exploring—I wouldn't come back again...

She was smiling at me, uncovering her teeth. She could read my thoughts before I could think them.

The skin of her face was in layers like an onion, like she'd been sunburnt, or had a skin disease. There were patches that had begun to peel. Her look was wet and gloating. Don't hurt me, I wanted to say. Please don't hurt me.

I'd begun to cry. My nose was running like a baby's. I thought I would crawl past the woman I would get to my feet and run past her and escape but the woman stood in my way blocking my way leaning over me breathing damp and warm her breath like a cow's breath in my face. Don't hurt me, I said, and she said, "You know you have to be punished—you and your pretty blond sister."

"She isn't my sister," I said.

"And what is her name?"

The woman was bending over me, quivering with laughter.

"Speak up, miss. What is it?"

"I don't know—" I started to say. But my voice said, "Mary Lou."

The woman's big breasts spilled down into her belly, I could feel her shaking with laughter. But she spoke sternly saying that Mary Lou and I had been very bad girls and we knew it her house was forbidden territory and we knew it hadn't we known all along that others had come to grief beneath its roof?

"No," I started to say. But my voice said, "Yes."

The woman laughed, crouching above me. "Now, miss, 'Melissa' as they call you—your parents don't know where you are at this very moment, do they?"

"I don't know."

"Do they?"

"No."

"They don't know anything about you, do they?—what you do, and what you think? You and 'Mary Lou.'"

"No."

She regarded me for a long moment, smiling. Her smile was wide and friendly.

"You're a spunky little girl, aren't you, with a mind of your own, aren't you, you and your pretty little sister. I bet your bottoms have been warmed many a time," the woman said, showing her big tobacco-stained teeth in a grin, "...your tender little asses."

I began to giggle. My bladder tightened.

"Hand that here, miss," the woman said. She took the willow switch from my fingers—I had forgotten I was holding it. "I will now administer punishment: take down your jeans. Take down your panties. Lie down on that mattress. Hurry." She spoke briskly now, she was all business. "Hurry, Melissa! *And* your panties! Or do you want me to pull them down for you?"

She was slapping the switch impatiently against the palm of her left hand, making a wet scolding noise with her lips. Scolding and teasing. Her skin shone in patches, stretched tight over the big hard bones of her face. Her eyes were small, crinkling smaller, black and damp. She was so big she had to position herself carefully over me to give herself proper balance and leverage so that she wouldn't fall. I could hear her hoarse eager breathing as it came to me from all sides like the wind.

I had done as she told me. It wasn't me doing these things but they were done. Don't hurt me, I whispered, lying on my stomach on the mattress, my arms stretched above me and my fingernails digging into the floor. The coarse wood with splinters pricking my skin. Don't hurt me O please but the woman paid no heed her warm wet breath louder now and the floorboards creaking beneath her weight. "Now, miss, now 'Melissa' as they call you—this will be our secret won't it..."

+ + +

When it was over she wiped at her mouth and said she would let me go today if I promised never to tell anybody if I sent my pretty little sister to her tomorrow.

She isn't my sister, I said, sobbing. When I could get my breath.

I had lost control of my bladder after all, I'd begun to pee even before the first swipe of the willow switch hit me on the buttocks, peeing in helpless spasms, and sobbing, and afterward the woman scolded me saying wasn't it a poor little baby wetting itself like that. But she sounded repentant too, stood well aside to let me pass, Off you go! Home you go! And don't forget!

And I ran out of the room hearing her laughter behind me and down the stairs running running as if I hadn't any weight my legs just blurry beneath me as if the air was water and I was swimming I ran out of the house and through the cornfield running in the cornfield sobbing as the cornstalks slapped at my face *Off you go! Home you go! And don't forget!*

I told Mary Lou about the Minton house and something that had happened to me there that was a secret and she didn't believe me at first saying with a jeer, "Was it a ghost? Was it Hans?" I said I couldn't tell. Couldn't tell what? she said. Couldn't tell, I said. Why not? she said.

"Because I promised."

"Promised who?" she said. She looked at me with her wide blue eyes like she was trying to hypnotize me. "You're a goddamned liar."

Later she started in again asking me what had happened what was the secret was it something to do with Hans? did he still like her? was he mad at her? and I said it didn't have anything to do with Hans not a thing to do with him. Twisting my mouth to show what I thought of him.

"Then who—?" Mary Lou asked.

"I told you it was a secret."

"Oh shit—what kind of a secret?"

"A secret."

"A secret *really?*"

I turned away from Mary Lou, trembling. My mouth kept twisting in a strange hurting smile. "Yes. A secret *really*," I said.

The last time I saw Mary Lou she wouldn't sit with me on the bus, walked past me holding her head high giving me a mean snippy look out of the corner of her eye. Then when she left for her stop she made sure she bumped me going by my seat, she leaned over to say, "I'll find out for myself, I hate you anyway," speaking loud enough for everybody on the bus to hear, "—I always have."

Once upon a time the fairy tales begin. But then they end and often you don't know really what has happened, what was meant to happen, you only know what you've been told, what the words suggest. Now that I have completed my story, filled up half my notebook with my handwriting that disappoints me, it is so shaky and childish—now the story is over I don't understand what it means. I know what happened in my life but I don't know what has happened in these pages.

Mary Lou was found murdered ten days after she said those words to me. Her body had been tossed into Elk Creek a quarter mile from the road and from the old Minton place. Where, it said in the paper, nobody had lived for fifteen years.

It said that Mary Lou had been thirteen years old at the time of her death. She'd been missing for seven days, had been the object of a country-wide search.

It said that nobody had lived in the Minton house for years but that derelicts sometimes sheltered there. It said that the body was unclothed and mutilated. There were no details.

This happened a long time ago.

The murderer (or murderers as the newspaper always said) was never found.

Hans Meunzer was arrested of course and kept in the county jail for three days while police questioned him but in the end they had to let him go, insufficient evidence to build a case it was explained in the newspaper though everybody knew he was the one wasn't he the one?—everybody knew. For years afterward they'd be saying that. Long after Hans was gone and the Siskins were gone, moved away nobody knew where.

Hans swore he hadn't done it, hadn't seen Mary Lou for weeks. There were people who testified in his behalf said he couldn't have done it for one thing he didn't have his brother's car any longer and he'd been working all that time. Working hard out in the fields—couldn't have slipped away long enough to do what police were saying he'd done. And Hans said over and over he was innocent. Sure he was innocent. Son of a bitch ought to be hanged my father said, everybody knew Hans was the one unless it was a derelict or a fisherman—fishermen often drove out to Elk Creek to fish for black bass, built fires on the creek bank and left messes behind—sometimes prowled around the Minton house too looking for things to steal. The police had records of automobile license plates belonging to some of these men, they questioned them but nothing came of it. Then there was that crazy man, that old hermit living in a tar-paper shanty near the Shaheen dump that everybody'd said ought to have been committed to the state hospital years ago. But everybody knew really it was Hans and Hans got out as quick as he could, just disappeared and not even his family knew where unless they were lying which probably they were though they claimed not.

Mother rocked me in her arms crying, the two of us crying, she told me that Mary Lou was happy now, Mary Lou was in Heaven now, Jesus Christ had taken her to live with Him and I knew that didn't I? I wanted to laugh but I didn't laugh. Mary Lou shouldn't have gone with boys, not a nasty boy like Hans, Mother said, she shouldn't have been sneaking around the way she did—I knew that didn't I? Mother's words filled my head flooding my head so there was no danger of laughing.

Jesus loves you too you know that don't you Melissa? Mother asked hugging me. I told her yes. I didn't laugh because I was crying.

They wouldn't let me go to the funeral, said it would scare me too much. Even though the casket was closed.

It's said that when you're older you remember things that happened a long time ago better than you remember things that have just happened and I have found that to be so.

For instance I can't remember when I bought this notebook at Woolworth's whether it was last week or last month or just a few days ago. I can't remember why I started writing in it, what purpose I told myself. But I remember Mary Lou stooping to say those words in my ear and I remember when Mary Lou's mother came over to ask us at suppertime a few days later if I had seen Mary Lou that day—I remember the very food on my plate, the mashed potatoes in a dry little mound. I remember hearing Mary Lou call my name standing out in the driveway cupping her hands to her mouth the way Mother hated her to do, it was white trash behavior

"'Lissa!" Mary Lou would call, and I'd call back, "Okay, I'm coming!" *Once upon a time.*

The Have-Nots

ELIZABETH HAND

Elizabeth Hand is the multiple-award-winning author of numerous novels and collections of short fiction. She is also a longtime reviewer for publications including the *Washington Post*, *Salon*, *Village Voice*, and the *Los Angeles Times*, and is a columnist for *The Magazine of Fantasy & Science Fiction*. *Available Dark*, the sequel to Shirley Jackson Award winner *Generation Loss*, and *Radiant Days*, a young adult novel about Arthur Rimbaud, were both published in 2012 to wide acclaim, as was *Errantry*, a new collection of her short fiction. She divides her time between the coast of Maine and North London.

Now you know Eddie Rule came and took that baby girl three days after she was born.

Actually, his mother took her, Nora Margaret. That was his mother's name, not the girl's. Marched right into that hospital room, Loretta said the nurse was checking her stitches Down There and Nora Margaret marched right in anyway, didn't give a tinker's damn.

I'm taking that baby, she said.

Pardon me? said the nurse. She didn't know Nora Margaret Rule from a hole in the ground.

Excuse *us*, she told the nurse, I think you better go now.

The hell you will, said Loretta; at least now that's what she says she said, but I knew Loretta since fourth grade and she never said a swear in her life 'til she met Eddie Rule, and let me tell you, he was such a goddamn son of a bitch, pardon my French, I would of swore, too.

Now, Alice Jean honey, let me explain something. That shade is just all wrong for you. You're a Summer Rose, remember, you got that blonde hair and blue eyes, you just *have* to go with the Love That Pink. That's the wonder of Mary Rose Cosmetics, everyone gets their own special coordinated color. I think the Salmon Joy is for Erika here, now see the difference?

I thought you would.

Now I'm sorry, I got distracted. But Loretta says now she should of told Nora Margaret off like that, anyhow, swears or not, and I wish she had.

We're married, Loretta said. Ask that nurse, she saw it, Mr. Proctor came down and did it before the baby came. The nurse was gone by then but Loretta showed me the license, it was real all right, she's still got it at home. They wanted to see it for the movie.

Well, you ain't married no more, says Nora Margaret. Loretta told me later, she was surprised a rich lady'd talk like that, but I told her Nora Margaret Rule had no more schooling than my dog King, she just married a rich man is all. Anyway she flaps some thing in front of Loretta's face, Loretta practically went into hysterics then and they called the doctor in. She got them to annex the marriage—

Pardon?

Oh. Well, whatever. Annul it, then, she went to court and had them fix it somehow, said 'cause her son is a Catholic and there was no priest it wasn't a real marriage. Loretta said if you're a Christian how come you're taking my baby and I'm gonna call the police.

Catholic, not Christian, Nora Margaret says, and don't waste your breath, Miss Missy.

Loretta says, It's *Missus*, and Nora Margaret says, Not anymore it ain't. And you know she really did, she took that little baby practically out of her mama's arms and took it away. Paid somebody to adopt it in Richmond and that was the last Loretta saw of it.

Erika, honey, I swear that color takes ten years off your life. Not that you need it. I swear. Alice Jean, don't you think so? I love it that we can compare like this, friends at home. That's why I love Mary Rose Cosmetics,

I can come right here to your house with everything and then later, in the middle of the night, you change your mind, why next day I can come right back and you can exchange that Salmon Joy for anything you like.

That Touch of Teal is *very* popular this year, Erika, you just go right ahead and try it. Kind of smudge it around your eyelid like that. There. I sold one to Suzanne Masters last week, she had that Dinner Dance at the Club to go to and it just matched her dress. I told her if I keep going like this, I'm gonna have that Mary Rose Cadillac by the end of summer and drive my kids to school in it.

I haven't forgotten I'm telling about Loretta's Cadillac, Alice Jean. You get too impatient. Let me give you a facial massage and masque, you got that hot water there, Erika? All right. Now this only takes a few minutes but I swear you will feel like a new woman. You need to relax more, Alice Jean.

There. Isn't that nice? I think it smells like that shampoo they use at Fashion Flair.

So that was, what, Nineteen fifty-six? Nineteen fifty-six. Loretta got out of the hospital and I got her a job at the Blue Moon. Now I swear to god every small town and every city I ever lived in had a diner called the Blue Moon. But it wasn't a bad place to work, just not what you'd want to do after you were married for three days to a Catholic whose rude mama came into the hospital and stole your baby and then gave it to a chiropractor and his wife in Richmond. Plus Nora Margaret said she was gonna change the baby's name—

Her name is Eloise, Loretta shouted. Eloise LeMay Rule.

Not anymore it ain't, Nora Margaret yelled back.

So she's gone forever, Eloise or whatever her name was. Eddie Rule is gone, too, his father sent him off to college, some place where they take people even if you got kicked out of high school without graduating and your mother's the kind of person says ain't. But let me tell you, it's an ill wind blows no one any good, 'cause Loretta hasn't seen him since then and that's the best thing ever happened to her. Good riddance to bad rubbish and I mean that. But of course she didn't feel like that then—

I love him, Terry! she'd tell me, and I'd say, Sure, honey, you love him, but he's gone now and don't do you any good to moon over him. We all thought it best not to bring up the baby at all. Nowadays they wouldn't do that, they'd have her going to some kind of Group, like now Loretta's been going to AA, some place where they'd all talk about having their babies taken away. Like when Noreen was on *Oprah*, they had all these people claimed to have seen him since he died—

Well, all right, Alice Jean, I *am* getting to it. Let me put some more warm water there—

Well, I'm sorry, was that too hot? I'm sorry, honey, I surely am. Erika, see if there's any ice there, will you?

All right. So we're at work one day, this is still at the Blue Moon, and *he* comes in. The Colonel was with him, we recognized the Colonel first 'cause of he's wearing this big hat, but let me tell you, it didn't take us more than a New York second to recognize him. He was famous then but it wasn't like later, he could still walk around like a regular person.

My god he's a handsome man, said Loretta. Sweet Jesus he sure is.

Yup, I said. I was Manageress-in-Training so I had to be more professional, though that was a dead-end job, too. Doing this Mary Rose thing is the best thing ever happened to me, god strike me if that isn't the truth. Erika, if you're still interested you let me know, 'cause I get extra points for signing up new people and it all goes towards the You-Know-What.

The one they had you wouldn't believe. One of the other girls saw it and told us, Look outside, and we did and there it was. Looked like it took up the whole parking lot, and that was before they opened the Piggly Wiggly next door.

Holy cow, said Loretta. That's the biggest goddamn Cadillac I ever saw. Pardon my French, I told you she started talking like that after Eddie. But she was right, it *was* a big car—but you all've seen it, least you saw it the way Loretta had it. Sure you have, oh, Erika honey, thank you—

Alice Jean, I *am* telling it! Here, put this ice there and see if that helps. If it swells up Mary Rose makes this Aloe Vera Nutrifying Lotion, Kenny Junior sunburned himself caddying after school last week and I gave him some and he said it really helped.

So they come in and sit down, I started to give them the booth in the back corner 'cause I thought, well, they're famous, maybe they'd like some privacy, but the Colonel said, No ma'am, we're on vacation, and then *he* said, Put us right here in the front window, it'll be good for business!

Which was just like him, because he meant it to be nice. He always was a nice man and good to his mother, I tell Kenny Junior he should pay attention to that. So anyway I sat them there and since I was in charge I had Loretta serve them. We were all feeling sorry for her, she just had that dinky little Half-Moon trailer to live in and some people in town thought she was just Bad Luck back in those days, she hadn't had a real date since Eddie left. Though she was really nice looking, she hadn't started drinking yet, not much at least, we used to have rum and Cokes sometimes after work but nobody thought anything of it back then.

The Colonel ordered a ribeye steak sandwich and he got fried chicken. Loretta says she doesn't remember, she was so nervous, but *I* remember. I told the director for the TV movie exactly what they had and even showed her how to set the platter. Just pay me my consulting fee, I told her.

I was only joking, Alice Jean. They're not really going to pay me for it.

Here's that Nutrifying Lotion. It doesn't smell as nice as the other but it sure feels good, doesn't it?

You're welcome, honey. I'm sure sorry about burning you like that.

Well, he said it was the best fried chicken he ever had, and as you know if you read that book his wife wrote about him after he was dead, that man loved fried chicken better than Saint John loved the Lord, even after he got to be so famous he had to have it sent up to him in disguise from Popeyes. And really Loretta did a real nice job, she brought the Colonel extra ketchup without him asking and extra napkins for the fried chicken, because it *was* a little greasy, but good, and she was so cute in that pink uniform and all that when they left he gave her his car. Just like that.

Brand-new Cadillac. They just walked downtown to Don Thomas's dealership and bought another one. Drove by and waved to us on their way out of town.

Well, Loretta just about fainted. He kissed her cheek and the Colonel shook her hand and took a picture. Later Hal Morehead from the *Reporter Dispatch* came and took another picture of her and the car, and WINY made the next day Loretta Dooley Day and played "Hound Dog" and "Love Me Tender" about sixty-three million times, I thought I was going to throw up if I heard that song one more time but it did get the point across. And of course Loretta had to learn to drive, but by then people were starting to show more interest and think maybe she wasn't bad luck after all, the absolute reverse in fact. Don Thomas came over, to see what model Cadillac it was this waitress got tipped with, and after a while he and Loretta started seeing each other. And I got promoted to Manager Full-Time. It was all good for business at the Blue Moon, I can tell you that.

But eventually it all settled down. She was still working at the Blue Moon, 'cause of course it was just a *car*, it wasn't like he gave her a million dollars or something. But she'd drive to work every day and park it out front, and people'd stop by just to see it, and then of course they'd come in to see *her*, and most of the time they'd have something to eat. I always recommended the fried chicken.

After a while Loretta stopped seeing Don Thomas. She found out he wasn't actually divorced from his wife after all, just separated, and his wife told him she was pregnant and Loretta put two and two together and told him he better find somewhere else to eat fried chicken, if he knew what was good for him. It was around then she got this weird idea for finding her daughter again.

Erika, I really do like the way he did your hair this time. Those red streaks really show off your eyes. With that color eye shadow you look like that actress in *Working Girl*. Doesn't she, Alice Jean? You know, what's-her-name's daughter. Kim Novak. The one married to what's-his-name.

Whoever.

So look at this, Loretta tells me one day at work. She'd been off for two days and drove in but I was in the back checking on the freezer 'cause the freon tube seized up, so I didn't see her drive up. Come on out, I want to show you something.

Well, okay, I said. Just a minute; and then I went outside.

And you know, she had just ruined that car.

It was sky-blue and black, that car, I swear it was the prettiest thing on earth. The TV movie director, she wanted to make it pink but I told her, Come on, you think a man like that would drive a *pink* car? Back then you wouldn't be caught dead in a pink car, less you were a fairy.

Pardon me, can't say that anymore. I mean a gay. But *you* know what I mean, right Alice Jean? Back then regular people did *not* drive pink cars around. This one was sky-blue.

Look at this, Erika—Mojave Turquoise! Since you're a Spring Rose you can wear that. Try this tester here. Alice Jean, that blusher takes ten years off your life, I am serious.

Did I tell you what she did?

All right. What she did was this: she spent that whole weekend off putting stuff on her car. I mean, *stuff*—old headlights painted green and blue and orange, rocking horses she took off their rockers and painted like carousel animals, Barbie dolls, you name it. All these old antennas she got at the dump and covered in foil and colored paper and stuck all over the car like—well, like these antennas stuck all over the car. There was even this Virgin Mary thing she put where a hood ornament would go, I think that was because of Eddie being a Catholic and having the marriage canceled. I mean, it looked *awful*. And I said, Loretta honey, what in god's name have you done to your car?

She got kind of defensive. What do you mean? she said.

What do I *mean*? I said. I *mean* why have you made the car that beautiful man gave you look like it belongs in Ripley's Believe It or Not?

It's *my* car, she said. She was mad but she also looked like she might cry. And I already was one girl short because Jocelyn Reny's son Peter, the older one who's at Fort Bragg now, had unexpectedly fallen off the roof of their house and broken his arm and she had to take him to the hospital. So I couldn't afford for Loretta to go home because she was crying because I insulted her car, which looked like a blind person had decorated it.

So I said, Well, it's very interesting Loretta, that's all. It's very unusual.

She smiled then and walked over to it. She'd put a bicycle wheel over the front grill, and stuck these little Troll dolls all around the edge of the wheel so it looked like a wheel with all these Troll things sticking on it. I mean, how she drove that car to work without getting arrested I don't know.

Thank you, she said. She started braiding one of the Trolls' hair. She was always good at things like that. Probably she should of gone to the Academy of Beauty and studied Cosmetology. That's another reason it was so sad about her little girl.

Really, I said. It's very interesting.

I had to think about the customers.

Thank you, she said again, and she adjusted another part of the front, where she had stuck these Rat Fink key chains and a flamingo like we have in our front yard. Thank you, Terry. I put a lot of work into it.

I didn't know what else to say, but I had to say something so we could end this conversation and get back to work. So I said, Well, they're sure gonna see you coming, Loretta, that's for sure.

I know, she said. That's what I want. That's the whole point. And she patted it like it was something she had just won on *Let's Make a Deal* instead of a car you wouldn't want to see clowns climbing out of at the Fork Union Fair.

She said, People'll see me coming and they'll talk about me, and everyone'll know who is in this car. Even if they've never been to this town, even if they're a complete and total stranger, they'll hear about me and know how to find me.

Then without another word she turned around and went inside, like nothing unusual had happened at all.

Well, I'll tell you, everyone in the tri-state area pretty well *did* know who owned that car already, because even though it had been a couple years now since she got it Loretta was sort of the town drunk and people knew her 'cause of that. And let's face it, a sky-blue Cadillac that the most famous man in the world gave you as a tip, who could forget about *that?* I mean, some people had forgotten, but then they recognized her for the other reason, so one way or the other Loretta Dooley was not exactly sneaking around Black Spot, Virginia, without somebody knowing about it. So I didn't get why she wanted people to see it was her driving this car that looked like a King Kone on wheels, unless she wanted to give them the chance to see her coming from about three miles away and stay home if they wanted to.

Later I understood better, how she had this kind of daydream that someday her daughter would figure out who her real mother was and start looking for her. And I guess in Loretta's mind somehow her daughter would hear about the story of what happened and come to Black Spot to find her. And then of course once she was here she'd hear about the lady with this famous car, which on top of everything else now it looks like Woolworth's blew up on it. And so that way she'd be able to find her mama. It was kind of a sad thing, to think Loretta had this crazy old idea and thought junking up her nice car would help things along. But I didn't have time to discuss Loretta's problems right then.

Although to tell you the truth, it did seem to cheer her up some. She was lonely a lot, and sort of quiet. Some people thought she was stuck up, because of the Cadillac, but it wasn't that. It was that Nora Margaret Rule took her baby girl and gave her to perfect strangers when she was only three days old. Up until then Loretta was fine as frog hair. And afterwards, well, she wasn't mean or anything. I mean, she was always nice to the customers and me and everybody, it's not like she was *ever* mean. But you could just sort of tell that maybe she felt like the only good thing that was ever going to happen to her already had, and let's face it, living in a rented Half-Moon trailer down on Delbarton and slinging hash at the Blue Moon is not what anyone wants to spend the rest of their life doing, even if you do own a famous Cadillac.

Which, incidentally, by this time was worth about zero money. All that junk she stuck on it weighed it down, and of course kids started trying to pull off the Rat Fink key chains and the baby dolls, and the antennas got snagged on branches and broke off. And to tell you the absolute truth, Loretta's driving wasn't all that great to begin with, so you can just imagine how that poor car looked after a few years.

He would roll over in his grave if he could see what you've done to his nice car, I told her once.

I'd be surprised there was room in his grave for him to turn in, Loretta said. She never forgave him for getting fat and running around on his wife and those other nasty things. Truth was, I think she never forgave him for not coming back and getting her and taking her the hell out of Black Spot.

Besides, why should he care, she sniffled. He never really gave a shit about me. It was just a publicity stunt, like Don said.

She really started crying then. He did tell her that once, Don Thomas did. I thought it was a real mean thing for him to say to her. Loretta is a *very* sensitive person.

Oh, honey, that's not true, I told her. I was trying to fix that damn freezer again and she'd stayed late, to keep me company and also 'cause her license had been suspended and she didn't want Sergeant Merdeck to see her driving. She thought in the dark he wouldn't be able to tell it was her but there was no way you could sneak that thing around, no way. Plus she'd had a few. I didn't say anything, but I could tell.

What?

Well, Alice Jean, all I can say is, if anyone ever had a good reason to drink, it was Loretta Dooley. I know some people do it just for fun. I cut back except for cookouts and parties sometimes. It just *ruins* your skin.

Why, thank you, Erika. I got it last quarter, for being Mary Rose's Most Improved Salesperson in the Southern Mid-Atlantic Area. Ken Senior gave me the gold chain for our anniversary so it's sort of double special. The Mary Rose Cadillac is the same color, only kind of darker, sort of more purple. It's got whitewalls, too. I could have the first one in the Southern Mid-Atlantic, if I get it.

Doesn't that Aloe Vera feel nice, Alice Jean? I keep it in the fridge—makes it sort of a treat to get burned!

Anyway, as I was saying, Loretta was pretty upset that night. I guess it had just all sort of gotten her depressed. It was right after they shut down the Merriam Brick Plant in Petrol, and at the Blue Moon everybody's hours were cut back, not that we were making any money to begin with. That was when I first started thinking about working for myself. Plus her landlord had given her notice, they were developing that part of Delbarton and he just figured he'd cash in, I guess. But I was only trying to be nice to her, cheer her up.

It's not true, Loretta, I told her. I think he really meant it to be a nice thing. I think he truly appreciated the service you gave him.

Well, you are wrong, Terry Westerburgh, she said. You are wrong, 'cause he just did not give a shit, about me or anyone else. Her eyes got this kind of look sometimes when she was drinking, like if you were made of paper they would just burn you up. She crumpled her Dixie cup and threw it on the floor and said, There are two kinds of people in this world, the Haves and the Have-Nots. And I am a Have-Not, and you know what *he* was.

Well, I got sort of P.O.'d then. I mean, here I was on my hands and knees, trying to fix that damn refrigerator, and it wasn't like Ken didn't have to work nights at Big Jim's Barbeque just so we'd get by, and here she was throwing Dixie cups on the floor like she was the Queen of Sheba.

Now you listen to me, *Miss* Dooley, I said. I was pretty aggravated. He worked for everything he ever got, that man did, he was poor as dirt when he started and until the day he died he never forgot where he came from. *That's* why he gave you that car. But you just go ahead and listen to Don Thomas if you want and see where it gets you.

I see where it got me, she said, too mad herself by now to even care who it was she was talking to, Number One, her oldest friend Terry Westerburgh, Number Two, her boss. It got me a shitty job I can't even work enough hours to make my rent. If I had a place to rent, which I don't.

Well, then you just see if you can find another place where you'll be happier, Miss Potty-mouth, I said, and I slammed the refrigerator shut and stomped out.

I was so mad. I shouldn't have to put up with that kind of talk. That was when I decided I was going to really have my own business someday, not work for some person who owns a diner. Sort of the first step towards working for Mary Rose Cosmetics, only of course I didn't know that then.

Erika honey, I know you would love it. You can set your own hours, sleep late as you want, plus you get all your makeup free! And you-know-who would like *that*!

But you know I felt terrible about five minutes after yelling at her. I went into the back room, but she was gone. I heard her leaving, that poor old car scraping along the ground like some dog that got run over. It's funny but I even had started to like that car in a way. I mean it really *did* get your attention. The kids loved it. We got so we'd save old toys, dolls and things, and parts from Ken's Buick and the lawnmower, and I'd bring them over and give them to Loretta and they'd all end up on her car. She had this giant Mr. Potato Head she put on the roof and these colored tennis balls she stuck on all the antennas and really, it was a hoot. Plus her nephew had rigged up some kind of lights that blinked all around the rearview window and Jocelyn's son Peter gave her this funny moose horn she could honk. It was really from the football team but none of us was supposed to know that.

I went outside but it was too late. I really felt terrible. Like Ann Landers says, you should always make your words sweet, 'cause you never know when you'll have to eat them. If I had to eat my words right then I would have thrown up. And so right then I decided to quit the Blue Moon. If it was making me into this mean unkind person, well, then it wasn't the job for me.

Alice Jean, you should kind of dab that Aloe Vera stuff off now, I think, honey, otherwise your pores turn a funny color. Here, use this—these are specially formulated for removing deep-down dirt and grime. Doesn't it smell refreshing!

Okay, this is the good part now. So Loretta is gone, and I felt real bad. I felt guilty, too, because I knew she'd had a few and all I could think of was her and her famous car going off the bridge into the reservoir. I thought of calling Bud Merdeck but then I thought, well, Loretta's not going to feel any better spending the night in the drunk tank, so I decided I'd go after her. She was supposed to get all moved out the next day, she was supposed to have started packing stuff that night. Her sister was going to let her stay with her until she found another place. And you know, she really was in a tight spot, because where are you going to find a decent place to live on what you make working fifteen hours a week at the Blue Moon?

So I got in my car and drove to her house. It was dark by then, and a bad night. It had been raining off and on and now it had finally stopped but it was so foggy, I drove with my low beams on the whole way. Once I even slowed down and opened the window and stuck my head out, 'cause I couldn't see otherwise.

You know where she used to live. Where those Hunters Glen condos are now. That used to be all fields, just these three mobile homes that Gus Brinzer used to rent out. Loretta had the nicest one but that's not saying much. After they sold them they found out the Hell's Angels used one of the others to make LSD in.

Well, I finally got there, but there was nobody home. I would've let myself in but when I peeked in the windows I saw all these boxes, and stuff thrown around everywhere, and—well, to tell you the truth, it was a terrible mess. I mean, it looked like the Hell's Angels had been living *there*. And I knew then, things were worse with Loretta than I'd known. I mean, here she was, my oldest friend plus I was her supervisor, but I just had no idea. If I'd known I would've done something, she had a lot of friends, really, but I just had no idea at all.

So I waited outside. There was a kind of metal stairs in front of the trailer but that was broken so I sat on my car. I was there for a long time. It was cold, the fog was real damp and just sank into you after a while. I was starting to worry, too; I mean I was starting to get so worried I was afraid I'd start to scream, thinking of all the horrible things that might've happened to Loretta and I was nasty to her. I was just getting ready to let myself in and call Ken, when I heard somebody walking down the road.

I turned around and it was her. She looked awful, like when you see movies and there's people been in a car wreck. There was no blood or anything but she was wet and her hair was wet and she had mud on her face and oh, I just screamed and ran over and started hugging her.

Loretta, thank god you're all right! What happened?

She made a noise like she was embarrassed and then she started to cry.

I wrecked it, she said. I put my arms around her, I didn't even care I had already changed out of my uniform. She said, I went down Lee Highway and rolled it into the reservoir.

Oh, my god! I said. You could have killed yourself, Loretta!

I know, she said. I had to swim out. It's in there so deep they'll never get it out. She really started crying then.

Why'd you do *that?* I said and started crying, too, but I stopped. I only had one clean tissue left, and I gave it to her.

Because it doesn't matter, she said. My whole life and nothing matters. I live *here*—she bent and picked up a rock and threw it and broke a window, I heard it—in this *dump*, and now I don't even live here anymore. I had a husband and a baby for three days, and twenty-seven years ago someone famous gave me a goddamn Cadillac as a tip, and that's it. That's my whole life. That's it, Terry. My whole life is right there.

Well, you know I wished I could of said something to her, but she was right. That was her whole life, right there.

I just wish I could've kept my baby, she said. She was crying so I could hardly hear what she said. If they'd of left me my baby girl I would've felt like I had something. Like you have Ken and Little Kenny. I would have had Eloise.

I started crying again then, too. I mean, god! It was just so *sad*. So then we sat for a little while but we didn't say anything. It was all just too depressing.

But after a while I started to think, Well, we have got to do something, we can't sit here all night in the mud, and I thought maybe I'd call Ken and see was it okay if Loretta came back with me and could stay at our house. I was just thinking of standing up and asking Loretta was it okay if I went inside to use the phone, when we heard it. It had started raining again, a little, and we had sat on that broken step in front of the trailer, 'cause there's an awning there.

Loretta stood up first. Oh, my god, she said. Shit.

I listened and stood, too. Shit, I said.

It was her car. That was obvious, I mean you couldn't mistake that car for anything else in the world. It sounded like it was having trouble getting over the last hill, where it was always overgrown and muddy anyway. And you figure a car that was in the bottom of the reservoir, it probably wouldn't run too well.

Shit, Loretta said again. That's it.

I knew just what she meant. I was thinking that Bud Merdeck had found it somehow and gotten Lynnwood Gentry to tow it out, and now how was Loretta going to pay for it, not to mention they could have arrested her, probably, for rolling a car into the reservoir on purpose. Especially that car.

And then it made this grinding nose, and suddenly it popped over the rise. The headlights were on, at least one of them was. The wheel that used to have the Trolls on it and now had this Big Bird sort of tied to it was all bent up and the antennas were all mashed together. Whoever was driving it tried to honk the moose horn but it hardly made a noise at all. It was just about the saddest car you ever saw.

Loretta and I looked at each other and she rubbed at her face, trying to get some of the mud off.

We better go see who it is, I whispered. If it's Lynnwood I'll call Ken and he'll talk to him.

Thank you, Terry, she said. She knew that was my way of making up with her.

We started walking to the car, slowly because of the rain and it was sloppy going. The car had stopped at the edge of the drive and waited with the motor running. It didn't sound too good either. Maybe better than you'd expect, but it was pretty sad, to think that car had come to this. As we walked up to it the door on the passenger side popped open.

Hello? It was this woman's voice, nobody we knew.

Hi, I said. I stopped, wondering if maybe Lynnwood had brought along his girlfriend Donna. He stays at the shop all night sometimes and on weekends she usually keeps him company.

But it wasn't Donna. It wasn't anybody that I recognized at all. This short woman, with dyed blonde hair. She stepped out of the car, jumping over the water. She had on nice clothes, not expensive or designer clothes but like a secretary's clothes, like she hadn't changed from work yet. She had a nice smile, and nice eyes—I know you wouldn't think you'd notice something like that in the dark but I did, I have a good eye for things like that. Mary Rose says that a great saleswoman needs an eye for detail.

Are you—? The woman started to say something, then she turned around and leaned back into the car, like she was asking the driver something. Then she turned around again and said, Is one of you Loretta Dooley?

That's me, said Loretta. She had this squinched-up tone. I knew she was nervous they were going to ask, Have you been drinking?

Instead the girl says, My name is Noreen Marcus.

Marcus? Loretta says.

That's right, says the girl. She glances back at the car, sort of nervously, but then it was like whoever was inside told her it was okay, so she goes on.

Noreen Marcus. My parents are Lowell and Angeline Marcus, in Richmond. I hitchhiked here. This man gave me a ride out by the reservoir. I'm your daughter.

My daughter? Loretta says, and *I'm* saying, Your *who?*

Ye-es—

And the girl stepped forward, holding up her skirt so it wouldn't get wet, and then she looked up, and it was like for the first time she got a good look at Loretta in the headlight. 'Cause she suddenly gave this scream and started laughing, and dropped her purse in the water and ran across and I started running, too, next to Loretta, only then at the last minute I stopped because I thought, Now wait a minute, this is something very special going on here between Loretta and this young woman who is her daughter, and so I stayed and waited a little while until they calmed down.

Well, Alice Jean, I knew it was her because she had Eddie Rule's eyes and his smile. He may have been a poor father but he did have a nice smile.

And so for a little while there was some crying and laughing and you can just imagine how we all felt. And all the while that old car just sat there, though whoever was inside turned the motor off after a while and smoked a cigarette. There was no radio in it but you could hear him sort of humming to himself.

And finally Loretta said, Well, for god's sakes let's go inside, we're getting soaked.

Well, wait a minute while I get my bag, said Noreen.

She went back to the car and stuck her head in and said something to whoever was in there.

Okay, now this is when I got goosebumps.

Because I couldn't hear what he was saying—it was too far away, and it wasn't like I wanted to eavesdrop or anything. I guess I sort of expected it must be old Eddie Rule inside. But now I could definitely hear his voice, and it wasn't Eddie Rule's voice at all. It was—

Well, *you* know whose voice it was.

Loretta knew, too. She stood by me with her arms crossed, shivering, and when she heard him she turned to me and opened her mouth and for a minute there I thought she was going to faint.

Oh, my god, she said, oh, my *god*—

Thank you for the ride, I heard Noreen yelling at him, and I could just barely make out his voice saying something back to her, goodbye I guess, something like that. Then she pulled this suitcase out of the car and stood back while it backed up.

Loretta! I said, elbowing her and then pulling her to me. Loretta, hurry up! Tell him thank you—

And she yelled, Thank you, thank you! and then she started running after the car, yelling and waving like she was crazy. Which we all were by then, all of us yelling and waving at him and laughing like we'd known each other all this time, when it'd really only been, like, five minutes. And the car just kept backing up 'til it got over the top of the hill, and then I guess he turned it around and drove off. And that was the last time anybody ever saw Loretta's famous Cadillac.

Afterwards we went inside and kind of dried off and then on the way to my house we stopped at Big Jim's and got a half-dozen Specials and went home. The Specials were so Ken Senior wouldn't be too mad about me being out so late.

And so that's how it happened. Next day of course the story got out, because there is no way, just no way, you can keep something like that a secret. Noreen says she thinks it was just a coincidence, she says everybody out here in Black Spot looks like him and who could tell the difference? Plus she said if it was really him wouldn't he have been in a fancy limousine, not some crazy fixed-up car her real mother drove into the reservoir.

But *I* said, Well, that's how you know it was really him. 'Cause it's like Loretta said, there's the Haves and there's the Have-Nots, and if you're a Have-Not you never forget what it's like to be poor and on your own. I mean how could he have sung "Heartbreak Hotel" otherwise? Noreen said, Well, I still have my doubts, but when she and her mama went on *Oprah* they played it up for all they could, I can tell you that. And like the TV movie director says, it doesn't really matter, does it? Because it's such a good story.

And I mean there's Noreen reunited with Loretta to prove it, not to mention how would you ever get a car like that out of the reservoir, *plus* where is that car now, I ask you? Because I saw it, too, and I hadn't had a thing to drink.

What do I think? Well, Erika honey, I guess it's just one of those things. Strange things happen sometimes and you just got to take the good with the bad, is all. But you won't hear me complaining about how it all turned out, not as long as business stays this good and I get that new Mary Rose Cadillac in the fall, no ma'am.

Closing Time

NEIL GAIMAN

Neil Gaiman is the Newbery Medal-winning author of *The Graveyard Book* and a *New York Times* bestseller. Several of his books, including *Coraline*, have been made into major motion pictures. He is also famous for the "Sandman" graphic novel series, and for numerous other books and comics for adult, young adult, and younger readers. He has won the Hugo, Nebula, Mythopoeic, World Fantasy, and other awards. He is also the author of powerful short stories and poems.

There are still clubs in London. Old ones, and mock-old, with elderly sofas and crackling fireplaces, newspapers, and traditions of speech or of silence, and new clubs, the Groucho and its many knockoffs, where actors and journalists go to be seen, to drink, to enjoy their glowering solitude, or even to talk. I have friends in both kinds of club, but am not myself a member of any club in London, not anymore.

Years ago, half a lifetime, when I was a young journalist, I joined a club. It existed solely to take advantage of the licensing laws of the day, which forced all pubs to stop serving drinks at eleven PM, closing time. This club, the Diogenes, was a one-room affair located above a record shop in a narrow alley just off the Tottenham Court Road. It was owned by a cheerful, chubby, alcohol-fueled woman called Nora, who would tell anyone who asked and even if they didn't that she'd called the club the Diogenes, darling, because she was still looking for an honest man. Up a narrow flight of steps, and, at Nora's whim, the door to the club would be open, or not. It kept irregular hours.

It was a place to go once the pubs closed, that was all it ever was, and despite Nora's doomed attempts to serve food or even to send out a cheery monthly newsletter to all her club's members reminding them that the club now served food, that was all it would ever be. I was saddened several years ago when I heard that Nora had died; and I was struck, to my surprise, with a real sense of desolation last month when, on a visit to England, walking down that alley, I tried to figure out where the Diogenes Club had been, and looked first in the wrong place, then saw the faded green cloth awnings shading the windows of a tapas restaurant above a mobile phone shop, and, painted on them, a stylized man in a barrel. It seemed almost indecent, and it set me remembering.

There were no fireplaces in the Diogenes Club, and no armchairs either, but still, stories were told.

Most of the people drinking there were men, although women passed through from time to time, and Nora had recently acquired a glamorous permanent fixture in the shape of a deputy, a blonde Polish émigré who called everybody "darlink" and who helped herself to drinks whenever she got behind the bar. When she was drunk, she would tell us that she was by rights a countess, back in Poland, and swear us all to secrecy.

There were actors and writers, of course. Film editors, broadcasters, police inspectors, and drunks. People who did not keep fixed hours. People who stayed out too late or who did not want to go home. Some nights there might be a dozen people there, or more. Other nights I'd wander in and I'd be the only person around—on those occasions I'd buy myself a single drink, drink it down, and then leave.

That night, it was raining, and there were four of us in the club after midnight.

Nora and her deputy were sitting up at the bar, working on their sitcom. It was about a chubby-but-cheerful woman who owned a drinking club, and her scatty deputy, an aristocratic foreign blonde who made amusing English mistakes. It would be like *Cheers*, Nora used to tell people. She named the comical Jewish landlord after me. Sometimes they would ask me to read a script.

There was an actor named Paul (commonly known as Paul-the-actor, to stop people confusing him with Paul-the-police-inspector or Paul-the-struck-off-plastic-surgeon, who were also regulars), a computer gaming magazine editor named Martyn, and me. We knew each other vaguely, and the three of us sat at a table by the window and watched the rain come down, misting and blurring the lights of the alley.

There was another man there, older by far than any of the three of us. He was cadaverous and gray-haired and painfully thin, and he sat alone in the corner and nursed a single whiskey. The elbows of his tweed jacket were patched with brown leather, I remember that quite vividly. He did not talk to us, or read, or do anything. He just sat, looking out at the rain and the alley beneath, and sometimes, he sipped his whiskey without any visible pleasure.

It was almost midnight, and Paul and Martyn and I had started telling ghost stories. I had just finished telling them a sworn-true ghostly account from my school days: the tale of the Green Hand. It had been an article of faith at my prep school that there was a disembodied, luminous hand that was seen, from time to time, by unfortunate schoolboys. If you saw the Green Hand you would die soon after. Fortunately, none of us were ever unlucky enough to encounter it, but there were sad tales of boys from before our time, boys who saw the Green Hand and whose thirteen-year-old hair had turned white overnight. According to school legend they were taken to the sanatorium, where they would expire after a week or so without ever being able to utter another word.

"Hang on," said Paul-the-actor. "If they never uttered another word, how did anyone know they'd seen the Green Hand? I mean, they could have seen anything."

As a boy, being told the stories, I had not thought to ask this, and now it was pointed out to me it did seem somewhat problematic.

"Perhaps they wrote something down," I suggested, a bit lamely.

We batted it about for a while, and agreed that the Green Hand was a most unsatisfactory sort of ghost. Then Paul told us a true story about a friend of his who had picked up a hitchhiker, and dropped her off at a place she said was her house, and when he went back the next morning, it turned out to be a cemetery. I mentioned that exactly the same thing had happened to a friend of mine as well. Martyn said that it had not only happened to a friend of his, but, because the hitchhiking girl looked so cold, the friend had lent her his coat, and the next morning, in the cemetery, he found his coat all neatly folded on her grave.

Martyn went and got another round of drinks, and we wondered why all these ghost women were zooming around the country all night and hitchhiking home, and Martyn said that probably living hitchhikers these days were the exception, not the rule.

And then one of us said, "I'll tell you a true story, if you like. It's a story I've never told a living soul. It's true—it happened to me, not to a friend of mine—but I don't know if it's a ghost story. It probably isn't."

This was over twenty years ago. I have forgotten so many things, but I have not forgotten that night, or how it ended.

This is the story that was told that night, in the Diogenes Club.

I was nine years old, or thereabouts, in the late 1960s, and I was attending a small private school not far from my home. I was only at that school less than a year—long enough to take a dislike to the school's owner, who had bought the school in order to close it and to sell the prime land on which it stood to property developers, which, shortly after I left, she did.

For a long time—a year or more—after the school closed the building stood empty before it was finally demolished and replaced by offices. Being a boy, I was also a burglar of sorts, and one day before it was knocked down, curious, I went back there. I wriggled through a half-open window and walked through empty classrooms that still smelled of chalk dust. I took only one thing from my visit, a painting I had done in Art of a little house with a red door knocker like a devil or an imp. It had my name on it, and it was up on a wall. I took it home.

When the school was still open I walked home each day, through the town, then down a dark road cut through sandstone hills and all grown over with trees, and past an abandoned gatehouse. Then there would be light, and the road would go past fields, and finally I would be home.

Back then there were so many old houses and estates, Victorian relics that stood in an empty half-life awaiting the bulldozers that would transform them and their ramshackle grounds into blandly identical landscapes of desirable modern residences, every house neatly arranged side by side around roads that went nowhere.

The other children I encountered on my way home were, in my memory, always boys. We did not know each other, but, like guerillas in occupied territory, we would exchange information. We were scared of adults, not each other. We did not have to know each other to run in twos or threes or in packs.

The day that I'm thinking of, I was walking home from school, and I met three boys in the road where it was at its darkest. They were looking for something in the ditches and the hedges and the weed-choked place in front of the abandoned gatehouse. They were older than me.

"What are you looking for?"

The tallest of them, a beanpole of a boy, with dark hair and a sharp face, said, "Look!" He held up several ripped-in-half pages from what must have been a very, very old pornographic magazine. The girls were all in black-and-white, and their hairstyles looked like the ones my great-aunts had in old photographs. Fragments of it had blown all over the road and into the abandoned gatehouse front garden.

I joined in the paper chase. Together, the three of us retrieved almost a whole copy of *The Gentleman's Relish* from that dark place. Then we climbed over a wall, into a deserted apple orchard, and looked at what we had gathered. Naked women from a long time ago. There is a smell, of fresh apples and of rotten apples moldering down into cider, which even today brings back the idea of the forbidden to me.

The smaller boys, who were still bigger than I was, were called Simon and Douglas, and the tall one, who might have been as old as fifteen, was called Jamie. I wondered if they were brothers. I did not ask.

When we had all looked at the magazine, they said, "We're going to hide this in our special place. Do you want to come along? You mustn't tell, if you do. You mustn't tell anyone."

They made me spit on my palm, and they spat on theirs, and we pressed our hands together.

Their special place was an abandoned metal water tower in a field by the entrance to the lane near to where I lived. We climbed a high ladder. The tower was painted a dull green on the outside, and inside it was orange with rust, which covered the floor and the walls. There was a wallet on the floor with no money in it, only some cigarette cards. Jamie showed them to me: each card held a painting of a cricketer from a long time ago. They put the pages of the magazine down on the floor of the water tower, and the wallet on top of it.

Then Douglas said, "I say we go back to the Swallows next."

My house was not far from the Swallows, a sprawling manor house set back from the road. It had been owned, my father had told me once, by the Earl of Tenterden, but when he had died his son, the new earl, had simply closed the place up. I had wandered to the edges of the grounds, but had not gone further in. It did not feel abandoned. The gardens were too well-cared-for, and where there were gardens there were gardeners. Somewhere there had to be an adult.

I told them this.

Jamie said, "Bet there's not. Probably just someone who comes in and cuts the grass once a month or something. You're not scared, are you? We've been there hundreds of times. Thousands."

Of course I was scared, and of course I said that I was not. We went up the main drive until we reached the main gates. They were closed, and we squeezed beneath the bars to get in.

Rhododendron bushes lined the drive. Before we got to the house there was what I took to be a groundskeeper's cottage, and beside it on the grass were some rusting metal cages, big enough to hold a hunting dog, or a boy. We walked past them, up to a horseshoe-shaped drive and right up to the front door of the Swallows. We peered inside, looking in the windows but seeing nothing. It was too dark inside.

We slipped around the house, through a rhododendron thicket and out again, into some kind of fairyland. It was a magical grotto, all rocks and delicate ferns and odd, exotic plants I'd never seen before: plants with purple leaves, and leaves like fronds, and small half-hidden flowers like jewels. A tiny stream wound through it, a rill of water running from rock to rock.

Douglas said, "I'm going to wee-wee in it." It was very matter-of-fact. He walked over to it, pulled down his shorts, and urinated in the stream, splashing on the rocks. The other boys did it, too, both of them pulling out their penises and standing beside him to piss into the stream.

I was shocked. I remember that. I suppose I was shocked by the joy they took in this, or just by the way they were doing something like that in such a special place, spoiling the clear water and the magic of the place, making it into a toilet. It seemed wrong.

When they were done, they did not put their penises away. They shook them. They pointed them at me. Jamie had hair growing at the base of his.

"We're cavaliers," said Jamie. "Do you know what that means?"

I knew about the English Civil War, Cavaliers (wrong but romantic) versus Roundheads (right but repulsive), but I didn't think that was what he was talking about. I shook my head.

"It means our willies aren't circumcised," he explained. "Are you a cavalier or a roundhead?"

I knew what they meant now. I muttered, "I'm a roundhead."

"Show us. Go on. Get it out."

"No. It's none of your business."

For a moment, I thought things were going to get nasty, but then Jamie laughed, and put his penis away, and the others did the same. They told dirty jokes to each other then, jokes I really didn't understand, for all that I was a bright child, but I heard and remembered them, and several weeks later was almost expelled from school for telling one of them to a boy who went home and told it to his parents.

The joke had the word *fuck* in it. That was the first time I ever heard the word, in a dirty joke in a fairy grotto.

The principal called my parents into the school, after I'd got in trouble, and said that I'd said something so bad they could not repeat it, not even to tell my parents what I'd done.

My mother asked me, when they got home that night.

"Fuck," I said.

"You must never, ever say that word," said my mother. She said this very firmly, and quietly, and for my own good. "That is the worst word anyone can say." I promised her that I wouldn't.

But after, amazed at the power a single word could have, I would whisper it to myself, when I was alone.

In the grotto, that autumn afternoon after school, the three big boys told jokes and they laughed and they laughed, and I laughed, too, although I did not understand any of what they were laughing about.

We moved on from the grotto. Into the formal gardens and over a small bridge that spanned a pond; we crossed it nervously, because it was out in the open, but we could see huge goldfish in the blackness of the pond below, which made it worthwhile. Then Jamie led Douglas and Simon and me down a gravel path into some woodland.

Unlike the gardens, the woods were abandoned and unkempt. They felt like there was no one around. The path was grown over. It led between trees and then, after a while, into a clearing.

In the clearing was a little house.

It was a playhouse, built perhaps forty years earlier for a child, or for children. The windows were Tudor style, leaded and crisscrossed into diamonds. The roof was mock Tudor. A stone path led straight from where we were to the front door.

Together, we walked up the path to the door.

Hanging from the door was a metal knocker. It was painted crimson and had been cast in the shape of some kind of imp, some kind of grinning pixie or demon, cross-legged, hanging by its hands from a hinge. Let me see...how can I describe this best? It wasn't a *good* thing. The expression on its face, for starters. I found myself wondering what kind of a person would hang something like that on a playhouse door.

It frightened me, there in that clearing, with the dusk gathering under the trees. I walked away from the house, back to a safe distance, and the others followed me.

"I think I have to go home now," I said.

It was the wrong thing to say. The three of them turned and laughed and jeered at me, called me pathetic, called me a baby. *They* weren't scared of the house, they said.

"I dare you!" said Jamie. "I dare you to knock on the door."

I shook my head.

"If you don't knock on the door," said Douglas, "you're too much of a baby ever to play with us again."

I had no desire ever to play with them again. They seemed like occupants of a land I was not yet ready to enter. But still, I did not want them to think me a baby.

"Go on. *We're* not scared," said Simon.

I try to remember the tone of voice he used. Was he frightened, too, and covering it with bravado? Or was he amused? It's been so long. I wish I knew.

I walked slowly back up the flagstone path to the house. I reached up, grabbed the grinning imp in my right hand, and banged it hard against the door.

Or rather, I tried to bang it hard, just to show the other three that I was not afraid at all. That I was not afraid of anything. But something happened, something I had not expected, and the knocker hit the door with a muffled sort of a thump.

"Now you have to go inside!" shouted Jamie. He was excited. I could hear it. I found myself wondering if they had known about this place already, before we came. If I was the first person they had brought there.

But I did not move.

"*You* go in," I said. "I knocked on the door. I did it like you said. Now you have to go inside. I dare you. I dare *all* of you."

I wasn't going in. I was perfectly certain of that. Not then. Not ever. I'd felt something move, I'd felt the knocker *twist* under my hand as I'd banged that grinning imp down on the door. I was not so old that I would deny my own senses.

They said nothing. They did not move.

Then, slowly, the door fell open. Perhaps they thought that I, standing by the door, had pushed it open. Perhaps they thought that I'd jarred it when I knocked. But I hadn't. I was certain of it. It opened because it was ready.

I should have run then. My heart was pounding in my chest. But the devil was in me, and instead of running I looked at the three big boys at the bottom of the path, and I simply said, "Or are you scared?"

They walked up the path toward the little house.

"It's getting dark," said Douglas.

Then the three boys walked past me, and one by one, reluctantly perhaps, they entered the playhouse. A white face turned to look at me as they went into that room, to ask why I wasn't following them in, I'll bet. But as Simon, who was the last of them, walked in, the door banged shut behind them, and I swear to God I did not touch it.

The imp grinned down at me from the wooden door, a vivid splash of crimson in the gray gloaming.

I walked around to the side of the playhouse and peered through all the windows, one by one, into the dark and empty room. Nothing moved in there. I wondered if the other three were inside hiding from me, pressed against the wall, trying their damnedest to stifle their giggles. I wondered if it was a big-boy game.

I didn't know. I couldn't tell.

I stood there in the courtyard of the playhouse, while the sky got darker, just waiting. The moon rose after a while, a big autumn moon the color of honey.

And then, after a while, the door opened, and nothing came out.

Now I was alone in the glade, as alone as if there had never been anyone else there at all. An owl hooted, and I realized that I was free to go. I turned and walked away, following a different path out of the glade, always keeping my distance from the main house. I climbed a fence in the moonlight, ripping the seat of my school shorts, and I walked—not ran, I didn't need to run—across a field of barley stubble, and over a stile, and into a flinty lane that would take me, if I followed it far enough, all the way to my house.

And soon enough, I was home.

My parents had not been worried, although they were irritated by the orange rust dust on my clothes, by the rip in my shorts. "Where were you, anyway?" my mother asked.

"I went for a walk," I said. "I lost track of time."

And that was where we left it.

It was almost two in the morning. The Polish countess had already gone. Now Nora began, noisily, to collect up the glasses and ashtrays and to wipe down the bar. "*This* place is haunted," she said, cheerfully. "Not that it's ever bothered me. I like a bit of company, darlings. If I didn't, I wouldn't have opened the club. Now, don't you have homes to go to?"

We said our good nights to Nora, and she made each of us kiss her on her cheek, and she closed the door of the Diogenes Club behind us. We walked down the narrow steps past the record shop, down into the alley and back into civilization.

The underground had stopped running hours ago, but there were always night buses, and cabs still out there for those who could afford them. (I couldn't. Not in those days.)

The Diogenes Club itself closed several years later, finished off by Nora's cancer and, I suppose, by the easy availability of late-night alcohol once the English licensing laws were changed. But I rarely went back after that night.

"Was there ever," asked Paul-the-actor, as we hit the street, "any news of those three boys? Did you see them again? Or were they reported as missing?"

"Neither," said the storyteller. "I mean, I never saw them again. And there was no local manhunt for three missing boys. Or if there was, I never heard about it."

"Is the playhouse still there?" asked Martyn.

"I don't know," admitted the storyteller.

"Well," said Martyn, as we reached the Tottenham Court Road and headed for the night bus stop, "I for one do not believe a word of it."

There were four of us, not three, out on the street long after closing time. I should have mentioned that before. There was still one of us who had not spoken, the elderly man with the leather elbow patches, who had left the club with the three of us. And now he spoke for the first time.

"I believe it," he said mildly. His voice was frail, almost apologetic. "I cannot explain it, but I believe it. Jamie died, you know, not long after Father did. It was Douglas who wouldn't go back, who sold the old place. He wanted them to tear it all down. But they kept the house itself, the Swallows. They weren't going to knock *that* down. I imagine that everything else must be gone by now."

It was a cold night, and the rain still spat occasional drizzle. I shivered, but only because I was cold.

"Those cages you mentioned," he said. "By the driveway. I haven't thought of them in fifty years. When we were bad he'd lock us up in them. We must have been bad a great deal, eh? Very naughty, naughty boys."

He was looking up and down the Tottenham Court Road, as if he were looking for something. Then he said, "Douglas killed himself, of course. Ten years ago. When I was still in the bin. So my memory's not as good. Not as good as it was. But that was Jamie all right, to the life. He'd never let us forget that he was the oldest. And you know, we weren't ever allowed in the playhouse. Father didn't build it for us." His voice quavered, and for a moment I could imagine this pale old man as a boy again. "Father had his own games."

And then he waved his arm and called "Taxi!" and a taxi pulled over to the curb. "Brown's Hotel," said the man, and he got in. He did not say good night to any of us. He pulled shut the door of the cab.

And in the closing of the cab door I could hear too many other doors closing. Doors in the past, which are gone now, and cannot be reopened.

Anna

F. PAUL WILSON

F. Paul Wilson is the award-winning, *New York Times* bestselling author of forty-plus books and many short stories spanning medical thrillers, science fiction, horror, adventure, and virtually everything in between. More than nine million copies of his books are in print in the United States and his work has been translated into twenty languages. He also has written for the stage, screen, and interactive media.

His latest thriller, *Cold City*, stars the notorious urban mercenary, Repairman Jack, and is the first of The Early Years Trilogy. *Dark City* follows soon.

He currently resides at the Jersey Shore and can be found online at www.repairmanjack.com.

The bushy-haired young man with long sideburns arrives on deck with two cups of coffee—one black for himself, the other laced with half-and-half and two sugars, the way his wife always takes it. Rows of blue plastic seats, half of them filled with tourists heading back to the mainland, sit bolted to the steel deck. He stops by a row under the awning. His wife's navy blue sweatshirt is draped over the back of one of the seats but she's not there. He looks around and doesn't see her. He asks a nearby couple, strangers, if they saw where his wife went but they say they didn't notice.

The man strolls through the ferry's crowded aft deck but doesn't see his wife. Still carrying the coffee, he ambles forward but she's not there either. He wanders the starboard side, checking out the tourists leaning on the rails, then does the same on the port side. No sign of her.

The man places the coffee on the seat with her sweatshirt and searches through the inner compartments and the snack bar. He begins to ask people if they've seen a blond woman in her mid-twenties wearing a flowered top and bell-bottom jeans. Sure, people say. Dozens of them. And they're right. The ferry carries numerous women fitting that description.

The man finds a member of the crew and tells him that his wife is missing. He is taken to the ferry's security officer who assures him that his wife is surely somewhere aboard—perhaps she's seasick and in one of the restrooms.

The man waits outside the women's rooms, asking at each if someone could check inside for his wife. When that yields nothing, he again wanders the various decks, going so far as to search the vehicle level where supply trucks and passengers' cars make the trip.

When the ferry reaches Hyannis, the man stands on the dock and watches every debarking passenger, but his wife is not among them.

He calls his father-in-law who lives outside Boston. He explains that they were on their way over for a surprise visit but now his daughter is missing. The father-in-law arrives in his chauffeur-driven Bentley and joins the young man in storming the offices of the Massachusetts Steamship Authority, demanding a thorough, stem-to-stern search of the ferry and too damned bad if that will delay its departure. The father-in-law is a rich man, influential in Massachusetts politics. The ferry is detained.

The state police are called to aid in the search. The Coast Guard sends out a helicopter to trace and retrace the ferry's route. But the wife is not to be found. No one sees her again. Ever.

"Ow!"

William Morley grabbed his right heel as pain spiked through it. His knee creaked and protested as he leaned back in the chair and pulled his foot up to where he could see it.

"I'll be damned!" he said as he spotted the two-inch splinter jutting from the heel of his sock.

Blood seeped through the white cotton, forming a crimson bull's-eye around the base of the splinter. Morley grabbed the end and yanked it free. The tip was stiletto sharp and red with his blood.

"Where the hell...?"

He'd been sitting here in his study, in his favorite rocker, reading the Sunday *Times*, his feet resting on the new maple footstool he'd bought just yesterday. How on earth had he picked up a splinter?

Keeping his bloody heel off the carpet, he limped into the bathroom, dabbed a little peroxide on the wound, then covered it with a Band-Aid.

When he returned to the footstool he checked the cushioned top and saw a small hole in the fabric where his heel had been resting. The splinter must have been lying in the stuffing. He didn't remember moving his foot before it pierced him, but he must have.

Morley had picked up the footstool at Danzer's overpriced furniture boutique on Lower Broadway. He'd gone in looking for something antiquey and come out with this brand-new piece. He'd spotted it from the front of the showroom; tucked in a far rear corner, it seemed to call to him. And once he'd seen the intricate grain—he couldn't remember seeing maple grained like this—and the elaborate carving along the edge of the seat and up and down the legs, he couldn't pass it up.

But careless as all hell for someone to leave a sharp piece of wood like that in the padding. If he were a different sort, he might sue. But what for? He had more than enough money, and he wouldn't want to break whoever did this exquisite carving.

He grabbed two of the stool's three legs and lifted it for a closer look. Marvelous grain, and—"

"Shit!" he cried, and dropped it as pain lanced his hand.

He gaped in wonder at the splinter—little more than an inch long this time—jutting from his palm. He plucked the slim little dagger and held it up.

How the hell...?

Morley knelt next to the overturned stool and inspected the leg he'd been holding. He spotted the source of the splinter—a slim, pale crevice in the darker surface of the lightly stained wood.

How on earth had that wound up in his skin? He could understand if he'd been sliding his hand along, but he'd simply been holding it. And next to the crevice—was that another splinter angled outward?

As he adjusted his reading glasses and leaned closer, the tiny piece of wood popped out of the leg and flew at his right eye.

Morley jerked back as it bounced harmlessly off the eyeglass lens. He lost his balance and fell onto his back, but he didn't stay down. He'd gained weight in his middle years and was carrying an extra thirty pounds on his medium frame, yet he managed to roll over and do a rapid if ungainly scramble away from the footstool on his hands and knees. At sixty-two he cherished his dignity, but panic had taken over.

My God! If I hadn't been wearing glasses—!

Thankfully, he was alone. He rose, brushed himself off, and regarded the footstool from a safe distance.

Really—a "safe distance" from a little piece of furniture? Ridiculous. But his stomach roiled at the thought of how close he'd come to having a pierced cornea. Something very, very wrong here.

Rubbing his hands over his arms to counter a creeping chill, Morley surveyed his domain, a turn-of-the-century townhouse on East Thirty-first Street in the Murray Hill section of Manhattan. He and Elaine had spent just shy of a million for it in the late eighties, and it was worth multiples of that now. Its four levels of hardwood floors, cherry wainscoting, intricately carved walnut moldings and cornices were all original. They'd spent a small fortune refurbishing the interior to its original Victorian splendor and furnishing it with period antiques. After the tumor in her breast finally took Elaine in 1995, he'd stayed on here, alone but not lonely. Over the years he'd gradually removed Elaine's touches, easing her influence from the decor until the place was all him. He'd become quite content as lord of the manor.

Until now. The footstool had attracted him because of its grain, and because the style of its carving fit so seamlessly with the rest of the furniture, but he wouldn't care now if it was a genuine one-of-a-kind Victorian. That thing had to go.

Tugging at his neat salt-and-pepper beard, Morley eyed the footstool from across the room. Question was...how was he going to get it out of here without touching it?

The owner of Mostly Maple was at the counter when Morley walked in. Though close to Morley in age, Hal Danzer was a polar opposite. Where Morley was thick, Danzer was thin, where Morley was bearded, Danzer was clean shaven, where Morley's thin hair was neatly trimmed, Danzer's was long and thick and tied into a short ponytail.

A gallimaufry of maple pieces of varying ages, ranging from ancient to brand new, surrounded them—claw-footed tables, wardrobes, breakfronts, secretaries, desks, dressers, even old kitchen phones. Morley liked maple too, but not to the exclusion of all other woods. Danzer had once told him that he had no firm guidelines regarding his stock other than it be of maple and strike his fancy.

Morley deposited the heavy-duty canvas duffel on the counter.

"I want to return this."

Danzer stared at him. "A canvas bag?"

"No." With difficulty he refrained from adding, *you idiot*. "What's inside."

Danzer opened the bag and peeked in. He frowned. "The footstool you bought Saturday? Something wrong with it?"

Hell, yes, something was wrong with it. Very wrong.

"Take it out and you'll see."

Morley certainly wasn't going to stick his hand in there. Last night he'd pulled the old bag out of the attic and very carefully slipped it over the stool. Then, using a broom handle, he'd upended the bag and pushed the stool the rest of the way in. He was *not* going to touch it again. Let Danzer find out firsthand, as it were, what was wrong with it.

Danzer reached in and pulled out the footstool by one of its three carved legs. Morley backed up a step, waiting for his yelp of pain.

Nothing.

Danzer held up the footstool and rotated it back and forth in the light.

Nothing.

"Looks okay to me."

Morley shifted his weight off his right foot—the heel was still tender. He glanced at his bandaged left hand. He hadn't imagined those splinters.

"There, on the other leg. See those gaps in the finish? That's where slivers popped out of the wood."

Danzer twisted the stool and squinted at the wood. "I'll be damned. You're right. Popped out, you say?"

Morley held up his bandaged and. "Right into my palm. My foot too." He left off mention of the near miss on his eye.

But why isn't anything happening to you? he wondered.

"Sorry about that. I'll replace it."

"Replace it?"

"Sure. I picked up three of them. They're identical."

Before Morley could protest, Danzer had ducked through the curtained doorway behind the counter. But come to think of it, how could he refuse a replacement? He couldn't say that this footstool, sitting inert on the counter, had assaulted him. And it *was* a beautiful little thing...

Danzer popped back through the curtain with another, a clone of the first. He set it on the counter.

"There you go. I checked this one over carefully and it's perfect."

Morley reached out, slowly, tentatively, and touched the wood with the fingertips of his left hand, ready to snatch them back at the first sharp sensation. But nothing happened. Gently he wrapped his hand around the leg. For an awful instant he thought he felt the carving writhe beneath his palm, but the feeling was gone before he could confirm it.

He sighed. Just wood. Heavily grained maple and nothing more.

"While I was inspecting it," Danzer said, "I noticed something interesting. Look here." He turned the stool on its side and pointed to a heavily grained area. "Check this out."

Remembering the near miss on his eye, Morley leaned closer, but not too.

"What am I looking for?"

"There, in the grain—isn't the grain just fabulous? You can see a name. Looks like 'Anna,' doesn't it?"

Simply hearing the name sent a whisper of unease through Morley. And damned if Danzer wasn't right. The word "*ANNA*" was indeed woven into the grain. Seeing the letters hidden like that only increased his discomfiture.

Why this unease? He didn't know anyone named Anna, could not remember *ever* knowing an Anna.

"And look," Danzer was saying. "It's here on the other one. Isn't that clever."

Again Morley looked where Danzer was pointing, and again made out the name "*ANNA*" worked into the grain.

Morley's tongue felt as dry as the wood that filled this store. "What's so clever?"

Danzer was grinning. "It's got to be the woodworker. She's doing a Hirschfeld."

Morley's brain seemed to be stuck in low gear. "What the hell are you talking about?"

"Hirschfeld—Al Hirschfeld, the illustrator. You've seen him a million times in the *Times* and *Playbill*. He does those line caricatures. And in every one of them for the last umpteen years he's hidden his daughter Nina's name in the drawing. This Anna is doing the same thing. The shop probably doesn't allow its woodworkers to sign their pieces, so she's sneaked her name into the grain. Probably no one else but her knows it's there."

"Except for us now."

"Yeah. Isn't it great? I just love stuff like this."

Morley said nothing as he watched the ebullient Danzer stuff the replacement footstool into the canvas duffel and hand it back.

"It's all yours."

Morley felt a little queasy, almost seasick. Part of him wanted to turn and run, but he knew he had to take that footstool home. Because it was signed, so cleverly inscribed, by Anna, whoever that was, and he must have it.

"Yes," he mumbled through the sawdust taste in his mouth. "All mine."

At home, Morley couldn't quite bring himself to put the footstool to immediate use. He removed it from the canvas bag without incurring another wound—a good sign in itself—and set it in a corner of his study. He felt a growing confidence that what had happened yesterday was an aberration, but he could not yet warm to the piece. Perhaps in time...when he'd figured out why the name Anna stirred up such unsettling echoes.

He heard the clank of the mail slot and went down to the first floor to collect the day's letters: a good-sized stack of the usual variety of junk circulars, come-ons, confirmation slips from his broker, and pitches from various charities. Very little of a personal nature.

Still shuffling through the envelopes, he had just reentered the study when his foot caught on something. Suddenly he was falling forward. The mail went flying as he flung out his arms to prevent himself from landing on his face. He hit the floor with a brain-jarring, rib-cracking thud that knocked the wind out of him.

It took a good half minute before he could breathe again. When he finally rolled over, he looked around to see what had tripped him—and froze.

The footstool sat dead center in the entry to the study.

A tremor rattled through Morley. He'd left the stool in the corner—he was certain of it. Or at least, pretty certain. He was more certain that furniture didn't move around on its own, so perhaps he hadn't put it in the corner, merely intended to, and hadn't got around to it yet.

Right now he wasn't certain of what he could be certain of.

Morley found himself wide awake at three a.m. He'd felt ridiculous stowing the footstool in a closet, but had to admit he felt safer with it tucked away behind a closed door two floors below. That name—*Anna*—was keeping him awake. He'd sifted through his memories, from boyhood to the present, and could not come up with a single Anna. The word was a palindrome, so reversing the order was futile; the only workable anagram was also worthless—he'd never known a "Nana" either.

So why had the sight of those letters set alarm bells ringing?

Not only was it driving him crazy, it was making him thirsty.

Morley reached for the bottle of Evian he kept on the night table—empty. Damn. He got out of bed in the dark and headed for the first floor. Enough light filtered through the windows from the city outside to allow him a faint view of where he was going, but as he neared the top of the stairs, he felt a growing unease in his gut. He slowed, then stopped. He didn't understand. He hadn't heard a noise, but he could feel the wiry hairs at the back of his neck rise in warning. Something not right here. He reached out, found the wall switch, and flicked it.

The footstool sat at the top of the stairway.

Morley's knees threatened to give way and he had to lean against the wall to keep them from crumbling. If he hadn't turned on the light he surely would have tripped over it and tumbled down the steps, very likely to his death.

"That footstool! Where did you get it?"

After a couple of seconds' pause, Danzer's voice came back over the line. "What? Who is this?"

Morley rubbed his eyes. He hadn't slept all night. After kicking the footstool down the hallway and locking it in a spare bedroom, he'd sat up the rest of the night with the room key clutched in his fist. As soon as ten a.m. rolled around—the time when Danzer opened his damn store—he'd started dialing.

"It's Bill Morley. Where did you buy that footstool?"

"At a regional woodworker's expo on Cape Cod."

"From whom? I need a name!"

"Why?"

"I just do! Are you going to tell me or not?"

"Hold your horses, will you? Let me look it up." Papers shuffled, then: "Here it is...Charles Ansbach. 'Custom and Original Woodwork.'"

"Charles? I thought it was supposed to be 'Anna.'"

Danzer laughed. "Oh, you mean because of the name in the grain. Who knows? Maybe this Anna works for him. Maybe she bought his business. Maybe—"

"Never mind! Where can I find this Charles Ansbach?"

"His address is 12 Spinnaker Lane, Nantucket."

"Nantucket?" Morley felt his palm begin to sweat where it clutched the receiver in a sudden death grip. "Did you say Nantucket?

"That's what's written here on his invoice."

Morley hung up the phone without saying good-bye and sat there trembling.

Nantucket...of all places, why did it have to be Nantucket? He'd buried his first wife, Julie, there. And he'd sworn he'd never set foot on that damn island again.

But now he must break that vow. He had to go back. How else could he find out who Anna was? And he must learn that. He doubted he would sleep a wink until he did.

At least he hadn't had to take the ferry. No matter how badly he wanted to track down this Anna person, nothing in the world could make him ride that ferry again.

After jetting in from LaGuardia, Morley stepped into one of the beat-up station wagons that passed for taxis on Nantucket and gave the overweight woman behind the wheel the address.

"Goin' to Charlie Ansbach's place, ay? You know him?"

"We've never met. Actually, I'm more interested in someone named Anna who works for him."

"Anna?" the woman said as they pulled away from the tiny airport. "Don't know of any Anna workin' for Charlie. Tell the truth, don't know of any Anna connected to Charlie at all."

That didn't bode well. Nantucket was less than fifteen miles long and barely four across at its widest point. The islanders were an insular group who weathered long, isolated off-seasons together; as a result they tended to know each other like kin, and were always into each other's business.

As the taxi took him toward town along Old South Road, Morley marveled at the changes since his last look in the seventies. Decades and an extended bull market had transformed the island. New construction was everywhere. Even now, in post-season October, with the oaks and maples turning gold and orange, new houses were going up. Nantucket ordinances allow little variation in architecture—clapboard or cedar shakes or else—but the newer buildings were identifiable by their unweathered siding.

Nantucket had always been an old-money island, a summer hideaway for the very wealthy from New York, Connecticut, and Massachusetts—Old Money attached to names that never made the papers. The Kennedys, the Carly Simons and James Taylors, the Spike Lees and other spotlight-hungry sorts preferred Martha's Vineyard. Morley remembered walking through town here in the summer when the island's population explodes, when the town would be thick with tourists fresh off the ferry for the day. They'd stroll Main Street or the docks in their pristine, designer leisure wear, ogling all the yachts. Salted among them would be these middle-aged men in faded jerseys and torn shorts stained with fish blood, who drove around in rusty Wagoneers and rumbling Country Squires. Deck hands? No, these were the owners of the yachts, who lived in the big houses up on Cliff Road and on the bluffs overlooking Brant Point. The more Old Money they had, the closer to homeless they looked.

"Seems to be houses everywhere," Morley said. "Whatever happened to the conservancy?"

"Alive and well," the driver replied. "It's got 48 percent of the land now, and more coming in. If nothing else, it'll guarantee that at least half of the island will remain in its natural state, God bless 'em."

Morley didn't offer an amen. The conservancy had been part of all his troubles here.

The cab skirted the north end of town and hooked up with Madaket Road. More new houses. If only he'd held onto the land longer after Julie's death, think what it might be worth now.

He shook his head. No looking back. He'd sold off the land piece by piece over the years, and made a handsome profit. Prudent investing had quadrupled the original yield. He had no complaints on that score.

He noticed groups of grouse-like birds here and there along the shoulder of the road, and asked the driver about them.

"Guinea hens. Cousins to the turkey, only dumber. We imported a bunch of them a few years ago and they're multiplying like crazy."

"For hunting?"

"No. For ticks. We're hoping they'll eat up the deer ticks. Lymes disease, you know."

Morley was tempted to tell her that it was *Lyme* disease—no terminal "s"—but decided against it.

Spinnaker Lane was a pair of sandy ruts through the dense thicket of bayberry and beach plum south of Eel Point Road. Number 12 turned out to be a well-weathered Cape Cod with a large work shed out back.

"Wait for me," Morley told the driver.

He heard the whine of an electric saw from the shed so he headed that way. He found an angular man with wild salty hair leaning over a table saw, skinning the bark off a log. A kiln sat in the far corner. The man looked up at Morley's approach, squinting his blue eyes through the smoke from the cigarette dangling at the corner of his mouth.

"Charles Ansbach?"

"That's me." His face was as weathered as the siding on his shed. "What's up?"

Morley decided to cut to the chase. These islanders would talk your head off about nothing if you gave them half the chance.

"I'm looking for Anna."

"Anna who?"

"She works for you."

"Sorry, mister. No Anna working for me, now or ever."

"Oh, no?" Morley said, feeling a flush of anger. He was in no mood for games. "Then why is she working her name into the grain of your furniture?"

Ansbach's blue eyes widened, then he grinned. "So, you spotted that too, ay?"

"Where is she?"

"Told you: ain't no Anna."

"Then *you're* doing it?"

"Ain't me, either. It's in the grain. Damnedest thing I ever seen." He glanced down and blew sawdust off the log he'd been working on. He pointed to a spot. "Here's more of it, right here."

Morley stepped closer and leaned over the table. The grain was less prominent in the unstained wood, but his gut began to crawl as he picked out the letters of "*ANNA*" fitted among the wavy lines.

"It's uncanny," he whispered.

"More than uncanny, mister. It's all through every piece of wood I got from that tree. Downright spooky, if you ask me."

"What tree?"

"From the old Lange place. When I heard they was taking down one of the big maples there, I went to see it. When I spotted the grain I realized it was a curly maple. You don't see many curly maples, and I never seen one like this—magnificent grain. I bought the whole tree. Kept some for myself and sold the rest to a coupla custom wood workers on the mainland. Got a good price for it too. But I never..."

Ansbach's voice faded into the growing roar that filled Morley's ears. The strength seemed to have deserted his legs and he slumped against the table.

Ansbach's voice cut through the roar. "Hey, mister, you all right?"

All right? No, he was not all right—he was *far* from all right. All right for him was somewhere out near Alpha Centauri. But he nodded and forced himself to straighten and stagger away.

"What's wrong, mister?" Ansbach called after him but Morley didn't reply, didn't wave good-bye. He sagged into the rear seat of the taxi and sat there trying to catch his breath.

"You look like you just seen a ghost!" the driver said.

"Do you know the old Lange place?" Morley gasped.

"Course. Ain't been a Lange there for a long time, though."

"Take me there."

My tree! My tree! Morley thought. Have they cut it down?

Perhaps not. Perhaps it had been another tree. He couldn't remember any other maples on the house property, and yet it must have been another tree, not *his* tree. Because if they'd cut down his tree they would have removed the stump. And in doing so they inevitably would have found Julie's bones.

The taxi pulled off Cliff Road and stopped in front of the Lange place. The house itself looked pretty much the same, but Morley barely recognized its surroundings. Once the only dwelling on a fifty-two-acre parcel between Cliff and Madaket Roads, it now stood surrounded by houses. Morley's doing. He'd sold them the land.

Panic gripped him as he searched the roof line and saw no maple branches peeking over from the backyard. He told the driver to wait again and hurried around the north corner of the house, passing a silver Mercedes SUV on the way. He caught his breath when he reached the rear. His maple was gone, and in its place sat...a picnic table.

As he staggered toward it, he noticed the table's base—a tree stump. His tree was gone but they hadn't pulled the stump!

Morley dropped into a chair by the table and almost wept with relief.

"Can I help you?"

Morley looked up and saw a mid-thirties yuppie type walking his way across the lawn. His expression was wary, verging on hostile. With good reason: Who was this stranger in his yard?

Morley rose from the chair and composed himself. "Sorry for intruding," he said. "I used to live here. I planted this tree back in the seventies."

The man's expression immediately softened. "No kidding? Are you Lange?"

"No. It was the Lange place before I moved in, and remained the Lange place while I was living here. It will always be known as the Lange place."

"So I've gathered."

"What happened to my tree?"

"It got damaged in that nor'easter last fall. Big branch tore off and stripped a lot of bark. I had a tree surgeon patch it up but by last spring it was obvious the tree was doomed. So I had it taken down. But I left the stump. Put it to pretty good use, don't you think?"

"Excellent use," Morley said with heartfelt sincerity. Bless you, sir.

"The center is drilled to hold an umbrella in season."

"How clever. It's a wonderful addition to the yard. Don't ever change it."

Morley suffered through a little more small talk before he could extract himself. He rode back to the airport in silent exhaustion. When he finally reached his first-class seat for the return to LaGuardia, he ordered a double Macallan on the rocks and settled back to try to sort out what the hell was going on. But when he glanced out his window and saw the Nantucket ferry chugging out of the harbor far below, the events of the most nerve-wracking and potentially catastrophic twenty-four hours of his life engulfed him in a screaming rush...

* * *

The trouble with Julie Lange was that she was a rich girl who didn't know how to play the part. She didn't appreciate the finer things money could buy. She was just as happy with something from the JCPenney's catalog as a one-of-a-kind designer piece. She had no desire for the style of life and level of comfort to which her new husband desperately wished to become accustomed.

But young Bill Morley hadn't realized this when he started courting her in the big-haired, long-sideburned, bell-bottomed late sixties and early seventies. All he knew was that she was pretty, bright, fun, and rich. And when they eventually married, he was ecstatic to learn that her father was giving them the Nantucket family summer house and adjacent acreage as a wedding present.

That was the good news. The bad news was that Julie wanted to live there year round. Bill had said he wanted to write, hadn't he? Nantucket would be the perfect place, especially in the winter when there were no distractions.

No distractions...a magnificent understatement. The damn island was virtually deserted in the winter. Bill contracted island fever early on and was a raw nerve by the time spring rolled around. He begged Julie to sell the place and move to the mainland.

But oh no, she couldn't sell the family home. She'd spent almost every summer of her life at the Lange place. Besides, who would want to leave Nantucket? It was the best place on earth.

She just couldn't see: the island was paradise to her, but to him it was hell on earth.

Bill fumed. He could *not* survive another winter on this island. He cudgeled his brain for a way out, and came up with a brilliant solution: How about we keep the house but sell off the fifty acres of undeveloped land and use the money from that to buy a place near Boston? We can live there in the winter and still summer here. Cool, huh?

But Julie simply laughed and said she couldn't bear the thought of anyone but a Lange living on the land where she'd roamed and camped out during her childhood. In fact, she'd been looking into donating it to the conservancy so that it would always remain in its wild, undeveloped state.

Which left Billy three choices, none of which was particularly appealing. He could stay with Julie on Nantucket and devolve into drooling incoherence.

Or he could file for divorce and never see this island again, but that would mean cutting himself off from the Lange estate, all of which would go to Julie when her old man died.

Or Julie could die.

He reluctantly opted for the last. He wasn't a killer, and not a particularly violent man, but an entire winter on this glorified sandbar had shaken something loose inside. And besides, he deserved to come out of this marriage with something more than a bad memory.

But he'd have to make his move soon, before Julie handed fifty acres of prime land over to the stupid damn conservancy.

So he convinced Julie that the backyard needed some landscaping. And on a bright Friday afternoon in June, after solidifying the plan and setting up all the props he'd need, Bill Morley sat on his back porch and watched the landscapers put the finishing touches on the free-form plantings in the backyard. He waved to them as they left, then waited for Julie to return from town where she'd been running errands and shopping and doing whatever she did.

Carrying a three-iron casually across a shoulder, he met her in the foyer when she came home, and she looked so bright, so cheery, so happy to be alive that he gave her one last chance to change her mind. But Julie barely listened. She brushed off the whole subject, saying she didn't want to talk about selling houses or land or moving because she had something to tell him.

Whatever it was, she never got the chance. He hit her with the golf club. Hard. Three times. She dropped to the floor like a sack of sand, not moving, not breathing.

As soon as it was dark, Bill began digging up one of the landscapers' plantings. He removed the burlap-wrapped root ball of a young maple and dug a much larger hole under it. Julie and the three iron went into the bottom of that, the maple went on top of her, and everything was packed down with a nice thick layer of dirt. He wheelbarrowed the leftover soil into the woods she'd planned to give away, and spread it in the brush. He cleaned up before dawn, took a nap, then headed for town.

He parked their car in the Steamship Authority lot and bought two tickets to Hyannis on the next ferry, making sure to purchase them with a credit card. Then he ducked into the men's room. In a stall, he turned one of Julie's dark blue sweatshirts inside out and squeezed into it—luckily she liked them big and baggy. He put on the fake mustache he'd bought in Falmouth two weeks before, added big, dark sunglasses, then pulled the sweatshirt hood over his head.

The mustachioed man paid cash for his ticket and waited in line with the rest of the ferry passengers. As he stood there, he used the cover of his sunglasses to check out the women with long blond hair, cataloguing their attire. He spotted at least four wearing flowered tops and bell-bottom jeans. Good. Now he knew what he'd say Julie was wearing.

Once aboard, the mustachioed man entered one of the ship's restrooms where he broke the sunglasses and threw them in the trash. After flushing the mustache he emerged as Bill Morley with the sweatshirt—now right-side out—balled in his hand. While passengers milled about the aft deck, he discreetly draped the sweatshirt over the back of a chair and headed for the snack bar.

After that he played an increasingly confused, frightened, and eventually panicked young husband looking for his lost wife. He'd gone to get her a cup of coffee, and when he came back she was...gone.

Morley smiled at how perfectly the plan had worked. The police and his father-in-law had been suspicious—wasn't the husband always suspect?—but hadn't been able to punch a hole in his story. And since Julie wasn't carrying a speck of life insurance, no clear motive.

The disguise had proved a big help. If he'd stood on line as Bill Morley, someone very well might have remembered that he'd been alone. But as it turned out, no one could say they'd noticed Bill Morley at all, with or without his wife, until he'd begun wandering the decks, looking for her.

But it had been his fellow passengers who'd helped him the most. A number of them swore they'd seen a woman aboard matching Julie's description. Of course they had—Morley had made sure of that. One couple even identified Julie's picture. As a result, the long, unsuccessful search focused on the thirty-mile ferry route. No one gave a thought to digging up the yard back on Nantucket.

Final consensus: 1) Julia Lange Morley either fell or jumped unnoticed from the ferry; or 2) she was a victim of foul play—killed or knocked unconscious and transported off the ferry in the trunk of one of the cars riding on the lower deck.

Neither seemed likely, but once one accepted the fact that Julie had embarked but not debarked, those were the possibilities that remained.

Morley had kept the house for a while but didn't live there. Instead he mortgaged it and used the money to lease an apartment in Greenwich Village. It was the disco seventies, with long nights of dancing, drugs, and debauchery. In the summers he rented out the Lange place for a tidy sum, and forced himself to pay a visit every so often. He was especially interested in the growth of a certain young maple—*his* maple.

And now it seemed his maple had come back to haunt him.

Haunt...poor choice of words.

And perhaps he should start calling it Julie's maple.

All right: What did he know—really *know?*

Whether through extreme coincidence, fate, or a manipulation of destiny, he had purchased a piece of maple furniture made from the very tree he'd placed over Julie's corpse nearly thirty years ago. That seemed to be the only hard fact he could rely on.

After that, the assumptions grew murky and fantastic. Much as he hated saying it, he had no choice: The wood from that tree appeared to be possessed.

Two days ago he would have laughed aloud at the very suggestion of a haunted footstool, but after numerous injuries and one potentially fatal close call, Morley was unable to muster even a sneer today.

He didn't believe in ghosts or haunted houses, let alone haunted footstools, but how else to explain the events of the past two days?

But just for the sake of argument, even if it *were* possible for Julie's soul or essence or whatever to become a part of that young maple as it grew—after all, its roots had fed on the nutrients released by her decomposing body—why wasn't *JULIE* worked into the grain? Why *ANNA*?

Morley's second scotch hit him and he felt his eyelids growing heavy. He let them close and drifted into a semiconscious state where floating woodgrains morphed from *JULIE* to *ANNA* and back again...*JULIE... ANNA...JULIE...ANNA...JULIE*—

"Dear God!" he cried, awakening with a start.

The flight attendant rushed to his side. "Is something wrong, sir?"

"No," he gasped. "I'm all right. Really."

But Morley wasn't all right. His insides were strangling themselves in a Gordian knot. He'd just had an inkling about Anna, and if he was correct, *nothing* was all right. Nothing at all.

As soon as Morley was through the airport gate, he found a seat, pulled out his cell phone, and dialed Nantucket information. He asked the operator to read off all the names on the short list of doctors practicing on the island. She did, but none of them rang a bell.

"He might not be in practice any more." Might not even be alive, though Morley prayed he was. "He was a GP—my wife saw him back in the seventies."

"That was probably Doc Lawrence. He's retired now but his home phone's listed."

Lawrence! Yes, that was it! He dialed the number and a moment later found himself talking to Charles Lawrence, MD, elderly, somewhat hard of hearing, but still in possession of most of his marbles.

"Of course I remember your wife. Saw Julie Lange at least twice a summer for one thing or another all the years she was growing up. Did they ever find her?"

"Not a trace."

"What a shame. Such a nice girl."

"She certainly was. But let me ask you something, Doctor. I was just out visiting the old place and it occurred to me that Julie had an appointment with you the day before she disappeared. Did you...discover anything that might have upset her?"

"Not at all. In fact, quite the opposite. She was absolutely overjoyed about being pregnant."

Morley was glad he was already sitting as all of LaGuardia seemed to tilt under him. Even so, he feared he might tumble from the chair.

"Hello?" Dr. Lawrence said. "Are you still there?"

"Yes," he croaked. His tongue felt like Velcro.

"You sound as if this is news to you. I assumed she told you."

"Yes, of course she did," Morley said, his mind racing. "That's why we were heading for the mainland—to surprise her father. I never had the heart to tell him after she..."

"Yeah, I know. That made it a double tragedy."

Morley extricated himself from the conversation as quickly as possible, then sat and stared at nothing, the cell phone resting in his sweating palm, cold damp terror clutching at his heart.

On the last day of her life, Julie had driven into town to run some errands and to see Doc Lawrence for "a check-up." A check-up...young Bill Morley had been too involved in planning his wife's demise to question her about that, but now he knew what had been going on. Julie must have missed her period. No such thing as a home pregnancy test back then, so she'd gone to the doctor to have it done. That was what she'd wanted to tell him before he cracked her skull with the three iron.

Julie had often talked about starting a family...not if—*when*. When she talked of a son, she never mentioned a name; but whenever she spoke of having a daughter, she knew what she wanted to call her. A name she loved.

Anna.

Julie had always intended to call her little girl Anna.

Morley felt weak. He closed his eyes. Something had invaded the wood of that tree, and the wood of that tree had invaded his house, his life. Was it Anna, the tiny little life that had been snuffed out along with her mother's, or was it Julie, seeking vengeance in the name of the child who would never be born?

How did it go? Heaven has no rage like love to hatred turned, Nor hell a fury like a woman scorned.

But what of a woman never allowed to be born?

Morley shuddered. It didn't matter who, really. Either way, measures had to be taken, and he knew exactly what he needed to do.

Night had fallen by the time Morley got home. He entered his house cautiously, turning on lights in each room, hallway, and staircase before he proceeded. When he reached the living room he went directly to the fireplace, opened the flue, and lit the kindling beneath the stack of aged logs on the grate.

He waited until he had a roaring fire, then went to the hall closet and removed a heavy winter blanket. With this tucked under his arm, Morley headed up the stairs—turning lights on as he went—to the floor where he'd locked the footstool in the spare bedroom.

He hesitated outside the door, heart pounding, hands trembling. He tried the knob—still locked, thank God. He turned the key and opened the door just enough to snake his hand in and turn on the light. Then, taking a deep breath, he pushed the door open.

The footstool lay on its side, exactly as he had left it.

He felt a little silly now. What had he been afraid of? Had he been half expecting it to jump at him?

But Morley was taking no chances. He threw the blanket over the stool, bundled it up, and carried it downstairs where he dumped it in front of the fireplace. Using the log tongs, he pulled the stool free and consigned it to the flames.

He watched the curly maple burn.

He wasn't sure what he expected next. A scream? The legs of the stool writhing in pain? None of that happened. It simply lay there atop the other logs and...burned. At one point he leaned closer, trying for one last peek at the name hidden in the grain, but the heat drove him back before he could find it.

Anna...his child's name...he thought he should feel something, but he was empty of all emotions except relief. He never knew her...how could he feel anything for her? And as for Julie...

"It's too bad you had to die," he whispered as the varnish on the wood bubbled and blackened. "But you left me no choice. And as for coming back and interfering with my life, that's not going to happen. I'd all but forgotten about you—and now I'll go about forgetting you again."

Morley watched the fabric and padding of the stool dissolve in a burst of flame, watched the wood of the seat and legs char and smoke and burn and crumble. He remained before the fire until every last splinter of the stool had been reduced to ash.

Finally he rose and yawned. A long, hard day, but a fruitful one. He looked around. His home was his again, purged of a malign influence. But how to keep it from reentering?

Easy: Morley resolved never to buy another stick of furniture that wasn't at least a hundred years old.

With that settled, he headed upstairs for a well-deserved night's rest. In his bedroom he pulled out the third drawer in his antique pine dresser. As he bent to retrieve a pair of pajamas, the top drawer slid open and slammed against his forehead.

Clutching his head, Morley staggered back. His foot caught on the leg of a chair—a chair that shouldn't have been there, *hadn't* been there a moment ago—and he tumbled to the floor. He landed on his back, groaning with the pain of the impact. As he opened his eyes, he looked up and saw the antique mahogany wardrobe tilting away from the wall, leaning over him, *falling!*

With a terrified cry he rolled out of the way. The heavy wardrobe landed with a floor-jarring crash just inches from his face. Morley started to struggle to his feet but froze when he saw the letters worked into the grain of the wardrobe's flank: *ANNA*.

With a hoarse cry he lunged away and rose to his hands and knees—just in time to see a two-foot splinter of wood stab through the oriental rug—exactly where he'd been only a heartbeat before. He clambered to his feet and ducked away as his dresser tumbled toward him. On its unfinished rear panel he saw the name *ANNA* wrapped around one of its knots.

Caught in the ice-fisted grip of blind, screaming panic, Morley lurched toward the door, dodging wooden spears that slashed through the rug.

Julie...Anna...or whoever or whatever it was had somehow seeped out of the footstool and infected the entire room. He had to get out!

Ahead of him he saw the heavy oak door begin to swing shut. No! He couldn't be trapped in here! He leaped forward and ducked through the door an instant before it slammed closed.

Gasping, Morley sagged against the hallway wall. Close. Too close. He—

Pain lanced into his ankle. He looked down and saw a foot-long splinter of floorboard piecing his flesh. And all up and down the hall the floorboards writhed and buckled, thrusting up jagged, quivering knife-sharp spikes.

Morley ran, dodging and leaping down the hall as wooden spears stabbed his lower legs, ripping his clothes. Where to go? Downstairs—out! He couldn't stay in the house—it was trying to kill him!

He reached the stairs and kept going. He felt the wooden treads tilting under his feet, trying to send him tumbling. He grabbed the banister and it exploded into splinters at his touch, peppering him with a thousand wooden nails. He slammed against the stairwell wall but managed to keep his footing until the next to last step when he tripped and landed on the tiled floor of the front foyer.

What now? his fear-crazed mind screamed. Would the tiles crack into ceramic daggers and cut him to shreds?

But the foyer floor lay cool and inert beneath him.

Of course, he thought, rising to his knees. It's not wood. Whatever was in the footstool has managed to infiltrate the wood of the house, but has no power over anything else. As long as I stay on a tile or linoleum floor—

Morley instinctively ducked at the sound of a loud *crack!* behind him, and felt something whiz past his head. When he looked up he saw one of the balusters from the staircase jutting from the wall, vibrating like an arrow in a bull's-eye. At that instant the upper border of the wainscoting splintered from the wall and stabbed him in the belly—not a deep wound, but it drew blood.

And then the entire foyer seemed to explode—the wainscoting panels shredding and flying at him, balusters zipping through the air, molding peeling from the ceiling and lancing at him.

Morley dashed for the front door. Moving in a crouch, he reached the handle and pulled. He sobbed with joy when it swung open. He stumbled into the cool night air and slammed the door shut behind him.

Battered, bruised, bleeding, he gripped the wrought iron railing—metal, cold, hard, wonderful, reliable metal—and slumped onto the granite slabs of his front steps where he sobbed and retched and thanked the stars that years ago he'd taken a contractor's advice and replaced the original oak door with a steel model. For security reasons, the contractor had said. That decision had just saved his life.

He'd lost his home. No place in that building was safe for him—even being this close to it could be dangerous. He fought to his feet and staggered across the glorious concrete of the sidewalk to lean against the magnificent steel of one of the parked cars. Safe.

And then something bounced off his head and dropped to the sidewalk. Morley squinted in the darkness. An acorn. Dear God!

He lurched away from the overhanging oak and didn't stop moving until he was a good dozen feet from the tree.

An accident? A coincidence? After all, it was October, the time of year when oaks began dropping acorns.

But how could he be sure that even the trees hadn't turned against him?

He needed a safe place where he could rest and tend his wounds and clear his head and not spend every moment fearing for his life. A place with no wood, a place where he could *think!* Tomorrow, in the light of day, he could solve this problem, but until then...

He knew the place. That newly restored hotel on West Thirty-fifth Street—The Deco. He'd been to an art show there last month and remembered how he'd loathed its decor—all gleaming steel and glass and chrome, so completely lacking in the warmth and richness of the wood that filled his home.

What a laugh! Now it seemed like Mecca, like Paradise.

The Deco wasn't far. Giving the scattered trees a wide berth, Morley began walking.

• • •

"Sir, you're bleeding," said the clerk at the reception desk. "Shall I call a doctor?"

I know damn well I'm bleeding, Morley wanted to shout, but held his tongue. He was in a foul mood, but at least he wasn't bleeding as much as before.

"I've already seen a doctor," he lied.

"May I ask what happened?"

This twerp of a desk clerk had a shaved head, a natty little mustache, and a pierced eyebrow that rose as he finished the question. His name tag read Wölf. Really.

"Automobile accident." Morley fumbled through his wallet. "My luggage is wrecked, but I still have this." He slapped his AmEx Platinum down on the black marble counter.

The clerk wiggled his eyebrow stud and picked up the card.

"I must stress one thing," Morley said. "I want a room with no wood in it. None. Got that?"

The stud dipped as the clerk frowned. "No wood...let me think...the only room that would fit that is the Presidential Suite. It was just refurbished in metal and glass. But the rate is—"

"Never mind the rate. I want it."

As the clerk nodded and got to work, Morley did a slow turn and looked around. What a wonderful place. Steel, brass, chrome, marble, glass, ceramic. Lovely because this was the way the future was supposed to look when the here-and-now was the future...a future without wood.

Lovely.

He did not let the bellhop go—though Morley had no luggage, the man had escorted him to the eighth floor—until he had made a careful inspection. The clerk had been right: not a stick of wood in the entire suite.

As soon as he was alone, Morley stripped and stepped into the shower. The water stung his wounds, but the warm flow eased his battered muscles and sluiced away the dried blood. He wrapped himself in the oversized terry cloth robe and headed straight for the bedroom.

As he reached for the covers he paused, struck by the huge chrome headboard. At its center, rising above the spread wings that stretched to the edges of the king-size mattress, was the giant head of a bald eagle with a wickedly pointed beak. So lifelike, Morley could almost imagine a predatory gleam in its metallic eye.

But no time for aesthetics tonight. He was exhausted. He craved the oblivion of sleep to escape the horrors of the day. Tomorrow, refreshed, clearheaded, he would tackle the problem head on, find a way to exorcise Julie or Anna from his home. But now, tonight...

Morley pulled back the covers and collapsed onto the silk sheets. Hello, Morpheus, good-bye Anna...

Wölf spots the night manager crossing the lobby and motions him over.

"Mr. Halpern, I just had a guest here who insisted on a room with no wood—absolutely no wood in it. I gave him the Presidential Suite. I believe that's all metal and glass and such, right?"

"It was until yesterday," Halpern says. He's fortyish and probably thinks the curly toupee makes him look thirtyish. It doesn't. "The designer moved in a new headboard. Said he found it in a Massachusetts wood shop. Brand new and carved out of heavily grained maple. But he went and had it coated with so many layers of chrome paint it looks like solid steel. Said he couldn't resist the eagle. Can't say as I blame him—looks like it came straight off the Chrysler Building."

"Should I inform the guest?"

"What? And disturb his sleep?" Halpern waves a dismissive hand and strolls away. "Let the man be. What he doesn't know won't hurt him."

Mr. Fiddlehead

JONATHAN CARROLL

Jonathan Carroll is the author of several acclaimed novels, including *The Land of Laughs*, *Voice of Our Shadow*, *Bones of the Moon*, *From the Teeth of Angels*, *After Silence*, *Black Cocktail*, *Outside the Dog Museum*, *A Child Across the Sky*, *Kissing the Beehive*, *The Marriage of Sticks*, *The Wooden Sea*, *White Apples*, *Glass Soup*, and *The Ghost in Love*. He has won the World Fantasy Award for his story "Friend's Best Man" and his short fiction has been collected in *The Panic Hand* and in *The Woman Who Married a Cloud*.

On my fortieth birthday Lenna Rhodes invited me over for lunch. That's the tradition—when one of us has a birthday, there's lunch, a nice present, and a laughing afternoon to cover the fact we've moved one more step down the staircase. We met years ago when we happened to marry into the same family: Six months after I said yes to Eric Rhodes, she said it to his brother Michael.

Lenna got the better end of *that* wishbone: She and Michael are still delighted with each other, while Eric and I fought about everything and nothing and then got divorced.

But to my surprise and relief, they were a great help to me during the divorce, even though there were obvious difficulties climbing over some of the thornbushes of family and blood allegiance.

She and Michael live in a big apartment on One-hundredth Street with long halls and not much light. But the gloom of the place is offset by their kids' toys everywhere, colorful jackets stacked on top of each other, and coffee cups with WORLD'S GREATEST MOM and DARTMOUTH written on the side. Theirs is a home full of love and hurry, children's drawings on the fridge alongside reminders to buy *La Stampa*. Michael owns a very elegant vintage fountain pen store, while Lenna freelances for *Newsweek*. Their apartment is like their life: high-ceilinged, thought-out, overflowing with interesting combinations and possibilities. It is always nice to go there and share it a while.

I felt pretty good about being forty years old. Finally there was some money in the bank and someone I liked, talking about a trip together to Egypt in the spring. Forty was a milestone but one that didn't mean much at the moment. I already thought of myself as being slightly middle-aged anyway, but I was healthy and had good prospects, so *so what!* to the beginning of my fifth decade.

"You cut your hair!"

"Do you like it?"

"You look very French."

"Yes, but do you *like* it?"

"I think so. I have to get used to it. Come on in."

We sat in the living room and ate. Elbow, their bull terrier, rested his head on my knee and never took his eyes off the table. After the meal was over we cleared the plates, and she handed me a small red box.

"I really hope you like them. I made them myself."

Inside the box were a pair of the most beautiful gold earrings I have ever seen.

"My God, Lenna. They're *exquisite*! You *made* these? I didn't know that you made jewelry."

She looked happily embarrassed. "You like them? They're real gold, believe it or not."

"I believe it. They're art! You *made* them, Lenna? I can't get over it. They're really works of art; they look like something by Klimt." I took them carefully out of the box and put them on.

She clapped her hands like a girl. "Oh, Juliet, they really do look good!"

Our friendship is important and goes back a long way, but this was a lifetime present—one you gave a spouse or someone who'd saved your life.

Before I could say that (or anything else), the lights went out. Her two young sons brought in the birthday cake, forty candles strong.

A few days later I was walking down Madison Avenue and, caught by something there, looked in a jewelry store window. There they were—my birthday earrings. The exact ones. Looking closer, open-mouthed, I saw the price tag. Five thousand dollars! I stood and gaped for what must have been minutes. I was shocked. Had she lied about making them? Or spent five thousand dollars for my birthday present? Lenna wasn't a liar, and she wasn't rich. All right, so she had them copied in brass or something and just *said* they were gold to make me feel good. That wasn't her way either. What the hell was going on?

The confusion emboldened me to walk right into the store. Or rather to walk right up and press the buzzer. Someone rang me in. The salesgirl who appeared from behind a curtain looked like she had graduated from Radcliffe with a degree in bluestocking. Maybe you had to to work in this place.

"Can I help you?"

"Yes. I'd like to see the pair of these earrings you have in the window."

Looking at my ears, she suddenly realized I had a very familiar five thousand dollars hanging from my earlobes. It changed everything: Her expression said she would be my slave—or friend—for life. "Of course, the Dixies."

"The what?" She smiled, like I was being very funny. It quickly dawned on me that she must have thought I knew very well what "Dixies" were, since I was wearing some.

She took them out of the window and put them carefully down in front of me on a blue velvet card. They were beautiful, and admiring them, I entirely forgot for a while I had some on.

"I'm so surprised you have a pair. They only came in a week ago."

Thinking fast, I said, "My husband bought them for me, and I like them so much I'm thinking of getting a pair for my sister. Tell me about the designer. What's his name, Dixie?"

"I don't know much, madam. Only that the owner knows who Dixie is, where they come from...and that whoever it is is a real genius. Apparently both Bulgari and people from the Memphis group have already been in, asking who it is and how they can contact him."

"How do you know it's a man?"

I put the earrings down and looked directly at her.

"Oh, I don't. It's just that the work is so masculine that I assumed it. Maybe you're right; maybe it *is* a woman." She picked one up and held it to the light. "Did you notice how they don't really reflect light so much as enhance it? Golden light you can own. I've never seen that. I envy you."

They were real. I went to a jeweler on Forty-seventh Street to have them appraised, then to the only other two stores in the city that sold "Dixies." No one knew anything about the creator or weren't talking if they did. Both dealers were very respectful and pleasant, but mum's the word when I asked about the jewelry's origin.

"The gentleman asked us not to give out information, madam. We must respect his wishes."

"But it *is* a man?"

A professional smile. "Yes."

"Could I contact him through you?"

"Yes, I'm sure that would be possible. Can I help with anything else, madam?"

"What other pieces did he design?"

"As far as I know, only the earrings, the fountain pen, and this key ring." He'd shown me the pen, which was nothing special. Now he brought out a small golden key ring shaped in a woman's profile. Lenna Rhodes's profile.

The doorbell tinkled when I walked into the store. Michael was with a customer and, smiling hello, gave me the sign he'd be over as soon as he was finished. He had started INK almost as soon as he got out of college, and from the beginning it was a success. Fountain pens are cranky, unforgiving things that demand full attention and patience. But they are also a handful of flash and old-world elegance: gratifying slowness that offers no reward other than the sight of shiny ink flowing wetly across a dry page. INK's customers were both rich and not so, but all of them had the same collector's fiery glint in their eyes and addict's desire for more.

A couple of times a month I'd work there when Michael needed an extra hand. It taught me to be cheered by old pieces of Bakelite and gold plate, as well as other people's passion for unimportant but lovely objects.

"Juliet, hi! Roger Peyton was in this morning and bought that yellow Parker Duofold. The one he's been looking at for months!"

"Finally. Did he pay full price?"

Michael grinned and looked away. "Rog can never afford full price. I let him do it in installments. What's up with you?"

"Did you ever hear of a Dixie pen? Looks a little like the Cartier Santos?"

"Dixie? No. It looks like the Santos?" The expression on his face said he was telling the truth.

I brought out the brochure from the jewelry store and, opening it to the pen photograph, handed it to him. His reaction was immediate.

"Why, that bastard! How much do I have to put up with?"

"You know him?"

Michael looked up from the photo, anger and confusion competing for first place on his face. "Do I know him? Sure I know him. He lives in my goddamned *house*, I know him so well! Dixie, huh? Cute name. Cute man.

"Wait. I'll show you something, Juliet. Just stay there. Don't move! That shit."

There's a mirror behind the front counter at INK. When Michael motored off to the back of the store, I looked at my reflection and said, "*Now* you did it."

He was back in no time. "Look at this. You want to see something beautiful? Look at this." He handed me something in a blue velvet case. I opened it and saw...the Dixie fountain pen.

"But you told me that you'd never heard of them."

His voice was hurt and loud. "It is *not* a Dixie fountain pen. It's a Sinbad. An original, solid-gold Sinbad made at the Benjamin Swire Fountain Pen Works in Konstanz, Germany, around 1915. There's a rumor the Italian futurist Antonio Sant'Elia did the design, but that's never been proven. Nice, isn't it?"

It was nice, but he was so angry I wouldn't have dared say it wasn't. I nodded eagerly. He took it back. "I've been selling pens twenty years, but I've only seen two of these in all that time. One of them was owned by Walt Disney, and I have the other. Collector's value? About seven thousand dollars."

"Won't the Dixie people get in trouble for copying it?"

"No, because I'm sure they either bought the design or there are small differences between the original and this one. Let me see that brochure again."

"But you have an original, Michael. It still holds its value."

"That's not the point. It's not the value that matters. I'd never sell this.

"You know the classic 'bathtub' Porsche? One of the strangest, greatest-looking cars of our time. Some smart, cynical person realized that and is now making fiberglass copies of the thing.

"But it's a lie car, Juliet; sniff it and it smells only of today—little plastic things and cleverly cut corners you can't see. Not important to the car but essential to the real *object*.

"The wonder of the thing was Porsche designed it so well and thoughtfully so long ago. That's art. But the art is in its original everything, not just the look or the convincing copy.

"I can guarantee you that your Dixie pen has too much plastic inside where you can't see and a gold point that probably has about a third as much gold on it as the original. It looks good, but they always miss the whole point with their cut corners.

"Look, you're going to find out sooner or later, so I think you better know now."

"What are you talking about?"

He brought a telephone up from beneath the counter and gestured for me to wait a bit. He called Lenna and in a few words told her about the Dixies, my discovery of them....

Michael was looking at me when he asked. "Did he tell you he was doing that, Lenna?"

Whatever her long answer was, it left his expression deadpan. "Well, I'm going to bring Juliet home. I want her to meet him. What? Because we've got to do something about it, Lenna! Maybe she'll have an idea of what to do. Do you think this is normal? Oh, you do? That's interesting. Do you think it's normal for *me*?" A dab of saliva popped off his lip and flew across the store.

When Michael opened the door, Lenna stood right on the other side, arms crossed tight over her chest. Her soft face was squinched into a tight challenge. "Whatever he told you probably isn't true, Juliet."

I put up both hands in surrender. "He didn't tell me anything, Lenna. I don't even want to *be* here. I just showed him a picture of a pen."

Which wasn't strictly true. I showed him a picture of a pen because I wanted to know more about Dixie and maybe my five-thousand-dollar earrings. Yes, sometimes I am nosy.

Both of the Rhodeses were calm and sound people. I don't think I'd ever seen them really disagree on anything important or raise their voices at each other.

Michael growled, "Where is he? Eating again?"

"Maybe. So what? You don't like what he eats anyway."

He turned to me. "Our guest is a vegetarian. His favorite food is plum pits."

"Oh, that's *mean*, Michael. That's really mean." She turned and left the room.

"So he is in the kitchen? Good. Come on, Juliet." He took my hand and pulled me behind on his stalk to their visitor.

Before we got to him I heard music. Ragtime piano. Scott Joplin?

A man sat at the table with his back to us. He had long red hair down over the collar of his sport jacket. One freckled hand was fiddling with the dial on a radio nearby.

"Mr. Fiddlehead? I'd like you to meet Lenna's best friend, Juliet Skotchdopole."

He turned, but even before he was all the way around, I knew I was sunk. What a face! Ethereally thin, with high cheekbones and deep-set green eyes that were both merry and profound. Those storybook eyes, the carroty hair, and freckles everywhere. How could freckles suddenly be so damned sexy? They were for children and cute advertisements. I wanted to touch every one on him.

"Hello, Juliet! Skotchdopole, is it? That's a good name. I wouldn't mind havin' it myself. It's a lot better than Fiddlehead, you know."

His deep voice lay in a hammock of a very strong Irish accent.

I put out a hand, and we shook. Looking down, I ran my thumb once quickly, softly across the top of his hand. I felt hot and dizzy, as if someone I wanted had put his hand gently between my legs for the first time.

He smiled. Maybe he sensed it. There was a plate of something on the table next to the radio.

To stop staring so embarrassingly at him, I focused on it and realized the plate was full of plum pits.

"Do you like them? They're delicious." He picked one off the shiny orange-brown pile and, putting the stony thing in his mouth, bit down on it. Something cracked loud, like he'd broken a tooth, but he kept his angel's smile on while crunching away on the plum pit.

I looked at Michael, who only shook his head. Lenna came into the kitchen and gave Mr. Fiddlehead a big hug and kiss. He only smiled and went on eating...pits.

"Juliet, the first thing you have to know is I lied about your birthday present. I didn't make those earrings—Mr. Fiddlehead did. But since he's me, I wasn't *really* lying." She smiled as if she was sure I understood what she was talking about. I looked at Michael for help, but he was poking around in the refrigerator. Beautiful Mr. Fiddlehead was still eating.

"What do you mean, he's 'you'?"

Michael took out a carton of milk and, at the same time, a plum, which he exaggeratedly offered his wife. She made a face at him and snatched it out of his hand. Biting it, she said, "Remember I told you I was an only child? Well, like a lot of lonely kids, I solved my problem the best way I could—by making up an imaginary friend."

My eyes widened. I looked at the red-headed man. He winked at me.

Lenna went on. "I made up Mr. Fiddlehead. I read and dreamed so much then that one day I put it all together into my idea of the perfect friend: First, his name would be Mr. Fiddlehead because I thought that was the funniest name in the world—something that would always make me laugh when I was sad. Then he had to come from Ireland because that was the home of all the leprechauns and fairies. In fact, I wanted a kind of life-size human leprechaun. He'd have red hair and green eyes and, whenever I wanted, the magical ability to make gold bracelets and jewelry for me out of thin air."

"Which explains the Dixie jewelry in the stores?"

Michael nodded. "He said he got bored just hanging around, so I suggested he do something useful. Everything was fine so long as it was just the earrings and key chain." He slammed the glass down on the counter. "But I didn't know about the fountain pen until today. What's with *that,* Fiddlehead?"

"Because I wanted to try me hand at it. I loved the one you showed me, so I thought I'd use that as my model. Why not? You can't improve on perfection. The only thing I did was put some more gold in it here and there."

I put my hand up like a student with a question. "But who's Dixie?"

Lenna smiled and said, "I am. That was the secret name I made up for myself when I was little. The only other person who knew it was my secret friend." She stuck her thumb in his direction.

"Wonderful! So now Dixie fountain pens, which are lousy rip-offs of Sinbads, will be bought by every asshole in New York who can afford to buy a Piaget watch or a Hermes briefcase. It makes me sick." Michael glared at the other man and waited belligerently for a reply.

Mr. Fiddlehead's reply was to laugh like Woody Woodpecker. Which cracked both Lenna and me up.

Which sent her husband storming out of the kitchen.

"Is it true?"

They both nodded.

"But I had an imaginary friend, too, when I was little! The Bimbergooner. But I've never seen him for real."

"Maybe you didn't make him real enough. Maybe you just cooked him up when you were sad or needed someone to talk to. In Lenna's case, the more she needed me, the more real I became. She needed me a lot. One day I was just there for good."

I looked at Lenna. "You mean he's been here since you were a girl? Living with you?"

She laughed. "No. As I grew up I needed him less. I was happier and had more friends. My life got fuller. So he was around less." She reached over and touched his shoulder.

He smiled, but it was a sad one, full of memories. "I can give her pots of gold and do great tricks. I've even been practicing ventriloquism and can throw my voice a little. But you'd be surprised how few women love ventriloquists.

"If you two'll excuse me, I think I'll go in the other room and watch TV with the boys. It's about time for *The Three Stooges*. Remember how much we loved that show, Lenna? I think we saw one episode at least ten times. The one where they open up the hairdressing salon down in Mexico?"

"I remember. You loved Moe, and I loved Curly."

They beamed at each other through the shared memory.

"But wait, if he's...what you say, how come he came back now?"

"You didn't know it, but Michael and I went through a *very* bad period a little while ago. He even moved out for two weeks, and we both thought that was it: no more marriage. One night I got into bed crying like a fool and wishing to hell Mr. Fiddlehead was around again to help me. And then suddenly there he was, standing in the bathroom door smiling at me." She squeezed his shoulder again. He covered her hand with his own.

"God, Lenna, what did you do?"

"Screamed! I didn't recognize him."

"What do you mean?"

"I mean he grew up! The Mr. Fiddlehead I imagined when I was a child was exactly my age. I guess as I got older, so did he. It makes sense."

"I'm going to sit down now. I have to sit down because this has been the strangest afternoon of my life." Mr. Fiddlehead jumped up and gave me his seat. I took it. He left the room for television with the boys. I watched him go. Without thinking, I picked up Michael's half-empty glass of milk and finished it. "Everything that you told me is true?"

She put up her right hand. "I swear on our friendship."

"That beautiful man out there is an old dream of yours?"

Her head recoiled. "Ooh, do you think he's beautiful? Really? I think he's kind of funny looking, to tell the truth. I love him as a friend, but"—

she looked guiltily at the door—"I'd never want to go *out* with him or anything."

But *I* did, so we did. After the first few dates I would have gone and hunted rats with him in the South Bronx if that's what he liked. I was completely gone for him. The line of a man's neck can change your life. The way he digs in his pockets for change can make the heart squawk and hands grow cold. How he touches your elbow or the button that is not closed on the cuff of his shirt are demons he's loosed without ever knowing it. They own us immediately. He was a thoroughly compelling man. I wanted to rise to the occasion of his presence in my life and become something more than I'd previously thought myself capable of.

I think he began to love me, too, but he didn't say things like that. Only that he was happy or that he wanted to share things he'd held in reserve all his life.

Because he knew sooner or later he'd have to go away (*where* he never said, and I stopped asking), he seemed to have thrown all caution to the wind. But before him, I'd never thrown anything away, caution included. I'd been a careful reader of timetables, made the bed tight and straight first thing every morning, and hated dishes in the sink. My life at forty was comfortably narrow and ordered. Going haywire or off the deep end wasn't in my repertoire, and normally people who did made me squint.

I realized I was in love *and* haywire the day I taught him to play racquetball. After we'd batted it around an hour, we were sitting in the gallery drinking Coke. He flicked sweat from his forehead with two fingers. A hot, intimate drop fell on my wrist. I put my hand over it quickly and rubbed it into my skin. He didn't see. I knew then I'd have to learn to put whatever expectations I had aside and just live purely in his jet stream, no matter where it took me.

That day I realized I'd sacrifice anything for him, and for a few hours I went around feeling like some kind of holy person, a zealot, love made flesh.

"Why does Michael let you stay?"

He took a cigarette from my pack. He'd begun smoking a week before and loved it. Almost as much as he liked to drink, he said. The perfect Irishman.

"Don't forget he was the one who left Lenna. Not vice versa. When he came back he was pretty much on his knees to her. He had to be. There wasn't a lot he could say about me being there. Especially after he found out who I was. Do you have any plum pits around?"

"Question two: Why in God's name do you eat those things?"

"That's easy: because plums are Lenna's favorite fruit. When she was a little girl, she'd have tea parties for just us two. Scott Joplin music, imaginary tea, and real plums. She'd eat the fruit, then put the pit on my plate to eat. Makes perfect sense."

I ran my hand through his red hair, loving the way my fingers got caught in all the thick curls. "That's disgusting. It's just like slavery! Why am I getting to the point where I don't like my best friend so much anymore?"

"If you like me, you should like her, Juliet—she made me."

I kissed his fingers. "*That* part I like. Would you consider moving in with me?"

He kissed my hand. "I would love to consider that, but I have to tell you I don't think I'll be around very much longer. But if you'd like, I'll stay with you until I, uh, have to go."

I sat up. "What are you talking about?"

He put his hand close to my face. "Look hard and you'll see."

It took a moment, but then there it was; from certain angles I was able to see right through the hand. It had become vaguely transparent.

"Lenna's happy again. It's the old story—when she's down she needs me and calls." He shrugged. "When she's happy again, I'm not needed, so she sends me away. Not consciously, but...look, we all know I'm her little Frankenstein monster. She can do what she wants with me. Even dream up that I like to eat fucking plum pits."

"It's so wrong!"

Sighing, he sat up and started pulling on his shirt. "It's wrong, but it's life, sweet girl. Not much we can do about it, you know."

"Yes, we can. We can do something."

His back was to me. I remember the first time I'd ever seen him. His back was to me then, too. The long red hair falling over his collar. When I didn't say anything more, he turned and looked at me over his shoulder, smiling.

"We can do something? What can we do?"

His eyes were gentle and loving, eyes I wanted to see for the rest of my life.

"We can make her sad. We can make her need you."

"What do you mean?"

"Just what I said, Fiddy. When she's sad she needs you. We have to decide what would make her sad a long time. Maybe something to do with Michael. Or the children."

His fingers had stopped moving over the buttons. Thin, artistic fingers. Freckles.

The Fooly

TERRY DOWLING

Terry Dowling is one of Australia's most awarded, versatile, and respected writers of science fiction, dark fantasy, and horror. In addition to having written the internationally acclaimed Tom Rynosseros saga and *Wormwood*, a collection of linked science fiction stories, he is the author of several excellent collections of horror fiction including *An Intimate Knowledge of the Night, Blackwater Days,* and the retrospective *Basic Black: Tales of Appropriate Fear.* This last won the 2007 International Horror Guild Award for Best Collection. Dowling's stories have been published in such anthologies as *Dreaming Down Under, Wizards, The Dark, Inferno,* and *Dreaming Again*, and been reprinted in *The Year's Best Science Fiction, The Year's Best SF, The Year's Best Fantasy, Best New Horror,* and many times in *The Year's Best Fantasy and Horror.*

It was a new town, a new chance, a new shortcut home from a new pub. All so similar, yet so different, walking this lonely road on this cool, windy night.

The choosing was what made it special for Charles Ratray. The chance to choose, the ability to do it. He had lost so much, before, during and after Katie, truth be told, but here he was, at the end of that hardest choice, here in Kareela instead of Karalta.

It wasn't so bad. Kareela was like any other small town really, a town you could walk out of in ten minutes it was so small; the Royal Exchange like any other small pub.

And this road across the fields could have been a dozen similar back-roads at Karalta, the same clumps of trees, same scrappy field-stone walls and barbed-wire fences, same grasses blowing in the cool night wind.

Some would ask then why relocate at all? But they didn't know, couldn't, or forgot to remember the handful of reasons that always changed everything for anyone.

Katie was there. Karalta was her place.

Warwick's too. *Their* place now.

Away was better. You had to know when to leave, how to manage it, no matter how demanding it was, how difficult.

And he *had* managed. And weren't they surprised now? If they were.

Charles stopped, just stood in the blowing dark and breathed in the night.

How good it was to be here, anywhere else.

"You're new," a voice said and Charles Ratray yelped in fright.

There was a figure leaning against a field-stone wall, a dark man-shape, darker in the darkness, with a glitter at the eyes.

"You startled me," Charles managed.

"That'll do for starters," the figure said. "It's all about persuasion, you see. You're new."

"Arrived last week. I'm the new day supervisor out at Fulton's dairy."

The eyes glittered. "I haven't seen you on the road."

"Should you have?"

"Well, it's my road, see? I'm here a lot."

"I can't see you very well. There's enough moonlight. I should be able—"

"Part of the effect," the figure said. "Adds to the mood. I'm a specialist in mood lighting." There was a hint of smile below the glitter.

"You're a fooly, aren't you?"

"A what?"

"You know, a fooly. Something in my mind. A figment. My mind is playing tricks."

"Well, in a sense that's right. I'm already tweaking your mind a bit, see? There'll be more later. It'll get worse once I start bringing up the fear. Slipping in a bit of terror and despair. Walk with me."

Charles had been walking home anyway. He started along the road again. The figure stepped away from the wall and joined him, walking in an odd crimped walk Charles found disconcerting.

"You're a ghost," Charles said.

"That's more like it."

"You don't seem very frightening."

"They all say that at first. That's the come-on, see. Start out easy. Build up to it. They never tell you about that in ghost stories. What it really involves."

"Like what?" Charles asked.

"How we adjust the mind, the feelings. Being in charge of something means everything. That's what it's all about, living or dead."

"I never knew."

"See? It's the thing that matters most. It's like a work of art really, judging the moment, bringing up the disquiet, the dread. Hard to believe it right now, I know, Mr—?"

"Ratray. Charles Ratray. Charles."

"Good, Charles. Always try for first names. That's part of it. I'm Billy. Billy Wine. See, much less threatening. They'll tell you about me in town."

"Then you should let them do that. I'll ask around. Do this another night."

"Too late, Charles. Charlie. Had your chance. They should have told you about Billy Wine already. Bad death. Awful death. Five people at the funeral. Disappointing all round, really."

"So now you're making up for it."

"That's it exactly. Hey, I like you, Charles. You're quick. You're interested."

"That won't change anything."

"Not a bit. Not at all. You took this road. But no one told you? No one at the pub? No one at the dairy?"

"About the road? No. Haven't been here long. Will I survive this?"

"Probably not. But you have to understand. I don't get many along this road so I like to draw it out. Sometimes I misjudge the heart business. Scare folks too much."

"I thought ghosts just gave you a quick scare and that was it."

"That's the quick shock approach. The public relations side of it. We can do far more. That name you said. Fooly. We like to bring the victim—the subject—the scaree—to the point where they're not sure if it's real or in their heads. You get much more panic once you get to that point."

"Maybe you could just give me a quick scare now and I can come back tomorrow night."

"Hey, you're a real kidder. You wouldn't, of course. Surprised no one told you about me though."

"Maybe you had something to do with that."

"Boy, you're quick. Charlie, I really like you. Where are you staying?"

"Out at the Dickerson place. Six-month lease."

"Well, there you go then. That explains it. They probably figured you for a relative of old Sam Dickerson. Shutters would've come down the minute you said."

"Or maybe you did something to stop them telling me."

Billy Wine grinned. "That too. Lots of things are possible."

Charles smiled to himself, at least meant to. It was actually rather pleasant walking in the night; windy, blustery really, but cool, not cold. The grass was soughing on the verge. The trees were tossing. There were house lights far off to the right—and more behind when he glanced back, the homes of people he didn't know yet, and right there, the patch of light where Kareela sat in the night, like the glow of a ship at sea.

He kept alert for the fear, the thinnest edge of terror, but felt nothing. Perhaps he was immune. Maybe it didn't work for him.

"Should be feeling it soon," the fooly said. "Your senses will go a bit, bring in weird stuff. You smelling the sea yet?"

Charles couldn't help it. He sniffed the wind.

And he did. He could. The salt tang, impossibly far away but there. Charles *smelled* it.

Billy Wine's eyes glittered, a paring of smile beneath. "Seabirds?"

They were barely there, thin, far-off, wheeling four, five fields away, but there.

"Why the sea?" Charles asked.

"Always loved the sea," Billy Wine said. "You hearing trains?"

Trains, yes! Nowhere near as surprising; there was a station at Kareela, after all.

"But steam trains!" the ghost of Billy Wine said, anticipating.

And that's what Charles heard, chuffling, snuffling, stolen back, there and gone, there and gone.

"Circus!"

A calliope whooped and jangled in the night, forlorn, distant, dangerous.

"Weeping!"

And, oh, there was. Full of ocean-lost, clown-sad, missed-train sorrow, desolate on the wind. Billy Wine brought it in. Made Charlie do the bringing.

"Getting you ready, Charlie, my man! Think now—all the things you've had taken from you. All the things you never got to say. All the bitter."

Not bitterness. Bitter. Billy had the way of it, the ghosting knack, sure enough.

Charles kept walking. "What can I give? What can I trade?"

"Trade? Don't need souls. Nothing to hold 'em in. Old fooly joke."

"Fooly?"

"Just using your terminology, Charlie, my man. Don't get excited! Maybe an invitation to the Exchange. That'd be worth something."

"I can go back. See what I can do."

"You wouldn't. You couldn't. They don't see you. They served you up."

"You did that," Charles said. "Stopped 'em warning. Tweaked their minds."

The eyes glittered. The paring of smile curved up.

"Taking care of business," Billy said. "It's what you do."

"I'm nearly home."

"You'll never get there." The smile sharpened. "Walking's getting harder, isn't it?"

It was. Suddenly was.

Charles felt so heavy. His legs were leaden, wooden, twin stumps of stone. This was feeding Billy, Charles saw. The power. The finesse.

Billy read the moment. "Time for a flourish. Look how scary I've become."

And he had. Oh, how he had, Charles saw, felt, knew.

That awful darkness. That blend of glitter-gaze, crimp-step and pared darkling smile. In spite of everything, knowing it was coming, Charles saw that Billy was the same but not the same. Never could be.

The wind was slippery now, pushing, coddling, blustery and black-handed. The grass blew, hushed and blew again, reeling them in. No, not them. Him. Him.

Billy Wine lunged, strode, tottered, stayed alongside yet flowed ahead, all at once. He was sharps, dagger edges, razor-gaze and guttering grin. The dark of him was too much, too close, too stinking hot.

But mostly it was the gut-wrench suicide cocktail inside Charles Ratray, three parts dread, two parts despair, one blossoming nip of revulsion slipped in sideways.

Charles could barely breathe. He staggered, breath to breath, inside and out, fighting to remember what breathing was, what walking was, what self was.

This deadly, crimp-stepped Billy truly was good at what he did.

Close up, there was his sudden, awful intimacy, while out there, oceans closed over ships, birds plucked at eyes, calliopes screamed into the fall of colliding trains, and Katie was denied, denying, again and again.

Charles screamed and stilted and propped, fought to breathe. No part of the night was satisfied to hold him. It pushed him away, hurled him from itself back into itself, made panic from the stilting, flailing pinwheel he had become. He screamed and yelled because Billy wanted him to.

Though Billy knew to stop, of course, to relax and savor, to settle for shades and ebb and flow. He had a whole night, a whole splendid, new-to-town Charlie Ratray to teach the last of all lessons.

But Charles managed to keep his sense of self through it all, did manage, and he let the Dickerson house be the focus, off in the distance, its single yard light showing where it was.

"I made it," Charles said, knowing how Billy would respond.

"Did you? Have you? Are you sure?"

The house swept away, one field, two, road threading between, single yard light jiggering, dancing off like a small tight comet.

"Too bad," Billy Wine said. "We're almost at the end of it."

"We are?"

"It'll be quick. You'll be fully aware." Billy sounded gleeful.

"But it's still early—"

"I know. And *do* be disappointed! That bad death I had. Only five people to see me off. It makes you hard."

"But you have the whole night. Surely there's more fear? More dread?"

"No need. All that's just window dressing anyway. Absolute clarity is best. Just the anguish. The disappointment. Enough despair. You go out knowing."

"Billy—"

"No more, Charlie. Time to go. It'll hurt just a bit. Well, quite a bit. Well, a lot actually, pain being what it is. But maybe you'll get to come back. Some do."

"Maybe I already have."

And Charles Ratray was gone, spiralling away as a twist of light on the wild dark air.

"Hey! What? What's that?" Billy Wine demanded, but knew, had even imagined the possibility, though had never ever expected it.

For who else watched the watchmen, hunted the hunters, haunted the haunters?

Who else fooled the foolies?

All that remained of Billy Wine stood on the dark windy road and felt the ache of disappointment tear at him again and again.

The Toll

PAUL WALTHER

Paul Walther has had stories in numerous small press and online magazines including *New Genre*, *Niteblade*, and *Horror Library*. His story "Splitfoot" was reprinted in *The Year's Best Fantasy and Horror* #21. In addition to writing stories, Paul has collaborated with filmmaker Brian Lilly on several screenplays through Brian's Lion Belly production company.

Paul lives in Hopkins, Minnesota, with his wife. You can find more information about Paul's stories and screenplays at: www.paulwalther.com.

The end of the summer is near. Maybe that's why the water of Pine Lake looks a little darker, a little more menacing. Maybe that's why the azure sky overhead appears mildly ominous, despite the lack of clouds.

Maybe that's what makes Bohanan look slightly malevolent on this day—instead of simply ridiculous, as he usually appears. Here he is, standing on the beach with his toes curled into the hot sand, his hand resting lightly on the calf of the lifeguard sitting high up in her wooden chair.

She is Mary Joan Schmitt, and as she looks down benevolently at the crown of his head she thinks she remembers her mother mentioning him—did he date an aunt, an aunt's friend? There is a story to Bohanan, she just can't remember what it is.

He's a tall man, skinny, with his stomach muscles well defined and his slender legs perfectly, darkly tanned. From a distance he looks younger than he is—the skimpy swim suit, the long, carefully tended hair, the flashy sunglasses on a thick cord—he could pass for any of the well-built young men strutting the beach. It's only up close that the illusion evaporates like one of those shimmering heat mirages hovering above the hot sand. His face is lined, and his sun-bleached hair is getting thin at the crown. His hands are veined and the skin is coarse. Another summer is ending and here is Bo, vainly trying to hold time still for another year.

It's been said that everybody is who they were in high school. Well, Jeffrey Bohanan is precisely who he was in high school. Exactly. He dresses the same way, talks the same way. His hair, though thinner, is styled in exactly the same way. He still has the same job—the very same job he started part time in high school and went full time to his senior year. And he still spends every single summer afternoon here at the beach, at Pine Beach, just as he did in high school.

Mary Joan Schmitt isn't staying the same. She has been changing—getting more tan and more blond as the summer goes on. Here, in late August, her skin is the color of a brown hen's egg and her eyebrows have actually disappeared. In two days when this summer is finally over, she is going to change some more. She is going to have a life.

As contemptuous as she is of Bo and his endless summer, she isn't really annoyed by his hand on her perfectly browned calf because she needs him. She's using Bo, right this instant. He's actually fulfilling a purpose, for once. How: Bo is a walking encyclopedia of death in the tiny town of Pine Lake. For twenty years he's worked at the Pine Lake Cemetery as a grounds keeper and he can tell you how many people have been killed in auto accidents, how many of cancer, how many from suicide. It's not like he has anything else to do with his time.

Mary Joan is quizzing him again today, warming him up for her real question. "Bo, how many people have died from poison?"

"One—but that was never totally proved."

"Motorcycles?"

"Two—three, if you count Morrie Murdoch—his blew up in the garage and burned the house down."

She lets a slight pause come between them, pretends to watch the water. Now, she thinks, is the time for her real question: "Drowning?" she asks.

"Five," he says calmly. He seems utterly unaware that his hand is gently stroking her leg.

"Five? That's just since you started?"

"Yes." Bo is also known for having a good idea of the historical statistics on cause of death. Whether he's reading tombstones or cemetery records or what, nobody knows, but his talent isn't just confined to who died of what during his tenure. He can give a solid number for a given cause right back to the inception of Pine Lake as a town. "You want the total? Maybe seventeen, eighteen, in all. Less than twenty."

"Twenty!" She almost falls off her chair. It seems like an impossibly high number for such a tiny community. On the other hand, the beach has been around a long time. In the lifeguard shack there are old photographs of the beach in the thirties, with lumpy black cars in the background, and in the twenties, when women wore funny bathing suits and everyone brought big hampers and stiff clothing. There are even a few very dim, very blurred, reproductions of what must be tintypes, or plates, or whatever they were, before Kodak. It doesn't matter; it all looks amazingly, depressingly, the same—except for certain details. None of the original buildings survived, of course. The bathrooms and concession stands popped up in the fifties and the big diving platforms out in the deep water were built in the seventies. That's when Mary's father was a lifeguard, in the silly seventies, when his hair was as long as hers is now. He met her mother here. His father was a lifeguard before that, macho and serious in old black and white photographs in the family album. Behind him the beach is the same; the lake is the same. The opposite shore is the same, with the dark spires of pine trees poking into the gray sky.

All the pictures are filled with monotone swimmers and sun bathers and kids frolicking in the water. And some of those people, it suddenly occurs to Mary, one at least, might be one of those who have drowned. One of the twenty.

"Depressing thought, eh?" says Bo, grinning. "What're you doing this fall?"

She's going away to college. Bo's problem is obvious—he's spent so long stuck in the summer after high school that all the women his own age have moved too far beyond him. They're all married, or divorced with kids, working at real jobs, not living with their mothers, driving their mothers' cars.

"You ever know any of them?"

"Who—the people who drowned? Nah. What's your worry?"

"No worry." And she's about to brush his hand away the way she would a biting horsefly, but the sun is going down. The beach closes, as it has for a hundred years, a little before dark. Not that Mary is afraid of the dark—not a chance.

As the sun sets, it shines right across the flat expanse of Pine Lake—as it has for a hundred, a thousand years—more. As it reaches the tops of the pines opposite, it is so low that it lights everything from behind, so that all the features are lost and the whole beach becomes a waving, shrieking, splashing, happy amalgam of people and liquid nearly inseparable by the naked eye.

To a lifeguard it's a dangerous time of the day, squinting into that blinding sun—especially hard for Mary. She has to take off her sunglasses to see anything in the water, and her sunglasses hold a secret. They are prescription lenses and without them...well, it's not that she can't see. Of course she can see. To continue lifeguard duty without her eyeglasses just because they're...eyeglasses, would be a dereliction of duty, if she couldn't see without them. She can.

Just not quite as well. She tried contact lenses but they would never work for her; it was like having a tarp draped over each suffocating eyeball. In the daytime, even in cloudy weather, nobody questions sunglasses on a browning, bleaching blond lifeguard. But at night—that would raise questions.

That's when her problems begin—when she takes off her sunglasses. Things look different with her sunglasses off—and not just lighter. With the sun going down and everything back lit and her eyesight impaired the water looks slightly...overpopulated.

Is that the best way to describe it?

The screaming, splashing, colorful multitude is suddenly joined by others. That's what Mary calls them when she thinks of them to herself. They are darker than the rest—completely thrown into shadow by the setting sun. They move with the rocking rhythm of the shining waves, heads inscrutable, bodies narrow, arms long and tipped with slender hands that extend above everything else, waving. Mary has been watching them all summer long and it seems as if their numbers increase as the summer wanes.

She's tried to find a rational explanation: it's possible that they're just people; that they only look different because they're a little farther out, just beyond the beach rope. It's not that they're any more blurred, after all, than anyone else in the water—or any less substantial looking. They're just not as colorful. Still, there's more than that. It isn't just how they look, it's how they move. That slow rocking motion, those long, waving arms—the general outline is human, but there is a serenity, a lifelessness, about them.

That brought Jeffrey Bohanan, and his peculiar knowledge, to mind. So now she has Bo, rubbing up against her leg like an adoring Irish setter, and she has thought of another good use for him.

"Bo," she asks. "How fast can you swim out to the far platform and back?"

"I don't know—four minutes?"

"No way! Not a chance you could do it that fast."

"It's a simple fact."

"I'd think it'd take you at least six, at your age."

"We'll show you."

He's got some kind of giant, overly complicated chronometer on his wrist—apparently waterproof—and he sets it with an electronic beep as he jogs down to the water. Mary watches as he wades through the shallow water to the rope, ducks under it, and begins paddling. She can see as he passes through the arm-waving legion of black figures. None seem to impede his path and he takes no notice of them. In fact, whether it is an optical illusion or not, he seems to pass right through one with his long-armed strokes toward the tall platform.

He touches off one of the platform's pilings and swims back through the ring of black figures. He splashes through the closer swimmers and hurries up the beach, stopping his watch with a triumphant gesture as he reaches her perch.

"There you go," he says, showing her the time: 3:52 minutes.

"Impressive," Mary says. "How's the water?"

"Fine. A little colder, just past the rope. Nothing scary."

"Who says I thought there was something scary?"

"Just like your mom; won't admit a thing."

"Bo, do us both a favor. Don't talk about my mother."

"You know she almost drowned out here?"

"Of course I do. That's how she met my dad."

"That's right. Dragged her right out of the water, the big hero. I remember now."

"You were there?"

"I'm always here; don't you know that?"

His hand is on her leg again, this time inside the thigh. She swings her whistle rope with the bundle of keys attached and hits him in the forehead.

"Ow!"

"Sorry, Bo. I wasn't looking."

"Well, keep an eye out."

It's odd to think of Bo knowing her mother when she was, well—her age. She cannot get the image of Bo, young, on the same beach with her mother, before she was...Mother.

As the sun sets and the final whistle blows, the swimmers come up the beach and drift into the parking lot. The dark figures in the water are long gone. As the sun touches the water they sink, waving their long arms and disappearing under the waves like tree branches overcome by a flood.

Mary comes out of the guard shack after she's changed into her clothes. She stands and looks at the still water of the beach in the increasing darkness. The lake is so calm now—without a ripple. Why does it make her think of the bodies of the drowned, sinking slowly, placidly, to their watery graves?

And Bo is right—her mother was almost one of those. If it wasn't for Dad, she would have slipped right under those waves and disappeared.

Walking to her car in the darkness, Mary thinks of how well she knows this beach. She was probably at this beach before her memory began—she's certain that she was, knowing her parents. It makes her smile to think that she was probably at this beach in the womb; that's how long she's been coming here. Wasn't she just a little tyke, taking her first stroke? Didn't she picnic for years with her parents up on the grass? This is where she first held her breath under water, had her first kiss, her first...all of it. And in three days she'll be gone, the way her mother thought she would be gone until she met Dad. The difference is that Mary is really going. She'll waste away her summer tan out East, where nobody knows her name.

She takes a deep breath of the pine-scented air, looks at the sky. It's still too early for stars: just the vague gray nothingness framed by the blackness of the pine trees, just the same old Chevrolet her parents gave her, just the same old asphalt parking lot she's burned her feet on a hundred times in the hot sun. A thousand times, maybe.

A thousand times. This thought sticks in her head because there is something next to her car—someone, standing, tall and thin and it had better be Bo, because...

"Bo," she says, disgusted. "What are you doing here?"

"Did I scare you?"

"No."

"Want to go for a ride?"

"No, Bo, I want to go home."

Mary has an odd revelation. He's a little bit frightening, standing there in the dark. She's never even thought of him as a full grown man before. She's never thought of him as a threat.

"You're not scared to be alone out here?"

"I'm not alone though, am I?"

He's too close, leaning in on her with claustrophobic intensity. She wonders for a moment if he means to kiss her—doesn't give him a chance, if that's his idea—pushes him away and turns to get into her car.

"There's plenty to be afraid of, out there."

"Out where?" But why is she even bothering to talk to this idiot? "Never mind. I've got to go."

So softly she's not sure she heard it: "You're not going anywhere."

"What?"

"Are you really going away to school? That's what your mother said she was doing, too."

"I know, I know. Then she met Dad. You think I haven't heard that corny story a million times?"

And then he's just Bo again, hopeful, pitiful, frozen in time like that cave man they found in the Alps, or wherever. She waves at him: "Say goodnight, Bo."

She's annoyed to find that he's unsettled her. On her way home the streets seem especially black, the houses abnormally bleak. The long, dark hands of the mysterious swimmers reach through her mind and cast shadows over her thoughts. There would be a certain comfort to leading the life Bo leads—unchanging, unchallenging. Perfected, in a way. As she drives by his cemetery, her brain disobeys her, sends her gaze up the dark and tombstone-covered hill.

Here and there little lights flicker—like candles, only larger and not as well defined as flames. Just a few, widely spaced throughout the graveyard, flickering silently above tombstones. She cocks her head, blinks her eyes, tries to identify the optical illusion. That's worse, though. The more she tries to see the cause of the illusion, the more the flickering lights defy easy explanation. An uneasy—and unfamiliar—dread rises in her throat and she turns her attention back to the road, bearing down on the gas pedal. When she dares to glance in the rearview mirror she can see someone standing at the cemetery gate—a tall, thin man silhouetted against the lit iron gates.

At night Mary dreams of the beach—empty and still on a moonlit night. She watches from the water just beyond the rope. She can see the beach but it is empty, and autumn leaves skitter across the sand. In the sky, low, black clouds seem to threaten snow. Where is summer, where is the warmth? She can feel the ice creeping in from the shores of the lake as if it is creeping into her own veins. On the desolate beach a lone figure moves—skinny, tall, somehow hideously evil.

When she wakes up it is Labor Day, the last day, the end, and Mary is exhausted. She feels as though she has spent the whole night running—or swimming. By ten in the morning it's seventy, by noon, eighty-seven. It's the last day of summer, the last day the beach is open, and for the lifeguards, it's like the last day of summer camp. Simmering romances are suddenly boiling over. A sense of ecstatic grief hangs over the guard shack. Mary is standing there, transfixed, looking at all those old pictures on the walls. The one that holds her gaze is the most mundane—who knows when it was taken. The beach is unadorned by any of the modern paraphernalia—no concession stand, no guard shack, no sun umbrellas or beach blankets or inflatable rafts, no lifeguard chairs down by the water. Just a plain sand beach apparently uninhabited by anything but some big pines, pines that must have been cut down a long time ago. Mary is struck by the sheer familiarity of it: without a single landmark it is clearly, by its shape and slope and location, this very same place. There are rocks near the water—not boulders but big stones—and inconvenient outcroppings of scrubby plants, and campfire smoke rising in the distance, but this is where they used to swim. This is where they've always gone swimming. In fact, up close, there are dark blurs that might be moving people on the sand, and as she looks closer, dark blurs in the water as well. The people have always been there, always, just unrecorded by the technology of the times. To Mary it's as if those people lived in a different universe—one of silence, one of landscapes uninhabited by humans except as blurs as fine and fleeting as the wings of a hummingbird.

And before that: what?

"Bo's looking for you," somebody tells her.

"Great."

She steps outside; the beach is crazy. It's so noisy it's impossible to pick out individual sounds, so busy it's impossible to separate one person from another. It looks like every square inch of sand has been covered with a blanket. Like one of those Wild Kingdom rookeries where the birds are sunning, mating, socializing, shoving each other for a nest near the water.

"It's a zoo," says Jane, coming up off the sand, swinging her whistle on its cord, "Good luck getting anybody to listen. Yoo-hoo, Mary, Bo's been looking for you."

"I heard."

Then Mary's down on the sand with a towel wrapped around her waist and her shades in place and Bo is upon her before she can even reach the chair. He must work nights, or something—but how can he?

"Been looking for you."

"I heard."

"Well," he says, taking up his position and laying a hand on her leg, "hell of a day, huh?"

"Hell of a day," she says, squinting, daring the dark shapes to come out in broad daylight, when her eyes are sharp.

There's no room for them, though. The water is absolutely frothy with bodies and out on the tall dock they're packed like arctic penguins pushing each other for space. It's a perfect, sunny day, a day for the record books at Pine Lake Beach, for history, and here she is, right in the middle of it.

"This is it, eh? Then it's winter."

"Buzz off, Bo. I didn't sleep well, I'm tired, and I'm really in no mood."

"What?"

"Buzz off! Christ, you must be twice my age. Why don't you get a life?"

Instead of getting angry he just stands there, silent. Mary swats his hand off her leg and he stands there still, either petrified or too dumb to know he's being brushed off.

"Just like your mother," he finally says.

"Yeah, except that I really am getting away."

"She did, too," he says, softly.

What is his problem? Anyone looking on would think they were in conversation, or collusion, or friends. He is like a stone, like an obelisk, sticking out of the sand at a slight angle. If they took one of those old pictures right now, Bo would be crystal clear, sharp, with all the rest of the beach blurred incomprehensibly around him.

"Why don't you go away," she says clearly, not taking her eyes from the water.

"I beat my time," he says cheerfully.

"What time?"

"My time—the time out to the dock and back I set with you. I beat it this morning."

"Whatever," she says. Is he really so stupid? "Anyway, you didn't set it with me. That was just a joke. I didn't mean for you to take it so seriously."

It's cruel, she knows, but...where does he get these crazy ideas?

His face has fallen; he looks suddenly old, suddenly his age. She feels a completely unwelcome rush of guilt and chagrin and pure meanness and is almost ready to recant, when—

"I had your mother," he says, surprising her.

"Drop dead."

"I laid her, before your father."

"Go away. I've had enough."

He has his hand on the inside of her thigh again. "He took her away from me. Did you know that?"

"No, I didn't know that. Should I care?"

"He owes me one." He looks so evil now she can hardly recognize his face. He is terrifying.

"Get away from me."

"That's the way you want it to be?"

"Get away from me!"

"Listen," he says softly, grinning horribly at her. "I think I hear a child crying."

God help her, she does too. Above the din of the beach, above the cacophony of sounds, impossibly, she hears a child screaming for help.

"Better go get it," Bo says.

"I don't see it!" she says, standing up in her chair, scanning the water.

"Right there," Bo says, pointing, and at the end of his outstretched finger a child magically appears, screaming and waving its arms, just beyond the rope. "Go get it," he says.

She blows short blasts on her whistle; leaps from the chair and throws down her sunglasses to find that the shapes are there, they are there in broad daylight. The child is crying, though, screaming, and she dashes into the water and takes long, broad strokes toward the rope. She goes under the float-studded rope like a dolphin, and on the other side—nothing. The child isn't there: she dives to find it.

Instant silence, instant calm.

The cold water envelopes Mary's head. Her eyes are open but the darkness of the water limits her vision as she dives deeper, reaching ahead with her outstretched arms to find the child's sinking body.

And then it all goes terribly wrong. At first she doesn't associate the horrible weight on her back with another human being, but as the arm swings around to force the air from her lungs, she catches a glimmer of that huge silver watch and sees her life escape to the surface in a boil of silver bubbles. Down, down, her attacker pushes her, and as her lungs scream for air an extraordinary thing happens. Instead of getting darker as she is pushed deeper, the water suddenly begins to get lighter. She pulls water into her lungs and it seems as if she can see sunlight coming up through the water, as if she can see the moving legs of swimmers below her.

Or are they above her?

There are people, people with their legs above her in the bright water—a wide variety of swimsuits—and bodies. There are fat legs in striped pants, naked hairy bodies from before township days, thick suits from the forties and the fifties, bikinis from the sixties. They tread water slowly; their pleasant, welcoming faces peer into the water as if it is a fun-house mirror. Mary knows it's wrong, and not just wrong but unbelievable: faces from the past, peering down at her like she's an errant fish swimming towards the beach, but their legs are real, solid in front of her face. Not as shadows, but in the pink and blue hues of human flesh under water, old as the lake, decrepit as casket-bound corpses, but real, real, and terrifying for that reason. Their hands reach down to pull her up.

Like a fever dream she knows them, knows their names and knows their faces, knows their lives as if they are neighbors, as if their families are something other than dry, dusty bones lying in the vaults up the road and up the hill. Cheerful, welcoming, smiling down through the sunny water, they trap her with their water-pruned fingers. Up there, she thinks longingly, things must never change; up there, they must live in summer every day.

She pulls herself toward the light, but as she breaks surface things are not at all what they had seemed they would be. She is all alone, and the beach she knows so well is as desolate as it was in her dream. The sand is packed hard and the water is stiff as ice. The final reminders of summer—abandoned Styrofoam cups and paper hot dog sheathes—blow across the empty sand on a cold wind. It is the day after the last day of summer, and she suddenly understands that it lasts forever here, all under the baleful eye of the gaunt, aging wolf who paces the frozen sand of the beach like a demon sentry, throwing back his head to howl a dark, deep and malevolent laugh.

Terrified, she submerges again. The water is warm, and friendly. She takes a deep breath of water and feels it flow into her with a heavy, calming surge. What was she so worried about a moment ago? She can't even remember. The happy faces smile down at her again. Their soft fingers caress her body, touch her convulsing mouth. She could stay here forever, warm and safe.

The Pennine Tower Restaurant

SIMON KURT UNSWORTH

Simon Kurt Unsworth was born in Manchester in 1972 and currently lives on a hill in the north of England with his wife and child awaiting the coming flood, where he writes essentially grumpy fiction (for which pursuit he was nominated for a 2008 World Fantasy Award for Best Short Story). His stories have been published in a number of anthologies, including *At Ease with the Dead, Shades of Darkness, Exotic Gothic 3, Gaslight Grotesque, Never Again,* and *Lovecraft Unbound*, and have been collected in *Lost Places, Quiet Houses*, and *Strange Gateways*. A fourth collection will launch the Spectral Press "Spectral Signature Editions" imprint in 2013. His stories have also been reprinted in four *Mammoth Book of Best New Horror* anthologies.

Introduction

This is not fiction.

I should, perhaps, explain how I came to write this. Before I became self-employed, I worked for a number of years in local government and the voluntary sector. I did not always enjoy the work, and I never really enjoyed being an employee, but there were some nice things about the experience. I met my wife whilst working for a charity in Manchester and my best friend (and subsequent godfather to my son) working for Liverpool City Council. Indeed, this aspect of the work is the one thing I miss now that I am self-employed, and that I enjoyed most at the time, meeting a wide range of people, some of whom I am proud to now call friends.

One department I dealt with was housing, and over a period of months I worked closely with a member of the committee dealing with planning applications; during this time we became, if not friends, then at least friendly acquaintances. We discovered a shared enjoyment of supernatural fiction and cold lager, that we had both spent time in Scotland and that both of us wanted to make a difference to the people's lives by doing our jobs well. This probably sounds like a cliché, I know, but nonetheless it was true of most of the people I met working for the council. No matter how hard or stressful the work or how much pressure people were under (and they were often under a lot) I rarely met anyone who didn't believe in the work that they did. Despite clients who were sometimes hostile, managers who didn't understand what their workers were doing, workloads that were unmanageable and a government obsessed with targets rather than client welfare, my colleagues carried on with little complaint because they believed in what they did and saw its benefit to the public they tried to serve.

My colleague from housing was involved in all sorts of council tasks and projects, and at the time struck me as a man who was working long hours and driving himself hard to do the best job he could. He was unceasingly cheerful, always helpful and for a few months, we supported each other and enjoyed each other's company. Like many of the relationships made at work, however, I lost contact with this person after I left and thought little about him until he got in touch by email out of the blue at the beginning of the year. The email read:

Hi Simon

Please help me. I know it's been a long time and we don't work together any more but I don't know who else to ask and we were friends enough for you to trust me, I hope. I know you've had some success with your writing, and I have a story that needs telling and you're the only person I know who has a chance of understanding it. Of believing me. I'm not after money for this, nor any recognition. I don't want you to name me at all if possible. I have a family and I'm the only income we have, and I can't afford to lose my job. I've been told that if I spread any more "rumours," I'll be fired. Rumours! Those stupid idiots won't see what I'm telling them is true. I can't risk my wage, but I can't afford to let this go either. People's lives are at risk.

What I want to tell you is amazing, unbelievable, but it's true. Everything can be checked—all the information is publically available. The Pennine Tower Restaurant is dangerous, and we have to do something. I don't know what. Something. Anything. Stop it opening again, keep it closed. Burn the place down if needs be. I've told the highest people at the council, but they didn't believe me, called me a liar. Most of them won't speak to me now. You're my only hope. Can you help me? Pray God that you can.

Please can we meet?

At the time, I was wary. Although it hasn't happened often, one of the things that I've noticed since getting published is that people seem to want to tell me ghost stories. Sometimes, these are "real" stories, sometimes fictions, and normally they're prefaced by the phrase "*Here's something you can use...*" I've never been entirely sure what people expect from me when they do that—to write the story but give them credit, perhaps, or tell them how to write it and then give them the name of a few friendly publishers? It's not a frequent thing, but it is an irritation, and I expected that this would be more of the same. I replied noncommittally and heard nothing for a few weeks. Then, another email appeared, then in short order, another and then more, each more desperate-sounding than the previous ones. Eventually, I agreed to meet, as much to stop the messages as anything. I thought it would be simple, that I would give him a chance to tell his story, and then walk away and forget it.

It was not.

We met in the car park of Forton Services, with the Pennine Tower Restaurant stretching up above us. My ex-colleague parked at the far end of the car park and when I got in the car, I was shocked by the change that had occurred in him. He looked ill, his hair dirty and his skin bad. The car was full of papers and folders and bags, and food wrappers were crumpled around my feet on the passenger side. The inside of the car smelled stale. *He* smelled stale. As he talked, I saw that he would not so much as glance at the restaurant, telling me the whole story sitting in the driver's seat and with the engine running.

At first, I wondered if this was a complex joke, however unlikely that might seem. It struck me as unlikely, though. There was an insistency about what I was told that made me think that, even if it weren't true, my ex-colleague believed it and I began to wonder about his sanity. He must have realised that I had my doubts, because at one point he said, "It's madness, I know, but it's true." I remember very clearly that this was the only point in the whole of our time together that he looked up at the restaurant, a darting look that lasted only a fraction of a moment. "It's an evil place. If it opens again, people will die," he said.

People will die.

The Pennine Tower isn't much to look at. A tower with a wide, circular top level, it looks shabby now, like a rusting flying saucer that's been abandoned. I'd always known that it was a restaurant, of course; my wife remembers eating there, and her friend ran it for a period in the early '80s. I also knew it had been shut down in the late '80s because of fire regulations or asbestos or something similar. It's a popular local landmark, and the subject of occasional retrospectives and campaigns to have it reopened. It's hardly threatening, and not the sort of place I would have imagined making anyone fearful.

At the end of our meeting, my ex-colleague said one last thing to me: "I know you don't believe me, but you can check it all out. Nothing I've told you is secret. I've written it all down. Here, take it. Check it. Please." He gave me a bag full of loose papers, printed sheets and cuttings and photocopies all covered in handwritten notes. On the top of the file was a report which he said he'd distributed as far as he could but which had been ignored.

"They think I'm mad," he said. "Or stupid or lying or drunk. Something. I don't know. I'm tired. Promise me you'll read it. Promise me. Write it up if you can. That building is *wrong* and people need to know. You need to tell them."

And then he was gone. Truthfully, I was glad to see him go. I've worked with mentally ill people in the past, and those with active psychoses frighten me even though I know that they're rarely a danger to anyone but themselves. I felt very sorry for my ex-colleague, and sorrier for his family who were going to have to deal with him and the results of his illness, but ultimately I was glad he was gone. I didn't read the papers straight away. Instead, I left them in my car and tried to pretend that they weren't there because reading them felt like it would be giving validity to my ex-colleague's paranoias. A few weeks later, I went to throw the bag away, but found that I couldn't; I remembered the way he had said, "People will die," and I thought that maybe I should at least look at what he'd given me. I hadn't promised, not exactly, but I had come close enough to feel guilty, I thought, if I didn't at least try. So I read them and then, because it seemed so preposterous, I reread them and then I made some checks and I found that everything he'd given me, every fact he'd written or copied or underlined, was true.

What follows is my collation and rewriting of the report and the mess of papers. It includes some of what I was told that overcast afternoon, and some things I found out later through my own research and through interviewing those people who were prepared to talk with me. I was as thorough as I could be and what I present here are the examples that have the most evidence to back them up, are the most provable, but bear in mind: *this is not all.* There are, literally, hundreds of incidents and suspicions, and suppositions that I could have included but haven't for reasons of space or because there was no proof. What I have included here is verifiable; I have checked the information as well as I can, and what I present is as detailed and accurate as I can make it. I have used footnotes to provide references (should specific ones exist) or to add additional information and/or clarification. I started this by hoping to provide you with an interesting story about a place, nothing more, but it has become something much bigger.

What you make of the following is up to you.

✦ ✦ ✦

Background

A little history first:

The Pennine Tower Restaurant is located at the motorway service station (Forton Services) adjacent to Junction 33 of the M6 motorway. It is 7 miles distant from the village of Forton, south of Lancaster and around 7 miles north of Preston. The restaurant is on the northbound carriageway, although the service station has sites on both sides of the road, linked by a covered footbridge.

Construction on the service station and the Pennine Tower Restaurant itself started midway through 1964 and was complete by early 1965. Originally owned by the Rank group, it was built because of its position (almost exactly halfway between London and Edinburgh) to capitalise on both the passing trade and also to tap into the large nearby catchment areas of Lancaster, Preston and Blackpool (whose inhabitants, it was anticipated, would want to travel to the new, futurist restaurant to enjoy its cutting-edge design and cosmopolitan menu). Forton was designed by the London-based firm T. P. Bennett, who allocated the work to Architect in Charge Bill Galloway and Job Architect Ray Anderson; both recall a stress-free build, with the exception of the death of one worker in a falling incident.[1]

The design of the restaurant itself is an unusual one and is clearly of its time; a twenty-metre-tall[2] steel-frame tower with two cantilevered floors, the lower providing an enclosed dining area and the upper an observation platform. Access to the restaurant was via two lifts and the spiral staircase that encircled them, whilst the restaurant itself consisted of 120 seats in a waiter-assisted silver service establishment. Tables were constructed against the outer wall, giving unparalleled views of the surrounding area. For those who preferred it, food could also be taken at American diner-style chairs lining counters looking into the kitchens. In its day, the Pennine

1 Not uncommon in the 1960s, a period when health and safety regulations were less stringent than today.

2 Original plans had the height of the tower at 33 metres, but this was reduced by 13 metres by the planning committee of the local council. The tower is constructed to allow the addition of a third floor, should permission ever be given.

Tower was a popular establishment, with people travelling from across the northwest just to experience this new dining experience whilst enjoying the excellent views.[3]

Ultimately, many factors worked against the success of the Pennine Tower, most obviously the cost of providing a silver service restaurant that could not seat more than 120. In an attempt to keep it operational, it was converted to a truckers' rest-stop and staff room but even this proved too expensive to run and, in 1989, the restaurant closed. The closure itself was due to the problems associated with evacuating 120 people down a narrow spiral staircase in the event of a fire or other emergency, and the consequent refusal to grant a fire safety certificate. The cost of fixing this (by constructing an external fire escape), along with the fact that asbestos had been used in the original construction (which, although stable, needs removing if members of the public are to be allowed back in) means that the building has not been used as a public venue since its closure.

The building was not completely closed, however. Most of its fixtures and fittings were removed and placed into storage and its space was partitioned, enabling its use as administrative offices. In 2001 it was refitted as a staff training venue, a capacity in which it continued to serve until early 2008 when the training function was relocated and the Pennine Tower was, essentially, mothballed. It is currently used for storage only.

Whilst there are no current plans to reopen the Pennine Tower Restaurant, this may one day change; many people believe it should be listed as a national heritage site due to its uniqueness, and should this happen the owners may be forced to carry out repairs/improvements. In these circumstances, they may see this as a reasonable opportunity to make the investment needed to reopen the venue as a viable business. Also, as building methods become more advanced (and often cheaper), there is the increased chance that reopening the restaurant will become an economically viable investment opportunity. Already, preliminary investigations have taken place into reopening just the observation platform.[4] Although the

3 It is well known that, early in their career, the Beatles often travelled to the Pennine Tower as it was one of the only places in the North West that offered the cosmopolitan experience of speed, travel and cappuccinos.

4 The current owners have denied this, although they did tell me that it is something

cost of this (somewhere in the region of £300,000)[5] is prohibitive in the current financial climate, this may change as construction technology or the economy improves.

1965 to the Present

There is another history for the Pennine Tower. Like most histories, it is made up of small things, tiny pieces that seem unrelated until they are placed together in a particular way, revealing that they are segments of a larger whole. This other history tells a different story about the Pennine Tower Restaurant, one of shadows and darkness and the conclusions it suggests are both uncomfortable and difficult to accept. It is a history formed into an apparent chain, one that links event to occurrence to suspicion and which leads to somewhere I suspect few of us will willingly go.

October 1964: The Health and Safety Executive report into the death of the workman (David Prentiss) killed during the building of the tower found that it was an accident, but witness statements taken at the time are interesting: "I looked up and saw Dave backing out onto the scaffold platform. He was holding his hands out in front of him and didn't look around. I shouted up, but it was like he didn't hear me. Even when he hit the scaffold, he never stopped moving. He just sort of slipped and fell. He never even looked back."[6] Prentiss' foreman, George Toms, described him that morning: "Dave was fine when he arrived, just as cheerful as ever. He was one of my best workers, always on time, knew what he was doing, never took risks, could be trusted to just get on. I sent him to the restaurant floor to carry on putting in the frames for the windows, just like he'd been doing for the last few days. I was in the staircase, and about half past eleven, I heard him shout something and then scream. I was just walking up to

---

that they may consider as they get "5 or 6" requests a day to visit the tower from people who stop at the service station below.

5 Also denied.

6 Statement given to police by fellow workman Alex Scott, October 13th 1964, released under *Freedom of Information Act* regulations.

see what the problem was when I heard everyone else start screaming and shouting and I found out he'd fallen."[7]

July 1965: On a sunny Wednesday afternoon, some 27 people in the Pennine Tower spend ten minutes listening to the "sound of something grunting and breathing like a large animal."[8] The noise seems to come from all around the restaurant at once. A full search of the building is carried out, but no explanation for it is found.

November 1966: The observation platform and the narrow balcony that runs around the outside of the restaurant floor (for use when outside access is required to carry out repairs) are found covered in dead birds. Several breeds of bird are identified as being among the dead (including pigeons, blackbirds, sparrows and seagulls), and although several autopsies are carried out by a local vet (Bay Veterinary Services), no cause of death is identified. The number of dead birds is estimated to be between one and two thousand.

February 1967: The restaurant's manager, Odette Wilkinson, is working late in the restaurant when she hears a sound like "faint breathing".[9] She watches as the contents of a work surface (including eggs, pans and cups) slide to the floor without anyone or anything touching them. When she tries to leave the kitchen, Wilkinson finds she cannot open the door. The breathing gets louder, to the point where she is convinced that someone is in the room with her. It is only when she screams that the sound stops and the door opens, banging her face and cutting her lip.

April 1968: Gina Reading, a cleaner, is found in the ladies' toilet of the restaurant weeping uncontrollably. She becomes hysterical when

---

7 Statement given to police by Foreman George Toms, October 13th 1964, released under *Freedom of Information Act* regulations.

8 Manager of the restaurant Michael Lovell, quoted in Lancaster *Guardian*, "Strange Sounds in New Restaurant Baffle Diners," July 22nd 1965, p. 5.

9 Rank Group Accident Report #271, Health and Safety Executive, released under the *Freedom of Information Act*.

approached, screaming about something "in the mirror," only calming down when she is forcibly removed from the building. She refuses to reenter the Pennine Tower and is allocated duties in other areas of Forton Services. Previously a "happy, cheerful girl,"[10] her mood changes dramatically in the months following this incident. In June 1969, Gina kills herself. Her suicide note says simply "I don't want to see it again."

September 1968: Two truckers, Daniel Moffat and Harvey Allen, are in the restaurant at around three in the morning. It is otherwise deserted although Moffat thinks that there may have been "a cleaner and a cook around."[11] Not well acquainted, they do know each other well enough to sit together and, according to Moffat, "...were chatting quite happily, just guys with similar concerns, the two of us driving and away from home in the middle of the night, when I heard a noise. I'm not sure that Harvey heard it at first, but I did. Jesus, it was horrible. It was like a grunting sound, like something massive was in there with us. I was looking around when I hear Harvey say, 'What's that?' and I said something like, 'I don't know, can you hear it too?' and then he shouted. I turned back to the table in time to see him stand up and back away. He looked frightened. No, not frightened, *terrified*. He was looking at something behind me and backing away from the table, staring at the window. He dropped his coffee and knocked over his chair, and all the time I could hear the noise, the sound of something panting or grunting from all around us. I don't mean it was echoing, or it was hard to tell where it was coming from, I mean it sounded like it was coming from everywhere at once. I looked around again, to see if I could see what Harvey was seeing, but there was just the empty restaurant and those big windows looking out so that you could see the road and the lights of the cars as they went along it.

"Harvey shouted again and I looked back around and he had fallen over and was on the floor and I knew he was having a heart attack or something. He'd gone red, bright red, he was twitching and he'd got spit coming out of the corner of his mouth. I shouted for help but it was

10 Desmond Reading, Gina's father, interviewed by SKU, January 2009.

11 In conversation with the author, January 2009.

useless. He was dead in seconds, and that fucking sound just carried on, all around me like something was huge and hungry."[12]

The coroner's report into the death finds that Allen had suffered a massive heart attack, despite having been given a clean bill of health by his GP only two weeks prior to his death.

August 1969: Alice Pearl stops for a meal in the Pennine Tower Restaurant. She is seen eating whilst seated at one of the tables that looks out over the Trough of Bowland, and has not been seen since. None of the staff or customers see her leave. Her car is found abandoned in Lancaster several days later with a driver's side window broken and steering column damaged. Alice was a sometime prostitute with known mental health problems, and the police put her disappearance down to "a chaotic lifestyle coupled with a desire not to be found."[13] The investigation into Alice's disappearance lasts only a few days, and is carried out by an inexperienced junior officer.

March 1971: George Harrison gives an interview in which he states: "There are some places you go, you know, that aren't happy. There's nothing you can point to, nothing obvious, they're just miserable, unhealthy places full of negative energy or worse. We used to go to somewhere, the four of us, and drink coffee and look out at the hills and the sea and enjoy the view, but we stopped because I always left feeling horrible. John too. I used to think things like that were only in old buildings, ghosts and the like, but I know different now. Age doesn't matter, there are places in the world that are just wrong."[14]

November 1974: Jennifer Ashe and her daughter, Rosemary, stop at Forton and visit the Pennine Tower Restaurant to eat. Jennifer is moving from Liverpool to Carlisle to escape an abusive husband, but vanishes from the toilet of the restaurant. Rosemary is found in a cubicle by herself,

12 Statement given at Lancaster Coroner's Court, December 1968.

13 Police statement quoted in *The Visitor*, August 21st 1969, p.3.

14 *Mission* magazine, Vol. 1, Issue 2, "Harrison Up Close and Personal," April 1971, p. 31–33.

her pants around her ankles and sitting in a puddle of urine. She is later diagnosed as being in severe shock and even as she recovers, the only thing she will say is "teeth." She is eventually committed to a long-stay mental institution, where she still remains. No trace of Jennifer is ever found. Suspicion initially falls on Jennifer's estranged husband, Rory, but he has an alibi for the time of Jennifer's disappearance. No charges are ever brought.[15]

December 1976: Nick Birchill vanishes mid-shift from his job as a cleaner in the Pennine Tower Restaurant. He is seen at 2:20 a.m. by two customers, who state that he seems cheerful and that he spoke to them, commiserating with them that they were visiting the restaurant in the middle of the night and so were missing the views. He goes out of sight, following the curve of the wall and mopping the floor. Perhaps five minutes later, the two customers hear a "terrible scream"[16] and the sound of something falling over. When they investigate, Birchill's mop is found on the floor and his overturned mop bucket next to it. Beside the spilled water are three drops of blood.

Police later discover that Birchill was in a considerable debt and come to the conclusion that he ran to escape his debtors. Several months later, on 16th April 1977, a badly burned and decomposed body is found in the Lancaster Canal. Although its teeth have been damaged and its features and fingerprints mostly destroyed, it is similar enough in shape and build for police to decide that it is Birchill and, accordingly, the case becomes a murder investigation, although one which makes little progress. In early 2003, following repeated applications from Birchill's mother, police test

15 One of the surviving investigating officers, DI Andrew Charlesworthy (Ret.), told me (on November 11th 2008): "This was a disappearance that made no sense, none. Jenny was a hard-working, stable woman, she loved her kid, she was well-liked and happy because she'd escaped the husband. We knew something had happened to her, but for the life of us, we couldn't find out what. We never found anything that pointed us towards someone. I mean, we were so convinced it was the husband, but his alibi was cast iron, watertight. It still bothers me. I wonder what happened, where she went and what happened to make that poor kid so damaged."

16 Transcript of police statement, released under *Freedom of Information Act.*

the body's DNA and discover that it is not, in fact, Birchill. The case is reopened as a missing person's enquiry and despite a high profile relaunch, including an appearance in a segment of the BBC TV show *Crimewatch*,[17] no witnesses are found and no new information discovered. The case remains open.

March 1978—The Maracott Photograph: John and Irene Maracott are travelling from Dundee to Bristol with their children Lucy and Mark. Whilst eating in the restaurant, they ask another customer to take their photograph. When developed, the photograph shows some unexpected details. Although at first dismissed by the Maracotts as faulty film, they eventually show the picture and the camera it was taken on to a friend, who persuades them to share it with the press. Initially printed by the local paper, it is quickly reprinted around the world and is the subject of much debate in both the mainstream press and specialist photographic and paranormal interest publications. An initial investigation carried out at the Kodak laboratories on both the picture and camera finds that there is "...no evidence of tampering or fakery."[18] Various explanations for the photograph are put forward, including that it is a complex hoax by the Maracotts themselves (with or without the aid of the person who took the picture, who has never been publically identified) or a weather inversion of some kind that caused heat patterns to form on the glass. It is also suggested that the images could be sunlight reflecting on puddles in the car park. Kodak dismisses all of these suggestions.[19]

In the early eighties, John Maracott sells the picture to a private picture library which licences its use strictly and refuses to allow its release for further investigation.[20] Most people who have seen and studied the picture

---

17 Broadcast date August 22nd 2003.

18 Internal scientific report, Kodak, March 1976, quoted in *The Times*, May 22nd 1979.

19 Also from the Kodak report quoted in *The Times*

20 I was unable to licence the picture for inclusion here because of the costs involved, although anyone interested in seeing it can do so relatively easily. Several scans of it (of varying quality) can be found online, although the best reproduction of it remains the one contained in the now out-of-print *Photographs of the Supernatural World* (Charles

agree that it shows something, although they disagree precisely what. In the picture, the Maracotts are seated at one of the tables, facing away from the windows and towards the camera. All are smiling, and are framed by the window. It is a bright day, and the view through the window should be excellent but it is obscured by what look like faces. There are three, two female and one male, apparently printed on the glass behind the group. All three have open mouths and closed eyes and appear to be in torment. Around the edges of the window frame are further shapes on the glass: jagged, uneven triangles that look not unlike shark's teeth. The family are insistent that the window was unmarked when the photograph was taken and that they saw no images on the glass.

June 1980: Travelling salesman Martin James is found on a sunny afternoon halfway down the spiral staircase, curled into a ball and weeping. He becomes violent when staff try to move him and both the police and ambulance service are called, finally having to inject James with a tranquiliser before they can calm him enough to remove him from the building. Once at hospital, he tells this story:[21]

I picked the hitchhiker up somewhere outside of Bolton and she told me that she wanted to go to Scotland. She said her name was Mary, but I thought it probably wasn't her real name. She was like lots of them, children trying to be adults, and she reminded me of my daughter. She looked so hungry and I said I'd buy her some food. All through the meal she kept telling me that she could hear a funny noise. I mean, I couldn't hear anything and I thought she was just having some sort of drug reaction, or she was high. She looked the sort, all thin and wasted and pathetic, like she needed a good hug and a warm bath and someone to love her and tell her everything was okay, you know?

Anyway, it got to the point where she wouldn't stay in the restaurant any more so I said we'd go and I followed her out. She wouldn't use the lifts, instead she went down the stairs and she was nearly running. She kept saying she could

---

Bramley, Edgington Press, 1979).

21 Transcript of police statement, released under *Freedom of Information Act.*

still hear it, and I said "What? What?" and she said "The animal" and then I lost sight of her for just a second. She got a bit far ahead of me, disappeared around the curve of the staircase. I couldn't hear her at all and when I got there, she'd gone. I went all the way to the bottom of the stairs and then looked around the shops and car park and went back to the place on the stairs where I'd seen her but there was no sign of her. As I stood there, wondering whether she'd just run fast, found another lift before I saw her, I heard something a bit like a choking sound and it sounded like her, and just for a minute I heard something else, something like the growls of a lion or wolf or something, something that's malicious, that eats for fun and not just for food. I turned to go down the stairs and it was below me so I turned to go up and it was above me and all around me and then I don't remember much till I woke up in the hospital bed.

Although the police investigate, they find no trace of a hitchhiker and no one remembers seeing James with a girl. However, his description of her is accurate enough for some investigators to believe that James had picked up Denise Arron. Arron is reported missing several weeks after the incident with James at the restaurant, having been last seen leaving her home on the day of the incident after an argument, and has not been seen since. She claimed at the time that she was going "to Scotland," which she has done before, staying with a friend for "a week or two"[22] before getting in contact. Arron has never been found, and (despite being repeatedly investigated and questioned by the police in relation to the disappearance) James sticks to his story for the remainder of his life, going as far as to repeat it on a documentary about missing teenagers shown by ITV in 1993,[23] two years before his death.

October 1982: Gordon Harrow vanishes from the toilets of the Pennine Tower Restaurant; he is 6 years old. His parents watch as he enters the toilet, and both his mother and father (Mary and Frederick) keep watch on the outer door leading to the cubicles. Both insist that Gordon does

22 Statement of Elise Mainwairing, Denise's friend, to police, repeated in conversation with the author.

23 *Lost Children*, ITV/Philips pictures, first shown May 26th 1993, Dir. Edward Hampson.

Gordon does not come out, and no one else enters whilst they watch. After ten minutes, Frederick goes to find Gordon but discovers that all the cubicles are empty. He alerts the restaurant manager, who immediately instigates a full search of the restaurant and the rest of the site, to no avail. The police are called, who also search. During the course of the next three weeks, the motorway is shut several times as over 1000 police and volunteers are organised into one of the biggest missing person hunts (including fingertips searches of the surrounding grounds and roads) that Lancashire has known. Rumours abound that Gordon has been taken by "gypsies" or "travellers," stories seized upon "by a national press keen to attack the increasing influx of foreign nationals and other perceived 'undesirables' into Britain."[24] No evidence of this is found, however, and Gordon's parents eventually become the main suspects in their son's disappearance "solely because no other suspects have been identified."[25] They are investigated by an increasingly desperate police force, and are questioned at length in the final week of October. The media interview a local psychic, Madame Rowena, who states that Gordon is "screaming" and is "somewhere close to the restaurant."[26] The police dismiss her claims, although the media continue to interview Madame Rowena whenever the case is mentioned. No trace of Gordon is found and he joins Alice, Jennifer and Nick as one of the region's unsolved disappearances.

October 1985: Britain suffers its worst motorway crash since the motorways were first opened when 13 people are killed and many more are seriously injured when a coach and ten cars collide close to Junction 33 and within sight of the Pennine Tower Restaurant. The incident happens on a clear, sunny day around six hundred yards before a point where the motorway narrows due to two closed lanes. The subsequent investigation

24 "Investigating the Investigations: How the Media Helps and Hinders the Police in Missing Persons' Cases," Dyer et al, *Community Care Magazine*, July 2001.

25 DCI Eric Banning, Lancashire Constabulary (Ret) during a telephone conversation with me, May 20th 2009.

26 *Lancaster Guardian*, November 2nd 1982, widely quoted by the national press in the weeks after.

and report state that the accident was caused by a combination of excessive speed and possible mechanical faults with one or more vehicles. However, in 1992, one of the survivors goes on record to state that these are not the only reasons: "I was several cars back from the coach and the car in the lane next to it, and we weren't going that fast. Suddenly the car ahead starts to wobble and veer across the lane. I saw the coach shift to get out of the car's way, but it wasn't fast enough. The next thing is the two crash into each other but before they hit together, I saw people on the coach pointing up at that building at the side of the road, the one that looks like a Frisbee on a pole. I didn't see anything myself, because I was too busy trying to avoid hitting the car in front of me." [27]

Other survivors of the accident have, generally, not wished to speak about their experiences—of the 7 remaining alive and contactable, none agreed to go on the record about what they saw or heard. However, one did agree to speak on the condition that their identity be hidden. They claim[28] that "there was something wrong with the windows of the restaurant. I was looking out of the car window and I happened to look up at [it] and the windows were grey, darker than they should have been, and it looked like they were moving, that the edges were flexible and ragged. Spikey. I went to say something to [the driver] but he'd already seen it. When I looked again, the windows looked huge, like they had opened up and they were completely black. I know that this must sound stupid, but it's the truth of what I saw. The windows had gone, somehow, and in their place were openings. I can't explain it any better than that."

August 1989: Workmen converting the restaurant to offices following its closure find badly mutilated cats' bodies on the observation floor, along with the bones of birds and at least one dog. A police veterinary surgeon identifies pieces from at least 17 different cats, although none of the corpses is whole. The crime is blamed on "local teens," [29] despite the fact that the

27 Paul Gallagher, quoted in *Accidents and Causes: Motorway Driving and Safety and the UK*, Chapter 6: Forton and Beyond, Dyson and Pimblett, University of Manchester, 1992.

28 In an email to me, dated January 11th 2009.

29 Lancaster *Guardian*, August 5th 1989.

doors were locked upon the workmen's arrival and there is no evidence of a break-in. How the animals got to the top of the tower remains a mystery, and no one is charged.

July 1991: Two bloody handprints are discovered on the inside wall of the restaurant below a window, and a further smear of blood is discovered covering 7 steps of the staircase between the ground and restaurant floors of the tower. The blood is tested and found to be of animal origin. Police dismiss the blood as "a prank" and blame "university students."[30]

November 1993: During the morning session of a training day, trainees are constantly interrupted by the sound of low growling. During the 10 to 15 minutes of the lunch break that the room is unoccupied one of the white boards in the training room is vandalised beyond repair, having been cracked and splintered and covered in "slimy liquid." One trainee says that the board looks "chewed." Despite the level of damage inflicted on the board (which is torn from the wall so forcefully that the pieces of the partition wall are also torn loose) and their proximity to the room, none of the delegates hears anything. An internal investigation puts the damage down to "probable trespassers," despite the fact that no one on site that day recalls seeing anyone suspicious-looking.[31]

June 1999: Nayan Gowda, a freelance photographer, is photographing the Pennine Tower for a proposed article on '60s architecture for the magazine *Architectural Review*. He takes 133 photographs during his visit to the tower, but finds when he develops them that almost all are entirely black or black and grey. In two, taken towards the windows "a shape like a shark's jaw"[32] can be seen.[33]

---

30 Statement to the press by DI Andrew Bellamy, Lancashire Constabulary, August 1st 1991.

31 All quotes from Incident Report #342 (Company records, held at HSE, released under *Freedom of Information Act*).

32 Nayan Gowda, quoted in *Fortean Times*, September 2000.

33 Both photographs copyright the Fortean Picture Library: www.forteantimes.com

November 2004: Gary Young is carrying out a site inspection on the mostly disused building for the Health and Safety Executive when he stops to ring his wife, Lorna. In the middle of the call, Lorna hears Young say "What's that?" presumably in response to something he has heard or seen. There is a brief pause and then he screams once and drops his phone. Lorna hears sounds she describes as "a dragging noise and a roar" and then her husband screams again. Panicked, Lorna breaks the call off and telephones the police, who have an officer on the scene within minutes. Young's phone is found on the floor of the former restaurant's kitchen area, and nearby are streaks in the dirt and dust on the floor. Young is found in the elevator, unconscious and battered. When he awakes, he claims to remember nothing about his ordeal and is diagnosed as suffering from severe concussion.

Several weeks later a homeless man with mental health problems, Neil McDonagh, is arrested at Forton and charged with drunkenness and public disorder offences. He is a regular visitor to the cafe and shops of the service station, and further investigations show he was there the day of the Young attack. He is charged with actual bodily harm in relation to this incident. McDonagh, whilst never denying his presence in the abandoned restaurant on the day of the attack, states his innocence and claims, consistently, that he saw Young attacked by "a great black thing from the walls and windows".[34] When asked to draw what he saw by his psychiatrist, he draws a picture of what looks like a crude mouth with large, uneven teeth. The picture is used as evidence during his trial, at which he is found guilty and remanded to the custody of a secure psychiatric unit.[35]

February 2006: Paramedics are called to attend to a delivery man who has had an asthma attack whilst carrying crates up to the first floor of the Pennine Tower. One paramedic leaves the tower shortly after arriving and refuses to reenter, saying only that she feels "stalked" in the building.

April 2007: During one of the regular inspections of the site, a large pool of liquid is found in the restaurant. It proves to be a mix of animal

34 Court transcript, Crown vs McDonagh, March 2005.

35 Permission to reprint the picture here was refused by McDonagh's family.

blood, cholesterol, glycocholic and taurocholic acids and lecithin.[36] The source of the liquid is not found.

Conclusion

Even faced with the discovery that the incidents my ex-colleague had written about in his notes and report were true, I did not believe that his conclusions were correct. After all, how could the Pennine Tower Restaurant be a danger to anyone who stepped inside it? It's a building, after all, a construction of concrete and steel and glass and wood, and nothing else. Looking at the separate events, I was struck by how easy it is to take random things and make them into a chain, creating links that do not exist. Once that is done *everything* seems to fit into the pattern you have imposed upon what is, essentially, patternless. Why are there fewer incidents after the restaurant closes to the public in the late 1980s? Because there are fewer people there in total or because there is a more sinister explanation? Are those incidents that have occurred since it closed the normal vandalism any isolated, underused building undergoes, or are they result of more malign forces working? And so it goes.

It is easy to see how psychosis starts. An unfortunate coincidence, a series of events or bad luck, get woven into a thread that implies a consciousness, a *directedness,* rather than the simple blind chaos of a universe that has no guiding hand to oversee it nor grand plan to guide it. Once you have an idea that a pattern exists, everything starts to fit the pattern. It even has a name, *confirmation bias,* and even then, it was what I believed was happening here. The things that had occurred at the Pennine Tower Restaurant over the years were, I told myself, a series of unrelated tragedies and mysteries and not related. Go to any place and I am sure you'd find a similar set of occurrences, particularly in places around roads and motorways which, by their very nature, imply movement and travel, escape and relocation. My ex-colleague's ideas were nonsense, a dark fairy story created by someone struggling to make sense

36 Common ingredients in bile.

of a world that was chaotic and threatening. Opening the Pennine Tower (assuming the asbestos and fire regulation issues which had led to its closure in the first place could be solved) would be no more dangerous than opening any other restaurant. However, two separate press reports changed my mind.

In late 2008, the Museum of Lancashire opened an exhibition celebrating the development of the British motorway system. One of the exhibits was a re-creation of a section of the Pennine Tower Restaurant, using an original table and chairs, tiles, plates and cutlery and even a section of the original flooring, all of which had been in storage since the late eighties or earlier. On 19th December, Malcolm Skilling visited the exhibit with his wife, Genie. He was particularly excited about the Forton section, having been a professional driver before retiring and therefore remembering the Pennine Tower well. Just before the museum closed for the night, Genie went to the toilet, leaving Malcolm at the Pennine Tower exhibit. *The Lancashire Evening Post* reported that:

> *By her reckoning, Genie was away for no more than five minutes. When she returned, Malcolm had vanished. A check with the guard on the front desk showed that Malcolm had not left the museum by that exit, and none of the emergency exits had been opened or alarms triggered. A thorough search of the museum revealed no sign of Malcolm except for his bag, which was lying on the floor by the table in the Pennine Tower Restaurant exhibit. Despite intensive investigations, no trace of him has been found and police are growing increasingly concerned for his safety.*[37]

I think that I might even have dismissed this, put it down to chance, were it not for the second article. I came across it several months after reading through the papers and cuttings given to me that first day in the car park. It has altered my perception of what has been happening, made me think more seriously about the importance of what I have written.

---

37 Lancashire *Evening Post*, "Local Man Still Missing," December 22nd, p.3.

In summer of 2009, the motorway exhibition moved from the Lancashire Museum to Lancaster's smaller museum. Several weeks later, in a light-hearted piece entitled "It's Official! Lancashire Is the Most Haunted County in the Country!"[38] published on July 23rd, it was reported that a guard carrying out his overnight rounds in the museum had heard a strange sound, which followed him for the duration of his hour-long patrol. It was, he says, like the "breathing of a huge dog."

This is not fiction.

Simon Kurt Unsworth
September 2009

38 Lancaster *Guardian*, "It's Official! Lancashire Is the Most Haunted County in the Country!," July 23rd, p.6 & 7.

Distress Call

CONNIE WILLIS

Connie Willis is an internationally known science fiction author and the winner of an unprecedented total of seven Nebula Awards and eleven Hugo Awards, and is the first author to have ever won both awards in all four fiction categories. In 2009 she was inducted into the Science Fiction Hall of Fame, and in 2012 was named a Nebula Grand Master of science fiction.

Willis is the author of *Doomsday Book*, winner of the Nebula and Hugo awards for Best Science Fiction Novel; *Lincoln's Dreams*, winner of the John W. Campbell Award for Best Science Fiction Novel; *Remake*; *Uncharted Territory*; *Bellwether*; *To Say Nothing of the Dog*, winner of the Hugo Award for Best Science Fiction Novel, and *Passage*; and the short story collections *Fire Watch*, *Impossible Things*, *Miracle and Other Christmas Stories*, and *The Winds of Marble Arch*, but she is probably most famous for her short stories, including "Fire Watch," "Even the Queen," and "The Last of the Winnebagos."

Her most recent novel is the Nebula- and Hugo-winning two-volume work entitled *Blackout* and *All Clear*, a time-travel saga set in World War II, in the middle of the evacuation of Dunkirk, the intelligence war, and the London Blitz.

She is currently working on a new novel about iPhones, Facebook, tweeting, and telepathy. It is, of course, a comedy.

Caroline was not in the room. Amy could hear her crying somewhere down the hall. Her crying sounded louder, as though some other, all-pervading sound had suddenly ceased. "The engines have stopped," Amy thought. "We are dead in the water. Something has happened," she thought. "Something terrible."

She had gone to get Caroline, to get her out of this house, and Caroline had run from her, sobbing in terror. Had run from Amy, her own mother.

She had found Caroline with the women, clinging onto their gray drifting skirts. They had dressed her like themselves. "When did they do that?" Amy thought frightenedly. "I have let things go too far."

She had said firmly, so they wouldn't know how frightened she was, "Get your things together, Caroline. We are going home."

"No!" Caroline had screamed, hiding behind their skirts. "I'm afraid. You'll hurt me again."

"Hurt you?" Amy said, bewildered and then furious. "*Hurt* you? Who has been telling you that, that I would hurt you?" She reached angrily into the protective circle of the women for Caroline's hand. "What have you been telling her?" she demanded.

Debra stepped forward, graceful as a ghost in the drifting gray, and smiled at Amy. "She wanted to know why she got so sick at the picnic," she had said.

Amy had had to hold her hands stiffly against her body to keep from slapping Debra. "What did you tell her?" she had said, and Caroline had shot past her, out the door and down the hall to the parlor.

Caroline had hidden under the big séance table in the parlor. Amy had gotten down on her knees and crawled toward her, but Caroline had backed away from her until she was almost hidden by the massive legs of the carved chair.

Amy had crawled out from under the table so she would not frighten her, and squatted back on her heels, her arms extended to the six-year-old. Caroline stayed huddled behind the chair. "Come here, Caroline," she had whispered, horrified that she should be reduced to having to say such a thing, "I won't hurt you, honey."

Caroline shook her head, the tears still wet on her face. "You'll poison me again," she whispered. Amy could hardly hear her.

"Poison?" Amy whispered. Caroline in her arms and dying, and then Jim, carrying her across the park to the house, she running after him, her heart pounding, running here because the police station was on the other side of the park and she had been afraid Caroline would die before Jim got her there. Jim carrying her here, to this house, which was so much closer. To these people. Thinking hysterically as Ismay took Caroline's limp body from Jim's arms, "We should not have brought her here."

"Somebody poisoned you," Amy had said, and knew it was true. She had been so shocked that for a long minute she had not been able to say anything. She'd crossed her hands on her breast as if she had been wounded there and whispered, so quietly some one standing behind her could not have heard her, her lips moving in almost silent prayer, "I would never hurt you, Caroline. I love you."

The sound of Caroline's crying was louder again, as though someone had opened a door. "I must go find Caroline," she said aloud, and tried to keep that brave thought in her mind as she went out the open door toward the sound of the crying. But before she reached the room where they had Caroline, she was saying over and over, like a prayer, "Something terrible has happened, something terrible has happened."

She stopped, standing in the open door, and looked back toward the parlor. The lamps in the hall wavered like candles and then steadied, dimmer than before. The hall was icy. "I should go back for my coat," Amy thought. "It will be cold on deck." And then the other thought, even colder, "I mustn't go in there. Something terrible has happened in the parlor."

Ismay had taken her into the parlor to wait while the doctor saw Caroline. Amy had been standing at the foot of the wide stairs, clutching the newel post, trying not to think, "She's going to die," for fear she would know it was true.

"Don't give up hope," one of the gray-haired women had said, patting Amy's clenched hands as she went up the stairs with a blanket. She was dressed in the floating gray all the women, even the young one, wore. They had clustered like spectres around Caroline's limp body, and Amy had thought, "It's some kind of cult. I shouldn't have brought her here." But the young one—Debra, Jim had called her—had gone immediately for the doctor. Debra had led the doctor up the stairs past Amy, saying, "The little girl collapsed in the park. They were having a picnic. Her father brought her here," and she had sounded so normal, in spite of the drifting ghost's dress, that Amy had begun to hope again.

"Hope persists, doesn't it?" someone said behind her. "Even with the most blatant evidence to the contrary."

"What do you mean?" Amy stammered. This was the man Jim had called Ismay. Debra and Ismay. How had he known their names?

"Did you know," he said, "it was nearly an hour before the passengers on the *Titanic* knew that she was sinking? Then they looked down at the lights still shining underneath the water on the lower decks and said, 'How pretty! Do you think perhaps we should get into a lifeboat?'"

Amy was very frightened at what this talk of sinking ships might mean, and she half-started up the stairs, but his hand closed over hers on the banister, and he said, "They won't let you up there. The doctor's still with her. And your husband." He moved his hand to her arm and led her into the parlor.

"Caroline's dead," she thought numbly, and looked unseeingly at the parlor.

"The body is like a ship. It does not die all at once. It is struck by death, the fatal iceberg brushing past, but it does not sink for several hours. And all that time, the passengers wander the decks, sending out S.O.S.'s to rescue ships that never come. Have you ever seen a ghost?"

"There were survivors on the *Titanic*," Amy said, her heart pounding so hard it hurt. "Help came."

"Ah, yes," Ismay said. "The *Carpathia* steamed boldly up at four in the morning. Captain Rostron stumbled about among the icebergs for nearly an hour, thinking he was in the wrong place. He was too late. She was already gone."

"No," Amy said, and she knew from the panicked sound of her heart that this conversation was not about sinking ships at all. "They weren't too late for the lifeboats."

"A few first-class passengers," Ismay said, as if the survivors did not matter. "Did you know that all the children in steerage drowned?"

Amy did not hear him. She had turned away from him and was looking at the parlor. "What?" she said blankly.

"I said, the *Californian* was only ten miles away. She thought their flares were fireworks."

"What?" she said again, and tried to get past him, but he was behind her, between her and the door, and she could not get out. "What is this place?" she said, and could not hear her voice above the sound of her heart.

Amy stood in the doorway, looking back to the parlor. "I must go back there," she thought clearly. "Something terrible has happened in the parlor."

"Mama!" Caroline said, and Amy turned and looked in through the open door.

The women stood motionless around the little girl, their hands reaching out awkwardly to comfort her, Debra kneeling at her feet. "They should be getting her lifebelt on," Amy thought. "They must get her up to the boat deck." Caroline held out her arms in joy toward Amy.

Amy said, "We're going home now, Caroline." But before she finished saying it, one of the women said, not interrupting but instead superimposing her words over Amy's so that Amy could not hear her own voice, "Your mother's gone, darling. She can't hurt you now."

"She is not gone," Caroline said. The three women looked up at the little girl and then anxiously at one another.

"You miss her, of course, but she's happy now. You must forget all the bad things and think of that," Debra said, patting Caroline's hand. Caroline yanked her hand away impatiently.

"Do you think we should give her a sedative?" said the woman who had spoken first. "Ismay said she might be difficult at first."

"Caroline," Amy said loudly. "Come here."

"No," said Debra, and at first Amy thought she was answering her, but she didn't reach out to restrain Caroline, and her voice sounded as it had when she was playing ghost at the séance. "Perhaps she does see her mother."

A shudder, like the sudden settling of a ship, went through the women.

"Caroline?" Debra asked carefully. "Where is your mother?"

"Right there," Caroline said, and pointed at Amy.

The women turned and looked at the doorway. "Perhaps she does see something," Debra said. "I think we should tell Ismay," and she went out the door past Amy and down the hall to the parlor.

"Oh, something terrible has happened in the parlor," Amy thought, "and Ismay has done it."

The parlor was the room she had seen from the park. Handing Caroline her glass of milk, she had looked at the heavy gray drapes in the windows and wondered what the gaudy Victorian house was like inside. She had imagined it like this room, rich woods and faded carpet, but the room they had hurried Caroline into upstairs was barren, a folding cot, gray walls, and she had thought again, "The house has been taken over by some kind of cult."

Near the windows was a large round table with chairs around it and candles burning in a candelabra in the center. One of the chairs was more massive than the others and heavily carved. "The captain's table," she thought, thinking of the *Titanic*, "and the captain sits in that chair."

She had turned away from Ismay, and in turning, seen what was behind her, dimly white in the darkness of the room. An iceberg. A catafalque. A bier. "I have seen it too late," Amy thought, and tried to get past Ismay, but he was at the door.

"The *Titanic* went down very fast," he said. "A little under two-and-a-half hours. People usually take longer. Ghosts have been seen for years afterwards, although it is my experience that they go down in a matter of hours."

"What is this place?" Amy said. "Who are you?"

"I am a man who sees ghosts, a spiritualist," Ismay said, and Amy nearly fainted with relief.

"You hold your séances in here," she said, relieved out of all proportion to his words. "You sit in this chair and call the ghosts," she said giddily, sitting down in the carved chair. "Come to us from the other side and all that. Have you ever had a ghost from the *Titanic*?"

"No," he said, coming around to face her. "Every ghost is his own *Titanic*."

He made her uneasy. She stood up and looked out the window. Across the park she could see the police station, and she was overcome by the same wild relief. The police within signaling distance and the doctor upstairs, and all the ghostly ladies only harmless tableturners who wanted to talk to their dead husbands. In this room Ismay would make the windows blow open and the candles go out, he would cause ghosts to hover above the catafalque, their hands folded peacefully across their breasts, and what, what had she been afraid of?

"I had a progenitor on the *Titanic*," he said. "Rather a cad actually. He made it off in one of the first boats. Did you know that the *Titanic* was the first ship to use the international distress signal? And the *Californian*, only ten miles away, would have been the first to receive it, a historic occasion, but the wireless operator had already gone to bed when the first messages went out."

"The *Carpathia* heard," Amy had said, and had walked past him and out the door, to go to where Caroline was already getting better. "Captain Rostron came."

"There were ice reports all day," Ismay had said, "but the *Titanic* ignored them."

Amy leaned against the wall after Debra passed, pressing her hands to her breast as though she had been wounded. "I must find Jim," she thought. "He will see she gets in one of the boats."

She had a very hard time with the stairs. They seemed to slant forward, and it took all her concentrated thought to climb them and she could not think how she would make Jim hear her, how she would convince him to save Caroline. Even the hall listed toward her, so that she struggled toward Debra's room as up a steep hill. When she came to the closed door, she had to stand a minute before she had the strength to put her hand on the doorknob. When she did, she thought the door must be locked. Then she looked down at her hand. She dropped it to her side, as if it had been injured.

Debra opened the door, leaning her graceful body against it. "Don't worry," she said.

"You can't just leave her in there," Jim said. "What about the police?"

"Why would the police come unless someone went to get them? We don't have any phones. The outside doors are locked. Who would go get them?"

"Caroline."

Amy came into the room.

Debra shook her head. "She's only six years old, and it isn't as if she saw anything. We told her her mother died in her sleep."

"No," Amy said. "That isn't true. I was murdered."

"I'd feel safer if Ismay had taken care of her, too. She might have seen something afterwards."

"She did," Debra said, and watched the color drain from Jim's face. "She thought she saw her mother this morning." She hesitated cruelly again. "Ismay has decided to have a séance," she said. She waited to see the effect on him and then said, "What are you afraid of? She's dead. She can't do anything to you." She went out the door.

"You poisoned her," Amy said to Jim. "She wasn't sick. She was poisoned. You planned the picnic. It was a trick to bring us here, to Debra, whose name you knew before. To bring us here so Ismay could murder me."

Jim was watching the door, the color slowly coming back into his face. He took a plastic prescription bottle out of his shirt pocket and rolled it in his hand. Amy thought of him standing in the park, looking first at the police station and then at the house with the gray curtains, measuring the distances and whistling, waiting for Caroline to drink her milk.

"I will not let you kill her," Amy said. "I am going to save Caroline." She tried to take the poison out of his hand.

Jim put the bottle back in his shirt pocket and opened the door.

She had gone to the séance because Caroline was better and she could not be frightened by anything, even Jim's unwillingness to leave. The windows had banged open and the curtains had drifted in, flickering the candles.

Amy had thought, "He is doing something under the table." She'd looked steadily through the candles' flame at him.

"Come to us, oh spirit," Ismay said. He was sitting next to the big carved chair, but not in it. "We call you. Come to us."

It was Debra, projected somehow above the bier though she had not let go of Amy's hand. Debra made up with greasepaint and dressed in flowing white. She hovered there, her hands crossed on her breast, and then drifted toward the table.

"Welcome, spirit," Ismay said. "What message do you bring us from beyond?"

"It is very peaceful," the ghost of Debra said.

Ismay slid his hand under the table. The stars were very bright, glittering off the ice. The ship hung like a jewel against the dark sky, its lights too low in the water. "He is doing something," Amy thought. "Something to frighten me." She tried to fight it, watching the phony ghost of Debra drift to the table. The candles guttered and went out as she passed. She drifted down into the carved chair. "I bring you word from your loved ones," she said, her hands resting on the carved arms. "They are at peace."

The stern of the ship began to rise into the air. There was a terrible sound as everything began to fall: the breaking glass of the chandeliers, the tinny vibrations of the piano as it slid down the boat deck, the people screaming as they struggled to hang onto the railings. The lights went out, flickered like candles, and went out again. The stern rose higher.

"No!" Amy blurted, standing up, still holding Jim's and Debra's hands.

Ismay did something under the table and the lights came on. The ghost of Debra disappeared. They were all looking at her.

"I heard...everything started to fall...the ship...we have to save them." She was very frightened.

"Some see the dead," Ismay said. "Some hear them. You should have been on the *Californian*. They didn't hear anything until the next morning." He waved the others out of the room. He was still seated at the table. The candles had relit themselves.

"Did you know that when the *Titanic* went down, she created a great whirlpool, so that all the people who were too close to her were pulled down, too?" he said, and she had bolted past him out the door, running to find Caroline, who had sobbed and run from her.

Jim left the door open and she hurried after him, but at the head of the stairs she stopped, too frightened to go down, afraid that the parlor would already be underwater. "I must hurry. I must save Caroline," she thought. "Before all the boats are away," and she went down the slanting stairs.

They were at the table in the parlor. "Come to us, Amy," Ismay said. "We call you. Can you hear us?"

"I hear you," Amy said clearly. "You murdered me."

Ismay was not looking at her. He was watching the carved chair, and there was someone in it. "I am happy here," the ghost of Amy said. Debra made up with greasepaint, sitting with her hands easily on the carved arms. "I wish you were here with me, darling Caroline."

"No!" Amy screamed, and tried to get across the table to the image of herself, but the floor was tilting so that she could hardly stand. "Don't listen to her," Amy sobbed. "Run! Run!"

Ismay turned to Caroline. "Would you like to see your mother, dear?" he said, and Amy flung herself upon him, beating against his chest. "Murderer! Murderer!"

"We'll go see her now," he said, and he moved from the table, holding Caroline's hand.

"Nuh-oh!" Amy shouted in a hiccup of despair and swung her arm against him with a force that should have knocked him against the table, spilling the candles into pools of wax. The candles burned steadily in the still air.

"Help, police! Murder!" she screamed, scrabbling at the window latches that would not open, hammering her hands against the windows that would not break. They could not hear her. They could not see her. Not even Ismay. She dropped her hands to her sides as if they were injured.

Ismay said, "The shipbuilder knew immediately, but the captain had to be told, and even then he didn't believe it."

She turned from the window. He was not looking at her, but the words had been intended for her. "You can see me," she said.

"Oh, yes, I can see you," he said, and stepped back from the bier. They had washed off the blood. They had pulled a sheet up to her breast and crossed her hands over it to hide the wound. Of course they could not see her, wandering the halls, shouting over their voices to be heard. Of course they could not hear her. She was here, had been here all along, with her useless hands crossed over her silent breast. Of course she could not open the door.

"I cannot save Caroline," she thought, and looked for her among the women, but they were all gone. "They have put her in the boats after all," she thought.

Ismay stood by the séance table, watching her. "We are on the ice," he said, smiling a little.

"Murderer," Amy said.

"I can't hear you, you know," Ismay said. "I can tell what you are saying sometimes by watching you. The word 'murderer' comes through quite clearly. But, my dear, you do not make a sound."

She looked down at her body, at her still face that would not make any sound again.

"The dead do make a sound," Ismay said. "Like a ship going down. S.O.S. S.O.S."

Amy looked up.

"Oh, my dear, I see you hope even yet. Isn't the human soul a stubborn thing? S.O.S. Save our ship. Imagine tapping out such a message when the ship cannot be saved. The *Titanic* was dead the moment she struck the iceberg, as you were the moment after I discovered you at your prayers. But it takes some time to go down. And till the very last the wireless operator stays at his post, tapping out messages no one will hear."

There was something there, hidden in what he had said, something about Caroline.

"It is apparently a real sound, dying cells releasing their stored energy, although *I* prefer to think of it as dying cells letting go of their last hope. It's down in the subsonic range, so its uses are limited. The lovely Debra and a few hidden speakers are far more practical in the long run. But it's useful at séances, although its effect is not usually as theatrical as it was on you."

He had reached under the table. The forward funnel toppled into the water, spraying sparks. There was a deafening crash as it fell, and then the sound of screams. The ship hung against the sky, nearly on end, for a long minute, then settled back at the stern and began to slide, slowly at first, then gaining speed, into the water.

She must not let him do this to her. There was something before, about her being at her prayers when he killed her. He thought she'd been kneeling under the table to pray, but she hadn't been. She'd been looking for Caroline.

He turned the sound off. "The range is, as I said, very limited, and the wireless operator on the *Californian* shuts down at midnight, fifteen minutes before the first call."

"The *Carpathia*," Amy said.

"Ah, yes," Ismay said. "The *Carpathia*. It's true I've had the police at my door several times, but they stumbled about in the front hall among the icebergs of apology and foolish explanation for an hour or so and then went away, thinking they were in the wrong place. By then, there was not even any wreckage for them to find."

"Caroline," Amy said.

"You think I would be so foolish as to let her lead the police in here? No, she will be in no position to lead them anywhere," Ismay said, misunderstanding.

Amy thought, "I must not let him distract me." There was something about Caroline. Something important. He had killed her at her prayers. At her prayers. "Why did you kill me?" she said, making an effort to form her words clearly so he could read them.

"For the most prosaic of reasons," he said. "Your husband paid me to. It seems he wants the lovely Debra. Did you think I was vain enough to murder you for trying to find out my tricks? Snooping about under my séance table like a child looking for clues?"

"He did not see Caroline under the table," she thought. "He does not know she saw me murdered." But that meant something, and she did not know what.

"He has paid me for Caroline, too," he said, and waited for her face.

"I won't let you," Amy said.

"You won't?" he said. "My dear, you still will not give up hope, will you? I could use your body as an altar on which to murder your beloved Caroline, and you could not lift a finger to stop me."

He had been standing by the séance table. Now she saw that he was leaning casually against the door. "The end is very near. I would like to stay and watch, but I must go find Caroline. Don't worry," he said. "I will find her. All the lifeboats are away." He shut the door.

"He did not see her hiding under the table when he murdered me," Amy thought, and now the other thought followed easily, mercilessly, "She is hiding there now."

"I must lock the door," she thought, and she waded toward it across the listing room. The lock was already under water, and she had to reach down to get to it, but when her hand closed on it, she saw that it was not the lock at all. It was her own stiff hand she touched. She had not moved at all.

"The end must be very near," she thought, "because I have no hope left at all. S.O.S.," she cried out pitifully, "S.O.S."

She stood very straight by her body, not touching it, and at first the slight list was not apparent, but after a long time, she put her hands out as if to brace herself, and her hands passed through and into her body's hands, and she foundered.

Caroline let the policemen in. They had a search warrant. Caroline said clearly and without a trace of tears, "They killed my mommy," and led them to the body.

"Yes," the captain said, pulling the sheet up over Amy's face. "I know."

"We have had a tragedy here, I'm afraid," Ismay said coming into the room. "The little girl's mother..."

"Was murdered," the captain said. "While she knelt by this table. With her hands crossed on her breast." Caroline silent behind the chair, watching. Amy's lips moving as if in prayer. The sudden explosion of blood from behind her hands, and Caroline backing against the wall, the tears knocked out of her. "Murdered by you," the captain said.

"You cannot possibly know that," Ismay said.

Jim ran in. He sank to his knees by Caroline and clutched her to him. "Oh, my Caroline, they've murdered her!" he sobbed. Caroline wriggled free and went and put her hand in the captain's.

"It's no use," Ismay said. "It would seem these gentlemen have received a message."

"Caroline!" Jim said, moving threateningly toward her. "What did you tell them?"

"Caroline didn't tell them anything," Ismay said. He reached under Jim's jacket into his shirt pocket and took out the medicine bottle. He handed it to Caroline. "You have been rescued," he said to her. "All the first class children were, except for little Lorraine Allison, only six years old. But your name isn't Lorraine. It's Caroline." He looked up at the captain. "And yours, I suppose, is Captain Rostron."

"Who sent a message?" Jim said hysterically. "How?"

"I don't know," Ismay said calmly. "I doubt if even these fine policemen know, in spite of their search warrant and their familiarity with the facts of the crime. But I will wager I know what the message was," he said, watching the captain's face. "'Come at once. We have struck a berg.'"

The Horn

STEPHEN GALLAGHER

Winner of British Fantasy and International Horror Guild awards, Stephen Gallagher is described by London newspaper *The Independent* as "the finest British writer of bestselling popular fiction since le Carré." His fourteen novels include *Nightmare, with Angel*, *Red, Red Robin*, and *The Spirit Box*, along with two collections of short fiction. His most recent novel is *The Bedlam Detective*, continuing the exploits of ex-Pinkerton man Sebastian Becker, first introduced in *The Kingdom of Bones*. A third Becker novel, *The Authentic William James*, is the current work in progress.

Extract from the court record, Crown v Robson, 24th September 1987:

COUNSEL: *You lured her to this quiet spot on the pretext that you were going to run away together.*
ROBSON: *I never promised her anything.*
COUNSEL: *Then you beat her senseless and left her for dead.*
ROBSON: *Hold on, chief! I tapped her once to calm her down, that's all.*
COUNSEL: *Are you now saying that you weren't responsible for her murder?*
ROBSON: *She was fit enough when I left her.*
COUNSEL: *So how do you suppose that she died?*
ROBSON: *That wouldn't be until the next morning.*
COUNSEL: *When, exactly?*
ROBSON: *Around the time they poured the concrete in, I expect.*

• • •

"We've got heat, we've got light, we've got shelter," Mick said. "The lads even left us some dirty books. We've got everything we'll need to ride out the bad weather, so why don't we just sit tight until it all blows over?"

It was just then that the lights flickered and failed and the coal effect on the two-bar electric fire went terminally dark. The bars themselves went more slowly, and the three of us could only watch their fading glow with a kind of bleak desperation. Sub-zero winds were still hammering at the walls of the little roadside hut, and I felt about as well-protected as a mouse under a shoebox in the middle of a stampede. I was cold already. It was quickly going to get worse.

The single flame of Mick's gas lighter put giants' shadows onto the walls and ceiling. "Winds must've brought the line down," he said.

The other man, whose name was David something or other, said, "Anything we could fix?"

"Not me, pal. I'd rather live."

"What do we do, then? Burn the furniture?"

"Then we'd have nowhere to sit." The big man who'd told us to call him Mick held the flame higher, and our shadows dived for cover. "Look, there's still candles and a gas ring. Nothing's altered. We can even have a brew."

"The kettle's electric and the water pipes are frozen," David said promptly. Mick looked at him, hard.

"I could really go off you," he said. "D'you know that?"

The candles were the dim, slow-burning kind in small tin dishes, and they'd been used before. The gas ring ran from a bottle under the table, and a kinked hose gave us a momentary problem in getting it going. The candles burned yellow, the gas burned blue, and our faces were white and scared-looking in the light that resulted.

Mick, David, me. Three separate stories of blizzard and breakdown and abandoned vehicles, three lifelines that probably wouldn't otherwise have crossed but which had come together in this fragile cabin at the side of a snowbound motorway.

"Well, here goes nothing," Mick said, and he grabbed a pan and went outside to get us some snow. The one called David went over to try the dead phone yet again.

I'd been the last to find the place, and I'd known immediately on entering that these two hadn't been travelling together. They were an unmatched and probably unmatchable pair. Mick weighed in at around eighteen stones and had the look of—well, there's no kind way of putting it, a slob however you might dress and groom him. If you had to guess his line of work you might well place him as one of those vendors who stand with their push-along wagons near to football grounds, selling hamburgers and hotdogs that have the look of having been poached in bodily fluids.

David (he'd told me his second name, but it hadn't stuck in my mind) was more like one of those people you'll often see driving a company car with a spare shirt on a hanger in the back; he'd said that he was "in sales," which I took to mean that he was a salesman. He was about my own age, and had reddish-blond hair so fine that he seemed to have no eyelashes.

The story as I understood it was that Mick had been aiming for the big service area about two miles further along the road, but had found his way blocked and had been forced to abandon his vanload of rubber hose in order to walk back to the only light that he'd seen in miles; when he'd made it to the hut he'd found David already there, crouched before the electric fire with a workman's donkey jacket that he'd found and thrown around his shoulders. I'd joined them about half an hour after that, and no one had arrived since; the weather was worsening by the minute and it seemed unlikely that anybody else was going to make it through. The motorway must have been closed for some time now.

"Jesus wept!" Mick gasped when he fell back in through the door three or four minutes later; I'd thought that he'd simply intended to take two steps out to fill the pan and then return, and so I said, "What kept you?"

Some of the colour started to seep back into him as he stood over the heat of the gas ring, hands spread like he was making a blessing. He'd have made a pretty rough-looking priest. "I went down for a look at the road," he said, "just in case there was any sign of a gritter going through."

"See anything?"

"I'm lucky I even found the way back. I didn't get more than twenty yards, and it blew up so hard that I might as well have been blind. Nothing else is moving out there. Looks like we're in for the duration."

"Oh, great," David said heavily.

"You want to stick your nose outside and see for yourself," Mick suggested. "It's worse than before—it's like walking into razor blades, and I'll tell you something else. When the wind gets up in those wires, it's just like voices. You listen long enough and honest to God, you start hearing your own name. You know what I reckon?"

"What?" I said.

"It's all the dead people they've scraped up. They're all cold and lonely out there." And he winked at me as he said this, I suspect because his back was turned to David and David couldn't see.

"For Christ's sake," David muttered darkly, and he went over to the other side of the hut and started rummaging around in the cupboards for mugs and tea bags.

Mick was grinning happily now, but I wasn't exactly sure why. Lowering my voice so that David wouldn't hear me—he'd half-disappeared headfirst into one of the cupboards by now—I said, "What's all that about?"

"Haven't you seen the noticeboard?" Mick said, and he pointed to the wall behind me. "Take a look. We've found a right little Happy House to get ourselves snowed into. Desmond was reading all about it when I got here."

"It's David," corrected a muffled voice from somewhere inside the furniture and Mick said, unruffled, "Of course it is."

I picked up one of the candles and took it over to the wall where the space alongside some lockers had been papered with old newspaper clippings. There were a few yellowing Page Three girls, but the rest of them were news stories. Some had photographs, and the photographs were all of mangled wreckage. It took me a moment to realise that they were all motorway crashes, and that the stretch of motorway where they'd taken place was the one that ran by under three feet of snow right outside.

"This must be where the lads wait for a callout when there's something nasty," Mick said from just behind me. He'd come around and was inspecting the collection over my shoulder. "Some of the things they must have seen, eh? Rather them than me."

Amen to that, I thought, although even in the dim and unsteady candlelight I found that I was browsing through the details in some of the pieces with the kind of detached fascination that I always seem to be able to manage when it's a question of someone else's misery. Entire families wiped out. A teenaged girl decapitated. Lorry drivers crushed when their cabs folded around them like stepped-upon Coke cans. An unwanted mistress—this one really got me looking twice—an unwanted mistress dumped, Jimmy Hoffa-style, into the wire skeleton of a bridge piling that had been boxed-up ready to take concrete the next morning. ENTOMBED ALIVE! the headline said, but even that paled next to the disaster involving the old folks' outing and the petfood truck full of offal.

I gathered from the collection that this hut was the base for the cleanup team who worked the road for some distance in either direction, and that they took an honest pride in their gruesome occupation; I imagined them trooping out to their breakdown wagon, whistling as they pulled on their jackets and thinking about next year's holidays. And then, at the other end of the drive, getting out with their bags and shovels to give their professional attention to the loved ones of some cheapskate who'd saved the cost of a cabin on the car ferry or skipped a night in a hotel to drive on through and get an extra half-day out of the holiday flat.

Where the team would be right now, I could only guess; I imagined that they'd moved along to the service area as soon as the weather had started to clamp down, because the hut was no place to be marooned out of choice. The Services would probably be starting to resemble a refugee centre by now, cut off but reasonably self-sufficient, and I wished that I could be there instead of here. The gas ring behind us was running with the valve wide-open, and still I could see my breath in the air in front of me.

David, over by the table, said, "Did you fill this?"

I tore myself away from the interesting stuff on the wall and followed Mick over to the ring, where David was peering into the aluminium pan. Where before it had been so overfilled with snow that it had looked like a big tub of ice cream, now it held about an inch of water.

Mick observed, "It melts down to nothing, doesn't it?" And then the silence that followed was like the slow race in a restaurant to reach for the bill.

But then, finally, I said, "I'll get us some more."

I don't know how to describe the way the cold hit me as I stepped out of the hut. It was almost like walking into a wall, much worse than it had been when I'd made my way up there. The wind was the most disorienting factor, filling my eyes with hail and battering me around so hard that I could barely draw breath; but then, thankfully, it dropped a little, and the air cleared enough for me to see without being blinded.

Visibility was somewhere between fifty and a hundred yards, beyond which everything just greyed-out as if reality couldn't hold together any further. I could see about half a dozen of the overhead sodium lights marching off in either direction, their illumination blanketed and diffused by the amount of snow clouding the air; of the motorway itself I could make out the parallel lines of the crash barriers as hardly more than pencilmarks sketched onto the snow, and that was it. A few of the lightweight plastic cones that had been used earlier to close off lanes had been blown around and had lodged themselves here and there like erratic missiles, but nothing else broke the even cover.

I didn't see what Mick had been talking about. I didn't hear any voices, just the wind in the wires somewhere off the road and out of sight. The sound meant nothing special to me.

I had a Baked Bean can, catering size, that was the only other clean-looking container that I'd been able to find, and I stooped and tried to fill it with snow. The newly fallen stuff was too fine, it just streamed away as I tried to load it in, but then I tried wedging it into snowball nuggets and did rather better. I was already starting to shake with the cold. I paused for a moment to wipe at my nose with the back of my glove, and realised with a kind of awe that I couldn't even feel the contact.

I fell back into the hut like a drowning man plucked from an icy sea. I'd been outside for less than a minute.

David looked up from the phone. I wouldn't have believed how welcoming the place could look with its candlelight and comparative warmth and the road gang's mugs set out ready, each with the name of an absent person written on the side in what looked like nail varnish. I did my best to make it look as if I had a grip on myself, and went over to set the rest of the snow to melt as Mick secured the door behind me.

"Still dead?" I said to David, with a nod at the phone.

"It's not exactly dead," he said, jiggling the cradle for about the hundredth time. "It's more like an open line with nothing on the other end."

"It'll be like a field telephone," Mick said from over by the door. "If nobody's plugged in, then there's no one to hear. How's it looking outside?"

"I'd still rather be in here than out there," I said.

Mick made the tea with a catering bag and some of that non-dairy whitener that looks and smells like paint. It was the worst I'd ever tasted, and the most welcome. The three of us pulled our chairs in close to get into the circle of warmth around the gas ring, and we grew heady on the monoxide fumes. Inevitably, the conversation returned to the clippings on the wall.

"You want to see it from their point of view," Mick said. "It'll be like working in a morgue. You get bad dreams for the first few weeks and then after that, it's just another job."

"How would you know?" David said.

"I've got a brother-in-law who's a nurse, he's just about seen it all. I mean, the likes of me and you, we don't know the half of what it's about."

David didn't comment, but I suspect that by then he was starting to read something personal into everything that Mick was saying. I believed that I'd recognised his type by now. Some people's reaction to pressure is to look around for someone convenient to dump on; they get angry, they get sarcastic, and if you pull through it tends to be in spite of them rather than with much in the way of help. I knew what Mick was talking about. I could imagine the team sitting there, patiently reading or playing cards while waiting for carnage. They were one up on us...we'd go through life telling ourselves that it was never going to happen, but they knew that it would. The knowledge wasn't even anything special to them.

Mick seemed to be the one who was holding us together, here. I'm not sure that right then I'd have wanted to rely on David for anything. He was frowning at the floor, his borrowed donkey jacket sitting uneasily on his shoulders. Had he really struggled from his car to the cabin in just a suit jacket and no overcoat? He must have seen the way that the weather was going before he set out, but he didn't look as if he'd taken any account of the possibility that he might have to step much beyond the warmth of a heated building or a moving car. Some people have too much faith in everything. I'm the opposite.

I'd been heading for my girlfriend's place over in the next county when I'd come to my own unscheduled journey's end. She was with a big retail chain who were moving her around and paying her peanuts, and I was just about holding down one of those jobs that they kept telling me might or might not turn out to be something permanent. The only way that we could ever get together was at weekends, hiding out from the landlady in her one-roomed flat. Mine must have been one of the last cars to get onto the road before they'd closed it; I'd had to stop as a jackknifed articulated lorry had been cleared from the sliproad, and then it took two policemen to get me rolling again because my tyres wouldn't grip on the icy surface. They advised me to stay in low gear and to keep my revs down, and I remember their last words to me as I managed to get moving again: *Rather you than me, pal.* It got worse as I went on. After half an hour in first gear, following the crash barrier like a blind man following a rail, the temperature needle crept up into the red zone and then finally both hoses blew. I stopped and taped them and topped up the water, but the engine seized soon after that.

Mick was the only one who seemed to be listening as I told them the story. He said, "I've been driving this route since they opened it. I've never known it this bad. It looks like the end of the world."

"You've got a knack of seeing the bright side, Mick," I told him.

"You haven't seen that road train about half a mile on," he said. "A big new wagon and two trailers. It was blocking the road all the way across, that's why I had to give up and walk back to the last light I'd seen. Those things are like dinosaurs, they'll go on through anything. But it couldn't get through this. What do you reckon, Desmond?"

"It's David! *David!*" His sudden shout was startling in the enclosed space of the cabin, and I think even Mick was surprised by the reaction he got.

"All right," he said, "I'm sorry."

"Well, bloody get it right, then!"

"I said I'm sorry. I was only asking what you thought."

"I just want to get home," David said miserably, looking down at the floor again as if he was embarrassed by his sudden outburst.

And then Mick said, with unexpected gentleness, "Nothing to argue with there, Dave."

It was then that the gas ring began to make a popping sound. We all turned to look and I heard somebody say *Oh, shit,* and then I realised that it had been me.

The flame didn't exactly go out, not right away, but it was obviously into some kind of terminal struggle. Mick reached under the table and heaved out the squat metal cylinder; when he raised it two-handed and gave it a shake, there sounded to be about a cupful of liquid sloshing around in the bottom.

"There's some left," David said hopefully.

"You always get some in the bottom," Mick said. "Still means it's empty."

There was another cylinder under the table and right at the back, but this one sounded just about the same. By now the ring was giving out no heat at all and making such a racket that nobody objected when Mick turned the valve to shut it off.

The silence got to us before the cold did. But the cold started getting to us a couple of minutes later.

We broke open the lockers in the hope of finding more coats or blankets, but all that we found were tools and empty lunch buckets and mud-encrusted work boots. David's earlier remark about burning the furniture no longer seemed like a joke, but the truth of it was that there wasn't much about the furniture that was combustible; the chairs were mostly tubular steel and the table was some kind of laminate over chipboard, which left a stack of soft-core porno magazines and a few paperbacks and one deck of cards. By now, the hut had turned from a haven into an icebox.

David was the one who put it into words.

He said, "We're going to have to go out and find somewhere else, aren't we?" He made it sound as if the place itself had done a number and betrayed us. "This is great," he said bitterly. "This really puts the fucking tin lid on it."

Possibly we could have stayed put, jogged on the spot a little, done our best to keep going in the sub-zero air until the worst of the weather receded and rescue came pushing through. But Mick was already going through the lockers for a second time, as if looking again for something that he'd already seen.

"The way I see it," he said, "there's only one thing we can do."

"The Services?" I hazarded.

"We'd never make it that far. It's more than two miles and it might as well be twenty. I reckon we can do maybe a quarter of that, at the most."

"Which gets us nowhere," David said.

"It gets us as far as that big road train that's blocking the carriageway." So saying, Mick reached into the third locker and came out with a short, hooked wrecking bar. Holding up the jemmy he went on, "If we can get into that and get its engine running, we can sit tight in the cab with the heater on."

"Until the fuel runs out," I said, probably a touch too pessimistically.

"Those things never run out. They've got tanks like swimming pools. We can either wait for the snowplough to find us or else strike out again as the weather improves. What do you think?"

"It'll have a radio," David said, with a sense of discovery that seemed to surprise even him.

We both looked at him.

"A CB radio," he said. "Don't most of these big trucks carry them? We can tell someone where we are."

"That we can, Dave," Mick said with a note of approval, and then he looked from him to me. "Are you game?"

"Let's go," I said, sounding about four hundred per cent more eager than I felt. But Mick raised a hand as if to say, slow down.

"Just wait on a minute," he said. "There's no point in all of us scrambling out together. What I reckon is, one of us strikes out and does the necessary, and then he sounds the horn as a signal for the others to follow."

"I wouldn't know what to do," David said bleakly.

"Me neither," I said.

"Well," Mick said, "since we're talking about breaking and entering and a little creative rewiring, I'd say that I'm the only one with the education in the appropriate subjects around here. Am I right?"

He was right, and as far as I was concerned he could make all the jibes about education that he wanted as long as he got us out of this. He turned up his collar and buttoned up his coat, and he pulled on his sheepskin gloves as I moved with him to the door. David decided to give the phone yet another try as I made ready to let Mick out into the unwelcoming night.

I said, "You're mad, you know that?"

"I had my brain surgically removed," Mick said. "I've been feeling much better without it." Then he turned serious. "I'm going to get down to the crash barrier and follow it along, otherwise there's no knowing where I may end up. Keep listening for the horn." He glanced at David. "And keep an eye on him."

"He'll be all right."

"If he messes you about, dump him. I mean it."

There was a blast of cold air for the brief second or so between Mick going out and me getting the door closed after him, and this time it stayed in there with us like some unwelcome dog that had dashed in and was standing its ground. David had slammed the phone down with a curse, as if its non-co-operation was a matter of deliberate choice, before settling on one of the chairs with his hands thrust deep into the pockets of his borrowed coat and the collar up over his nose to recirculate the heat of his breath. He looked like some odd kind of animal retreating into its blue worsted shell.

"I heard what he said, you know." His voice was muffled by the thick material, and sounded distant.

"He didn't mean anything by it."

"Yeah, I bet. And who does he think he is? Scott of the Antarctic?"

"I don't care if he's Scotty of the *Enterprise*. If he gets us out of trouble he'll be okay by me."

He settled in deeper. "Well, don't go worrying about me. I'm no dead-weight."

"Never said I thought you were."

There was silence for a while.

Then he said, "Pretty serious, though, isn't it?"

Yes, I was thinking, it was pretty serious...but it could have been worse. Worse was being sliced in two at a combined speed of a hundred and fifty miles an hour, just because someone else chose the day of your trip to cross the central reservation and come looking for suicide in the oncoming traffic. Worse was being buried alive in concrete, so deep that even X-rays couldn't find you. It was sitting with your hands on the wheel while your head lay on the back seat. It was any one of the fifty or so examples of a messy and uncontrolled exit to be found in the road gang's private Black Museum over there on the wall.

"We've still got options," I said. "That puts us one step ahead."

"As long as he makes it," David said.

The next twenty or thirty minutes seemed to last forever. David wasn't great company, particularly after the way that Mick's parting words had stung him. I wondered what I ought to expect; more of the ball-and-chain act, or would he become dangerously gung-ho? If the latter, then I was going to be happy to let him go out first.

Finally, the wind dropped a little and we heard the distant sound of a horn.

I said, with some relief, "Our call, I think."

David said that he was ready. I asked him if he wanted to take one last shot at the phone, but he said no.

"The greaseball was right in one thing," he said. "You listen for long enough, and you do start to hear them calling your name."

I let him go out ahead of me.

My spirit of optimism took an instant hammering as the door was banging shut behind us; compared to this brutal storm, the wind that had set the wires keening on my last excursion had been a precise and delicate instrument. All sound and sense was destroyed on contact, and I was beginning to panic when I felt David's rough grip on my arm, shoving me forward into the blind haze. The snow had drifted high in places, masking the contours of the ground beneath and making progress even more difficult; we stumbled and floundered downhill toward the road surface, and as we descended from the more exposed slopes the wind mercifully lessened. We got across to the central crash barrier, a constant mist of snow streaming from its knife-edged top, but by then I'd become as disoriented as if I'd been popped into a box and shaken.

"Which way?" I shouted, and David had to put his face right up to my ear to make himself heard.

"Northbound!" he roared.

"What?"

"This way!" And he gave me a hard push to get me moving.

I wouldn't have believed how heavy the going could be. It went from thigh-deep to waist-deep and then back to thigh-deep again, and the barrier disappeared for entire stretches so that we had to navigate by the yellow sodium lights above us. I'd break the trail for a while, and then David would move up and replace me. Any tracks that Mick might have left had been obliterated, but then there was the sound of the distant horn to lead us on whenever the storm took out a beat to let it through.

He'd made it. So would I.

I reckoned that we'd been going for about three hours, although a more rational part of my mind knew that it had actually been closer to fifteen minutes, when we reached the first place where we could stop and rest. It was a flyover bridge, too high and too wide to feel like much of a shelter but offering a respite from the cutting edge of the wind. We staggered in so all-over numb that we might as well have been on Novocaine drips for the last quarter hour, and we collapsed against the wall like footsoldiers in some forgotten war.

"Are you okay?" I said to David, my voice oddly flattened by the carpet of snow that had blown in under the bridge.

"You must be fucking joking," he gasped, and that was all I could get out of him.

I tried to knock off some of the dry snow that had crusted onto my clothing. I didn't want to risk any of it melting and soaking through only to refreeze as we pushed on. It came off in chunks. David was hunkered down and hugging himself, presenting as small an area for heat loss as he could. If we stayed here for too long, we might end up staying here for good.

I listened for the horn.

Even though the bridge was open at the sides there was an enclosed, somehow isolated feeling about that few yards of shelter; it was brighter here than outside because there was nothing clouding the air between the sodium lights and the reflecting snow and, as I'd already noticed when I'd spoken to David, sounds went dead as if they'd run into something soft. There was scaffolding around the bridge support across the carriageway, but I could still make out the spraycanned graffiti in amongst the repair work behind it as if through a grid; it read ROBSON YOUR DEAD WHEN YOU GET OUT, and it had been written in red. My favourite graffiti was one that I'd seen on a beachfront building, the simple and elegant I FEEL A BIT NORMAL TODAY, but it was a beachfront that seemed about a million miles away from the here and now.

The wind outside must have dropped a little because a snatch of the horn came through, and it sounded closer than ever. It acted on David like a goad. He suddenly lurched to his feet and set out again, stumbling and flailing his arms as if he hadn't quite brought his limbs under control yet. Wearily, I wondered if I'd ever be able to raise the energy to follow; but even as I was wondering, I was starting to move. David was muttering as he went, but I couldn't hear anything of what he was saying.

I stumbled, because there seemed to be all kinds of jumbled crap under the snow here; my foot hooked up what looked like a length of compressor hose, and I had to kick it off. Over on what would normally be the hard shoulder I could see the half-buried shapes of machinery, big generators with tow-hitches and a small dumper that might have been the answer to our prayers if it hadn't been jacked-up with a wheel missing. It looked as if, until the bad weather had intervened, they'd been drilling out the concrete like a bad tooth; canvas on the scaffolding had concealed the work, but the canvas had been ripped by a through-wind to leave only a few flapping shreds around the hole. The cage of reinforcing wire inside the piling had been exposed, and the wire had been burst outward as if by a silent explosion. It looked as if they'd gone so far, and then the freeze-up had enlarged the hole further.

I suppose I could have thought about it harder. But there are some things, you can think about them as hard as you like but you'll never anticipate what you're actually going to see.

And the sight that I was concentrating on, to the exclusion of just about everything else, was that of the road train firming-up in the blizzard about a hundred yards ahead.

The first details that I made out were its hazard lights, and there were plenty of them; almost enough to define its shape, rather like those diagrams that take a scattered handful of stars and connect them up into some improbable-looking constellation. They were flashing on and off in time with the horn, and they were about the most welcome warning that I'd ever seen. Ahead of me, David was striding out like a wind-up toy that nothing could stop.

It was a big Continental articulated rig in three jackknifed sections, a true monster of the road that would look like a landslide on the move. The distant *parp-parp* that had led us so far had now become a deep, regular airhorn bellow as we'd drawn closer. David tried to break into a run for the cab, but he had to be close to exhaustion by now.

We helped each other up and in. An alarm beeper was sounding off inside the cab and in synchronisation with the horn and the lights. There was no sign of Mick anywhere.

I said, "Where is he?"

"God knows," David said, studying a dash that looked like a piece of the Space Shuttle. "He might at least have left the engine running."

"Maybe he didn't get that far."

But David pointed to a bunch of wires that had been pulled out to hang behind the steering column. "What's that, then?" he said. "Heinz spaghetti? You check the radio."

I checked the radio.

"I don't think it's working," I said.

Sixty seconds after our entry, the alarms cut and the horn stopped. The silence almost hurt.

David had found the starter by now, and he was trying it; the first couple of times it stayed dead, but he jiggled the hanging wires like a child patting a balloon into the air and this must have helped some weak connection, because on the third attempt the engine somewhere beneath the cab floor turned over without any hesitation at all. After a few seconds, it caught; but then, almost immediately, it faded away and died again.

"Bastard thing," David said, and tried again; but there was no persuading it to catch for a second time.

He flopped back heavily in the driver's seat. I said, "Maybe we can just stay here anyway."

"There's still no heat," he said. "It may seem warmer, but that's just the comparison with being outside. If we can't get the blowers going, I don't see any advantage over being back in the hut."

He tried the starter again, but still nothing.

"There's your reason why," he said suddenly, and pointed to a part of the dashboard display. If what he was pointing to was the fuel level readout, it was reading something like empty.

"*These things never run out*," he said bitterly, in what I assume he intended to be mimicry of Mick's voice. "*They've got tanks like swimming pools*." And he punched the steering wheel hard, and flopped back in the driver's seat again with a face as dark as a bruised plum.

And somewhere out in the night, another horn began to sound.

We both listened, lost it for a while as the wind howled, and then heard it again. Our signal was being repeated from somewhere further along the road.

"Here we go," David said wearily, and he opened the door on the far side of the cab to climb down. This time he didn't even flinch when the hail hit him. All right, I wanted to say, Case proven, you're no deadweight, now why don't we just try sticking it out here a while longer, but instead I levered myself up and clambered awkwardly across the cab. I could have dropped and slept, right there. And probably died, ready-chilled and prepared for the morgue, but at that moment I hardly felt as if it would matter.

Mick's sheepskin gloves were on the cab floor.

I reached down and picked them up. I wasn't hallucinating them, they were real enough. He must have taken them off for the delicate work of hotwiring...but how come he'd allowed himself to be parted from them? I was wearing my clumsy ski gloves, and even inside these my hands were feeling dead from the knuckles out. If Mick had gone the distance to the next stranded lorry, as the sounding of this second horn seemed to suggest, then I reckoned that he'd better not be planning any piano practice for a while.

I slid out of the cab and hit the snow again. I was now on the northern side of the big vehicle. David had launched off without me, hooked by the call like some deep-sea fish being drawn up to the gaffe. The horn wasn't so regular this time, but it was coming through more clearly.

And me, I wasn't happy.

The forgotten gloves were only one part of it. Another part of it was the fact that you didn't put a rig and its cargo, total value anything from a quarter of a million up, into the hands of a driver who's going to be walking the hard shoulder with a can to get some diesel because he let the tanks get empty. And the radio—the radio should have been working, even if only to give out white noise to match the scene on the other side of the glass.

I was looking around the side of the road train when I fell over Mick's body in the snow. He was lying face-down and already he was half covered by drift, which for a moment gave me the absurd hope that he might have been insulated from the chilling effect of the wind and might be basically okay. But when I tried to turn him over he was as stiff as a wet sheet hung out in winter, and when I finally got him onto his back I could see that there was a spike of reinforcing wire from the concrete flyover driven right up under his chin. I could see it passing up through his open mouth as if his head were something spitted for a barbecue. His eyes were half-open, but plugged with ice. The short jemmy was still in his ungloved hand, held tightly like a defensive weapon that he'd never managed to use.

This had happened right by the big diesel tanks behind the cab. The tanks themselves had been slashed open so that all the oil had run out and gone straight down into the snow. And when I say slashed, I mean raked open in four parallel lines as if by fingernails, not just spiked or holed by something sharp.

David had stopped, and was looking back; but he was too far away to see anything and only just on the verge of being seen, a smudgy ghost painted in smoke. He beckoned me on with a big, broad gesture that looked like he was trying to hook something out of the air, and even though I yelled *"No! Don't go! That isn't him!,"* he simply shouted back something inaudible and turned away. He walked on, and the blizzard sucked him in.

And from somewhere beyond him came the sound of the horn, the mating call of some dark mistress of nightmares with her skin oiled and her back arched and her long silver knives at the ready.

I started to run after him.

I call it running, although it wasn't much in the way of progress. I reckon you could have lit up a small town with the energy that I burned just to close up the distance between David and me. Close it up I did, but not enough. He didn't even glance back. I saw him duck at a near-miss from something windborne and I felt my heart stop for a moment, but I think it was only one of the plastic cones or some other piece of road debris. David couldn't have been distracted by nuns dancing naked in the air by that stage, because he was now within sight of the next truck.

The truck.

It was much older than the first one, and not so much of a giant. It was over on the far side of the barrier and facing my way; it looked as if it had come to a long, sliding halt before being abandoned and half-buried where it stood. It had a crouched, malevolent look, its engine running and breathing steam, pale headlamps like sickbed eyes. David reached the cab and pounded on the side to be let in, and I stopped at the crash barrier and could only watch.

The horn ceased. The door opened. The cab's interior light blinked on, but the insides of the windows were all steamed up and runny and there was only the vague shape of someone visible. David had already hoisted himself halfway up with his foot in the stirrup over the wheel, but now I saw him hesitate. The door had swung out and was screening whatever confronted him...and then suddenly he was gone, jerked in at an impossible speed, and the door was slammed and the light went out. I winced at the loud, long and intense muffled screaming that began to come from the cab, but I knew there was nothing that I could do. I thought about those long slashes in the diesel tank and, for David's sake, I could only hope that whatever was happening would be over quickly.

It wasn't.

And when it finally ended, and after the long silence that followed, I saw the door opening out a crack like a trap being reset. Light streamed out into the snow-mist, a narrow slice falling like a rain of something solid. I looked up at the truck's windows and saw that the now-lit windshield had been sprayed red on the inside like the jug of a blender, and it was just starting a slow wash-down as the cab sweat began to trickle through it. I watched a while longer, but I couldn't see anything moving.

I was calculating my chances of making it through to the service area. What had seemed like a complete impossibility before now had the look of the most attractive available option. I had to have covered a good part of the distance already, didn't I? And having just had a glimpse of the alternative, I was suddenly finding that the prospect of pressing on had a certain appeal.

The first move would be to cross the carriageway and put as much distance as possible between me and the truck. There was nothing that I could do for David now, and it made no sense to stay out where the overhead lights made a tunnel of day through the blizzard. It was as I was striking out at an angle across a field of white that had once been the fast lane, a stumbling and deep-frozen body with a white-hot core of fear, that the horn began again.

That was okay, that suited me fine. As long as somebody was leaning on the button then they weren't out here with me, and that was exactly the way that I wanted it. I was trying to remember the route from the times that I'd driven it before; my guess was that I was just about to come to an exposed and elevated curve that would swing out to overlook a reservoir before entering the hills where the service area would be sheltered. I wouldn't be able to see much, if any, of this, but I'd know it because the intensity of the wind was bound to increase; high-sided vehicles took a battering on this stretch at the best of times. I'd have to watch my footing. On a clear night I'd have been able to see right out to the lights of some mill town several miles out and below, but for now all that I could see was a dense white swirling. In my mind I could see myself holding one of those Christmas-scene paperweights, the kind that you shake and then watch as the contents settle, but in mine there was a tiny figure of David hammering on the glass and calling soundlessly to be let out. I saw myself shaking the globe once, and I saw the storm turn pink.

Stupid, I know—I wasn't responsible for anybody, and I certainly hadn't got behind him and boosted him up into the arms of whatever had been waiting in the cab. But I suppose that when you've just seen somebody meet an end roughly comparable to the act of walking into an aircraft propeller, it's bound to overheat your imagination just a little. Maybe that could explain some of what came later.

But somehow, I don't think so.

The truck horn was starting to recede behind me. The notes were longer now, like the moan of some trapped beast tiring of its struggles. Great, fine, I was thinking, you just stay there and keep at it, when the storm brightened and a dark figure suddenly rose before me.

It was my own shadow, cast forward into the blizzard way out beyond the edge of the road so that it seemed to stand in the air over nothing. I looked back and saw that there was some kind of a spotlight being operated from the cab of the truck, the kind that turns on a mount fixed to the body and stays however you leave it. This one was pointing straight at me; it went on past, and I realised that I was too small and too far away to spot with any ease. And there was probably so much snow sticking to me on the windward side that I'd be tough to spot even at close range.

Any relief that I felt was short-lived, though, because just a few seconds later the spotlight picked up the line of my trail through the snowfield. The bright light and the low angle exaggerated it and left no room for any doubt. The light stopped roving, and the horn stopped sounding only a moment later.

There followed a silence that I didn't like, filled with unstated menace.

And then the cab door opened, and its occupant stepped down to the road.

I don't know what I'd been expecting. Anything but this. She was small, and slight. Her light summer dress was torn and soiled and her hair was lank and dusty and blowing across her face. Her arms were bare, but she seemed oblivious to the cold and the wind. She started out toward the point where my trail angled out across the road, and I knew that I ought to be turning and running but I couldn't come unglued. She was walking barefoot on the snow and leaving no mark; I saw her bend to touch the barrier as she stepped over, and it might have been a stile out in the countryside somewhere in the warmest part of the spring.

I finally turned to run. I got a brief impression of another of those plastic cones tumbling by in the wind, and then it bopped me as I walked right into it. I went down. I tried to struggle to get up but it was as if I'd had my wires pulled and crossed so that none of the messages were getting through in the right order.

I could hear her light tread over the wind as she approached.

She came up and stood right over me. Her skin was as white as marble, and veined with blue; I couldn't see her face for the halo of light from the cab spotlight behind her. All I could see was her ruined hair blowing around a pitiless darkness in which something was watching me.

Louie, she whispered.

Louie? I thought. Who's Louie? Because it sure isn't me. I opened my mouth to say something similar and I think I made one tiny, almost inaudible croak. The wind dropped and the night grew still, and then it was like her eyes turned on like blazing torches in the ravaged pit of her face as she bent down toward me, and I could feel their heat and the breath of corruption warming my frostbitten skin. I could see now that her hair was matted with concrete, and that patches of it had been torn out. The exposed skin was like that of a plucked grouse that had been hanging in a cellar for far too long a time.

Louie, she said again, this time with a kind of nightmare tenderness, and she took hold of my dead-feeling face in her dead-looking hands and I realised with terror that she was raising me up for a kiss. I saw the darkness roaring in like an airshaft straight down to hell and I wanted to scream, but instead I think I just peed myself.

She stopped only inches away. She lowered me again. I think she'd just realised that I wasn't the one she was looking for.

Then she raised her hand and I saw the state of her fingers, and I knew how she'd caused the damage that she'd done to the diesel tank. I shut my eyes because I knew that this was going to be it. I stayed with my eyes shut and I waited and I waited, and after I'd waited for what seemed like the entire running time of *Conan the Barbarian* I managed to unstick one eye and look up.

She was still there, but she wasn't looking at me. She seemed to be listening for something. I listened too, but all I could hear was the wind in the wires overhead.

And then, only once and very faintly, the single blast of a horn.

Louie? she said. And she started to rise.

Most of what I know now is what I've learned since. Louis Robson was a construction services manager who drove a Mercedes, and she was a supermarket checkout trainee. How she ever believed that he'd desert his wife and run away with her will be one of those eternal mysteries like, why do old cars run better when they've been washed and waxed; but he must have made the promise one time and she must have replayed it over and over until finally, he told her to meet him one night with her bags packed and a goodbye-don't-look-for-me letter ready to mail. The place where she was to wait was one of his company's site offices by the new motorway; he'd pull in outside and sound the all clear on the car's horn. Except that it was a signal that she would have to wait a long time to hear because when she got there, he was already waiting in the dark with a lug wrench. He dropped her unconscious body into a prepared mould for a bridge piling and threw her cardboard suitcase after, and then he put the sealed letter into the post without realising that it mentioned him by name. This was all five years before.

I don't know if it was just the signal, or whether there was room for anything beyond obsession in the dark, tangled worm-pit of what was left of her mind; but she lurched stiffly upright and then, like a dead ship drawn to some distant beacon, she set off in what she thought was the direction of the sound.

The blade of the snowplough hit her square-on as she stepped out into the road.

She wasn't thrown; it was more like she exploded under gas pressure from within, a release of the bottled-up forces of five years' worth of corruption. She went up like an eyeball in a vacuum chamber, and the entire blade and windshield of the plough were sprayed with something that stuck like tar and stank like ordure. Rags of foul hide were flung over a hundred-yard radius, showering down onto the snow with a soft pattering sound. The destruction was so complete that nothing would ever be pieced together to suggest anything remotely human. The plough had stopped and I could see men in orange Day-Glo overjackets climbing out, stunned and uncertain of what they'd seen, and I managed to get up to my knees and to wave my arms over my head.

"Anybody else with you?" they asked me when we were all inside and I was holding a thermos cup of coffee so hot that it could have blanched meat. "No sign of anybody?"

I'd told them that I'd seen some kind of a bird fly into the blade, and it had all happened so fast that nobody had a better story to offer. They'd told me their names, and I'd recognised them from the tea mugs back in the hut that they'd been forced to abandon as a base for a while. I said that I hadn't seen anybody else. Then one of them asked me how long I'd been out there and I said, it seemed like forever.

"You know the police have jacked it in and closed the road for the night," one of them said. "We wouldn't have come out at all if it hadn't been for somebody hearing your horn solo one time when the wind dropped. You've got no idea how lucky you are."

I raised my face out of the steam. We all swayed as the big chained wheels turned the snow into dirt beneath us as we swung around for the return journey, and somebody put a hand out to the seat in front to steady himself. They'd find Mick and David when the thaw set in, and I'd say that I didn't know a damn thing about either of them. And did I really have no idea of how lucky I was?

"No," I said pleasantly. "I don't expect I do."

And I thought, You really want to bet?

Everybody Goes

MICHAEL MARSHALL SMITH

Michael Marshall Smith is a bestselling novelist and screenwriter, writing under several different names. His first novel, *Only Forward*, won the August Derleth and Philip K. Dick awards. *Spares* and *One of Us* were optioned for film by DreamWorks and Warner Brothers, and the Straw Men trilogy—*The Straw Men*, *The Lonely Dead*, and *Blood of Angels*—were international bestsellers. His Steel Dagger-nominated novel *The Intruders* is currently in series development with the BBC. His most recent novels are *Bad Things* and *The Servants*, the latter, a short novel published under the new pseudonym M. M. Smith.

He is a three-time winner of the British Fantasy Award for short fiction, and his stories are collected in two volumes: *What You Make It* and *More Tomorrow & Other Stories* (which won the International Horror Guild Award).

You can find more information about him and his work at: http://www.michaelmarshallsmith.com.

I saw a man yesterday. I was coming back from the waste ground with Matt and Joey and we were calling Joey dumb because he'd seen this huge spider and he thought it was a black widow or something when it was just, like, a *spider*, and I saw the man.

We were walking down the road towards the block and laughing and I just happened to look up and there was this man down the end of the street, tall, walking up towards us. We turned off the road before he got to us, and I forgot about him.

Anyway, Matt had to go home then because his family eats early and his mom raises hell if he isn't back in time to wash up and so I just hung out for a while with Joey and then he went home too. Nothing much happened in the evening.

This morning I got up early because we were going down to the creek for the day and it's a long walk. I made some sandwiches and put them in a bag, and I grabbed an apple and put that in too. Then I went down to knock on Matt's door.

His mom answered and let me in. She's okay really, and quite nice-looking for a mom, but she's kind of strict. She's the only person in the world who calls me Peter instead of Pete. Matt's room always looks like it's just been tidied, which is quite cool actually though it must be a real pain to keep up. At least you know where everything is.

We went down and got Joey. Matt seemed kind of quiet on the way down as if there was something he wanted to tell me, but he didn't. I figured that if he wanted to, sooner or later he would. That's how it is with best friends. You don't have to be always talking. The point will come round soon enough.

Joey wasn't ready so we had to hang round while he finished his breakfast. His dad's kind of weird. He sits and reads the paper at the table and just grunts at it every now and then. I don't think I could eat breakfast with someone who did that. I think I would find it disturbing. Must be something you get into when you grow up, I guess.

Anyway, *finally* Joey was ready and we left the block. The sun was pretty hot already though it was only nine in the morning and I was glad I was only wearing a T shirt. Matt's mom made him wear a sweatshirt in case there was a sudden blizzard or something and I knew he was going to be pretty baked by the end of the day but you can't tell moms anything.

As we were walking away from the block towards the waste ground I looked back and I saw the man again, standing on the opposite side of the street, looking at the block. He was staring up at the top floor and then I thought he turned and looked at us, but it was difficult to tell because the sun was shining right in my eyes.

We walked and ran through the waste ground, not hanging around much because we'd been there yesterday. We checked on the fort but it was still there. Sometimes other kids come and mess it up but it was okay today.

Matt got Joey a good one with a scrunched-up leaf. He put it on the back of his hand when Joey was looking the other way and then he started staring at it and saying "Pete..." in this really scared voice; and I saw what he was doing and pretended to be scared too and Joey bought it.

"I told you," he says—and he's backing away—"I *told* you there was black widows..." and we could have kept it going but I started laughing. Joey looked confused for a second and then he just grunted as if he was reading his dad's paper and so we jumped on him and called him Dad all afternoon.

We didn't get to the creek till nearly lunch time, and Matt took his sweatshirt off and tied it round his waist. It's a couple miles from the block, way past the waste ground and out into the bush. It's a good creek though. It's so good we don't go there too often, like we don't want to wear it out.

You just walk along the bush, not seeing anything, and then suddenly there you are, and there's this baby canyon cut into the earth. It gets a little deeper every year, I think, except when there's no rain. Maybe it gets deeper then too, I don't know. The sides are about ten feet deep and this year there was rain so there's plenty of water at the bottom and you have to be careful climbing down because otherwise you can slip and end up in the mud.

Matt went down first. He's best at climbing, and really quick. He went down first so that if Joey slipped he might not fall all the way in. For me, if Joey slips, he slips, but Matt's good like that. Probably comes from having such a tidy room.

Joey made it down okay this time, hold the front page, and I went last. The best way to get down is to put your back to the creek, slide your feet down, and then let them go until you're hanging onto the edge of the canyon with your hands. Then you just have to scuttle. As I was lowering myself down I noticed how far you could see across the plain, looking right along about a foot up from the ground. There's nothing to see for miles, nothing but bushes and dust. I think the man was there too, off in the distance, but it was difficult to be sure and then I slipped and nearly ended up in the creek myself, which would have been a real pain and Joey would have gone on about it forever.

We walked along the creek for a while and then came to the ocean. It's not really the ocean, it's just a bit where the canyon widens out into almost a circle that's about fifteen feet across. It's deeper than the rest of the creek, and the water isn't so clear, but it's really cool. When you're down there you can't see anything but this circle of sky, and you know there's nothing else for miles around. There's this old door there which we call our ship and we pull it to one side of the ocean and we all try to get on and float it to the middle. Usually it's kind of messy and I know Matt and Joey are thinking there's going to be trouble when their moms see their clothes, but today we somehow got it right and we floated right to the middle with only a little bit of water coming up.

We played our game for a while and then we just sat there for a long time and talked and stuff. I was thinking how good it was to be there and there was a pause and then Joey tried to say something of his own like that. It didn't come out very well, but we knew what he meant so we told him to shut up and made as if we were going to push him in. Matt pretended he had a spider on his leg just by suddenly looking scared and staring and Joey laughed, and I realised that that's where jokes come from. It was our own joke, that no one else would ever understand and that they would never forget however old they got.

Matt looked at me one time, as if he was about to say what was on his mind, but then Joey said something dumb and he didn't. We just sat there and kept talking about things and moving around so we didn't get burnt too bad. Once when I looked up at the rim of the canyon I thought maybe there was a head peeking over the side but there probably wasn't.

Joey has a watch and so we knew when it was four o'clock. Four o'clock is the latest we can leave so that Matt gets back for dinner in time. We walked back towards the waste ground, not running. The sun had tired us out and we weren't in any hurry to get back because it had been a good afternoon, and they always finish when you split up. You can't get back to them the next day, especially if you try to do the same thing again.

When we got back to the street we were late and so Matt and Joey ran on ahead. I would have run with them but I saw that the man was standing down the other side of the block, and I wanted to watch him to see what he was going to do. Matt waited back a second after Joey had run and said he'd see me after dinner. Then he ran, and I just hung around for a while.

The man was looking back up at the block again, like he was looking for something. He knew I was hanging around, but he didn't come over right away, as if he was nervous. I went and sat on the wall and messed about with some stones. I wasn't in any hurry.

"Excuse me," says this voice, and I looked up to see the man standing over me. The slanting sun was in his eyes and he was shading them with his hand. He had a nice suit on and he was younger than people's parents are, but not much. "You live here, don't you?"

I nodded, and looked up at his face. He looked familiar.

"I used to live here too," he said, "when I was a kid. On the top floor." Then he laughed, and I recognised him from the sound. "A long time ago now. Came back after all these years to see if it had changed."

I didn't say anything.

"Hasn't much, still looks the same." He turned and looked again at the block, then back past me towards the waste ground. "Guys still playing out there on the 'ground?"

"Yeah," I said, "it's cool. We have a fort there."

"And the creek?"

He knew we still played there: he'd been watching. I knew what he really wanted to ask, so I just nodded. The man nodded too, as if he didn't know what to say next. Or more like he knew what he wanted to say, but didn't know how to go about it.

"My name's Tom Spivey," he said, and then stopped. I nodded again. The man laughed, embarrassed. "This is going to sound very weird, but...I've seen you around today, and yesterday." He laughed again, running his hand through his hair, and then finally asked what was on his mind. "Your name isn't Pete, by any chance?"

I looked up into his eyes, then away.

"No," I said. "It's Jim."

The man looked confused for a moment, then relieved. He said a couple more things about the block, and then he went away. Back to the city, or wherever.

After dinner I saw Matt out in the back car park, behind the block. We talked about the afternoon some, so he could get warmed up, and then he told me what was on his mind.

His family was moving on. His dad had got a better job somewhere else. They'd be going in a week.

We talked a little more, and then he went back inside, looking different somehow, as if he'd already gone.

I stayed out, sitting on the wall, thinking about missing people. I wasn't feeling sad, just tired. Sure I was going to miss Matt. He was my best friend. I'd missed Tom for a while, but then someone else came along. And then someone else, and someone else. There's always new people. They come, and then they go. Maybe Matt would return some day. Sometimes they do come back. But everybody goes.

Transfigured Night

RICHARD BOWES

Richard Bowes has published seven books and fifty short stories. He has won two World Fantasy Awards, an International Horror Guild Award and a Million Writers Award. In 2013 he has four books coming out: his Lambda Award-winning novel, *Minions of the Moon* will be reprinted by Lethe Press; Lethe will also publish a new novel *Dust Devil on a Quiet Street*; Aqueduct Press will bring out a modern fairy tale collection *The Queen, the Cambion and Seven Others*; and Fairwood Press will release *If Angels Fight*, which includes the eponymous World Fantasy Award-winning novelette and thirteen other stories. His web page is: rickbowes.com.

"I remember this street, this house," the one she calls the Guest tells Frieda. She stands in her big, tile-floored kitchen kneading dough. Outside the windows, beyond the screened porch, summer light pours down on hollyhocks in the back yard. "I lived around here till I was fourteen," he says and touches the pocket of his denim jacket, feels the small leather sack and the relic inside it. When he does, a tingling in his spine, a tightness at the bottom of his stomach, confirm that here, on re-gentrified Sears Hill, twenty minutes by Red Line from downtown Boston, all the conditions exist to complete a magic circle.

She looks out the window at tree-shaded, rambling, turn-of-the-century houses just like hers. "This must have been a great neighborhood to grow up in, it's like where the family lived in *Father Knows Best* or something. I can't believe we own this."

Frieda was raised rootless on army bases all over Western Europe and the American South. "And I can't believe I'm seeing you again and that my street is where you were born. You were always so mysterious, even about your name. That's why we started calling you the Guest, remember?"

He smiles at the name and doesn't explain to her that Sears Avenue at the top of the hill was the best street in the neighborhood. Back when his father was working his way through the maze of city government, they lived in a small house close to the subway and Cray Square. His parents' big ambition was to be able to move. He'd felt like a guest in the neighborhood even when he lived here.

She asks, "Is there anyone still around that you know?"

"I know a guy called Ron who I'm sure is still around." Frieda is going to ask more, but the Guest distracts her by saying, "The gray house at the end of this block is haunted, a place they dared you to go on Halloween. A couple of crazy old women lived there. One of them took a shot at the bunch of us once with an old pistol her father had brought back from the Civil War. One kid, Chicky Boyle, got grazed in the shoulder and had to go to the hospital. I think he ended up as a cop."

She smiles, liking that, the ghosts, the local history, the insight into his past. Her smile, just as he remembers, narrows her eyes, creases the skin above them, gives her a wicked look. Frieda brushes back a strand of loose, honey-colored hair from her forehead.

He made up the story of the old lady and the pistol right on the spot. The atmosphere he's trying for is nostalgia slightly tinged with mystery. He wants to remind Frieda of when she was young and going to Radcliff and he came through her life a few times a year bringing unorthodox excitement, a whiff of danger. To remind himself of why he's there, the Guest touches the pocket, feels the sack and the finger inside it and knows he's coming home.

"This is going in the oven now," Frieda tells him, opening the door, sticking in the bread. It's a parent's habit, he realizes, to announce what you're doing as you do it. From upstairs comes the sound of children, Jesse, age five, and one of her little friends at play. Three-year-old Calvin, the other child, is watching *Sesame Street*. There is an au pair, a blond young woman from Finland. He wonders if she's going to be a problem.

"Let's sit outside for a little while," Frieda says. "Jas should be home soon and I could use an ice tea. Do you want a beer?"

"Tea is fine, if you have it." He stands up, hooks his thumbs in his jeans pockets like the kid he once was, the hustler he's sometimes been.

Frieda catches that as she pours amber tea out of a plastic pitcher from the fridge. She brushes her bare arm against his bare wrist and says, "I can't get over how good you look."

Eroticism is part of the mood he wants to create, but establishing that seemed to be no problem. "You're doing just fine yourself," he says, looking her up and down, winking when he catches her eye. As always, Frieda feels a little something lacking in her life with Jason.

Out on the porch, shaded from the summer sun, they listen to lazy Tuesday afternoon sounds, a lawn mower two yards over, a short burst from a car radio passing down Sears Avenue. She's wearing a t-shirt and tennis shorts. Her long legs, firm and tanned, are stretched out in front of her. "Tell me about this neighborhood when you were growing up," she says. "We've only been here a couple of years. It so...." She pauses for the polite word. "So polarized. Blacks and Spanish at the bottom of the hill, white preppies up on the top."

"This part of Dorchester was all white and Catholic. I noticed just now that the trade school down in Cray Square is a Family Planning and Community Health Center. We had none of that back then." He smiles as he talks and insects buzz and both of them listen for the sound of Jason coming home.

As he embroiders old tales of derring-do, of dodging homicidal nuns and re-enacting cowboy movies in vacant lots, he thinks back to what must have been the summer of '58. That's when he was ten and had lost his best friend. Summer vacation then was another country. July stretched like a prairie. A buddy moved several neighborhoods away and it was as if he'd fallen off the edge of the world. Adults, parents in particular, were the natural forces, their whims as devastating as hurricanes or forest fires.

Bobby's family had moved to Quincy at the start of that summer. Each kid was too tough to let on how much it hurt. So neither set of parents thought to let the two boys visit or stay over.

Bobby's parents didn't much like him hanging around with their son anyway and the Guest's parents never liked his friends. So that summer, when the ball games broke up in the baking, endless afternoons and the kids drifted off in twos and threes, he found himself left behind and missing Bobby.

Then one day, some instinct made the ten-year-old savage crouch in the hot sun and run a finger along the blade of a pocket knife. With blood on the blade, he sketched two figures in the playground dust and drew a circle around them. With the same bloody finger, he touched the black of his hi-tops and murmured, "Give me a new best friend." Adding that most solemn incantation, "Black magic, no changes, no nothing."

A shadow fell over him. Standing up fast, he saw a kid in jeans, t-shirt and sneakers like the ones he wore, a kid with a black crew cut instead of dirty orange like Bobby's or blond like his own. The kid asked, "Watcha doing?" and smiled a crooked little smile like one who knew already but couldn't quite believe it.

Erasing his drawings with one foot, he answered, "Nothing." They circled warily like two dogs sniffing. "You live around here?" he asked because he had never seen this kid before.

"We just moved in." The new boy gestured toward Cray Square. "What about you?"

He pointed up the hill toward his parents' house and asked, "What school you go to?"

"My mother doesn't know yet." There was something funny about the way the kid talked. "Where do you go?"

"St. Michael's. What's your name?"

"Ron. What's yours?"

Thinking back to that key meeting of his life, the Guest remembers hesitating for a moment. The name his parents had bestowed on him was Timothy Conroy and he resented it and them. He was tired of being a Tim or Timmy, didn't like being called Conroy. Out of nowhere, he said, "TC," and liked the sound. It was an alias. The first of many.

His new friend, Ron, lived with just his mother in a three-room apartment down on Cray Square. Previously, they had lived in Baltimore, distant, exotic, mean. Ron couldn't remember his father. His mother worked evenings and was home during the day, sleeping a lot.

TC never saw her. He and Ron would no sooner be in the front door than her voice would float out of the darkened bedroom. "There's a dollar on the table, take it and go to the movies." Sometimes they would spend the afternoon down the street at the Dorchester Strand. The old "Chester," huge, cold, almost deserted at mid-week, reminded him of a secret cavern.

Ron was real tough and knew more stuff than anyone. TC brought his new friend home but his parents were too busy even to notice that Ron called their son TC.

He liked knowing a kid who lived with an invisible mother and without a father. It was a secret he didn't want to share.

When he thought of his family, neighborhood and school, the image that came was of a huge unblinking eye watching over him. With Ron, he found a way of dodging that gaze.

When the two of them weren't playing ball or at the movies, they hung around Cray Square where commuters from the MTA station mingled with shoppers from the A&P, the Five & Dime, the hardware and clothes stores and bakeries, the bars, the liquor stores, the dim little places on side streets.

The first day they knew each other, Ron took TC to a store called Max's on the ground floor of the building where he lived. The windows of Max's were grime darkened. On the counter were newspapers, cigarettes, some stale candy and pretzels. In a corner was a cooler full of bottled soft drinks. On shelves over the radiator were dusty stacks of magazines and paperback books with their covers torn off.

The magazines were old *True Detective* and *Uncanny Tales*, with dates from the early fifties. The books were paperback westerns and mysteries and science fiction. Some of them were two stories stuck together, one upside down from the other.

The guy who worked at Max's and seemed to run the place was called Cy.

Cy was gray-haired, smoked cigarettes and let the two boys paw through the old magazines for as long as they wanted. Customers were infrequent during the day. A curtained opening on the wall behind the counter led to a dark corridor.

Sometimes when it was quiet, they heard the sound of muffled voices, of phones ringing somewhere in the distance.

TC discovered early that his friend had a lot of trouble reading. But Ron liked to be read to. Sometimes they would sit for hours on a board placed over the radiator and he would read aloud. Sometimes he looked up and Cy would be watching through half-shut eyes. Sometimes Cy would give them free Cokes and show them magazines they might have missed, dumb ones with nothing but pictures of women and men in bathing suits.

Once, while TC was totally absorbed in reading *True Tales of War in the Pacific,* Cy came up quietly and touched his neck with an ice cold bottle. When he jumped, Cy sort of laughed.

At a certain time late in the afternoon, business would pick up. A wall phone behind the counter would start to ring. Guys Cy knew would show up to talk to him. When that happened, Cy would tell the boys to take whatever they were reading and get out.

One time, escorting them out the door, Cy hooked his hands into the top of their jeans. TC felt fingers slip between skin and denim, find the elastic band of his briefs and give it a sharp yank. "Have a pair of wedgies on me," said the man.

Outside, Ron looked back for a long moment and said, "Let's do a stake-out, keep track of who goes in and out." For the rest of the afternoon, from the MTA station across the street they watched the sparse traffic at Max's. Eventually, TC had to go home for dinner. When he came back, Ron was still watching the front of Max's from the station waiting room. A guy in a hat left the store. "Okay, that's the last one I saw go in there." Ron told him.

By then it had started to get dark. Street lamps were on, stores that were still open threw light out onto the street, the neon marquee of the Chester glowed, trolleys sparked on the overhead wires.

Knowing he should already be home, TC said, "I gotta go." But made no effort to walk away from his friend. Across the street, Cy put up the "closed" sign, locked the door and drew the shade. Moviegoers straggled into the theater, a group of teenagers roared through the square in a convertible. "My parents are going to kill me," he told Ron.

The door of Max's opened and two guys walked out putting on their hats. "I didn't see them go in," Ron told him. "There's a way we can look in through the back, tomorrow."

Recently, they had read a story, "Secrets of the Atomic Squad," about a ring of Russian spies in New York. "Maybe Cy's a communist," he told Ron. The door opened and another guy left, this one lighting a cigar.

"Cy's a fucking ass bandit," Ron said without taking his eyes off the door. TC nodded as if he knew what his friend meant. That night he ran home long after dark, expecting the worst.

Coming up the street, he saw all the lights on in the house. As he tried to slip into the kitchen door, his mother, putting drinks on a tray, spotted him and cried, "Here he is!" like she did when she was very angry or very happy. "Come on and see the people." All the people were his father's political friends. Some shook his hand, slapped him on the back, told him he was growing. He finally got to go upstairs to his room.

The next morning after breakfast, he was in Cray Square yelling, "Hi-yo Ron," at his friend's window.

Ron came out saying. "My ma's still asleep." They went down the hall to the back of the building, past the super's apartment and out into a kind of courtyard. There, Ron flattened himself against the wall next to a screen door and glanced inside. Then he pulled back and TC stuck his eye a careful inch around the corner to see a room with nothing in it but a long table, a bunch of chairs, a blackboard and some big fans. On the table were ashtrays, pads of paper and more telephones than he had ever seen in one place. The door at the far end of the room opened and Cy came in. TC realized this room was behind Max's and ducked his head back. Cy hadn't seen him.

The two of them must have stayed for hours, saying nothing, peeking into the empty room. Late in the morning, men started to arrive, guys wearing hats, smoking cigars. Someone said, "Saratoga." Someone else said, "He's got dough, runs a six-for-five operation up in Lynn someplace." Then the phones started to ring and all the talk was numbers and names which TC didn't understand. The last time he peeked around the corner, half a dozen men, most of them still wearing their hats, were talking on phones. Another stood at the blackboard writing something.

He remembered telling Ron later, when they were on the street again, "Those guys are Commies."

Ron just said, "You gotta not tell what we saw."

"But the FBI...."

Ron smiled the same slit-eyed, slightly incredulous smile he had the first time they'd met. "We only tell if I say so. Otherwise you and me aren't friends." TC nodded. Ron knew about more stuff than any adult.

That afternoon, he sat in Max's, intensely involved in reading *Curse of the Indian Drum*. Then Ron nudged him. Cy had shut the door and drawn the shades. He stood at the counter with two open ice Cold cokes. Ron nodded for TC to go first. When he reached for the bottle, Cy said, "Let's see what you got," and yanked his pants and shorts down.

In panic and humiliation, TC froze. Cy held him with one arm and started stroking him. For a long minute, Ron didn't move, just watched the scene. The man said, "See how much he enjoys this. Get over here so I can do you too."

"Ass bandit," Ron said real loud. "I'm gonna tell the cops." Cy jumped away. "And he's gonna tell his parents. His father works for the mayor. He'll tell them about those guys in the back room." As TC pulled up his pants, he heard Ron say, "What have you got in the register? I want that. I want twenty dollars."

Cy's hand trembled as he took out his wallet, thrust bills at the boy. "Little bastard, little pimp. Here. Don't come back to this store again."

All those years later, sitting on a porch in the back yard of one of the nicest houses on the hill, the Guest can recall two more things from that long-ago afternoon. The first was that he took *Curse of the Indian Drums* with him and finished reading it to Ron under a tree in his parents' yard. The other was that Ron split the money with him and told him he had done good.

While remembering that, the Guest tells his amused hostess, "One of the nuns at St. Michael's had a black mustache she used to wax at night."

Then, out front, a car door slams. Upstairs, a kid yells, "Daddy!"

Frieda rises to her feet and says, "Just sit here. Let's surprise him." She touches his shoulder, getting up. He takes the gesture as a promise that things will be like old times and together they will handle Jason.

He turns his chair, positions himself so that his face is in shadow, his legs thrust out in front of him. The attitude, the hair that still curls over his ears, the faded denim jacket and jeans, the white sneakers and t-shirt all aim for an effect of youth.

"What kind of a surprise?" he hears a voice ask from inside the house. He touches the relic in his pocket for luck.

Frieda says something and Jason replies, "Someone?" sounding a little tired, a bit put out, a hard-working man home at the end of a day. Jason comes out the door and stops. He has lost most of his hair and is wearing a gray summer suit, a tie loosened on his striped collar.

The man sees first what appears to be a kid lounging on his patio and his eyes narrow, his mouth opens slightly. The Guest knows he still has a hook into this guy before he rises, saying, "Hi, Jas."

"My God." Jason pretends that what he just exhibited was nearsighted curiosity. "How long has it been? Ten years? You look exactly the same." As he says it, Jason, corporate lawyer, is looking at the face in front of him, assessing the thin gold earrings, seeking lines beside the eyes, slackness around the jaw, maybe a gray hair or two that the Guest hasn't caught.

Frieda, smiling at him from behind her husband, says, "I was thinking that it's uncanny the way he can show up in our lives. Turns out he's a local boy. He spent the afternoon telling me about growing up around here. I asked him to stay for dinner. Maybe relive some old times." She wiggles her eyebrows a little on that.

Jason, still examining for flaws, says, "Around here! I remember you saying you lived in Boston. But you grew up around here?" Jason's disbelief has to do with Cray Square as it now is, the huge MBTA station as it's now known, covered with graffiti and gang symbols, the empty store fronts, the corner bars with plywood in their windows.

"Years ago," the visitor tells them. "Before my parents split. We moved away in the early sixties. The place has gone through some tough times since then." The thing that links the old Cray Square to this evening is Ron.

Then Jason the attorney is sitting opposite him, still guessing the exact amount of the Guest's annual income, asking, "What are you doing these days?"

"Freelance. Video and television. I'm doing special effects. There's a new horror series called *Hour of the Wolf*, a syndicated thing."

"You've given up acting?" Frieda seems sad at the loss, although she's never seen his work. "Do you ever see Slade and Daphne?" she asks.

He doesn't let his smile fade as he says, "Saw them just the other day. Slade was directing some of the *Hour of the Wolf* episodes." To stop the questions, he starts talking to them about Hollywood and the series which really is in syndication. His connection with it, however, won't be on the credit crawl.

The Guest has a few funny, slightly worn Hollywood stories that he can recite on automatic pilot. He renders for Frieda and Jason an acting lesson he once attended. "By that time, half of us are bare-ass and I am wearing a cowboy hat, period, and this lunatic drama teacher is saying in this preposterous, phony Hungarian accent...."

Both of them are hysterical. Frieda gets up saying, "Let's see about dinner. You are staying, of course."

He stands up, looking uncertain. Jason stands up too and says, "He's staying. Can I get you something besides that watery tea? A drink, a beer?"

The Guest makes a move toward the kitchen saying, "A beer, but let me get it."

Jason puts a hand on his chest and says, "Sit down. We have a lot to talk about." The hand describes a barely perceptible circular motion. The look in Jason's eyes is quizzical, concerned not with the other's reaction but with his own. The first time the Guest saw that look in another was when Cy had his hand in his jockey shorts.

He smiles and sinks back into the chair and knows that his hosts are talking about him in the kitchen, imagines their conversation. Jason saying, "He's staying for dinner and...?"

"Why are you asking that way?"

"What about after dinner?"

"We talk. What else?"

"What else? When did an evening with him ever consist just of talk? I think he's a little strung out. I think he's carrying his worldly possessions on him. I wonder about AIDS.

You ever see anybody come out from L.A. who takes the subway, for Christ's sake?"

"He looks good, though. You're not going to deny that."

When Jason comes back with two John Adams beers sweating in their bottles, he's changed into sandals, shorts and a tennis shirt. "You're sure you don't want something stronger?" he asks.

The Guest shakes his head, reaches his hand not toward the leather sack in his jacket but to a plastic bag in a front pocket of his pants. "I have something here that may liven things up," he says.

Jason smiles and says, "Maybe later. After dinner." On his way here, the Guest noticed that the block where Ron and his mother lived, where Cy served as a front man for a bookie operation, had disappeared. A semi-trashed Kentucky Fried Chicken place occupies part of the site. The rest is a car wash. But he can still sense Ron's presence, not just in Cray Square but up here as well.

Events that began over three decades before are ready to come full cycle. In the plastic bag in his pants are several joints, each a grass, opium and angel-dust cocktail. On the street, they call them, "Pimp's Kisses," because of the way they can screw your head.

A beer or two along with cheese and pâté makes the time before dinner pass easily. Then Jesse and Kevin come out with the au pair. Kevin is shy, staring at the Guest with big, mistrustful eyes. But Jesse turns on the charm, smiles like a blond-haired little imp. She looks right at him and asks, "Are you on television?"

The Guest sees right away how she fits into his plans. He's nice to the children, smiling, but not going overboard, not getting them excited. He wants them sound asleep that night.

The au pair's name is Kristi and she's eighteen. In high heels and a dress he's seen worn better by others, she looks dull and knowing at the same time. She'll be out with friends till after midnight. "I will be letting myself in," she says.

A horn sounds out front and she turns to go. Her return could be a problem, the Guest realizes. Aside from that, everything goes well.

At one point, while Frieda is getting the kids fed and settled down, Jason stands up saying, "The news is on." He looks at the Guest who shrugs and smiles. "Not interested, huh?" Jason asks. "Well, I guess I can miss one day's worth of the Amazing White House Adventures. So tell me more about the project that you're working on with Slade. We were out there about a year ago and saw him and Daphne."

The Guest smiles, guessing that his name hadn't come up. It was before he re-entered the lives of certain old acquaintances. He says, "We're in the preparation stages right now. But I'm doing special effects. Like I said."

"Blood and gore?" Jason asks.

That's so apt that the Guest laughs aloud. "Piping hot and plenty of it. The time has come for me to think about making a career." Again he smiles and makes the slight involuntary gesture to his jacket. In the pocket is a soft, leather pouch. Inside the pouch, wrapped tightly in plastic, is the right index finger of Slade Bennet. It's the very finger with which Slade jabbed him the chest the night before in L.A. and called him a parasitic crazy.

"You were always into a kind of black magic," Jason says.

Suspicion still flickers, as if he wonders what price there may be for youthful crimes. He has no idea how Slade and Daphne Bennet found the past intertwined with the present when a third party joined them in bed for the last time.

Just then, Frieda comes out the door with a serving dish and apologizes for things having taken so long. The food is yuppie health fare, fresh pasta and bread she's just baked.

The bread seems to be mostly crust. Bugs smash themselves against the screens. The smell of charring steak wafts through the yards. Somewhere out on Sears Avenue, yuppified, fortified Sears Avenue, a car door slams. Much further down the hill, a ghetto blaster sounds.

With dinner there is wine and there are candles. The Guest drinks a careful glass as his hosts recall high times and night frolics twenty years back. "I remember," Frieda says after several glasses. "You always hung a picture of a crimson skull at the foot of the bed. And they said you had been in a porn movie and I thought you were the prettiest and wickedest boy. You did too," she tells Jason.

Jason has had a few glasses of wine but still looks strained when talk turns to polymorphous tumbles. At this point, the Guest feels a bare foot work its way under his pants leg. Frieda is ready. She was always ready. Jason says nothing. But the Guest notices sweat on the top of his head even though a breeze from the harbor has cooled the evening down.

From his pants pocket, the Guest removes the baggy with the joints. Frieda looks and giggles in the flickering light. He lights the joint on a candle, appears to draw on it without actually inhaling and hands it to her first. She takes it saying, "I haven't done this in years."

Jason shakes his head when the joint comes his way. He'll have to be coaxed, just as in the old days he had to be coaxed into bed even though he wanted the threesome the most of any of them. Frieda giggles softly to herself, saying, "Wow, it's been so long. Two tokes and my head feels like it's flying off." In the process of getting Jason to inhale, the Guest takes in a little more smoke than he intends. The night appears transfigured. Bugs hum like helicopters. The lights in neighbors' windows are exploding stars. When the couple is finally wrecked, they start to drift away into private orbits. "Just say no," Frieda says several times laughing. "Jesus," Jason says, looking around in wonder, "Jesus." He draws long and hard on a dead joint. The Guest, getting them back to business, begins to play touchy-feely games, massaging both their necks, unhooking her bra, opening his shirt. "It's like twenty years ago," they both say at different moments.

The Guest remembers how, twenty years ago, they provided a warm bed, some meals, a little amusement on his way to and from more interesting assignments. Once before, his path from childhood to this night led him to Cray Square in its time of ruin and to Ron the Eternal.

✦ ✦ ✦

Around 1970, sometimes still called TC but with school, family and the draft well behind him, he wandered back to Boston and found himself living with a coven of speed freaks.

The combination of a police bust and a burn artist led to the collapse of that frenzied scene. One winter evening he found himself unable to sleep or sit down. The only other one of the company left was a kid, a girl named Sally who said she knew someone with pills that would bring them in for a landing.

They had slept together a few times. Sally was skinny but cute, from somewhere in Tennessee, a drifter in the alternate country of drugs and hassle that had sprung up across America.

Nerves jumping, lids rasping on his eyeballs, freezing, screaming, promising anything, he scraped together some money. It was nearly midnight when they drove in her ancient van to meet the connection. He could think only of getting relief.

Suddenly, he recognized familiar ground: the brick pile of St. Michael's church in the moonlight, old streetcar tracks shining in the street. The apartment block where Cy had diddled little boys was a dark, boarded-up hulk. "Hey," he said, "I grew up around here."

"You lived here?" Sally asked with awe in her voice.

"This is the baddest part of the city. Black dealers shoot each other right in the train station." She sounded respectful for the first time.

Seeing the apartment house reminded him of Ron. They had been closest those first summers they knew each other. A couple of times they broke into houses on the Hill when he knew the owners were on vacation. Older kids got blamed for that. Afterwards, the two of them rode the MTA downtown and found guys on whom they pulled the same trick that had worked on Cy. Sometimes Ron did to him things like Cy had and more.

Since Ron went to public school when he went at all, and started having trouble with the police, they drifted apart even before TC's parents moved out of the neighborhood. They said it was to get him away from bad influences. Just before TC left, Ron began working at Max's in the afternoon, Cy having disappeared.

Hanging a right that night in 1970, Sally drove up Sears Hill and stopped in front of what he remembered as the MacCready's. He had gone to St. Michael's with their youngest son. Now, a hearse with skulls and crossbones painted all over it was parked in the driveway and a guy with hair in braids down to his waist answered the door, packing a gun.

The connection was a man with white hair, a young-old face free of wrinkles and huge, blue, unblinking eyes. Sitting cross-legged on a pile of cushions in Mrs. MacCready's former dining room, the man dealt what was supposed to be Tuinal out of a big plastic bag beside him.

Sally and TC both took a couple immediately, that much he was sure of. The next thing he remembered was waking up with an aching bladder to feel hands on his body, a voice saying,

"Someone has taken pretty good care of this young man."

He realized that he lay on a hard and unyielding surface. Trying to move, he discovered that his legs were pulled taut.

Attempting to sit up, he found he couldn't move his hands. When he focused his eyes, he saw that he was naked on a cellar floor under a bare bulb. His hands were cuffed in back of him and his feet were tied by a length of cord to an iron ring on one wall.

Twisting his head toward the voice. He found the white-haired dealer gazing down at him. The man with the braids stood bare-chested, dressed in a black leather vest and pants. TC got his mouth to work. "Can you let me up? I have to take a piss."

The man in leather didn't move or change expression as he pointed at the floor and said, "Go ahead."

Looking down, TC realized that the whole floor was painted as a target and he lay on the bull's eye. Beneath him, a rust-stained sluice ran to a drain. It hit him that the stain was dried blood, that this was a killing floor and he was marked for slaughter. "Listen," he said, "people are expecting me."

"That," said the white-haired man, "is not what your girlfriend seems to think."

"Sally doesn't know me. She's a runaway. I have family around here." The white-haired man just smiled. "I know people, I know...." Desperate, he faltered trying to think of someone who might still live in the neighborhood. From a circle of blood and dark magic, he said. "I know a guy called Ron."

They all heard the steps above them when he said that. Both men looked toward the stairs. "Well?" the white-haired man asked doing a double take. "I thought you were…gone. We're sure about the girl. What about this guy?"

Rolling over on the floor, he saw a tall guy in sunglasses give a familiar smirk of disbelief and say, "TC! Where have you been?" And, "We have to talk."

Ron told him about how they were making a little film, outlined the scenario, made it clear that, old friends or not, if TC refused he wasn't leaving the cellar alive. TC felt no overwhelming reluctance. He had been looking for something to do with his life, waiting without knowing it for Ron to reappear and show him the path through shadows.

The white-haired connection turned out to be the director of the epic. A guy named Harry Ring was the camera man. Sally, drugged out of her skull, lay on the cellar floor with a collar around her neck, her hands and feet bound. They told her she was going to star in a porn flick and she was willing.

Everyone, TC, Ron, the big guy with the leather vest, Harry Ring, one or two others, screwed her. Between takes, they massaged her brain with downs and meth. TC wondered if she recognized him when the camera rolled and he stepped forward wearing a black jockstrap and cross belt and carrying a knife. When he cut Sally's throat from ear to ear, the camera was on the blood spurting off his chest and down the drain. Sally tried to stand but instead just slumped.

He felt that this was the second time that Ron had saved his life. He stayed with his old friend for a couple of days. It seemed people were after Ron. The law and others. Early one morning, TC looked out the window and saw Ron and the guy in black leather loading up the hearse. When he pulled on his clothes and went out, Ron said, "See you next time we both get back this way."

At quarter to eleven, the three people on the back porch rise at the same moment and go into the kitchen. Jason stops, says, "Security," and with great concentration and stoned dignity, switches on lights at the rear of the property. Swaying slightly, he leans for a moment against the Guest. Frieda carries two candles carefully, lighting the way as if to a ceremony. As they climb the stairs, a child turns over in the dark and says, "Mommy," and all three of them freeze. Then there's silence and they continue on to the master bedroom.

"We're not going through with this," Jason says. But he's the one who gets the condoms out of the adjoining bathroom before returning to watch the Guest undress his wife. In the flickering candlelight, Frieda glows pink and luxuriant as a rococo nymph. And Jason, once they get his clothes off, is hairy and dark as a satyr. About the Guest they both exclaim,

"You look really great." Not adding, probably not thinking,

"For someone our age."

When the three are on the bed, all goes pretty much as it did twenty years before. First Jason watches another man make love to his woman. Then Jason looks aside as she and that man make love to him. The couple seem impressed with themselves. The third party is a practiced performer.

As the three of them lie on the huge bed, nestled against the cold from the air conditioner, Frieda asks him, "Hey, where did you go just now?" Her voices slurs as more of the Pimp's Kiss kicks in. "You keep going away," she says beginning to drift away herself. The Guest notices that cable news is on with the sound off: old men in suits stride across airport tarmacs; a weeping black woman talks to reporters.

From somewhere downstairs, a phone rings once, twice. Jason stirs suddenly. An answering machine in the room kicks on. Kristi, the au pair, says, "Hello. I am calling to say I will be back there tomorrow morning before seven if that is okay."

Frieda giggles, "Caught up in the wild Boston night life." The Guest is relieved; one big problem is removed. But now the couple is awake and Frieda is looking at the screen where police remove body bags from a house high on a canyon wall. Before she can recognize it as a place she's visited, the Guest hugs husband and wife, draws them both to him, psyches himself to perform again. Behind them, Slade and Daphne are being carried out of their house in L.A.

The stimulus the Guest draws on to perform one last time for Jason and Frieda is his memory of that cellar down the street. Remembering the fact of his own escape, his knowledge of how close he is to escaping again, excites him.

When he's done, the couple sleeps, breathing deep, drugged sighs. The candles have gone out and all the light in the room comes from the television. The Guest lies still, thinks about how events have carried him back to this place.

For a while, in certain circles, he heard rumors that Ron was in jail or in Thailand or both. Then the story from ones who said they'd seen it was that Ron was dead but he hadn't believed it. Actually, he hadn't thought much about Ron until a couple of days ago when he suddenly needed him very badly. And it was only the night before when he became sure he remembered how to reach his old friend dead or alive.

Until recently, he had been taking it easy, living on money saved, favors owed. But more time had passed than he realized and suddenly the money and favors dried up. Two days back, he went to Palo Alto and talked to Harry Ring, the camera man on that very first film. He and Harry had worked together after that, creating several twenty-minute epics much prized by ghouls and connoisseurs. Long ago he had left the name TC behind and taken others. But that was the one by which Ring still knew him.

He proposed to Harry that they do something similar again. But Mr. Ring had gotten rich running a video outlet chain. He refused to put up the money. When his old partner pointed out certain blood ties between them, Harry said. "What are you going to do, TC, take me to court? Say we made snuff films fifteen years ago? Tell them that entitles you to twenty grand of my money now? Get out, you fucking freak."

As he spoke, Harry's hand moved towards a desk drawer. But TC was in great shape and very angry. He smashed Harry Ring onto the floor, opened the drawer and shot him several times with the gun he found there. Then he stood motionless for a long moment, thinking about what had happened. He was still broke and out of favors. And now he was in a corner.

Maybe hearing his old name gave him the first clue. Blinds on the windows were drawn against the sun outside. On a blank TV screen behind the desk, a kid's face appeared for a second, then flickered and disappeared. He recognized the face as Ron's from back when they first met.

That's when he knew that once again his oldest friend was trying to rescue him. The outline of his escape began to form. The first attempt was Slade and Daphne's in Los Angeles.

Slade, it turned out, had forgotten his origins, had forgotten the time before the rock videos, before he directed the movie *Blood Savage*. As a young film student in Boston, Slade had teamed up with his visitor and Harry Ring on some wild numbers on and off camera.

By then, TC wasn't looking for money. He was working his way back to Ron. The path he chose ran through his own past. With Harry's gun pointed at them, Slade and his wife helped him create a crude but effective film. First, all the way around the bed, he drew a circle just like the one that had been present the first two times Ron had appeared to him.

Then Slade rode Daphne, both of them looking into the camera, terrified. TC stepped into the scene, climbed onto the bed just as had in the old days. But this time, as a climax, he shot each of them through the back of the head. It sort of summed up his career in motion pictures.

Now blood was present, as it had been those other times. In the silence that followed the killings, he saw the dark-haired kid looking at him from out of a mirror. The image flickered and disappeared. But before it did, he realized where Ron was standing and knew that he still hadn't done things right.

Seeing that reminded him of another couple from the old days, Jason and Frieda. He had heard about their beautiful old house near Cray Square and thought of it as just a strange coincidence. But staring at the mirror, he understood how they lay on his pathway back to Ron.

More than enough money lay around Slade's for the plane ticket to Boston. As a way of linking the rituals, he left the film in the camera and Harry's gun at the scene. To draw luck and power from what went before, he cut off Slade's right index finger and took it with him.

The next night, in Jason and Frieda's bedroom, the Guest stands, strips the case from a pillow, twists it into a tight cord. Going toward the bed, he decides to do Frieda first.

Jason lies face down, motionless, as the Guest slips the pillowcase around the wife's neck. She stirs. The Guest knows how to do this cleanly and quickly. He lifts the upper part of her body. Then he brings his knee up behind her neck at the same time that he pulls her head back. The neck snaps.

Jason is up and headed for the door. It's closed. As he turns the knob, the Guest hits him behind the ear with a karate chop, stunning him. Jason falls and is hit again. This time a candlestick smashes in the side of his head. Then the Guest smothers him, knowing he was wise to kill Frieda first. If she'd been awakened and found him murdering her husband, she would have yelled, screamed, tried to save Jason. The Guest wants this prelude to the ritual to happen as quickly and quietly as possible.

He sits on the floor for a few minutes regaining his breath. On television, a pair of heads move their mouths. This time, Ron doesn't have to appear on the screen. His presence is all around.

The Guest drags Jason back to the bed, places him parallel to his wife. No need to disturb them further now that their part is done. With a sheet pulled over Jason's head, he and Frieda seem as lithe and young as the first time all three of them slept together. The Guest thinks of this as his gift to them.

The electric clock reads ten after one when he goes to his jacket, pulls out the leather bag, removes the baggy with the finger. Remembering not to breathe through his mouth, he dips it in the blood from Jason's wound. With his jacket over his shoulder, he closes the door and goes into the hall.

A stair creaks beneath him as he descends. At the back of the house, one of the kids turns over in deep sleep. Through the beveled window on the front door, light from a street lamp seems diffuse, phosphorescent. In the round hall mirror, as he passes it, his skin is dead white. Thick carpet muffles his passage to the kitchen. Beyond the porch, security lights glow in the back yard.

The tiles are cool underfoot as he pauses a moment, making sure he's flicking the right switch. The lights die. He waits in absolute silence, gazing into the dark yard. Something stirs under the trees. A figure with a familiar smile nods impatiently.

The Guest turns his attention back to the kitchen. With the bloody finger, he draws a circle on the tile floor. From the rack placed carefully beyond the reach of small hands, he selects a sharp knife. Back upstairs, he slings his jacket over his arm. The children have separate rooms. He passes the boy's and goes directly to Jesse, waits again in darkness until he makes out her form on the bed.

When he first saw the kids, he knew that innocent blood was what he needed. Killing her parents was a practical matter. They would have interfered. Killing her brother isn't necessary. For a sacrifice, only the best will do.

Jesse starts awake as he bends and picks her up. She tries to cry but he puts his hand over her mouth. She struggles as they go down the stairs, but he holds her firmly. Her little heart beats against his chest all the way. Standing in the middle of the circle, he holds the child in front of him and picks up the knife.

The jacket falls away and she screams for her mother. Outside on Sears Avenue, a car pulls up in front of the house. Upstairs, the small boy starts to cry. The knife slashes down and blood spurts. He holds Jesse above his head, bathes himself in her innocence and whispers, "Black magic, no changes, no nothing." The squirming child above him grows still.

Locks turn on the front door. The au pair calls, "Hello? I came home after all." But all that is distant. The Guest sees night over Sears Hill transformed to bright afternoon.

Before him, Ron, tough and lonely, just moved in from Baltimore, crouches on the playground and summons a friend. Most of what TC has seen since 1958 fades before his hi-tops touch the circle drawn in the dust. But even the traces make him smile at the things he knows and this new kid doesn't.

Hula Ville

JAMES P. BLAYLOCK

James P. Blaylock has been publishing stories and novels since 1975—more than twenty novels and story collections in all. In 1977, *Unearth* magazine published his story "The Ape-box Affair," arguably the first American steampunk story. Over the years he has won the Philip K. Dick Memorial Award for his novel *Homunculus* and two World Fantasy Awards. His short story "Unidentified Objects" was nominated for an O. Henry Award. His most recently published novels are *The Knights of the Cornerstone*, set in the California desert, *The Ebb Tide*, a steampunk adventure set in London and the Lake District, and its companion volume, *The Affair of the Chalk Cliffs*. He is currently finishing up a novel titled *The Aylesford Skull*.

"...and the windows of the sky were opened."

When I was twelve years old, I awoke in the night to find a strange man standing at the foot of my bed, regarding me as I slept. Moonlight through the window cast what appeared to be the shadow of wings against the wall behind him. Instead of being terrified, I was filled with a radiant joy, and as he faded from existence it came into my head that I had been visited by an angel. The idea, you'll say, is absurd. I should have known a hallucination when I saw one, even at that young age. And I'll admit that the shadow on the wall might have had more to do with the moonlight and the shrubbery outside the window than with wings.

The mundane and rational explanation is perhaps always the most useful, whether it's right or wrong. It puts a safe and tidy end to otherwise incredible things: it was merely a hallucination, a shadow, a hoax, temporary insanity, swamp gas, a weather balloon—but not an angel. One can dismiss the very idea of angels and fall asleep. In the morning the sun will shine—no moonlight, no shadows.

But for a long time I lay awake, marveling at the angel, remembering the arch of its wings and the dim outline of the feathers, and it was gray dawn outside before I drifted off to sleep again, awakening hours later with the memory still going around in my head but tinged with a vague feeling of discontent. A door had opened on a mystery but then had closed before I had gotten a good glimpse at what lay on the other side, and I very much wished that it would open again—which is a little too much like wishing that a windmill were in fact a giant, and then having the wish come true.

Twenty years ago, when I was living alone in San Bernardino, off Highland Avenue at the edge of the California desert, I spent my weekends driving through the Mojave or down to Anza Borego or up 395 into the White Mountains. I was looking for something—the Lost Dutchman's Mine, let's say—although only in a figurative sense. I was never that sort of prospector. I was haunted by the continual impression that something was pending in the small world that I inhabited at that time in my life, a world circumscribed by the open highways and starry night skies of the desert in a changing season.

I carried a book of maps titled *California Desert Trails* that I bought at the Hula Ville Desert Museum out in Hesperia one afternoon. The museum was marked with a big plywood sign—the cut-out, garish image of a hula dancer with the words "The Hula Girl" painted underneath. It came into my mind that this was the definite article, and I pulled off the road and into the empty gravel parking lot. A cold wind blew down off the hills, picking up sand in little wind devils and making the two or three acres of Joshua trees and yucca seem even more desolate than it was.

The proprietor, an old-timer named Marion Walsh, stood behind the counter in the museum itself—a bunkhouse-shaped building knocked together out of rough-cut lumber. He had written and published *California*

Desert Trails himself—had drawn the maps and typed in the footnotes concerning UFO sightings and abandoned mines and other bits of arcane information about out-of-the-way desert places. I had the idea of working through the book methodically, page by page, covering all the ground.

Some months later, on a cool November afternoon, page twenty-eight sent me out Highway 10 to Desert Center, where Route 177 angles away north past the Granite Mountains, a narrow, twelve-mile range of lonesome, rocky peaks. The southernmost peak, according to Walsh's map, was called "Angels Peak" because a storefront preacher claimed to have seen an angel there in 1932 and for a few years thereafter had led pilgrims from San Bernardino, Riverside, and Redlands into the area for baptism in a shallow pool among the rocks.

From the highway, the Granite Range is nearly indistinguishable from the hundreds of other dry ranges that rise out of the desert floor in that part of the country. I had often driven past it before without turning my head to look at it. On this day there were heavy clouds gathering on the Arizona horizon, and the radio broadcast flash-flood warnings across the Mojave and down into Imperial County. As I angled up 177 at Desert Center and got a good look at the sky, I nearly turned around and headed home. A storm in the desert can be a uniquely beautiful thing, although it can change the demeanor of the landscape in an instant.

At the southern edge of the range, an overgrown and rutted dirt track winds back into the hills, quickly losing sight of the highway and climbing some five hundred feet before dead-ending at a rockslide. The road hasn't been maintained for fifty years, and there's nothing to identify it any longer—no marker and no highway turnout. Despite the map, I passed it twice before I got out of the car and began searching on foot, looking for the compacted and rutted soil of what had once been the road but was now overgrown with greasewood and scattered with boulders. The air was full of the scent of creosote and sage and the sound of the wind. Even in a pickup truck it was slow going once I left the highway, and it took me nearly fifteen minutes to drive the mile and a half around to the east-facing slope.

The map marked a place where a big Joshua tree hid a cut in the rock wall of the hillside. The cut begins as a little defile scarcely wide enough to pass through, but it soon opens into a narrow gorge that leads upward into a box canyon with steeply sloping rock walls. It's at the top of this hidden canyon, maybe a thousand feet below Angels Peak, that a stand of fan palms clusters around a natural spring that bubbles out of the mountainside, the water spreading out a few feet into a clear shallow pool before sinking away into the sand.

The spring itself, flowing out of a fissure in apparently solid rock, is utterly mythological, as if in some lost age a Moses wandering in the desert had struck the rock with a staff and water had issued forth. A profusion of desert primrose and paintbrush grow in the canyon, and a scattering of Panamint daisies a hundred-odd miles from their usual home to the north. There's a holy, lonesome beauty to the place, and a profound silence in the empty ridges and rocky peaks and in the deep expanse of the desert sky.

I intended to hike to the peak above the spring, a climb that would have been unpleasant in the summer heat. From there I would have a panoramic view of the storm moving in over the desert, although I would have to hurry, because the sky was darkening at an alarming rate. I heard the sound of distant thunder about ten minutes after losing sight of the canyon, and within moments immense drops began to fall, scenting the air with the intoxicating smell of rain on dry stone. It would have been sensible to turn around and return to the car, given the ominous nature of the clouds and the solid chance that the storm would wash out what was left of the old road, but at the time I wasn't inclined to be sensible. What I was searching for I couldn't rationally say—gold, perhaps, or fool's gold. I stepped under an outcropping of rock and was sheltered for a moment from the windblown rain and then came out of it onto a high ledge that was completely open to the weather and sky.

I could see for a hundred miles around three points of the compass, and although it might have been my imagination, I fancied that I could detect the thin, blue, sunlit ribbon of the Colorado River away to the east. There were scattered clearings in the clouds through which the sun still poured its golden beams, illuminating ragged patches of the desert floor, the light quickly swept away by dark curtains of moving rain. Lightning flashed, striking the distant ridges and washes, and the sound of thunder rumbled more or less continually.

The peak lay hidden above, very near by my reckoning, and with the rain at my back I clambered upward in a crouch from boulder to boulder and across angled planes of decomposing granite, hearing sharp, successive cracks of thunder, much louder and closer now. I finally found myself looking out across a vast rock face cut with open fissures. The granite surface was rough, and there was only a small chance of slipping, so I stepped out onto it, finding fingerholds and toeholds in the cracks and craning my neck to see whether there was any hope of getting entirely across to a line of ragged crags just below the peak.

It was then that I saw an immense nest built in among the crags on a flat area partly overgrown with greasewood. It lay in the shelter of a deep overhang that was evidently the mouth of a cave, its entrance partly blocked by boulders. Through the blur of rain and shadow and brush, the nest was difficult to see clearly, but it was apparently woven of palm fronds and was as incongruous in that part of the desert as was the spring in the canyon below. It was large enough for a family of condors, but there were no condors within two hundred and fifty miles. I inched toward it to get a better view, making out what appeared to be the arch of a massively heavy wing, the rainwater glistening on feathers of burnished gold.

Above, in the hollow of the cave mouth and half-hidden by boulders, something moved—a man, it seemed to me, perhaps stepping back out of sight. I had seen him out of the corner of my eye, just a shifting image that might as easily have been the shadow of moving clouds. The rain stopped abruptly then, and the clouds parted, and in that instant the creature in the nest turned to face me. I saw that there was another next to it, and in that one brief moment of sharp, sunlit clarity, I believe I either lost my mind or recovered it.

The sky went dark, rain fell in a sudden torrent, and a lightning flash struck the rock not twenty feet above me and blasted me from my handhold. The crack of thunder was simultaneous, deafeningly loud. I slid away down the rock face, scrabbling with my boots and hands to slow my fall, the air smelling of ozone and gunpowder. The rain pounded down so heavily now that I was blinded by it as I lurched to a stop against a spur of rock, where I lay for a moment gathering my wits. The only safe route lay upward again, but when I reached blindly for the base of a nearby bush, I lost my footing again and fell, rolling onto my side, frantic to stop myself but sliding and tumbling uncontrollably for the last twenty feet before slamming to a halt on a sandy little plateau where a clump of brush was stalky enough to bear my weight.

I lay there dazed, having hit my head in the fall, aware but unconcerned that the rain was washing blood into my eyes and mouth. I was strangely at peace, no doubt because of the knock on the head, and I listened to the thunder recede into the west as the worst of the storm passed away overhead. How long I lay there I can't say, but it's certain that I lost consciousness or fell asleep. How I found my way back down to the spring is a mystery. I have only scattered memories—more like dreams than memories—a recollection of floating, of being carried. It's quite common, of course, for a concussion to cause delusion and a temporary lapse of memory, and certainly the most sensible explanation is that I climbed back down to the canyon myself before passing out again beside the spring.

When I awoke I was full of a strange elation, a joy that I hadn't felt since that nighttime visitation during my childhood. I washed my abraded hands in the spring and stumbled back down the trail to my car. The dirt track was all but washed out by the storm, and it was a small miracle that I managed to make my way across the rutted desert floor to the highway.

The winged creatures that looked up at me from that nest in the crags had human faces, or at least that was the memory that possessed me when I awoke beside the spring in the hidden canyon, still picturing the creatures in my mind. The footprints in the sand beside me were half-full of sunlit water but there was no one besides myself at the spring and no sound except the splashing of water and the muted rumbling of distant thunder. Unfortunately there's no field guide that identifies the footprints of angels.

It was the next February, under a bright, cool winter sun, that I revisited the Granite Range. I spent the better part of the day searching through the crags and canyons. There was no storm now, and the trek up to Angels Peak was comparatively easy. I couldn't find the nest, although I found a few dry shreds of palm frond scattered among the crags, as well as several long feathers that I took along with me as souvenirs.

There's nothing unusual about finding a mummy in the desert, usually the dried body of a snakebitten prospector who had wandered too far out into the hills, the corpse air-drying for years in a tarpaper shack or a tin mine. There was an account of one in the Special Collections Library at the University of Redlands. It was in an unpublished history of Riverside County written by a woman named Maybelle Brewer, who was active in the Quill and Plume Society in San Bernardino in the 1930s. The history relates the story of a curious mummy discovered in the Kaiser Mine out near Eagle Mountain at the edge of the Joshua Tree National Park, perhaps ten air miles from the northern edge of the Granite Range. The mummy was taken, appropriately, to the Angels Rest Funeral Home in Desert Center, where it was warehoused "pending identification." It disappeared, however, on the same night that it arrived, almost certainly stolen by an employee, who disappeared with it.

With the theft, its existence ceased to be fact and became rumor, and rumor suggested that the mummy had leathery wings protruding from its shoulders, wings with the feathers still attached, and was about the size of a year-old child curled up in a fetal position. A reward was offered for its return. When it resurfaced years later in a Victorville carnival, the reward had long since been forgotten. The statute of limitations on stolen mummies turns out to be brief, even on mummified angels. Whether the winged mummy on display in the sideshow was the Eagle Mountain mummy remains to be seen, but it's probable that it was, and it's equally probable that it was finally sold to Marion Walsh out at Hula Ville some time in the late 1960s, along with the Hula Girl and other painted carnival signs and a small, gasoline-driven kiddy train, which Walsh set up behind the museum.

Hula Ville is marked with a star on page eighty-two, the last page of the Desert Trails map, and there's a brief but glowing description of the place, written, of course, by Marion Walsh himself, along with a photo of a sign that reads, "Hula Ville, State Landmark # 939."

I drove back out there on a winter afternoon not too long ago, my first visit to the museum since buying the guidebook years earlier. There were the same couple of acres of Joshua trees and yucca, and the same plywood carnival signs and suspended bottles. Time and the weather had taken their toll on the place since my previous visit. The painted signs were faded by the desert sun, and the bottles were rainbowed and nearly opaque. Many of them had broken, and the glass shards lay in the weeds and gravel. Part of the museum roof had blown off, and scraps of ragged tarpaper fluttered in the wind. The kiddy train tracks still lay in an oval behind the museum, but the train cars were gone, all except the engine, which had been pushed some distance away and tipped over. A big tumbleweed had grown up through it. A pickup-truck camper was parked near the museum. There was a light on inside and the sound of a television through an open window.

I walked around, taking a look at the place, reading the grave markers on Boot Hill—Dead Eye Toby and Steam Train Wagner and Freeway Annie—allegedly the names of friends of Walsh who had died years back. There were half a dozen "gates" built on the property, although virtually no fences. I passed through all of the gates as the sun traveled down the sky.

The idea of a freestanding gate appealed to me, calling up the suggestion of doors to nowhere, of windows in the sky.

After a time the curtains moved in the camper window, and then the television fell silent and Walsh came out. He looked older and just about as worn-out as Hula Ville itself. I asked him how he was doing, and he told me he felt a little "old-fashioned" these days. It was likely that he'd had a couple of drinks. He said he remembered me, though, from years back, and the fact that I had bought the book of maps, which he said was out of print now. I told him that I had worked through the entire book and had ended up back here, and he nodded his head as if what I'd said had stood to reason.

He showed me around, recollecting where he had gotten this or that artifact, describing the effect of desert sunlight on glass bottles and phone pole insulators, talking about the years he had spent as a card-carrying member of the Pacific Coast Showmen's Association back in the old days. It was evening, and the sun was setting over the hills. We sat in a pair of aluminum lawn chairs and watched the shadows lengthen, talking about places we'd been in the desert and what we'd seen there.

I told him that I'd spent some time camping in the Granite Range, and he assumed I meant the range up in the Mojave, near China Lake. "That's UFO territory," he told me. He had seen a few saucers himself over the years. One time out in Joshua Tree he had spotted three glowing disks heading due east, fast and low in the night sky. And then there was a time in Indian Wells when he'd seen moving lights circling overhead—some kind of Tinkertoy airship that hovered for a good ten minutes before lifting straight up into the sky and losing itself among the stars. He'd had plenty of time to take a photo, which he fetched now out of the camper. Like most UFO photos, however, it wasn't really conclusive. I couldn't tell the starship from the stars, and although he pointed out which were which, he might as well have been pointing out stars in a strangely shaped constellation. UFOs were like ghosts, he said—one of the things that people believe in and always have, even though there's no evidence of them nor ever has been. Which goes to show you, he told me, that evidence is overrated.

I thought about that one for a moment, and then I told him about the nest of angels that I'd seen out in the Granite Range, and my getting down off the mountain with no credible explanation aside from water-filled footprints in the sand. He shrugged. "Like I said," he told me, "you spend enough years in the desert and you see some things." He tended to think that a man shouldn't make too much of them, though, unless he had nothing better to do with his time. "I suppose that's why you came out here," he said. "You heard about my angel, didn't you?"

"Page eighty-two sent me out here," I told him.

"Same thing," he said. "You just want to *look* at him?"

"I want to buy him."

He thought about it for a moment, looking out at the hills. "Why don't you buy the Hula Girl?" he said. "We could tie her down on top of your pickup truck. You'd be happier with the Hula Girl."

"I didn't come out here to buy the Hula Girl."

"No, I don't suppose you did," he said.

We got up out of the lawn chairs and walked over to the museum. He unlocked the padlock hanging in the hasp and pushed the door open. When it jammed against the buckled floorboards, he yanked up on the knob and forced the door open and then found the light switch. The old displays of geodes and desert rose and petrified palm were covered with dust, and the newspaper clippings pinned to the walls were yellow and brittle—articles about silver strikes and UFO sightings and Vegas entertainers. There were a couple of dozen old perfume bottles, purple from years in the sun, displayed beneath glass along with the dried bodies of flies that had found their way under the glass and then couldn't find their way out. It came into my head that even the Hula Ville Museum had mummified over the years, but I kept the thought to myself.

"That's my wife's collection," Walsh said, gesturing at the perfume bottles. "She died back in '72 and I never remarried."

I nodded but couldn't think of anything relevant to say, so I stated the obvious: "She collected perfume bottles."

"Yes, she did. Everything else that she left behind I got rid of over the years, but I kept these as a display. Most people are fascinated by old bottles. Remind them of the past, I guess. That's why I kept them in the first place—something of hers to hold onto. After a while, though, it's just evidence that you can't hold onto anything, and then they're just empty bottles."

He opened a cupboard and hauled out a wooden case. Inside lay the mummified angel, visible under a glass lid. Walsh set it on top of the counter and stood aside. "Go ahead and open it up," he said. "Used to be sealed with rubber weather strip, but it dried out. Take a good look."

I opened the lid, letting the overhead light shine into the box. The mummy's flesh was desiccated, and it was salted with its own grainy dust. The shreds of dried skin still stretched over brown bone were striated like jerky. Broken feathers lay on the bottom of the box, still golden brown after all these years and nearly identical to the feathers I'd picked up out in the Granite Range. The wing bones showed through what was left of the skin and feathers. Its hands were drawn up into fists but hadn't quite closed, and I could see its overgrown fingernails. He was still curled in a fetal position, staring out of empty eye sockets at his own dislocated knees.

I looked closely at the joint between the wing and shoulder blade, searching for the telltale stitches that would be evident now that the body had decomposed. But there was no sign that the creature had been sewn together. Instead there were dry strands of connective ligament and pieces of flesh that made the wings seem entirely natural.

"It's no hoax," Walsh said.

"I didn't think it was," I told him.

"Is it worth fifty bucks to you?"

"What's it worth to you?" I asked him. Truthfully, I would have paid him more than fifty dollars for it, and it was certain he could use the money.

"Fifty bucks, just like I said. It was worth more than that once, but that was a long damned time ago. Just give me the fifty."

I counted out the bills, and we went outside. We walked to my truck, and he opened the door so that I could set the mummy's case in on the seat. I went around and climbed into the cab and put the key in the ignition. "Do yourself a favor," he said, bending over to look in through the rolled-down window. "Don't shellac this damned mummy and set up a shrine or something. And don't spend too much curiosity on what you saw up there in the hills twenty years ago. Whatever it was is long gone."

I thought for a moment about the dried-out strips of palm fronds and the feathers I'd found out in the mountains, the articles I'd cut out of newspapers over the years and the books I'd bought during my travels and underlined with marking pens. I nodded at him and started the engine.

"May it do you more good than it did me," he said.

I told him that I'd stop by when I passed that way again.

Three miles down the highway my car died. There was the sudden silence of the engine shutting down, and the indicator lights on the dash came on. I realized that the headlights were dim as I pulled off to the side of the road, thankful for the moonlight. The battery was stone dead—maybe a bad alternator. I had no cell phone at the time, and still don't, and so I turned on my emergency flashers and sat in the silent car, considering whether to walk back up to Hula Ville or wait for a Good Samaritan to stop and give me a jump-start or a lift into town.

I turned on the dome light, which was flickery dim, and looked at the mummy. After a time, I got out of the car and opened the hood and then leaned against the front fender. The wind had died down, and the night was almost warm. Off to the west there was a glow on the horizon from the lights of Victorville, and the stars out that way were dim. But overhead they were bright, and an enormous moon was rising over the hills. I listened to the perfect desert silence and watched the sky for shooting stars.

A shadow fell across the fender, and I turned around, startled to see a man standing beside the car, looking at me. Where he had come from I can't say. There was no other car visible, and I certainly hadn't passed any pedestrians since leaving Hula Ville. There were a good three or four miles of open highway ahead before the rural route that I was traveling met Highway 15 above the Cajon Pass. Had he walked down from the highway? Heading where? Hula Ville?

"Where did you come from?" I asked. He was a big man, but in no way threatening. He didn't look much like an angel, but then neither did the mummy on the front seat.

He nodded his head in the general direction of the desert. "I thought maybe you needed a hand."

"The battery's dead," I told him. "I've got jumper cables, but if you don't have a car, then they won't do us any good."

He looked at the engine. "Give it a try," he said, so I climbed into the cab and turned the key. He was hidden by the hood, but through the gap where the hood was raised up away from the car, I saw that he had laid his hands on the distributor. "Go ahead," he said. I bent down over the wheel to see as well as I could and turned the key. A spray of sparks like a pinwheel going off shot out from under the hood. The engine turned over, and I gunned it a couple of times and then backed off slowly on the accelerator, feathering it a little bit to keep it from dying. When I was certain it wouldn't stall, I climbed out of the cab.

He was a good distance from the car now, a shadowy figure lit by moonlight, disappearing into the desert. Very quickly he was lost among the shadows of the Joshua trees, and the night was empty again and silent except for the rumble of the engine. I went around to the driver's side of the truck and got in, switching on the headlights, which were bright enough now to illuminate a mile of highway.

The wooden case on the seat was empty except for dust. I owned a fifty-dollar packing crate with a glass lid. I sat there staring at it for a long time then pulled back out onto the highway and drove home.

It turns out that state landmarks, like angels and mummies, are prone to passing away without notice, and Hula Ville disappeared almost overnight a couple of months ago, replaced by a strip mall. I never did get back out there until it was gone, and I don't know what happened to Marion Walsh. The Hula Girl had been carted away, and the Joshua trees and gates and Boot Hill and hanging bottles had been bulldozed and buried beneath fill dirt pushed down from an adjacent hillside. The same tumbleweeds that blew through Hula Ville now blow across the hot asphalt of a parking lot.

The Bedroom Light

JEFFREY FORD

Jeffrey Ford is the author of eight novels (most recently *The Shadow Year*) and four collections of short stories (most recently *Crackpot Palace*). He is the recipient of the World Fantasy Award, Shirley Jackson Award, Edgar Allan Poe Award, and the Nebula Award. His story, "The Drowned Life," was recently included in *The Oxford Book of American Short Stories, 2nd Ed.* His stories have recently been published in *After: Nineteen Stories of Apocalypse and Dystopia* edited by Ellen Datlow and Terri Windling and *The Magazine of Fantasy & Science Fiction.*

He lives in Ohio with his wife and sons. You can find him online at: http://www.well-builtcity.com.

They each decided, separately, that they wouldn't discuss it that night. The autumn breeze sounded in the tree outside the open kitchen window and traveled all through the second-story apartment of the old Victorian house. It twirled the hanging plant over the sink, flapped the ancient magazine photo of Veronica Lake tacked to his office door, spun the clown mobile in the empty bedroom, and, beneath it, set the wicker rocker to life. In their bedroom it tilted the fabric shade of the antique floor lamp that stood in the corner by the front window. Allison looked at the reflection of them lying beneath the covers in the mirror set into the top of the armoire while Bill looked at their reflection in the glass of the hand-colored print, *Moon Over Miami*, that hung on the wall above her. The huge gray cat, Mama, her belly skimming the floor, padded quietly into the room and snuck through the partially open door of the armoire.

Bill rolled over to face Allison and ran his hand softly down the length of her arm. "Today, while I was writing," he said, "I heard, coming up through the grate beneath my desk, Tana, getting yelled at by her mother."

"Demon seed?" said Allison.

He laughed quietly. "Yeah." He stopped rubbing her arm. "I got out of my chair, got down on the floor, and turned my ear to the grate."

She smiled.

"So the mom's telling Tana, 'You'll listen to me, I'm the mother. I'm in charge and you'll do what I say.' Then there was a pause, and I hear this voice. Man, this was like no kid's voice, but it *was* Tana, and she says, 'No, Mommy, I'm in charge and you will listen to me.'"

"Get outa here," Allison said and pushed him gently in the chest.

"God's honest truth. So then Cindy makes a feeble attempt to get back in power. 'I'm the Mommy,' she yells, but I could tell she meant to say it with more force, and it came out cracked and weak. And then there's a pause, and Tana comes back with, 'You're wrong, Mommy. I am in charge and you will listen to me.'"

"Creep show," Allison said.

"It got really quiet then, so I put my ear down closer. My head was on the damn floor. That's when I heard Cindy weeping."

Allison gave a shiver, half fake, and handed Bill one of her pillows. He put it behind his head with the rest of his stack. "Did I tell you what Phil told me?" she said.

"No," he said.

"He told me that when he's walking down the street and he sees her on one side of the road, he crosses over to the opposite side."

"I don't blame him," he said, laughing.

"He told you about the dog, right?" she said, pulling the covers up over her shoulder.

Bill shook his head.

"He said the people who live in the apartment on the second floor next door—the young guy with the limp and his wife, Rhoda—they used to have a beagle that they kept on their porch all day while they were at work."

"Over here," he said and pointed at the wall.

"Yeah. They gave it water and food, the whole thing, and had a long leash attached to its collar. Anyway, one day Phil's walking down to the Busy-Bee to get coffee and cigarettes and he sees Tana standing under the porch, looking up at the dog. She was talking to it. Phil said that the dog was getting worked up, so he told Tana to leave it alone. She shot him a 'don't fuck with me' stare. He was worried how it might look, him talking to the kid, so he went on his way. That afternoon the dog was discovered strangled, hanging by the leash off the second-story porch."

"He never told me that. Shit. And come to think about it, I never told *you* this...I was sitting in my office just the other day, writing, and all of a sudden I feel something on my back, like it's tingling. I turn around, and there she is, standing in the doorway to the office, holding Mama like a baby doll, just staring at me. I jumped out of my chair, and I said, like, 'I didn't hear you knock.' I was a little scared actually, so I asked her if she wanted a cookie. At first she didn't say anything, but just looked at me with that...if I was writing a story about her I'd describe her face as *dour*—an old lady face minus the wrinkles...Then, get this, she says in that low, flat voice, 'Do you Lambada?'"

"What the fuck?" Allison said and laughed. "She didn't say that."

"No," he said, "that's what she said, she asked me if I *Lambada*. What the hell is it anyway? I told her no, and then she turned and split."

"Lambada, I think..." she said, and broke out laughing again, "I think it's some kind of South American Dance."

"What would have happened if I said yes?" he asked.

"Lambada," she whispered, shaking her head.

"Phil's got the right strategy with her," he said.

"But I don't like her coming up here in the middle of the day uninvited," said Allison.

"I'll have to start locking the door after you go to work," said Bill.

"This place...there's something very...I don't know." She sighed. "Like you ever lean against a wall? It kind of gives like flesh," she said.

"That's just the lathing...it's separating away from the sheet rock cause the place is so old. I know what you mean, though, with that egg shell smoothness and the pliancy when you touch it—spongy-weird."

"I'm talking there's a sinister factor to this place. The oriental carpets, the lion's paw tub, the old heavy furniture—the gravity of the past that was here when we moved in. I can't put my finger on it. At first I thought it was quaint, but then I realized it didn't stop there."

"Like melancholy?" he asked.

"Yeah, exactly—a sadness."

"Just think about it. You've got Corky and Cindy down there, hitting the sauce and each other almost every night. They must have had to buy a whole new set of dishes after last weekend. Then you got the kid...nuff said there. What about next door, over here on this side, the guy who washes his underwear on the fucking clothes line with the hose? That guy's also classically deranged."

"I forgot about him," she said.

"Well," he said, "let's not forget about him. I watch him from the kitchen window. I can see right down through the tree branches and across the yard into his dining room. He sits there every night for hours, reading that big fat book."

"I've seen him down there," she said. "Sometimes when I wake up at three a.m. and go into the kitchen for a glass of water, I notice him down there reading. Is it the Bible?"

"Could be the fucking phone book for all I know."

"Cindy told me that when they got Tana that yippie little dog,...Shotzy, Potzy...whatever, the kid was walking on that side of the house over by the old guy's property, and he came out his backdoor, and yelled at her, 'If I find your dog in my yard, I'll kill it.' Now, I know Tana's demon seed and all, but she's still a little kid...Cindy didn't tell Corky because she was afraid he'd Cork off and kick the crap out of the old guy."

"What, instead of her for once? Hey, you never know, maybe the old man's just trying to protect himself from Tana's...*animal magic*," said Bill. "You know, Cindy swears the kid brought a dead bird back to life. She just kind of slips that in in the middle of a 'hey, the weather's nice' kind of conversation."

"Yeah, I've caught that tale," said Allison. There was a pause. "But do you get my over all point here?" She opened her hands to illustrate the broadness of the concept. "Like we're talking some kind of hovering, negative funk."

"Amorphous and pungent," he said.

"I've felt it ever since the first week we moved in here," she said.

"Does it have anything to do with the old woman who answered the door with her pants around her ankles?"

"Olive Harker?" she said. "Corky's illustrious mom?"

"Remember, Olive hadta get shipped out for us to move in. Maybe she cursed the joint...you know, put the Lambada on it."

"It wasn't her so much," said Allison. "I first felt it the day the cat pissed in the sugar bowl."

He stopped rubbing her forehead. "Right in front of me—between bites of French toast," he said. "That cat sucks."

"Don't talk about Mama that way," she said.

"It baahhhs like a lamb and eats flies. I hate it," he said.

"She's good. Three whole weeks gone and she still came back, didn't she? You shouldn't have thrown her out."

"I didn't throw her, I drop kicked her. She made a perfect arc, right over the back fence. But the question is, or at least the point is, if I follow you, is how strange is it that she pissed right in the sugar bowl—jumped up on the table, made a bee line for it, parked right over it and pissed like there was no tomorrow?"

"That's what I'm getting at," said Allison. "It fulfills no evolutionary need. It's just grim."

"Maybe it's us," he said. "Maybe we're haunting ourselves."

"I saw Corky digging a big hole out in the yard the other day," she said. "His back's full of ink—an angel being torn apart by demons...I was more interested in the hole he was digging cause I haven't heard any yipping out of Potzy for a few days."

"Don't worry," he said. "I'm ready for him."

"How?" she asked.

"Last Thursday, when I went out garbage picking and found Veronica's picture, I brought back a busted off rake handle. I wound duct tape around one end for a grip. It's in the kitchen behind the door for when Corky gets shit faced and starts up the stairs. Then I'm gonna grab that thing and beat his ass."

"Hey, do you remember that guy Keith back in college?" she asked.

"McCurly, yeah," he said. "He did the apple dance. What made you think of him?"

She nodded. "Every time he flapped his arms the apple rolled off his head, remember?"

"He danced to Steve Miller's 'Fly Like an Eagle,'" Bill said. "What a fuckin' fruitcake. I remember Oshea telling me that he ended up working for the government."

"Well, remember that time he was telling us he was reading *The Amityville Horror?*"

"Yeah," he said.

"McCurly said that one of the pieces of proof that the author used in the book to nail down his case that the house was really haunted was that they found an evil shit in the toilet bowl. Remember that?"

"Yeah."

"You said to him, 'What do you mean by an *evil* shit?' And McCurly looked like he didn't get your question."

"But what he eventually said was, 'It was heinous.' I asked him if he could explain that and he said, 'Really gross.'"

They laughed.

She touched his face as if to make him quiet, and said, "That's the point. We paint the unknown with the Devil's shit to make it make sense."

"Heavy," said Bill. A few seconds passed in silence.

"Right...?" she said.

"That Amityville House was only like two towns over from where I grew up," he told her. "New people were in there and it was all fixed up. I'd go out drinking with my friends all night. You know, the Callahans, and Wolfy, and Angelo, and Benny the Bear, and at the end of the night we'd have these cases of empty beer bottles in the car. So around that time the movie of *Amityville Horror* came out. We went to see it and laughed our asses off—come on, Brolin? Steiger we're talking. One of the things that cracked us up big time was the voice saying, 'Get out. For God's sake get the hell out.' I don't want to get into it now but Steiger and the flies...baby, well worth the price of admission. So we decided we're gonna drive to the Amityville Horror House and scream, 'Get the hell out,' and throw our empties on the lawn."

"That's retarded," she said.

"We did it, but then we kept doing it, and not just to the Amityville Horror House. Every time we did it, I'd crack like hell. It was so fucking stupid it made me laugh. Plus we were high as kites. We did it to people we knew and didn't know and we did it a lot to the high school coaches we'd had for different sports. There was this one guy, though, we did it to the most—Coach Pinhead. Crew cut, face as smooth as an ass, goggly eyes, and his favorite joke was to say 'How Long is a Chinaman.' He was a soccer coach, a real douche bag, but we swung by his house every weekend night for like three months, dropped the empties and yelled 'Pinhead!!!' before peeling out on his lawn. We called the whole thing a 'Piercing Pinhead.'"

"Could you imagine how pissed off you'd be today if some kids did that to you," she said.

"Yeah," he said, "I know. But get this. I was talking to Mike Callahan about five years later. When he was working selling furniture and married to that rich girl. I saw him at my mother's funeral. He told me that he found out later on that Pinhead died of pancreatic cancer. All that time we were doing the Piercing Pinheads, screaming in the middle of the night outside his house, tormenting him, the poor guy was in there, in his bedroom, dying by inches."

"That's haunted," said Allison.

"Tell me about it," he said and then rolled closer to kiss her.

They kissed and then lay quiet, both listening to the sound of the leaves blowing outside. She began to doze off, but before her eyes closed all the way, she said, "Who's getting the light?"

"You," said Bill.

"Come on," she said, "I've got an early shift tomorrow."

"Come on? I've gotten the damn light every night for the past two weeks."

"That's cause it's your job," she said.

"Fuck that," he said but started to get up. Just then the light went out.

She opened her eyes slightly, grinning. "Sometimes it pays to be haunted," she said.

Bill looked around the darkened room and said, as if to everywhere at once, "Thank you."

The light blinked on and then off.

"Maybe the bulb's loose," he said.

The light blinked repeatedly on and off and then died again.

"That's freaky," she said, but freaky wasn't going to stop her from falling asleep. Her eyes slowly closed and before he could kiss her again on the forehead, she was lightly snoring.

Bill lay there in the dark, wide awake, thinking about their conversation and about the lamp. He thought about ghosts in Miami, beneath swaying palm trees, doing the Lambada by moonlight. Finally, he whispered, "Light, are you really haunted?"

Nothing.

A long time passed, and then he asked, "Are you Olive?"

The light stayed off.

"Are you Pinhead?"

Just darkness.

"Are you Tana?" he said. He waited for a sign, but nothing. Eventually he closed his eyes and thought about work. He worked at Nescron, a book store housed in the bottom floor of a block-long, four-story warehouse—timbers and stone—built in the 1800s. All used books. The owner, Stan, had started, decades earlier, in the scrap paper business and over time had amassed tons of old books. The upper three floors of the warehouse were packed with unopened boxes and crates from everywhere in the world. Bill's job was to crawl in amid the piles of boxes, slit them open and mine their cargo, picking out volumes for the literature section in the store downstairs. Days would pass at work and he'd see no one. He'd penetrated so deeply into the morass of the third floor that sometimes he'd get scared, having the same feeling he'd had when he and Allison had gone to Montana three months earlier to recuperate and they were way up in the mountains and came upon a freshly killed and half-eaten antelope beside a water hole. Amidst the piles of books, he felt for the second time in his life that he was really "out there."

"I expect someday to find a pine box up on the third floor holding the corpse of Henry Miller," he'd told Allison at dinner one night.

"Who's Henry Miller?" she'd asked.

He'd found troves of classics and first editions and even signed volumes for the store down below, and Stan had praised his efforts at excavating the upper floors. As the months went on, Bill was making a neat little stack of goodies for himself, planning to shove them in a paper sac and spirit them home with him when he closed up some Monday night. An early edition of Longfellow's translation of Dante, an actual illuminated manuscript with gold leaf, a signed, first edition of *Call of the Wild*, an 1885 edition of *The Scarlet Letter* were just some of the treasures.

Recently at work he'd begun to get an odd feeling when he was deep within the wilderness of books, not the usual fear of loneliness, but the opposite, that he was not alone. Twice in the last week, he'd thought he'd heard whispering, and once, the sudden quiet tumult of a distant avalanche of books. He'd asked down below in the store if anyone else was working the third floor, and he was told that he was the only one. Then, only the previous day, he couldn't locate his cache of horded books. It was possible that he was disoriented, but in the very spot he'd thought they'd be, he instead found one tall slim volume. It was a book of fairy tales illustrated by an artist named Segur. The animals depicted in the illustrations walked upright with personality, and the children, in powder-blue snowscapes surrounded by Christmas mice, were pale, staring zombies. The colors were odd, slightly washed out and the sizes of the creatures and people were haphazard.

Without realizing it, Bill fell asleep and his thoughts of work melted into a dream of the writer Henry Miller. He woke suddenly a little while later to the sound of Allison's voice, the room still in darkness. "Bill," she said again and pushed his shoulder, "you awake?"

"Yeah," he said.

"I had a dream," said Allison. "Oh my god..."

"Sounds like a good one," he said.

"Maybe, maybe," she said.

He could tell she was waiting for him to ask what it was about. Finally he asked her, "So what happened?"

She drew close to him and he put his arm around her. She whispered, "Lothianne."

"Lothianne?" said Bill

"A woman with three arms," said Allison. "She had an arm coming out of the upper part of her back, and the hand on it had two thumbs instead of a pinky and a thumb, so it wouldn't be either righty or lefty. The elbow only bent up and down, not side to side."

"Yow," said Bill.

"Her complexion was light blue, and her hair was dark and wild, but not long. And she wore this dress with an extra arm hole in the back. This dress was plain, like something out of the Dust Bowl, gray and reached to the ankles, and I remembered my fifth grade teacher, Mrs. Donnelly, the mean old bitch, having worn the exact one back in grade school when we spent a whole year reading *The Last Days of Pompeii*."

"Did the three-arm woman look like your teacher?" asked Bill.

"No but she was stupid and mean like her. She had a dour face, familiar and frightening. Anyway, Lothianne wandered the woods with a pet jay that flew above her and sometimes perched in that tangled hair. I think she might have been a cannibal. She lived underground in like a woman-size rabbit warren."

"Charming," he said.

"I was a little girl and my sister and I were running hard toward this house in the distance, away from the woods, just in front of a wave of nighttime. I knew we had to reach the house before the darkness swept over us. The blue jay swooped down and, as I tried to catch my breath, it spit into my mouth. It tasted like fire and spread to my arms and legs. My running went dream slow, my legs dream heavy. My sister screamed toward the house. Then, like a rusty engine, I seized altogether and fell over."

"You know, in China, they eat Bird Spit Soup..." he said.

"Shut up," she said. "The next thing I know, I come to and Lothianne and me are on a raft, in a swiftly moving stream, tethered to a giant willow tree that's growing right in the middle of the flow. Lothianne has a lantern in one hand, and in the other she's holding the end of a long vine that's tied in a noose around my neck. The moon's out, shining through the willow whips and reflecting off the running water, and I'm so scared.

"She says, 'Time to practice drowning' and kicks me in the back. I fall into the water. Under the surface I'm looking up and the moonlight allows me to see the stones and plants around me. There are speckled fish swimming by. Just before I'm out of air, she reels me in. This happens three times, and on the last time, when she reels me in, she vanishes, and I'm flying above the stream and surrounding hills and woods, and I'm watching things growing—huge plants like asparagus, sprouting leaves and twining and twirling and growing in the moonlight. Even in night, it was so perfectly clear."

"Jeez," said Bill.

Allison was silent for a while. Eventually she propped herself up on her elbow and said, "It was frightening but it struck me as a 'creative' dream cause of the end."

"A three-armed woman," said Bill. "Rembrandt once did an etching of a three-armed woman having sex with a guy."

"I was wondering if the noose around my neck was symbolic of an umbilical cord..."

He stared at her. "Why?" he finally said.

She was about to answer but the bedroom light blinked on and off, on and off, on and off, without stopping, like a strobe light, and from somewhere or everywhere in the room came the sound of low moaning.

Bill threw the covers off, sat straight up and said, "What the fuck?"

Allison, wide-eyed, her glance darting here and there, said, "Bill..."

The light show finally ended in darkness, but the sound grew louder, more strange, like a high-pitched growling that seemed to make the glass of the windows vibrate. She grabbed his shoulder and pointed to the armoire. He turned, and as he did, Mama the cat came bursting out of the standing closet, the door swinging wildly. She screeched and spun in incredibly fast circles on the rug next to the bed.

"Jesus Christ," yelled Bill, and lifted his feet, afraid the cat might claw him. "Get the fuck outa here!" he yelled at it.

Mama took off out of the bedroom, still screeching. Allison jumped out of the bed and took off after the cat. Bill cautiously brought up the rear. They found Mama in the bathroom, on the floor next to the lion paw tub, writhing.

"Look," said Bill, peering over Allison's shoulder, "she's attacking her own ass. What the hell..."

"Oh, man," said Allison. "Check it out." She pointed as Mama pulled this long furry lump out of herself with her teeth.

"That's it for me," he said, backing away from the bathroom doorway.

"Bill, here comes another. It's alive."

"Alive?" he said, sitting down on a chair in the kitchen. "I thought it was a mohair turd."

"No, you ass, she's having a kitten. I never realized she was pregnant. Must be from the time you kicked her out."

Bill sat there staring at Allison's figure illuminated by the bulb she'd switched on in the bathroom.

"This is amazing, you should come see it," she called over her shoulder to him.

"I'll pass," he said. He turned then and looked through the open kitchen window, down across the yard toward the old man's house. For the first time he could remember, his neighbor wasn't there, reading the big book. The usual rectangle of light was now a dark empty space.

Later, he found Allison sitting in the wicker rocker, beneath the clown mobile, in the otherwise empty bedroom. The light was on, and she rocked, slowly, a rolled up towel cradled in her arms. "Come see," she said to him, smiling. "The first was stillborn, and this is the only other one, but it lived. It's a little girl."

He didn't want to, but she seemed so pleased. He took a step closer. She pulled back a corner of the towel, and there was a small, wet face with blue eyes.

"We have to think of a name," she said.

Spectral Evidence[1]

GEMMA FILES

Born in England and raised in Toronto, Canada, Gemma Files has been a film critic, teacher, and screenwriter, and is currently a wife and mother. She won the 1999 International Horror Guild Award for her story "The Emperor's Old Bones," and the 2006 ChiZine/Leisure Books Short Story Contest with the story reprinted herein, "Spectral Evidence," Her fiction has been published in two collections: *Kissing Carrion* and *The Worm in Every Heart*, and five of her stories were adapted into episodes of *The Hunger*, an anthology TV show produced by Ridley and Tony Scott. She has also published two chapbooks of poetry. In 2010, her first novel—*A Book of Tongues,* Part One of the Hexslinger Series—was published, followed in 2011 by *A Rope of Thorns,* the second novel in the series. The third and final installment, *A Tree of Bones,* was published in May 2012, just in time for the Mayan Apocalypse. She is currently at work on a novel with no gay outlaws or Aztec gods in it whatsoever.

"The dust still rains and reigns."
—Stephen Jay Gould, *Illuminations: A Bestiary*

Preliminary Notes

The following set of photographs was found during a routine reorganization of the Freihoeven Institute's ParaPsych Department files, a little over half a year after the official coroner's inquest which ruled medium Emma Yee Slaughter's death either an outright accident

1 Metaphorical license, naturally: Nothing here constitutes proper legal "evidence" of anything, by any stretch of the imagination.

or unprovable misadventure. Taken with what appears to have been a disposable drug-store camera, the photographs had been stuffed into a sealed, blank envelope and then tucked inside the supplemental material file attached to Case #FI4400879, Experiment #58B (attempts at partial ectoplasmic facial reconstruction, conducted under laboratory conditions).

Scribbles on the back of each separate photo, transcribed here, appear to be jotted notes done in black ink—type of pen not readily identifiable—crossbred with samples of automatic writing done by a blue felt-tipped pen with a fine nib; graphological analysis reveals two distinct sets of handwriting. The original messages run diagonally across the underside of the paper from left to right, while the additional commentary sometimes doubles back across itself so that sentences overlap. Where indicated, supplementary lines have often been written backwards. Footnotes provide additional exegesis.[2]

....

Photograph #1:[3]

Indistinct interior[4] of a dimly lit suburban house (foliage inconsistent with downtown Toronto is observable through one smallish window to left-hand side); the location seems to be a living room, decorated in classic polyester print, plastic-wrapped couch 1970s style. A stuffed, moulting sloth (*Bradypus pallidus*), mounted on a small wooden stand, sits off-centre on the glass-topped coffee-table.

Notes: "House A, April. Apported object was later traced back to Lurhninger

2 All footnotes were compiled throughout March of 2006 by Sylvester Horse-Kicker, Freihoeven Placement Programme intern, at the request of Dr Guilden Abbott.

3 Photographs, as indicated, are not themselves numbered; numbers assigned are solely the result of random shuffling. The fact that—when viewed in the order they achieved through this process—the eventual array appears to "tell a story" (Dr Abbott's notes, March 3/06) must be viewed entirely as coincidence.

4 Most photos in the sequence are best described as "indistinct."

Naturalichmuseum in Bonn, Germany. Occupants denied all knowledge of how it got there, paid us $800 to burn it where they could observe. Daughter of family said it followed her from room to room. She woke up in bed with it lying next to her."[5]

Commentary (Forwards): "Edentata or toothless ones: Sloths, anteaters, armadillos. Living fossils. A natural incidence of time travel; time travel on a personal scale, living in two places at once, bilocation. Phenomena as observed. I love you baby you said, I can't do it without you, I cut the key, you turn it. But who opens the door, and to what? Who knows for sure what comes through?"[6]

---

5 Research prompted by details in commentary has since indicated that "House A" may be 1276 Brightening Lane, Mimico, owned by William MacVain and family. On April 15, 2004, at the request of MacVain himself, Slaughter and her Freihoeven control partner, Imre Madach, were sent to investigate on-site poltergeist activity. Activity had apparently ceased by April 20, when they filed their report; the report contains no mention of monetary reimbursement for services, which the Freihoeven's internal code of conduct (of course) strongly discourages.

N.B.: "There remains the question of exactly how McVain knew *who* to contact initially, not to mention the further question of who inside the programme might have authorized Madach and Slaughter's travelling expenses—though grantedly, travel to Mimico [a suburb of the Greater Toronto Area, easily reached by following the Queen Street streetcar line to its conclusion] wouldn't have cost them much, unless they did it by taxi. Inquiries into why any letters, e-mails or phone calls exchanged between McVain and Madach/Slaughter seem not to have been properly logged are also currently ongoing." (Dr Abbott, ibid.)

6 Samples sent to Graphology for comparison suggest the initial notes on each photo were made by Madach, while the backwards commentary comes closest to a hurried, clumsy imitation of Slaughter's normal penmanship. Forward commentary, on the other hand, can probably be attributed to former Freihoeven intern Eden Marozzi, who was found dead in her apartment on Christmas 2005; going by records left behind, Marozzi had apparently been assisting Madach with his work on Slaughter's unfinished channelling experiments. As we all know, it was Madach's proven presence in her apartment at the time of Marozzi's death—as revealed by evidence gathered during the Metro Toronto Police Department's initial crime scene investigation—which, along with a lack of plausible alibi, would eventually lead to

Commentary (Backwards): "Apports are often difficult without help, so try using lucifuges for guidance. Circle is paramount; Tetragrammaton must be invoked. They have no names."[7]

....

Photograph #2:

Equally dim, angled upwards to trace what may be marks of fire damage—scorching of wallpaper, slight bubbling of plaster—moving from ceiling of kitchen down *towards* sink. The highest concentration of soot seems to be at the uppermost point. Wallpaper has a juniper-berry and leaf motif.[8]

Notes: "House D, May. We were becoming popular in certain circles. Family had two children, both sons, both under three years old; nanny reported the younger one was playing in his high-chair during breakfast when his 'Teddy-thing' suddenly caught fire.[9] Subsequent damage was estimated at $4,000; we received an additional $2,000 for making sure it wouldn't happen again."

---

his subsequent arrest on charges of murder in the second degree.

7 "Mention of 'lucifuges' would seem to indicate Slaughter—and Madach?—were using hierarchical magic to accelerate or control—generate?—poltergeist activity at McVain house. Worth further inquiry, after cataloguing rest of photos." (Dr Abbott, ibid.)

8 Attempts to identify this location have, thus far, proved inconclusive. Dr Abbott is undecided, but tentatively calls it either 542 McCaul or 71B Spinster, both of which were visited by Slaughter and Madach in connection with repeated pyrokinetic poltergeist incidents. Since one family has moved out leaving no forwarding address, however, while the other proved spectacularly uncooperative, no more detailed analysis seems forthcoming.

9 If we assume the photo *was* taken at 71B Spinster, it may be relevant to record that the child in question sustained burns severe enough to require partial amputation of three fingers from his left hand.

Commentary (Forwards): "We need something more spectacular, baby, a display, like Hollywood. Fire eats without being eaten, consumes unconsumed, as energy attracts. Come at once from whatever part of the world and answer my questions. Come at once, visibly and pleasantly, to do whatever I desire. Come, fulfil my desires and persist unto the end in accordance to my will. I conjure thee by Him to whom all creatures are obedient, and by the name of Him who rules over thee.[10] So this one goes out to the one I love, the one who left me behind, a simple prop to occupy his time. And why Teddy-'thing,' anyway? God knows I couldn't tell what it was before, afterwards."

Commentary (Backwards): "By this time, I can only think they were already watching me closely."[11]

....

Photograph #3:

Murky yet identifiable three-quarter study of Slaughter, who appears to be in light mediumistic control-trance. Orbs[12] hover over her right eye, pineal gland and heart chakra, roughly the same areas in which she would later develop simultaneous (and fatal) aneurysms. She sits in a rust-red La-Z-Boy recliner, feet elevated, with a dust-covered television screen barely visible to her extreme right, in the background of the frame.

---

10 This "anthology incantation" seems to have been compiled from several different ones, all of which appear in the legendary grimoire *Lemegeteon*. Dr Abbott confirms that the Freihoeven's library copy of this text was misplaced for several days in November of 2004, half a year prior to when the first photo was taken; this theft coincides with Madach's brief tenure as volunteer assistant librarian, before forming an experimental field-team with Slaughter.

11 By "they," this commentator may mean the aforementioned lucifuges or fly-the-lights, elemental spirits identified with fire, who Eliphas Levi calls notoriously difficult to control and naturally "hateful towards mortals."

12 Sphere-shaped visual deformities of the emulsion or pixels, often observed at sites where teams are trying to record various psychic phenomena.

Notes: "House H, July. Inclement weather with continual smog-warning. Séance performed at the request of surviving family-members, with express aim of contacting their deceased father; a control spirit was used to produce and animate an ectoplasmic husk patterned after his totem photograph, freely donated for use as a guided meditational aid. Mother cashed out RRSPs and eldest daughter's college fund in order to assemble the $15,000 required to remove 'curse'[13] afflicting their bloodline."

Commentary (Forwards): "But he died of natural causes so it's not so bad, right, not like we did anything really, and if you keep having those migraines then maybe you should take something, maybe you should just relax, baby, let me help you, let me. Don't be like that, let me, why you gotta be that way? Palpitations, you say that like it's a bad thing, that's what I love about you, baby, you have such a big heart: A big fat heart full of love and warmth and plaque and knots and pain. So just breathe, just breathe, just breathe, go do some yoga, take a pill, calm the hell down. You know we can't stop yet."

Commentary (Backwards): "Them either."

....

Photograph #4:

Close-angled shot of greasy black writing sprawled across what looks like the tiled wall of a bathroom shower-stall; letters vary radically in size, are imperfectly formed, seem (according to Graphology) inconsistent with "tool-bearing hands."[14] Letters read: "aLWaYs TheRe."[15]

Notes: "Automatic writing observed at Apartment C, renewed five separate

13 "This just gets better and better." (Dr Abbott, ibid.)

14 "'Tool-bearing'? Most messages of this type are produced telekinetically." (Dr Abbott, ibid)

15 Naturally enough, opinions vary as to who (or what) might be responsible for these markings.

times over a period of eight days. When advised that a cleansing exorcism was the best option, owner refused to cooperate."[16]

Commentary (Forward): "We have to stop we can't. We have to stop we can't. We have to stop stop stop we can't can't can't, oh Christ I want to STOP this, what are you, stupid? There's too much at stake, we're in too deep, no going back. WE CAN'T STOP NOW."

Commentary (Backwards): "Behold, I shall show you a great mystery, for we shall not all sleep, but we shall all be changed. And you can consider this my formal letter of resignation."

....

Photographs #5 to #9:

After close examination by various Freihoeven staff-members, Photographs #5 through #8 have been conclusively proven to show one of the Institute's own experimental labs. The blurry image in the extreme foreground of each seems most consistent with an adjustable Remote Viewing diorama[17] which was set up in Lab Four from approximately September 15 to December 15, 2005. Much of the background area of each photo, on the other hand, has apparently been obscured by new visuals somehow imposed over an original image, by unidentifiable means;

16 The single shortest annotation. This photo has since been tentatively identified—within a fairly narrow margin of error—as having been taken inside Slaughter's former condo, the site of her death. Even more significant, in hindsight, may be Dr Abbott's recollection (confirmed through studying her coroner's inquest file) that Slaughter's body was found in her bathtub on August 23/05, partially immersed in shallow water.

17 Invented by Dr Abbott as part of his 1978 dissertational work at the University of Toronto, these are often used as a meditational aid during guided remote viewing sessions: The "navigator" or non-psychic team-member will set the diorama up to roughly approximate the area he/she wants the viewer to access, then talk them through it on a detail-by-detail level until their trance becomes deep enough that they can guide themselves on the rest of their mental journey.

portions of the emulsion have been either destroyed or significantly altered, creating a visual illusion not unlike the "chiaroscuro" effect observed in certain Renaissance paintings which, while being restored, turn out to have been painted over a primary image that the artist may have wanted to either alter or conceal.[18]

As usual, even these partially subliminal secondary images are best described as indistinct and difficult to identify and/or categorize. Nevertheless, extensive analysis has revealed certain constants, i.e.:

- That background areas correspond with rough approximations of Photos #1 through #4, with the exception/addition of:
- A figure, face always angled away from "the camera," whose physical proportions seem to match those observed in photos taken of Slaughter, pre-mortem.[19]

---

18 "This is a prime example of what is commonly called "spirit photography"—in this case, a Directed Imagery experiment involving Marozzi that may have been infiltrated by outside influences, producing the photo. These influences may have been, as Slaughter's commentary suggests, lucifuges originally suborned into helping her and Madach perpetrate their various psychic frauds; since Slaughter, the person with genuine paranatural power in their equation, was probably the one who did the actual invocation, the lucifuges would have seen her as their primary oppressor, and directed their revenge against her in specific. Even were we to take all of the above as being empirically "true," however, once the lucifuges' malefic influence had already brought about Slaughter's death (if that is, indeed, what actually happened), one would tend to assume that they would have no further interest in the case...or that, if they did, their campaign would shift focus onto Madach, the sole surviving author of the original invocation. And in that case, why harass Marozzi at all?" (Dr Abbott, ibid.)

19 Note to self: Why am I here? Wasn't there some other, slightly less insane, place I could have gotten a summer job in? I *knew* Eden; a sweet girl, if easily influenced, overly fascinated by/with psychic phenomena and those Freihoeven members who claimed to work with/produce them. Emma Slaughter looked at me in the halls once as I passed by, and I dreamed about it for a week—still felt her watching me, wherever I went. Is this relevant? Is recording stuff like this *science*? (S. Horse-Kicker, March 2/06)*

*"A valid question, Sylvester. Thanks for your input." (Dr Abbott, ibid.)

Photo #9 was taken elsewhere; the diorama shown in Photos #5 through #8 is notably absent. A grey-painted stretch of wall, the hinge of a partially open door and the angle of lens during exposure all suggest that the camera may have been mounted on a tripod inside one of the Freihoeven's many industrial-sized storage closets, but not enough distinguishing marks are visible to establish exactly which one (there are six on Floor Three alone, for example, near the location of Lab Four).

Notes [collated into list-form for easy reading]:

(#5) "Subject was asked to visualize inside of House X. One hour fifty-three minutes allowed for session; results varyingly successful."

(#6) "Subject was asked to visualize interior of Facility H, no specific target. Agreed to deepen trance through application of Batch 33. Three hours ten minutes allowed for session; results varyingly successful."

(#7) "Subject was asked to visualize office area within Facility H, with specific reference to files stored on Public Servant G's computer. Five hours seventeen minutes allowed for session; results inconclusive overall."

(#8) "Subject was asked to visualize home office area inside House Z, with specific reference to correspondence stored in file-cabinet with plaster gargoyle on top of it.[20] Given sample of handwriting to meditate on, with double dose of Batch 33. Session interrupted at eight hours two minutes, after subject began to spasm; results inconclusive."

(#9) "Subject entered trance on own time, without instruction, after having self-injected a triple dose of Batch 33; session interrupted after approximately one hour, when subject was accidentally discovered by navigator. Limited amnesia observed after recuperation. Having no idea what image is meant to represent, impossible to say if session was successful or not."

Commentary (Forwards) [as above]:

(#5) Unintelligible scrawls.

20 "That sounds like *my* office. Investigate? I have vague recollection of anonymous notes sent to me last year, shortly before Emma's death..." (Dr Abbott, ibid.)

(#6) Same.

(#7) Same, interrupted only by a shaky but repetitive attempt to form the letters E, Y, S.

(#8) In very different handwriting, far more like that usually used for backwards commentary: "See here, see there, trying so hard, how could I help but answer? Because he likes girls who see things, yes he does; little pig, little pig, let me come in. This world's a big wide open place, up and down and all in between. Not so fun to see around corners when you know what's waiting, is it?"

(#9) Back to unintelligible scrawls.

Commentary (Backwards) [as above]:

(#5) "can"
(#6) "you"
(#7) "hear"
(#8) "me"
(#9) "now"

Photograph #10:

At first misidentified as one of the actual MTPD crime-scene photos taken at the Marozzi apartment on Christmas Day, 2005, this image also demonstrates "spirit photography" alterations of a subtly different (yet far more disturbing) sort. Analysis has revealed that the apparent main image, that of Eden Marozzi's bedroom and corpse, is actually incongruent with other elements in the photo—specifically, the time visible on Marozzi's bedside clock, which places this as having been taken a good three hours prior to what forensic experts established as her physical T.O.D.

Further examinations, including x-rays administered at the Institute's expense, have since concluded that this first image has been recorded not on the photograph's own emulsion but on a thin, rock-hard layer of biological substance[21] overlaid carefully on the original photo. Beneath this substance is a simple holiday-style snap, probably taken with the camera on a timer, that shows Marozzi and Madach embracing at Marozzi's kitchen table, both wearing party-hats and smiling. The remains of a Christmas dinner surround them; if one looks closely at the bottom centre of the photo, an opened jewel-box explains the ring visible on Marozzi's finger.

In the mirror behind them, however, a third figure—familiar from the previous array of "guided" photos—can be glimpsed sitting next to them, its hand half-raised, as though just about to touch Marozzi on the shoulder.

Notes: "Merry Christmas, Eve, from your Adam. A new Paradise begins."

Commentary (Forwards): "Fruit of knowledge, fruit of sin, snake's gift. This is what you want? This is what you get: The bitter pill. Fly the lights, lights out; out, out, brief candle! Goodbye, my lover. Goodbye, my friend. Goodbye, little girl who didn't know enough not to get in between. You can tell her I picked the wallpaper out myself. Ask her: How you like me now? Pretty good oh God God God God God"

Commentary (Backwards): "And on that note—did it really never occur to you that allowing someone used to working outside her body to be *dis*embodied might not be the world's best idea, after all?"[22]

---

21 Possibly ectoplasm, a substance occasionally exuded during séances, made up of various dead material from the medium's body.

22 To this last bit of commentary, Dr Abbott asks that a partial transcript of his most recent interview with Freihoeven psychic control-group member Carraclough Devize—held March 4/06, during which he showed her what are now tentatively called the Slaughter/Madach/Marozzi photos—be appended to this report:

> Devize: (After 120-second pause) Oh, no. Christ, that's sad.
>
> Abbott: What is, Carra?
>
> Devize: That. Don't you...no, of course you don't. There, in that corner, warping the uppermost stains. See? You'll have to strain a bit.
>
> Abbott: Is that...an orb?
>
> Devize: That's *Emma*, Doc. Face-on, finally. God, so *sad*.
>
> Abbott: (After 72-second pause) I'm afraid I'm still not—

....

Conclusion:

With Imre Madach in jail, Emma Yee Slaughter and Eden Marozzi dead, and the official files closed on all three, the discovery of the preceding photographic array would seem—though, naturally, interesting in its own right—fairly extraneous to any new interpretation of the extant facts of the case.

Recommendations

- From now on, access to/possession of library books on the Freihoeven collection's "hazardous" list must obviously be tracked far more effectively.
- In the initial screening process for evaluating prospective Freihoeven employees, whether contracted freelancers or in-house, far more emphasis needs to be placed on psychological mapping. Issues thus revealed need to be recorded and rechecked, rigorously, on a regular monthly basis.
- Similarly, field-work teams should be routinely broken up after three complete assignments together, and the partners rotated into other departments. This will hopefully prevent either side of the equation developing an unhealthy dependence on the other.
- Finally, the Institute itself needs to undergo a thorough

Devize: (Cuts him off) I know. But there she is, right there. Just about to take shape.

Abbott: Not fly-the-lights?

Devize: *Emma* had fly-the-lights, like mice or roaches, except mice and roaches don't usually...anyway. But Madach, and that poor little spoon-bender wannabe Barbie of his? By the end, what *they* had—was Emma.

psychic cleansing, as soon as possible; lingering influences must be dispelled through expulsion or exorcism, and the wards must be redrawn over the entire building. Outside experts, rather than Freihoeven employees, should be used for this task (Dr Abbott suggests consulting Maccabee Roke, Nan van Hool, Father Akinwale Oja S.J. or—as a last resort—Jude Hark Chiu-wai as to promising/economical local prospects).

- Photographs #1 through #10 will be properly refiled under #FI5556701 (cross-referentials: Madach, Marozzi, Slaughter).

Filed and signed: Sylvester Horse-Kicker, March 5/06
Witnessed: Dr Guilden Abbott, March 5/06

Two Houses

KELLY LINK

Kelly Link is the multi-award-winning author of three short-story collections. With her husband, Gavin J. Grant, she runs Small Beer Press, and edits the occasional anthology as well as the zine *Lady Churchill's Rosebud Wristlet*. She and Gavin live with their daughter, Ursula, in Northampton, Massachusetts. For more information, check out her website here: http://kellylink.net/.

Soft music woke the sleepers in the spaceship *House of Secrets*. They opened their eyes to soft pink light, crept from their narrow beds.

The chamber too was small, and the sleepers floated gracelessly within it. They stretched out their arms, scratched their heads. There were three of them, two women and one man.

There was the ship as well. Her name was Maureen. She monitored the risen sleepers, their heart rates, the dilation of their pupils, each flare of their nostrils.

She was a spirit of the air; a soothing, subliminal hum; an alchemical sequence of smells and emanations.

"Maureen, you old witch! Bread, fresh from my mother's oven. Caraway seeds!" Gwenda said. "Oh, and old books. A library? The day in the library when I decided that I would go to space one day. I was twelve."

They inhaled. Stretched again, then slowly somersaulted. Arcane chemical processes initiated by Maureen occurred within their bodies.

"A tidal smell,'" said Sullivan. "Mangrove trees, and the sea caught in a hundred basins at their roots. I spent a summer in a place like that. Arrived with one girl and left with her sister."

"Oranges. A whole grove of orange trees, all warm from the sun, and someone's just picked one. I can smell the peel, coming away." That was Mei. "Oh, and coffee! With cinnamon in it! The way he used to make it for me."

"Maureen?" said Gwenda. "Who else is awake?"

There were six crew aboard *House of Secrets*. Five women and one man. They were over ninety years into their mission. They had much longer still to go.

"Portia and Aune and Sisi are all awake," Maureen said. "They're in the Great Room, arranging the surprise party for you."

There was always a surprise party.

They threw off the long sleep. Each rose or sank toward the curve of the bulkhead, opened cunning drawers and disappeared into them to be poked and prodded and examined and massaged. The smell of cinnamon went away, was replaced by something astringent. The rosy light grew stronger.

Gwenda's hair and eyebrows had grown back in her sleep. There was a fine down of hair on her arms and legs. She got rid of it all. She checked her personal log while making her toilet. The date was March 12, 2149. She'd been asleep for seven years.

Long-limbed Sisi poked her head through the iris door as Gwenda swung out of her drawer. "New tattoo?"

It was an old joke between them.

Head to toes Gwenda was covered in the most extraordinary pictures. There was a Dürer and a Doré; a Chinese dragon and a Celtic cross; there was a winged man holding a hellbaby; a pack of wolves chasing the Queen of Diamonds across blood-stained ice; a green-haired girl on a playground rocket; the Statue of Liberty and the State Flag of Illinois; passages from the Book of Revelations and a hundred other marvels. There was the ship *House of Secrets* on the back of Gwenda's right hand, and its sister *House of Mystery* on her left.

Sisi had a Tarot deck. Her mother had given it to her. Sullivan had a copy of *Moby-Dick*, and Portia a four-carat diamond in a platinum setting. Mei brought her knitting needles.

Gwenda had her tattoos. She'd left everything else behind.

The Great Room was, strictly speaking, neither Great nor a Room. But it was the heart and the brain and the soul of the ship.

The door irised. Entering, the sleepers staggered under the onslaught.

"Dear God," Mei said.

"We each picked a theme this time! Even Maureen!" Portia said, shouting to be heard above the music. She had on something ridiculous with silver fringe down both pant legs. Gwenda looked down and took in what she was now wearing. Damn Maureen anyhow.

"Go on!" Portia yelled. "Guess!"

"Easy," Sullivan yelled back. White petals seethed around them, chased by silky-coated dogs. "Westminster dog show. Cherry blossom season, and, um, that's Shakespeare over there, right? Little pointy beard?"

Mei said, "Does that count as a theme? Shakespeare?"

"Strobe lights," Gwenda shouted. "And, uh, terrible music, the kind of music that only Aune could love. A Finnish disco. Dogs, disco, cherry blossoms, uh, Shakespeare. Is that everything?"

Portia launched herself in their direction, showered indiscriminate kisses. "Sully didn't say which year, for the dog show."

"Oh, please," Sullivan said. "Maureen, I beg you. Turn down the music a little?"

"2009," Portia said. "2009! The Sussex Spaniel Clussex Three D Grinchy Glee wins. An excellent year!"

After that it was the usual sort of party. They all danced, the way you could only dance in micro gravity. It was all good fun. When dinner was ready, Maureen sent away the Finnish dance music, the dogs, the cherry blossoms. You could hear Shakespeare say to Mei, "I always dreamed of being an astronaut." And then he vanished.

Once there had been two ships. It was considered standard practice, in the Third Age of Space Travel, to build more than one ship at a time, to send companion ships out on their long voyages. Redundancy enhances resilience, or so they like to say. Sister ships *Seeker* and *Messenger*, called *House of Secrets* and *House of Mystery* by their crews, had left Earth on a summer day in the year 2059.

House of Secrets had seen her twin disappear in a wink, a blink. First there, then nowhere. That had been thirty years ago. Space was full of mysteries. Space was full of secrets.

Dinner was Beef Wellington (fake) with asparagus and new potatoes (both real) and sourdough rolls (realish). The experimental chickens were laying again, and so there was chocolate soufflé for dessert. Maureen increased gravity, because waking up was always a special occasion and even fake Beef Wellington requires suitable gravity. Mei threw rolls across the table at Gwenda. "Look at that, will you?" she said. "Every now and then a girl likes to watch something fall."

Aune supplied bulbs of something alcoholic. No one asked what it was. Aune worked with eukaryotes and Archaea. "I made enough to get us lit," she said. "Just a little lit. Because today is Portia's birthday."

"Here's to me!" Portia said. "How old am I anyway? Never mind, who's counting."

"To Portia," Aune said. "Forever youngish."

"To Proxima Centauri," Sullivan said. "Getting closer every day. Not that much closer.

"Here's to all us Goldilocks. Here's to just right."

"To Maureen," Sisi said. "And old friends." She squeezed Gwenda's hand.

"To our *House of Secrets*," Mei said.

"To *House of Mystery*," Sisi said. They all turned and looked at her. Sisi squeezed Gwenda's hand again. They drank.

"We didn't get you anything, Portia," Sullivan said.

Portia said, "I'll take a foot rub. Or wait, I know! We'll tell stories. Ones I haven't heard before."

"We should go over the log," Aune said.

"The log can lie there," Portia said. "Damn the log."

"The log can wait," Mei agreed. "Let's sit here a while longer, and talk about nothing."

Sisi cleared her throat. "There's just one thing," she said. "We ought to tell them the one thing."

"My *party*," Portia said.

"What?" Gwenda asked Sisi.

"It's nothing," Sisi said. "Nothing at all. Only the mind playing tricks. You know how it goes."

"Maureen?" Sullivan said. "What are they talking about, please?"

Maureen blew through the room, a vinegar breeze. "Approximately thirty-one hours ago Sisi was in the Control Room. She performed several usual tasks, then asked me to bring up our immediate course. I did so. Twelve seconds later, I observed that her heart rate had gone up. When I asked her if something was wrong, she said, 'Do you see it, too, Maureen?' I asked Sisi to tell me what she was seeing. Sisi said, '*House of Mystery*. Over to starboard. It was there. Then it was gone.' I told Sisi I had not seen it. We called up charts, but nothing was recorded there. I broadcast on all channels, and no one answered. No one has seen *House of Mystery* in the intervening time."

"Sisi?" Gwenda said.

"It was there," Sisi said. "Swear to God, I saw it. Like looking in a mirror. So near I could almost touch it."

They all began to talk at once.

"Do you think—

"Just a trick of the imagination—

"It disappeared like that. Remember?" Sullivan snapped his fingers. "Why couldn't it come back again the same way?"

"No!" Portia said. She slammed her hand down on the table. "I don't want to talk about this, to rehash all this again. Don't you remember? We talked and talked and we theorized and we rationalized and what difference did it make?"

"Portia?" Maureen said. "I will formulate something for you, if you are distraught."

"No," Portia said. "I don't want anything. I'm *fine*."

"It wasn't really there," Sisi said. "It wasn't there and I wish I hadn't seen it." There were tears in her eyes. One fell out and lifted away from her cheek.

"Had you been drinking?" Sullivan said. "Maureen, what did you find in Sisi's blood?"

"Nothing that shouldn't have been there," Maureen said.

"I wasn't high, and I hadn't had anything to drink," Sisi said.

"But we haven't stopped drinking since," Aune said. She tossed back another bulb. "Maureen sobers us up and we just climb that mountain again. Cheers."

Mei said, "I'm just glad it wasn't me who saw it. And I don't want to talk about it either. Not right now. Not right after waking up."

"That's settled," Portia said. "Bring up the lights again, Maureen, please. I'd like something fancy. Something with history. An old English country house, roaring fireplace, suits of armor, tapestries, bluebells, sheep, moors, detectives in deerstalkers, Cathy scratching at the windows. You know."

That breeze ran up and down the room again. The table sank back into the floor. The curved walls receded, extruding furnishings, two panting greyhounds. They were in a Great Hall instead of the Great Room. Tapestries hung on plaster walls, threadbare and musty, so real that Gwenda sneezed. There were flagstones, blackened beams. A roaring fire. Through the mullioned windows a gardener and his boy were cutting roses.

You could smell the cold rising off stones, the yew log upon the fire, the roses and the dust of centuries.

"Halfmark House," Maureen said. "Built in 1508. Queen Elizabeth came here on a progress in 1575 that nearly bankrupted the Halfmark family. Churchill spent a weekend in December of 1942. There are many photos. Additionally, it is reported to be the second-most haunted manor in England. There are three monks and a Grey Lady, a White Lady, a yellow fog, and a stag."

"It's exactly what I wanted," Portia said. "To float around like a ghost in an old English manor. Could you reduce gravity just a bit, Maureen?"

"I like you, my girl," Aune said. "But you are a strange one."

"Funny old Aune," Portia said. "Funny old all of us." She made a wheel of herself and rolled around the room. Hair seethed around her face in the way that Gwenda hated.

"Let's each pick one of Gwenda's tattoos," Sisi said. "And make up a story about it."

"Dibs on the phoenix," Sullivan said. "You can never go wrong with a phoenix."

"No," Portia said. "Let's tell ghost stories. Aune, you start. Maureen can provide the special effects."

"I don't know any ghost stories," Aune said, slowly. "I know stories about trolls. No. Wait. I have one ghost story. It was a story that my great-grandmother told about the farm in Pirkanmaa where she grew up."

The gardeners and the rose bushes disappeared. Now, through the windows you could see a neat little farm and rocky fields, sloping up toward the twilight bulk of a coniferous forest.

"Yes," Aune said. "Exactly like that. I visited once when I was just a girl. The farm was in ruins. Now the world will have changed again. Maybe there is another farm or maybe it is all forest now." She paused for a moment, so that they all could imagine it. "My great-grandmother was a girl of eight or nine. She went to school for part of the year. The rest of the year she and her brothers and sisters did the work of the farm. My great-grandmother's work was to take the cows to a meadow where the pasturage was rich in clover and sweet grasses. The cows were very big and she was very small, but they knew to come when she called them. In the evening she brought the herd home again. The path went along a ridge. On the near side she and her cows passed a closer meadow that her family did not use even though the pasturage looked very fine to my great-grandmother. There was a brook down in the meadow, and an old tree, a grand old man. There was a rock under the tree, a great slab that looked like something like a table."

Outside the windows of the English manor, a tree formed itself in a grassy, sunken meadow.

"My great-grandmother didn't like that meadow. Sometimes when she looked down she saw people sitting all around the table that the rock made.

They were eating and drinking. They wore old-fashioned clothing, the kind her own great-grandmother would have worn. She knew that they had been dead a very long time."

"Ugh," Mei said. "Look!"

"Yes," Aune said in her calm, uninflected voice. "Like that. One day my great-grandmother, her name was Aune, too, I should have said that first, I suppose, one day Aune was leading her cows home along the ridge and she looked down into the meadow. She saw the people eating and drinking at their table. And while she was looking down, they turned and looked at her. They began to wave at her, to beckon that she should come down and sit with them and eat and drink. But instead she turned away and went home and told her mother what had happened. And after that, her older brother, who was a very unimaginative boy, had the job of taking the cattle to the far pasture."

The people at the table were waving at Gwenda and Mei and Portia and the rest of them now. Sullivan waved back.

"Ooh," Portia said. "That was a good one. Creepy! Maureen, didn't you think so?"

"It was a good story," Maureen said. "I liked the cows."

"So not the point, Maureen," Portia said. "Anyway."

"I have a story," Sullivan said. "In the broad outlines it's a bit like Aune's story."

"You could change things," Portia said. "I wouldn't mind."

"I'll just tell it the way I heard it," Sullivan said. "Anyhow it's Kentucky, not Finland, and there aren't any cows. That is, there were cows, because it's another farm, but not in the story. Sorry, Maureen. It's a story my grandfather told me."

The gardeners were outside the windows again. There was beginning to be something ghostly about them, Gwenda thought. You knew that they would just come and go, always doing the same things. Perhaps this was what it had been like to be rich and looked after by so many servants, all of them practically invisible—just like Maureen, really, or even more so—for all the notice you had to take of them. They might as well have been ghosts. Or was it the rich who had been the ghosts? Capricious, exerting great pressure without ever really having to set a foot on the ground, nothing their servants dared look at for any length of time without drawing malicious attention?

Never mind, they were all ghosts now.

What an odd string of thoughts. She was sure that while she had been alive on Earth nothing like this had ever been in her head. Out here, suspended between one place and another, of course crew went a little crazy. It was almost luxurious, how crazy you were allowed to be.

She and Sisi lay cushioned on the air, arms wrapped around each other's waists so as not to go flying away. They floated just above the silky ears of one of the greyhounds. The sensation of heat from the fireplace furred one arm, one leg, burned pleasantly along one side of her face. If something disastrous were to happen now, if a meteor were to crash through a bulkhead, if a fire broke out in the Long Gallery, if a seam ruptured and they all went flying into space, could she and Sisi keep hold of one another? She resolved she would. She would not let go.

Sullivan had the most wonderful voice for telling stories. He was describing the part of Kentucky where his family still lived. They hunted wild pigs that lived in the forest. Went to church on Sundays. There was a tornado.

Rain beat at the mullioned windows. You could smell the ozone beading on the glass. Trees thrashed and groaned.

After the tornado passed through, men came to Sullivan's grandfather's house. They were going to look for a girl who had gone missing. Sullivan's grandfather, a young man at the time, went with them. The hunting trails were all gone. Parts of the forest had been flattened. Sullivan's grandfather was with the group that found the girl. A tree had fallen across her body and cut her almost in two. She was dragging herself along the ground.

"After that," Sullivan said, "my grandfather only hunted in those woods a time or two. Then he never hunted there again. He said that he knew what it was to hear a ghost walk, but he'd never heard one crawl before."

"Look!" Portia said. Outside the window something was crawling along the floor of the forest. "Shut it off, Maureen! Shut it off! Shut it off!"

The gardeners again, with their terrible shears.

"No more old-people ghost stories," Portia said. "Okay?"

Sullivan pushed himself up toward the white-washed ceiling. "You're a brat, Portia," he said.

"I know," Portia said. "I know! I guess you spooked me. So it must have been a good ghost story, right?"

"Right," Sullivan said, mollified. "I guess it was."

"That poor girl," Aune said. "To relive that moment over and over again. Who would want that, to be a ghost?"

"Maybe it isn't always bad?" Mei said. "Maybe there are happy, well adjusted ghosts?"

"I never saw the point," Sullivan said. "I mean, ghosts appear as a warning. So what's the warning in that story I told you? Don't get caught in the forest during a tornado? Don't get cut in half? Don't die?"

"I thought they were more like a recording," Gwenda said. "Not really there at all. Just an echo, recorded somehow and then being played back, what they did, what happened to them."

Sisi said, "But Aune's ghosts—the other Aune—they looked at her. They wanted her to come down and eat with them. What would have happened then?"

"Nothing good," Aune said.

"Maybe it's genetic," Mei said. "Seeing ghosts. That kind of thing."

"Then Aune and I would be prone," Sullivan said.

"Not me," Sisi said comfortably. "I've never seen a ghost." She thought for a minute. "Unless I did. You know. *House of Mystery*. No. It wasn't a ghost. How could a ship be a ghost?"

"Maureen?" Gwenda said. "Do you know any ghost stories?"

Maureen said, "I have all of the stories of Edith Wharton and M. R. James and many others in my library. Would you like to hear one?"

"No thanks," Portia said. "I want a real story. And then Sullivan will give me a foot rub, and then we can all take a nap before breakfast. Mei, you must know a ghost story. No old people though. I want a sexy ghost story."

"God, no," Mei said. "No sexy ghosts for me. Thank God."

"I have a story," Sisi said. "It isn't mine, of course. Like I said, I've never seen a ghost."

"Go on," Portia said. "Tell your ghost story."

"Not my ghost story," Sisi said. "And not really a ghost story. I'm not sure what it was. It was the story of a man that I dated for a few months."

"A boyfriend story!" Sullivan said. "I love your boyfriend stories, Sisi! Which one?"

We could go all the way to Proxima Centauri and back and Sisi still wouldn't have run out of stories about her boyfriends, Gwenda thought. And in the meantime all they are to us are ghost stories, and all we'll ever be to them is the same. Stories their grandchildren tell *their* grandchildren.

"I don't think I've told any of you about him," Sisi was saying. "This was during the period when they weren't building new ships. Remember? They kept sending us out to do fundraising? I was supposed to be some kind of Ambassadress for Space. Emphasis on the slinky little dress. I was supposed to be seductive and also noble and representative of everything that made it worth going to space for. I did a good enough job that they sent me over to meet a consortium of investors and big shots in London. I met all sorts of guys, but the only one I clicked with was this one dude, Liam. Okay. Here's where it gets complicated for a bit. Liam's mother was English. She came from this old family, lots of money and not a lot of supervision and by the time she was a teenager, she was a total wreck. Into booze, hard drugs, recreational Satanism, you name it. Got kicked out of school after school after school, and after that she got kicked out of all of the best rehab programs too. In the end, her family kicked her out. Gave her money to go away. She ended up in prison for a couple of years, had a baby. That was Liam. Bounced around Europe for a while, then when Liam was about seven or eight, she found God and got herself cleaned up. By this point her father and mother were both dead. One of the superbugs. Her brother had inherited everything. She went back to the ancestral pile—imagine a place like this, okay?—and tried to make things good with her brother. Are you with me so far?"

"So it's a real old-fashioned English ghost story," Portia said.

"You have no idea," Sisi said. "You have no idea. So her brother was kind of a jerk. And let me emphasize, once again, this was a rich family, like you have no idea. The mother and the father and brother were into collecting art. Contemporary stuff. Video installations, performance art, stuff that was really far out. They commissioned this one artist, an American, to come and do a site-specific installation. That's what Liam called it. It was supposed to be a commentary on the transatlantic exchange, the post-colonial relationship between England and the US, something like that. And what he did was, he bought a ranch house out in a suburb in Arizona, the same state, by the way, where you can still go and see the original London Bridge. This artist bought the suburban ranch, circa 1980, and the furniture in it and everything else, down to the rolls of toilet paper and the cans of soup in the cupboards. And he had the house dismantled with all of the pieces numbered, and plenty of photographs and video so he would know exactly where everything went, and it all got shipped over to England and then he built it all again on the family's estate. And simultaneously, he had a second house built from scratch just a couple hundred yards away. This second house was an exact replica, from the foundation to the pictures on the wall to the cans of soup on the shelves in the kitchen."

"Why would anybody ever bother to do that?" Mei said.

"Don't ask me," Sisi said. "If I had that much money, I'd spend it on shoes and booze and vacations for me and all of my friends."

"Hear, hear," Gwenda said. They all raised their bulbs and drank.

"This stuff is ferocious, Aune," Sisi said. "I think it's changing my mitochondria."

"Quite possibly," Aune said. "Cheers."

"Anyway, this double installation won some award. Got lots of attention. The whole point was that nobody knew which house was which. Then the superbug took out the mom and dad, and a couple of years after that, Liam's mother the black sheep came home. And her brother said to her, I don't want you living in the family home with me. But I'll let you live on the estate. I'll even give you a job with the housekeeping staff. And in exchange you'll live in my installation. Which was, apparently, something that the artist had really wanted to make part of the project, to find a family to come and live in it.

"This jerk brother said, 'You and my nephew can come and live in my installation. I'll even let you pick which house.'

"Liam's mother went away and talked to God about it. Then she came back and moved into one of the houses."

"How did she decide which house she wanted to live in?" Sullivan said.

"That's a great question," Sisi said. "I have no idea. Maybe God told her? Look, what I was interested in at the time was Liam. I know why he liked me. Here I was, this South African girl with an American passport, dreadlocks and cowboy boots, talking about how I was going to get in a rocket and go up in space, just as soon as I could. What man doesn't like a girl who doesn't plan to stick around?

"What I don't know is why I liked him so much. The thing is, he wasn't really a good-looking guy. He wasn't bad-looking either, okay? He had a nice round English butt. His hair wasn't terrible. But there was something about him, you just knew he was going to get you into trouble. The good kind of trouble. When I met him, his mother was dead. His uncle was dead too. They weren't a lucky family. They had money instead of luck. The brother had never married, and he'd left Liam everything.

"We went out for dinner. We gave each other all the right kind of signals, but then he took me back to my hotel. He said he wanted to take me up to his country house for the weekend. It sounded like fun. I guess I was picturing one of those little thatched cottages you see in detective series. But it was like this instead." Sisi gestured around. "Big old pile. Except with video screens in the corners showing mice eating each other and little kids eating cereal. Nice, right?

"He said we were going to go for a walk around the estate. Romantic, right? We walked out about a mile through this typical South of England landscape and then suddenly we're approaching this weather-beaten, rotting stucco house that looked like every ranch house I'd ever seen in a gone-to-seed neighborhood in the Southwest, y'all. This house was all by itself on a green English hill. It looked seriously wrong. Maybe it had looked better before the other one had burned down, or at least more intentionally weird, the way an art installation should, but anyway. Actually, I don't think so. I think it always looked wrong."

"Go back a second," Mei said. "What happened to the other house?"

"I'll get to that in a minute," Sisi said. "So there we are in front of this horrible house, and Liam picked me up and carried me across the threshold like we were newlyweds. He dropped me on a rotting tan couch and said, 'I was hoping you would spend the night with me.' I said, 'You mean back at your place?' He said, 'I mean here.'

"I said to him, 'You're going to have to explain.' And so he did, and now we're back at the part where Liam and his mother moved into the installation."

"This story isn't like the other stories," Maureen said.

"You know, I've never told this story before," Sisi said. "The rest of it, I'm not even sure I know how to tell it."

"Liam and his mother moved into the installation," Portia prompted.

"Yeah. Liam's mummy picked a house and they moved in. Liam's just this little kid. A bit abnormal because of how they'd been living. And there are all these weird rules, like they aren't allowed to eat any of the food on the shelves in the kitchen. Because that's part of the installation. Instead the mother has a mini-fridge in the closet in her bedroom. Oh, and there are clothes in the closets in the bedrooms. And there's a TV, but it's an old one and the installation artist set up so it only plays shows that were current in the early nineties in the U.S., which was the last time the house was occupied.

"And there are weird stains on the carpets in some of the rooms. Big brown stains.

"But Liam doesn't care so much about that. He gets to pick his own bedroom, which seems to be set up for a boy maybe a year or two older than Liam is. There's a model train set on the floor, which Liam can play with, as long as he's careful. And there are comic books, good ones that Liam hasn't read before. There are cowboys on the sheets. There's a big stain here, in the corner, under the window.

"And he's allowed to go into the other bedrooms, as long as he doesn't mess anything up. There's a pink bedroom, with twin beds. Lots of boring girls' clothes and a stain in the closet, and a diary, hidden in a shoebox, which Liam doesn't see any point in reading. There's a room for an older boy, too, with posters of actresses that Liam doesn't recognize, and lots of American sports stuff. Football, but not the right kind.

"Liam's mother sleeps in the pink bedroom. You would expect her to take the master bedroom, but she doesn't like the bed. She says it isn't comfortable. Anyway, there's a stain on it that goes right through the duvet, through the sheets. It's as if the stain came up *through* the mattress.

"I think I'm beginning to see the shape of this story," Gwenda says.

"You bet," Sisi says. "But remember, there are two houses. Liam's mummy is responsible for looking after both houses. She also volunteers at the church down in the village. Liam goes to the village school. For the first two weeks, the other boys beat him up, and then they lose interest and after that everyone leaves him alone. In the afternoons he comes back and plays in his two houses. Sometimes he falls asleep in one house, watching TV, and when he wakes up he isn't sure where he is. Sometimes his uncle comes by to invite him to go for a walk on the estate, or to go fishing. He likes his uncle. Sometimes they walk up to the manor house, and play billiards. His uncle arranges for him to have riding lessons, and that's the best thing in the world. He gets to pretend that he's a cowboy. Maybe that's why he liked me. Those boots.

"Sometimes he plays cops and robbers. He used to know some pretty bad guys, back before his mother got religion, and Liam isn't exactly sure which he is yet, a good guy or a bad guy. He has a complicated relationship with his mother. Life is better than it used to be, but religion takes up about the same amount of space as the drugs did. It doesn't leave much room for Liam.

"Anyway, there are some cop shows on the TV. After a few months he's seen them all at least once. There's one called CSI, and it's all about fingerprints and murder and blood. And Liam starts to get an idea about the stain in his bedroom, and the stain in the master bedroom, and the other stains, the ones in the living room, on the plaid sofa and over behind the La-Z-Boy that you mostly don't notice at first, because it's hidden. There's one stain up on the wallpaper in the living room, and after a while it starts to look a lot like a handprint.

"So Liam starts to wonder if something bad happened in his house. And in that other house. He's older now, maybe ten or eleven. He wants to know why are there two houses, exactly the same, next door to each other? How could there have been a murder—okay, a series of murders, where everything happened exactly the same way twice? He doesn't want to ask his mother, because lately when he tries to talk to his mother, all she does is quote Bible verses at him. He doesn't want to ask his uncle about it either, because the older Liam gets, the more he can see that even when his uncle is being super nice, he's still not all that nice. The only reason he's nice to Liam is because Liam is his heir.

"His uncle has showed him some of the other pieces in his art collection, and he tells Liam that he envies him, getting to be a part of an actual installation. Liam knows his house came from America. He knows the name of the artist who designed the installation. So that's enough to go online and find out what's going on, which is that, sure enough, the original house, the one the artist bought and brought over, is a murder house. Some high-school kid went nuts in the middle of the night and killed his whole family with a hammer. And this artist, his idea was based on something the robber barons did at the turn of the previous century, which was buy up castles abroad and have them brought over stone by stone to be rebuilt in Texas, or upstate Pennsylvania, or wherever. And if there was a ghost, they paid even more money. So that was idea number one, to flip that. But then he had idea number two, which was, What makes a haunted house? If you take it to pieces and transport it all the way across the Atlantic Ocean, does the ghost (ghosts, in this case) come with it, if you put it back together exactly the way it was? And if you can put a haunted house back together again, piece by piece by piece, can you build your own from scratch if you recreate all of the pieces? And idea number three, forget the ghosts, can the real live people who go and walk around in one house or the other, or even better, the ones who live in a house without knowing which house is which, would they know which one was real and which one was ersatz? Would they see real ghosts in the real house? Imagine they saw ghosts in the fake one?"

"So which house were they living in?" Sullivan asked.

"Does it really matter which house they were living in?" Sisi said. "I mean, Liam spent time in both houses. He said he never knew which house was real. Which house was haunted. The artist was the only one with that piece of information. He even used real blood to recreate the stains.

"I'll tell the rest of the story as quickly as I can. So by the time Liam brought me to see his ancestral home, one of the installation houses had burned down. Liam's mother did it. Maybe for religious reasons? Liam was kind of vague about why. I got the feeling it had to do with his teenage years. They went on living there, you see. Liam got older, and

I'm guessing his mother caught him fooling around with a girl or smoking pot, something, in the house that they didn't live in. By this point she had become convinced that one of the houses was occupied by unquiet spirits, but she couldn't make up her mind which. And in any case, it didn't do any good. If there were ghosts in the other house, they just moved in next door once it burned down. I mean, why not? Everything was already set up exactly the way that they liked it."

"Wait, so there were ghosts?" Gwenda said.

"Liam said there were. He said he never saw them, but later on, when he lived in other places, he realized that there must have been ghosts. In both places. Both houses. Other places just felt empty to him. He said to think of it like maybe you grew up in place where there was always a party going on, all the time, or a bar fight, one that went on for years, or maybe just somewhere where the TV was always on. And then you leave the party, or you get thrown out of the bar, and all of a sudden you realize you're all alone. Like, you just can't sleep as well without that TV on. You can't get to sleep. He said he was always on high alert when he was away from the murder house, because something was missing and he couldn't figure out what. I think that's what I picked up on. That extra vibration, that twitchy radar."

"That's sick," Sullivan said.

"Yeah," Sisi said. "That relationship was over real quick. So that's my ghost story."

Mei said, "So what happened?"

"He'd brought a picnic dinner with us. Lobster and champagne and the works. We sat and ate at the kitchen table while he told me about his childhood. Then he gave me the tour. Showed me all the stains where those people died, like they were holy relics. I kept looking out the window, and seeing the sun get lower and lower. I didn't want to be in that house after it got dark."

They were all in that house now, flicking through those rooms, one after another. "Maureen?" Mei said. "Can you change it back?"

"Of course," Maureen said. Once again there were the greyhounds, the garden, the fire and the roses. Shadows slicked the flagstones, blotted and clung to the tapestries.

"Better," Sisi said. "Thank you. You went and found it online, didn't you, Maureen? That was exactly the way I remember it. I went outside to think and have a cigarette. Yeah, I know. Bad astronaut. But I still kind of wanted to sleep with this guy. Just once. So he was messed up, so what? Sometimes messed up sex is the best. When I came back inside the house, I still hadn't made up my mind. And then I made up my mind in a hurry. Because this guy? I went to look for him and he was down on the floor in that little boy's bedroom. Under the window, okay? On top of that *stain*. He was rolling around on the floor. You know, the way cats do? He had this look on his face. Like when they get catnip. I got out of there in a hurry. Drove away in his Land Rover. The keys were still in the ignition. Left it at a transport café and hitched the rest of the way home and never saw him again."

"You win," Portia said. "I don't know what you win, but you win. That guy was *wrong*."

"What about the artist? I mean, what he did," Mei said. "That Liam guy would have been okay if it weren't for what he did. Right? I mean, it's something to think about. Say we find some nice Goldilocks planet. If the conditions are suitable, and we grow some trees and some cows, do we get the table with the ghosts sitting around it? If there is such a thing as ghosts, do we bring our ghosts with us? Are they here now? If we tell Maureen to build a haunted house around us right now, does she have to make the ghosts? Or do they just show up?"

Maureen said, "It would be an interesting experiment."

The Great Room began to change around them. The couch came first.

"Maureen!" Portia said. "Don't you dare!"

Gwenda said, "But we don't need to run that experiment. I mean, isn't it already running?" She appealed to the others, to Sullivan, to Aune. "You know. I mean, you know what I mean?"

"Not really," Sisi said. "What do you mean?"

Gwenda looked at the others. Then Sisi again. Sisi stretched luxuriously and turned in the air. Gwenda thought of the stain on the carpet, the man rolling upon it like a cat.

"Gwenda, my love. What are you trying to say?" Sisi said.

"I know a ghost story," Maureen said. "I know one after all. Do you want to hear it?"

Before anyone could answer, they were in the Great Room again, except they were somehow outside it too. They floated, somehow, in a great nothingness. But there was the table again with dinner upon it, where they had sat.

The room grew darker and colder and the lost crew of the ship *House of Mystery* sat around the table.

That sister crew, those old friends, they looked up from their meal, from their conversation. They turned and regarded the crew of the ship *House of Secrets*. They wore dress uniforms, as if in celebration, but they had been maimed by some catastrophe. They lifted their ruined hands and beckoned, smiling.

There was a smell of char and chemicals and blood that Gwenda almost knew.

And then it was her own friends around the table. Mei, Sullivan, Portia, Aune, Sisi. She saw herself sitting there, hacked almost in two. She beckoned to herself with a blackened hand, then vanished.

The Great Room reshaped itself out of nothingness and horror. They were back in the English country house. The air was full of sour spray. Someone had thrown up. Someone else sobbed.

Aune said, "Maureen, that was unkind."

Maureen said nothing. She went about the room like a ghost, coaxing the vomit into a great ball.

"The hell was that?" Sisi said. "Maureen? What were you thinking? Gwenda? My darling, are you okay?" She reached for Gwenda's hand, but Gwenda pushed away from her.

She wriggled away in a great spasm, her arms extended to catch the wall. Going before her on the one hand, the ship *House of Secrets* and on the other, *House of Mystery*. She could no longer tell the one from the other.

Where Angels Come In

ADAM L. G. NEVILL

Adam L. G. Nevill was born in Birmingham, England, in 1969 and grew up in England and New Zealand. He is the author of the supernatural horror novels *Banquet for the Damned*, *Apartment 16*, *The Ritual*, and *Last Days*.

He lives in Birmingham and can be contacted through www.adamlgnevill.com.

One side of my body is full of toothache. Right in the middle of the bones. While the skin and muscles have a chilly pins-and-needles tingle that won't ever turn back into the warmth of a healthy arm and leg. Which is why Nanna Alice is here; sitting on the chair at the foot of my bed, her crumpled face in shadow. But the milky light that comes through the net curtains finds a sparkle in her quick eyes and gleams on the yellowish grin that hasn't changed since my mother let her into the house, made her a cup of tea and showed her into my room. Nanna Alice smells like the inside of overflow pipes at the back of the council houses.

"Least you still got one 'alf," she says. She has a metal brace on her thin leg. The foot at the end of the caliper is inside a baby's shoe. Even though it's rude, I can't stop staring. Her normal leg is fat. "They took me leg and one arm." Using her normal fingers, she picks the dead hand from a pocket in her cardigan and plops it on to her lap. Small and grey, it reminds me of a doll's hand. I don't look for long.

She leans forward in her chair so I can smell the tea on her breath. "Show me where you was touched, luv."

I unbutton my pyjama top and roll on to my good side. Podgy fingertips press around the shrivelled skin at the top of my arm, but she doesn't touch the see-through parts where the fingertips and thumb once held me. Her eyes go big and her lips pull back to show gums more black than purple. Against her thigh, the doll hand shakes. She coughs, sits back in her chair. Cradles the tiny hand and rubs it with living fingers. When I cover my shoulder, she watches that part of me without blinking. Seems disappointed to see it covered so soon. Wets her lips. "Tell us what 'appened, luv."

Propping myself up in the pillows, I peer out the window and swallow the big lump in my throat. Dizzy and a bit sickish, I don't want to remember what happened. Not ever.

Across the street inside the spiky metal fence built around the park, I can see the usual circle of mothers. Huddled into their coats and sitting on benches beside pushchairs, or holding the leads of tugging dogs, they watch the children play. Upon the climbing frames and on the wet grass, the kids race about and shriek and laugh and fall and cry. Wrapped up in scarves and padded coats, they swarm among hungry pigeons and seagulls; thousands of small white and grey shapes, pecking around the little stamping feet. Sometimes the birds panic and rise in curving squadrons, trying to get their plump bodies into the air with flap-cracky wings. And the children are blind with their own fear and excitement in brief tornadoes of dusty feathers, red feet, cruel beaks and startled eyes. But they are safe here—the children and the birds—closely watched by tense mothers and kept inside the stockade of iron railings: the only place outdoors the children are allowed to play since I came back, alone.

A lot of things go missing in our town: cats, dogs, children. And they never come back. Except for me and Nanna Alice. We came home, or at least half of us did.

Lying in my sick bed, pale in the face and weak in the heart, I drink medicines, read books and watch the children play from my bedroom window. Sometimes I sleep. But only when I have to. Because when I sink away from the safety of home and a watching parent, I go back to the white house on the hill.

For the Nanna Alice, the time she went inside the big white place as a little girl, is a special occasion; like she's grateful. Our dad calls her a "silly old fool" and doesn't want her in our house. He doesn't know she's here today. But when a child vanishes, or someone dies, lots of the mothers ask the Nanna to visit them. "She can see things and feel things the rest of us don't," my mom says. Like the two police ladies, and the mothers of the two girls who went missing last winter, and Pickering's parents, my mom just wants to know what happened to me.

At least when I'm awake, I can read, watch television, and listen to my mom and sisters downstairs. But in dreams I have no choice: I go back to the white house on the hill, where old things with skipping feet circle me, then rush in close to show their faces.

"Tell us, luv. Tell us about the 'ouse," Nanna Alice says. Can't think why she's smiling like that. No adult likes to talk about the beautiful, tall house on the hill. Even our dads who come home from the industry, smelling of plastic and beer, look uncomfortable if their kids say they can hear the ladies crying again: above their heads, but deep inside their ears at the same time, calling from the distance, from the hill, from inside us. Our parents can't hear it anymore, but they remember the sound from when they were small. It's like people are trapped and calling out for help. And when no one comes, they get real angry. "Foxes," the parents tell us, but don't look you in the eye when they say it.

For a long time after what people call "my accident" I was unconscious in the hospital. After I woke up, I was so weak I stayed there for another three months. Gradually, one half of my body got stronger and I was allowed home. That's when the questions began. Not just about my injuries, but about my mate Pickering, who they never found. And now crazy Nanna Alice wants to know every single thing I can remember and all of the dreams too. Only I never know what is real and what came out of the coma with me.

For years, we talked about going up there. All the kids do. Pickering, Ritchie and me wanted to be the bravest boys in our school. We wanted to break in there and come out with treasure to use as proof that we'd been inside, and not just looked in through the gate like all the others we knew.

Some people say the house and its grounds was once a place where old, rich people lived after they retired from owning the industry, the land, the laws, our houses, our town, us. Others say it was built on an old well and the ground is contaminated. A teacher told us it used to be a hospital and is still full of germs. Our dad said it was an asylum for lunatics that closed down over a hundred years ago and has stayed empty ever since because it's falling to pieces and is too expensive to repair. That's why kids should never go there: you could be crushed by bricks or fall through a floor. Nanna Alice says it's a place "where angels come in." But we all know it's the place where the missing things are. Every street in the miles of our town has lost a pet or knows a family who's lost a child. And every time the police search the big house, they find nothing. No one remembers the big gate being open.

So on a Friday morning when all the kids in our area were walking to school, me, Ritchie and Pickering sneaked off, the other way. Through the allotments, where me and Pickering were once caught smashing deck chairs and bean poles; through the woods full of broken glass and dogshit; over the canal bridge; across the potato fields with our heads down so the farmer wouldn't see us; and over the railway tracks until we couldn't even see the roofs of the last houses in our town. Talking about the hidden treasure, we stopped by the old ice-cream van with four flat tyres, to throw rocks and stare at the faded menu on the little counter, our mouths watering as we made selections that would never be served. On the other side of the woods that surround the estate, we could see the chimneys of the big, white mansion above the trees.

Although Pickering had been walking out front the whole time telling us he wasn't scared of security guards or watch dogs, or even ghosts—"cus you can just put your hand froo 'em"—when we reached the bottom of the wooded hill, no one said anything or even looked at each other. Part of me always believed we would turn back at the black gate, because the fun part was telling stories about the house and planning the expedition and imagining terrible things. Going inside was different because lots of the missing kids had talked about the house before they disappeared. And some of the young men who broke in there for a laugh always came away a bit funny in the head, but our dad said that was because of drugs.

Even the trees around the estate were different, like they were too still and silent and the air between them real cold. But we still went up through the trees and found the high brick wall that surrounds the grounds. There was barbed wire and broken glass set into concrete on top of it. We followed the wall until we reached the black iron gate. Seeing the PRIVATE PROPERTY: TRESPASSERS WILL BE PROSECUTED sign made shivers go up my neck and under my hair. The gate is higher than a house with a curved top made from iron spikes, set between two pillars with big stone balls on top.

"I heard them balls roll off and kill trespassers," Ritchie said. I'd heard the same thing, but when Ritchie said that I just knew he wasn't going in with us.

We wrapped our hands around the cold black bars of the gate and peered through at the long flagstone path that goes up the hill, between avenues of trees and old statues hidden by branches and weeds. All the uncut grass of the lawns was as high as my waist and the old flower beds were wild with colour. At the summit was the tall, white house with big windows. Sunlight glinted off the glass. Above all the chimneys, the sky was blue. "Princesses lived there," Pickering whispered.

"Can you see anyone?" Ritchie asked. He was shivering with excitement and had to take a pee. He tried to rush it over some nettles—we were fighting a war against nettles and wasps that summer—but got half of it down his legs.

"It's empty," Pickering whispered. "'Cept for 'idden treasure. Darren's brother got this owl inside a big glass. I seen it. Looks like it's still alive. At night, it moves it's 'ead."

Ritchie and I looked at each other; everyone knows the stories about the animals or birds inside the glass that people find up there. There's one about a lamb with no fur, inside a tank of green water that someone's uncle found when he was a boy. It still blinks its little black eyes. And someone said they found skeletons of children all dressed up in old clothes, holding hands.

All rubbish; because I know what's really inside there. Pickering had seen nothing, but if we challenged him he'd start yelling, "Have so! Have so!" and me and Ritchie weren't happy with anything but whispering near the gate.

"Let's just watch and see what happens. We can go in another day," Ritchie couldn't help himself saying.

"You're chickening out," Pickering said, kicking at Ritchie's legs. "I'll tell everyone Ritchie pissed his pants."

Ritchie's face went white, his bottom lip quivered. Like me, he was imagining crowds of swooping kids shouting, "Piss pot. Piss pot." Once the crowds find a coward, they'll hunt him every day until he's pushed out to the edges of the playground where the failures stand and watch. Every kid in town knows this place takes away brothers, sisters, cats and dogs, but when we hear the cries from the hill, it's our duty to force one another out here. It's a part of our town and always has been. Pickering is one of the toughest kids in school; he had to go.

"I'm going in first," Pick' said, standing back and sizing up the gate. "Watch where I put my hands and feet." And it didn't take him long to get over. There was a little wobble at the top when he swung a leg between two spikes, but not long after he was standing on the other side, grinning at us. To me, it now looked like there was a little ladder built into the gate—where the metal vines and thorns curved between the long poles, you could see the pattern of steps for small hands and feet. I'd heard that little girls always found a secret wooden door in the brick wall that no one else can find when they look for it. But that might just be another story.

If I didn't go over and the raid was a success, I didn't want to spend the rest of my life being a piss pot and wishing I'd gone with Pick'. We could be heroes together. And I was full of the same crazy feeling that makes me climb oak trees to the very top branches, stare up at the sky and let go with my hands for a few seconds knowing that if I fall I will die.

When I climbed away from whispering Ritchie on the ground, the squeaks and groans of the gate were so loud I was sure I could be heard all the way up the hill and inside the house. When I got to the top and was getting ready to swing a leg over, Pick' said, "Don't cut your balls off." But I couldn't smile, or even breathe. My arms and legs started to shake. It was much higher up there than it looked from the ground. With one leg over, between the spikes, panic came up my throat. If one hand slipped off the worn metal I imagined my whole weight forcing the spike through my thigh, and how I would hang there, dripping. Then I looked up toward the house and I felt there was a face behind every window, watching me.

Many of the stories about the white place on the hill suddenly filled my head: how you only see the red eyes of the thing that drains your blood; how it's kiddy-fiddlers that hide in there and torture captives for days before burying them alive, which is why no one ever finds the missing children; and some say the thing that makes the crying noise might look like a beautiful lady when you first see her, but she soon changes once she's holding you.

"Hurry up. It's easy," Pick' said from way down below. Ever so slowly, I lifted my second leg over, then lowered myself down the other side. He was right; it wasn't a hard climb at all; kids could do it.

I stood in hot sunshine on the other side of the gate, smiling. The light was brighter over there too; glinting off all the white stone and glass up on the hill. And the air seemed weird—real thick and warm. When I looked back through the gate, the world around Ritchie—who stood alone biting his bottom lip—looked grey and dull like it was November or something. Around us, the overgrown grass was so glossy it hurt your eyes to look at it. Reds, yellows, purples, oranges and lemons of the flowers flowed inside my head and I could taste hot summer in my mouth. Around the trees, statues and flagstone path, the air was a bit wavy and my skin felt so good and warm I shivered. Closed my eyes. "Beautiful," I said; a word I wouldn't usually use around Pick'. "This is where I want to live," he said, his eyes and face one big smile. Then we both started to laugh. We hugged each other, which we'd never done before. Anything I ever worried about seemed silly now. I felt taller. Could go anywhere, do anything I liked. I know Pick' felt the same.

Protected by the overhanging tree branches and long grasses, we kept to the side of the path and began walking up the hill. But after a while, I started to feel a bit nervous as we got closer to the top. The house looked bigger than I thought it was down by the gate. Even though we could see no one and hear nothing, I also felt like I'd walked into this big, crowded, but silent place where lots of eyes were watching me. Following me.

We stopped walking by the first statue that wasn't totally covered in green moss and dead leaves. Through the low branches of a tree, we could still see the two naked children, standing together on the stone block. One boy and one girl. They were both smiling, but not in a nice way, because we could see too much of their teeth. "They's all open on the chest," Pickering said. And he was right; their dry stone skin was peeled back on the breastbone and in their outstretched hands they held small lumps of stone with veins carved into them—their own little hearts. The good feeling I had down by the gate was completely gone now.

Sunlight shone through the trees and striped us with shadows and bright slashes. Eyes big and mouths dry, we walked on and checked some of the other statues we passed. You couldn't help it; it's like they made you stare at them to work out what was sticking through the leaves and branches and ivy. There was one horrible cloth thing that seemed too real to be made from stone. Its face was so nasty, I couldn't look for long. Standing under it gave me the queer feeling that it was swaying from side to side, ready to jump off the stone block and come at us.

Pick' walked ahead of me a little bit, but soon stopped to see another. He shrunk in its shadow, then peered at his shoes. I caught up with him but didn't look too long either. Beside the statue of the ugly man in a cloak and big hat, was a smaller shape covered in a robe and hood, with something coming out of a sleeve that reminded me of snakes.

I didn't want to go any further and knew I'd be seeing these statues in my sleep for a long time. Looking down the hill at the gate, I was surprised to see how far away it was now. "Think I'm going back," I said to Pick'.

Pickering looked at me, but never called me a chicken; he didn't want to start a fight and be on his own in here. "Let's just go into the house quick," he said. "And get something. Otherwise no one will believe us."

But being just a bit closer to the white house with all the staring windows made me sick with nerves. It was four storeys high and must have had hundreds of rooms inside. All the windows upstairs were dark so we couldn't see beyond the glass. Downstairs, they were all boarded up against trespassers. "They's all empty, I bet," Pickering said to try and make us feel better. But it didn't do much for me; he didn't seem so smart or hard now; just a stupid kid who hadn't got a clue.

"Nah," I said.

He walked away from me. "Well I am. I'll say you waited outside." His voice was too soft to carry the usual threat. But all the same, I suddenly couldn't stand the thought of his grinning, triumphant face while Ritchie and I were considered piss pots, especially after I'd climbed the gate and come this far. My part would mean nothing if he went further than me.

We never looked at any more of the statues. If we had, I don't think we'd have ever got to the wide stone steps that went up to the big iron doors of the house. Didn't seem to take us long to reach the house either. Even taking small, slow, reluctant steps got us there real quick. On legs full of warm water I followed Pickering up to the doors.

"Why is they made of metal?" he asked me. I never had an answer. He pressed both hands against the doors. One of them creaked but never opened. "They's locked," he said.

Secretly relieved, I took a step away from the doors. As all the ground floor windows were boarded over too, it looked like we could go home. Then, as Pickering shoved at the creaky door again, this time with his shoulder and his body at an angle, I'm sure I saw movement in a window on the second floor. Something whitish. Behind the glass, it was like a shape appeared out of the darkness and then sank back into it, quick but graceful. I thought of a carp surfacing in a cloudy pond before vanishing the same moment you saw its pale back. "Pick'!" I hissed at him.

There was a clunk inside the door Pickering was straining his body against. "It's open," he cried out, and stared into the narrow gap between the two iron doors. But I couldn't help thinking the door had been opened from inside.

"I wouldn't," I said to him. He just smiled and waved at me to come over and help as he pushed to make a bigger space. I stood still and watched the windows upstairs. The widening door made a grinding sound against the floor. Without another word, he walked inside the big white house.

Silence hummed in my ears. Sweat trickled down my face. I wanted to run down to the gate.

After a few seconds, Pickering's face appeared in the doorway. "Quick. Come an' look at all the birds." He was breathless with excitement.

I peered through the gap at a big, empty hallway and could see a staircase going up to the next floor. Pickering was standing in the middle of the hall, not moving. He was looking at the ground. At all the dried-up birds on the wooden floorboards. Hundreds of dead pigeons. I went in.

No carpets, or curtains, or light bulbs, just bare floorboards, white walls, and two closed doors on either side of the hall. On the floor, most of the birds still had feathers but looked real thin. Some were just bones. Others were dust. "They get in and they got nuffin' to eat." Pickering said. "We should collect all the skulls." He crunched across the floor and tried the doors at either side of the hall, yanking the handles up and down. "Locked," he said. "Both of 'em locked. Let's go up them stairs. See if there's summat in the rooms."

I flinched at every creak caused by our feet on the stairs. I told him to walk at the sides like me. He wasn't listening, just going up fast on his plumpish legs. I caught up with him at the first turn in the stairs and began to feel real strange again. The air was weird; hot and thin like we were in a tiny space. We were both all sweaty under our school uniforms from just walking up one flight of stairs. I had to lean against a wall while he shone his torch up at the next floor. All we could see were the plain walls of a dusty corridor. A bit of sunlight was getting in from somewhere upstairs, but not much. "Come on," he said, without turning his head to look at me.

"I'm going outside," I said. "I can't breathe." But as I moved to go back down the first flight of stairs, I heard a door creak open and then close, below us. I stopped still and heard my heart banging against my ear drums from the inside. The sweat turned to frost on my face and neck and under my hair. Real quick, and sideways, something moved across the shaft of light falling through the open front door. My eyeballs went cold and I felt dizzy. Out the corner of my eye, I could see Pickering's white face, watching me from above on the next flight of stairs. He turned the torch off with a loud click.

It moved again, back the way it had come, but paused this time at the edge of the long rectangle of white light on the hall floor. And started to sniff at the dirty ground. It was the way she moved down there that made me feel light as a feather and ready to faint. Least I think it was a *she*. But when people get that old you can't always tell. There wasn't much hair on the head and the skin was yellow. She looked more like a puppet made of bones and dressed in a grubby nightie than an old lady. And could old ladies move so fast? Sideways like a crab, looking backwards at the open door, so I couldn't see the face properly, which I was glad of.

If I moved too quick, I'm sure it would look up and see me. I took two slow side-steps to get behind the wall of the next staircase where Pickering was hiding. He looked like he was about to cry. Like me, I knew all he could hear was his own heartbeat.

Then we heard the sound of another door open from somewhere downstairs, out of sight. We knelt down, trembling against each other and peered around the corner of the staircase to make sure the old thing wasn't coming up the stairs, sideways. But a second figure had now appeared down there. I nearly cried when I saw it skittering around by the door. It moved quicker than the first one with the help of two black sticks. Bent right over with a hump for a back, it was covered in a dusty black dress that swished over the floor. What I could see of the face through the veil was all pinched and as sickly-white as grubs under wet bark. When she made the whistling sound, it hurt my ears deep inside and made my bones feel cold.

Pickering's face was wild with fear. I was seeing too much of his eyes. "Is they old ladies?" he said in a voice that sounded all broken.

I grabbed his arm. "We got to get out. Maybe there's a window, or another door 'round the back." Which meant we had to go up these stairs, run through the building to find another way down to the ground-floor, before breaking our way out.

I took another peek down the stairs to see what they were doing, but wished I hadn't. There were two more of them. A tall man with legs like sticks was looking up at us with a face that never changed because it had no lips or eyelids or nose. He wore a creased suit with a gold watch chain on the waistcoat, and was standing behind a wicker chair. In the chair was a bundle wrapped in tartan blankets. Above the coverings I could see a small head inside a cloth cap. The face was yellow as corn in a tin. The first two were standing by the open door so we couldn't get out.

Running up the stairs into an even hotter darkness on the next floor, my whole body felt baggy and clumsy and my knees chipped together. Pickering went first with the torch and used his elbows so I couldn't overtake. I bumped into his back and kicked his heels. Inside his fast breathing, I could hear him sniffing at tears. "Is they comin'?" he kept saying. I didn't have the breath to answer and kept running through the long corridor, between dozens of closed doors, to get to the end. I looked straight ahead and was sure I would freeze up if one of the doors suddenly opened. And with our feet making such a bumping on the floorboards, I can't say I was surprised when I heard the click of a lock behind us. We both made the mistake of looking back.

At first we thought it was waving at us, but then realised the skinny figure in the dirty nightdress was moving its long arms through the air to attract the attention of the others that had followed us up the stairwell. We could hear the scuffle and swish as they came through the dark behind us. But how could this one see us, I thought, with all those rusty bandages around its head? Then we heard another of those horrible whistles, followed by more doors opening real quick like things were in a hurry to get out of the rooms.

At the end of the corridor, there was another stairwell with more light in it that fell from a high window three floors up. But the glass must have been dirty and greenish, because everything around us on the stairs looked like it was underwater. When he turned to bolt down them stairs, I saw Pick's face was all shiny with tears and the front of his trousers had a dark patch spreading down one leg.

It was real hard to get down them stairs and back to the ground. It was like we had no strength left in our bodies, as if the fear was draining it through the slappy, tripping soles of our feet. But it was more than the terror slowing us down; the air was so thin and dry it was hard to get our breath in and out of our lungs fast enough. My shirt was stuck to my back and I was dripping under the arms. Pick's hair was wet and he was slowing right down, so I overtook him.

At the bottom of the stairs I ran into another long, empty corridor of closed doors and greyish light, that ran through the back of the building. Just looking all the way down it, made me bend over with my hands on my knees to rest. But Pickering just ploughed right into me from behind and knocked me over. He ran across my body and stamped on my hand. "They's comin'," he whined in a tearful voice and went stumbling down the passage. I got back to my feet and started down the corridor after him. Which never felt like a good idea to me; if some of them things were waiting in the hall by the front doors, while others were coming up fast behind us, we'd get ourselves trapped. I thought about opening a door and trying to kick out the boards over a window in one of the ground-floor rooms. Plenty of them old things seemed to come out of rooms when we ran past them, like we were waking them up, but they never came out of every room. So we would just have to take a chance. I called out to Pick' to stop. I was wheezing like Billy Skid at school who's got asthma, so maybe Pickering never heard me, because he kept on running toward the end. I looked back at the stairwell we'd just come out of, then looked about at the doors in the passage. As I was wondering which one to pick, a little voice said, "Do you want to hide in here."

I jumped into the air and cried out like I'd trod on a snake. Stared at where the voice came from. I could see a crack between this big brownish door and the doorframe. Part of a little girl's face peeked out. "They won't see you. We can play with my dolls." She smiled and opened the door wider. She had a really white face inside a black bonnet all covered in ribbons. The rims of her dark eyes were bright red like she'd been crying for a long time.

My chest was hurting and my eyes were stinging with sweat. Pickering was too far ahead of me to catch him up. I could hear his feet banging away on loose floorboards, way off in the darkness, and I didn't think I could run any further. I nodded at the girl. She stood aside and opened the door wider. The bottom of her black dress swept through the dust. "Quickly," she said with an excited smile, and then looked down the corridor, to see if anything was coming. "Most of them are blind, but they can hear things."

I moved through the doorway. Brushed past her. Smelled something gone bad. Put a picture in my head of the dead cat, squashed flat in the woods, that I found one time on a hot day. But over that smell was something like the bottom of my granny's old wardrobe, with the one broken door and little iron keys in the locks that don't work any more.

Softly, the little girl closed the door behind us, and walked off across the wooden floor with her head held high, like a "little Madam" my dad would say. Light was getting into this room from some red and green windows up near the high ceiling. Two big chains hung down holding lights with no bulbs, and there was a stage at one end with a thick greenish curtain pulled across the front. Little footlights stuck up at the front of the stage. It must have been a ballroom once.

Looking for a way out—behind me, to the side, up ahead, everywhere—I followed the little girl in the black bonnet over to the stage and up the stairs at the side. She disappeared through the curtains without making a sound, and I followed because I could think of nowhere else to go and I wanted a friend in here. The long curtains smelled so bad around my face, I put a hand over my mouth.

She asked my name and where I lived. I told her like I was talking to a teacher who's just caught me doing something wrong, even giving her my house number. "We didn't mean to trespass," I said. "We never stole nothing." She cocked her head to one side and frowned like she was trying to remember something. Then she smiled and said, "All of these are mine. I found them." She drew my attention to the dolls on the floor; little shapes of people I couldn't see properly in the dark. She sat down among them and started to pick them up one at a time to show me, but I was too nervous to pay much attention and I didn't like the look of the cloth animal with its fur worn down to the grubby material. It had stitched up eyes and no ears; the arms and legs were too long for its body. And I didn't like the way the little, dirty head was stiff and upright like it was watching me.

Behind us, the rest of the stage was in darkness with a faint glow of white wall in the distance. Peering from the stage at the boarded-up windows down the right side of the dance floor, I could see some bright daylight around the edge of two big hardboard sheets nailed over patio doors. There was a breeze coming through. Must have been a place where someone got in before. "I got to go," I said to the girl behind me, who was whispering to her animals and dolls. I was about to step through the curtains and head for the daylight when I heard the rushing of a crowd in the corridor that me and Pickering had just run through—feet shuffling, canes tapping, wheels squeaking and two hooting sounds. It all seemed to go on for ages. A long parade I didn't want to see.

As it went past, the main door clicked open and something glided into the ballroom. I pulled back from the curtains and held my breath. The little girl kept mumbling to the nasty toys. I wanted to cover my ears. Another crazy part of me wanted it all to end; wanted me to step out from behind the curtains and offer myself to the tall figure down there on the dance-floor, holding the tatty parasol over its head. It spun around quickly like it was moving on tiny, silent wheels under its long musty skirts. Sniffing at the air. For me. Under the white net attached to the brim of the rotten hat and tucked into the high collars of the dress, I saw a bit of face that looked like skin on a rice pudding. I would have screamed but there was no air inside me.

I looked down to where the little girl had been sitting. She had gone, but something was moving on the floor. Squirming. For a moment, it looked like all her toys were trembling, but when I squinted at the Dolly with bits of curly white hair on its head, it was lying perfectly still where she had dropped it. The little girl may have hidden me, but I was glad she had gone.

Way off in the stifling distance of the big house, I heard a scream; full of all the panic and terror and woe in the whole world. The figure with the little umbrella spun right around on the dance-floor and then rushed out of the ballroom toward the sound.

I slipped out from behind the curtains. A busy chattering sound came from the distance. It got louder until it echoed through the corridor and ballroom and almost covered the sounds of the wailing boy. It sounded like his cries were swirling round and round, bouncing off walls and closed doors, like he was running somewhere far off inside the house, in a circle that he couldn't get out of.

I crept down the stairs at the side of the stage and ran across to the long strip of burning sunlight I could see shining through one side of the patio doors. I pulled at the big rectangle of wood until it splintered and I could see broken glass in a doorframe and lots of thick grass outside.

For the first time since I'd seen the first figure scratching about the front entrance, I truly believed I could escape. I could climb through the gap I was making, run around the outside of the house and then go down the hill to the gate, while they were all busy inside with the crying boy. But just as my breathing went all quick and shaky with the glee of escape, I heard a *whump* sound on the floor behind me, like something had just dropped to the floor from the stage. Teeny vibrations tickled the soles of my feet. Then

I heard something coming across the floor toward me—a shuffle, like a body dragging itself real quick.

Couldn't bear to look behind me and see another one close up. I snatched at the board and pulled with all my strength at the bit not nailed down, so the whole thing bent and made a gap. Sideways, I squeezed a leg, hip, arm and shoulder out. Then my head was suddenly bathed in warm sunlight and fresh air.

It must have reached out then and grabbed my left arm under the shoulder. The fingers and thumb were so cold they burned my skin. And even though my face was in daylight, everything went dark in my eyes except for little white flashes, like when you stand up too quick. I wanted to be sick. Tried to pull away, but one side of my body was all slow and heavy and full of pins and needles.

I let go off the hardboard sheet. It slapped shut like a mouse trap. I fell through the gap and into the grass outside. Behind my head, I heard a sound like celery snapping. Something shrieked into my ear which made me go deafish for a week.

Sitting down in the grass outside, I was sick down my jumper. Mucus and bits of spaghetti hoops that looked all white and smelled real bad. I looked at the door I had fallen out of. Through my bleary eyes I saw an arm that was mostly bone, stuck between the wood and door-frame. I made myself roll away and then get to my feet on the grass that was flattened down.

Moving around the outside of the house, back toward the front of the building and the path that would take me down to the gate, I wondered if I'd bashed my left side. The shoulder and hip were achy and cold and stiff. It was hard to move. I wondered if that's what broken bones felt like. All my skin was wet with sweat too, but I was shivery and cold. I just wanted to lie down in the long grass. Twice I stopped to be sick. Only spit came out with burping sounds.

Near the front of the house, I got down on my good side and started to crawl, real slow, through the long grass, down the hill, making sure the path was on my left so I didn't get lost in the meadow. I only took one look back at the house and will wish forever that I never did.

One side of the front door was still open from where we went in.

I could see a crowd, bustling in the sunlight that fell on their raggedy clothes. They were making a hooting sound and fighting over something; a small shape that looked dark and wet. It was all limp. Between the thin, snatching hands, it came apart, piece by piece.

In my room, at the end of my bed, Nanna Alice has closed her eyes. But she's not sleeping. She's just sitting quietly and rubbing her doll hand like she's polishing treasure.

Hunger, An Introduction

PETER STRAUB

Peter Straub is the author of eighteen novels, including *Ghost Story*, *Koko*, *Mr. X*, two collaborations with Stephen King, *The Talisman* and *Black House*, and his most recent, *A Dark Matter*. He has also written two volumes of poetry and three collections of short fiction. He edited *Conjunctions 39: The New Wave Fabulists*, Library of America's *H. P. Lovecraft: Tales*, the LoA's *American Fantastic Tales*, and *Poe's Children*.

He has won the British Fantasy Award, ten Bram Stoker Awards, two International Horror Guild Awards, and four World Fantasy Awards. In 1998, he was named Grand Master at the World Horror Convention. He has also been honored with the Lifetime Achievement Award given by the World Fantasy Convention and the Barnes & Noble Writers for Writers Award. The University of Wisconsin and Columbia University honored him with Distinguished Alumnus Awards.

You can find Peter on Twitter as @peterstraubnyc.

I have a sturdy first sentence all prepared, and as soon as I settle down and get used to the reversal of our usual roles I'll give you the pleasure. Okay. Here goes. *Considering that everyone dies sooner or later, people know surprisingly little about ghosts.* Is my point clear? Every person on earth, whether saint or turd, is going to wind up as a ghost, but not one of them, I mean, of *you* people, knows the first thing about them. Almost everything written, spoken, or imagined about the subject is, I'm sorry, absolute junk. It's disgusting. I'm speaking from the heart here, I'm laying it on the line—disgusting. All it would take to get this business right is some common, everyday, sensible thinking, but sensible thinking is easier to ask for than to get, believe you me.

I see that I have already jumped my own gun, because the second sentence I intended to deliver was: *In fact, when it comes to the subject of ghosts, human beings are completely clueless.* And the third sentence, after which I am going to scrap my prepared text and speak from the heart, is: *A lot of us are kind of steamed about that.*

For! The most common notion about ghosts, the granddaddy, is the one that parades as grown-up reason, shakes its head, grins, fixes you with a steely glint that asks if you're kidding, and says: Ghosts don't exist.

Wrong.

Sorry, wrong.

Sorry, I know, you'd feel better if you could persuade yourself that accounts of encounters with beings previously but not presently alive are fictional. Doesn't matter how many people say they have seen a woman in black moving back and forth behind the window from which in 1892 the chambermaid Ethel Carroway defenestrated a newborn infant fathered by a seagoing rogue named Captain Starbuck, thousands of fools might swear to having seen Ethel's shade drag itself past that window, it don't, sorry, it doesn't matter, they're all deluded. They saw a breeze twitch the curtain and imagined the rest. *They want you to think they're interesting.* You're too clever for that one. You know what happens to people after they chuck it, and one thing that's sure is, they don't turn into ghosts. At the moment of death, people either (1) depart this and all other possible spheres, leaving their bodies to fade out in a messier, more time-consuming fashion; or (2) leave behind the poor old skinbag as their immortal part soars heavenward, rejoicing, or plummets wailing to eternal torment; or (3) shuffle out of one skinbag, take a few turns around the celestial block, and reincarnate in a different, fresher skinbag, thereupon starting all over again. Isn't that more or less the menu? Extinction, moral payback, or rebirth. During my own life, for example, I favored (1), a good clean departure.

Now we come to one of my personal bugaboos or, I could say, anathemas, in memory of someone I have to bring in sooner or later anyhow, my former employer, Mr. Harold McNair, a gentleman with an autodidact's fondness for big words. Mr. McNair once said to me, *Dishonesty is my particular anathema.* One other time, he used the word *peculation*. Peculation was his anathema, too. Mr. Harold McNair was confident of his personal relationship to his savior, and as a result he was also pretty confident that what lay ahead of him, after a dignified leave-taking in the big bed on the third floor, was a one-way excursion to paradise. As I say, he was pretty sure about that. Maybe now and then the thought came to him that a depraved, greedy, mean-spirited weasel like himself might have some trouble squeaking through the pearly gates, no matter how many Sundays he strutted over to the church on Abercrombie Road to lip-synch to the hymns and nod over the sermon—yes, maybe Harold McNair had more doubts than he let on. When it came down to what we have to call the crunch, he did not go peacefully. How he went was screeching and sweating and cursing, trying to shield his head from the hammer and struggling to get back on his feet, for all the world as though he feared spending eternity as a rasher of bacon. And if asked his opinion on the existence of ghosts, this big-shot retail magnate would probably have nodded slowly, sucked his lower lip, pondered mightily, and opined—

All right, I never actually heard the position of my former employer in re ghostly beings despite our many, ofttimes tediously lengthy colloquies. Harold McNair spoke to me of many things, of the anathemas dishonesty and peculation, of yet more anathemas, including the fair sex, any human being under the age of twenty, folk of the Hebraic, Afric, or Papist persuasions, customers who demand twenty minutes of a salesman's attention and then sashay out without making a purchase, customers—*female* customers—who return undergarments soiled by use, residents of California or New York, all Europeans, especially bogtrotters and greaseballs, eggheads, per-fessers, pinkos, idiots who hold hands in public, all music but the operettas of Gilbert and Sullivan, all literature not of the "improving" variety, tight shoes, small print, lumpy potatoes, dogs of any description, and much else. He delivered himself so thoroughly on the topics that excited his indignation that he never got around to describing his vision of the afterlife, even while sputtering and screeching as the hammer sought out the tender spots on his tough little noggin. Yet I know what Mr. McNair would have said.

Though ghosts may fail to be nonexistent, they are at least comfortingly small in number.

Wrong. This way of thinking disregards the difference between Ghosts Visible, like poor Ethel Carroway, who dropped that baby from the fourth-floor window of the Oliphant Hotel, and Invisible, which is exactly like pretending there is no difference between living Visibles, like Mr. Harold McNair, and Living Invisibles, which, in spite of everything, is what I was back then, not to mention most everyone else, when you get down to it. Most people are about as visible to others as the headlines on a week-old newspaper.

I desire with my entire heart to tell you what I am looking at, I yearn to describe the visible world as seen from my vantage point beside the great azalea bush on my old enemy's front lawn on Tulip Lane, the spot I head for every day at this time. That would clear up this whole *numbers* confusion right away. But before I can get into describing what I can see, I must at last get around to introducing myself, since that's the point of my being here today.

Francis T. Wardwell is my handle, Frank Wardwell as I was known, and old Frank can already feel himself getting heated up over the third numbskull idea the run of people have about ghosts, so he better take care of that one before going any further. The third idea is: Ghosts are ghosts because they are unhappy. Far too many of you out there believe that every wandering spirit is atoning for some old heart-stuffed misery, which is why they suppose Ethel drifts past that window now and again.

Ask yourself, now. Is anything that simple, even in what *you* call experience? Are all the criminals in jail? Are all the innocent free? And if the price of misery is misery, what is the price of joy? In what coin do you pay for that, laddy: shekels, sweat, or sleepless nights?

Though in every moment of my youthful existence I was sustained by a most glorious secret that was mine alone, I too was acquainted with shekels, sweat, and what the poets call white nights. No child of luxury, I. Francis Wardwell, Frank to his chums, born to parents on the ragged-most fringe of the lower middle class, was catapulted into corporeality a great distance from the nearest silver spoon. We were urban poor (lower-middle-class poor, that is), not rural poor, and I feel deeply within myself that a country landscape such as that of which I was deprived would have yielded to my infant self a fund of riches sorely needed. (Mark the first sounding of the hunger theme, to which we will return betimes.) Is not Nature a friend and tutor to the observant child? Does it not offer a steady flow of stuff like psychic nutrient to the developing boy? Experts say it does, or so I hear, and also that much do I recall from my reading, which was always far, far in advance of my grade level. (I was reading on the *college level* before I was out of short pants.) Old-time poets all said Nature is a better teacher than any other. In my case, blocked off by city walls from the wise friend Nature, I was forced to feed my infant mind on the harsher realities of brick, barbed wire, and peacock-feather oil slicks. That I went as far as I did is testimony to my resilient soul-strength. Forbidden was I to wander 'mongst the heather and cowslips, the foxgloves, purple vetch, tiger lilies, loosestrife, and hawkweed on country lanes; no larks or thrushes had I for company, and we never even heard of nightingales where I came from. I wandered, when I had that luxury—that is, when I wasn't running my guts out to get away from a long-nosed, red-eyed, smirking Boy Teuteburg—through unclean city streets past taverns and boardinghouses, and for streaky gold-red sunsets I had neon signs. The air was not, to put it good and plain, fresh. The animals, when not domestic, were rodentine. And from the seventh grade on, at a time when I suffered under the tyranny of a termaganty black-haired witch-thing named Missus Barksdale, who hated me because I knew more than she did, I was forced to endure the further injustice of after-school employment. Daily had I to trudge from the humiliations delivered upon my head by the witch-thing, Missus Barfsbottom, humiliations earned only through an inability to conceal entirely the mirth her errors caused in me, from sadistic, unwarranted humiliations delivered upon the head of one of the topmost scholars ever seen at that crummy school, then to trudge through sordiosities to the place of my employment, Dockweder's Hardware, where I took up my broom and swept, swept, swept.

For shekels! In the sense of measly, greasy coins of low denomination in little number! Earned by my childish sweat, the honest sorrowful perspiration, each salty drop nonaccidentally just exactly like a tear (and that, Miss Doggybreath, is what you call a metaphor, not a methapor, as your warty mustachy cakehole misinformed the massed seventh grade of the Daniel Webster State Graded School in the winter of 1928), of a promising, I mean really and truly *promising* lad, an intelligent lad, a lad deserving of the finest this world had to offer in the way of breaks and opportunities, what you might want to call and I looking back am virtually forced to call a Shining Boy!

Who day and night had to check over his shoulder for the approach of, who had to strain his innocent ears in case he could hear the footfalls of, who was made to quench his glorious shining spirit because he had to live in total awful fear of the subhuman, soulless, snakelike figure of Boy Teuteburg. Who would crouch behind garbage cans and conceal himself in doorways, was a lurker in alleys, would drag at his narrow cigarette with his narrow shoulders against the bricks and squint out from under the narrow brim of the cap on his narrow head, was a low being of no conscience or intelligence or any other merits altogether. A Boy Teuteburg is not a fellow for your flowery fields and rending sunsets. And such as this, a lowly brutal creature with no promise to him at all save the promise to wind up in jail, became yet another, perhaps the most severe, bane of the Shining Boy's existence.

Between Daniel Webster State Graded School and Dockweder's Hardware Emporium would this young terrorist lurk of an afternoon, stealing some worthless titbit there, hawking on the sidewalk there, blowing his nose by pressing two fingers against one nostril, leaning over and firing, then repeating the gesture on the opposite side, all the while skulking along, flicking his puny red eyes over the passing throng (as *Dickens* had it) in search of children younger than he, any children in actual fact, but in most especial one certain child. This, you may have divined, was yours truly. I knew myself the object of Boy Teuteburg's special hatred because of what befell the child-me on those occasions when I managed to set sail from one place to another in convoy with other kidlings of my generation—other sparrows of the street (as *Blake* might put it)—to subsume myself within the shelter of a nattering throng of classmates. We all feared Boy, having suffered under his psychotic despotism through year after year of grade-school. Our collective relief at his eventual graduation (he was sixteen!) chilled to dread when we discovered that his release from the eighth grade meant only that Boy had been freed to prowl eternally about Daniel Webster, a shark awaiting shoals of smaller fishes. (A *simile*, Missus Doggybark, a *simile*.) There he was, smirking as he tightened his skinny lips to draw on his skinny cigarette—circling. Let us say our convoy of joking lads rounds the corner of Erie Street by the Oliphant Hotel and spreads across the sidewalk as we carry on toward Third Street, home for some, Dockweder's and the broom for me. Then a stoaty shadow separates from the entrance of Candies & Newsagent, a thrill of fear passes through us, red eyes ignite and blaze, some dreary brat begins to weep, and the rest of us scatter as Boy charges, already raising his sharp and pointy fists. And of all these larking children, which particular boy was his intended target? That child least like himself—the one he hated most—myself—and I knew why. Scatter though I would 'mongst my peers, rushing first to this one then to that, my friends, their morality stunted by the same brutal landscape which had shaped our tormentor, would'st thrust me away, abandon me, sacrifice me for their own ends. It was me, I mean I, he searched out, and we all knew it. Soon the others refused to leave the school in my presence, and I walked alone once more. Oft were the days when the body that wielded the broom ached with bruises, when the eyes within the body were dimmed with tears of pain and sorrow, and the nose of the body contained screws of tissue paper within each nostril, purpose of, to staunch the flow of blood.

Oft, too, were the nights when from a multiplicity of causes young Frank Wardwell lay sleepless abed. His concave boyish tummy begged for sustenance, for the evening repast may have been but bread and sop, and the day's beating meant that certain much-favored positions were out of the question. Yet hunger and pain were as nothing when compared to the primary reason sleep refused to grant its healing balm. This was terror. Day came when night bowed out, and day brought Boy Teuteburg. So fearsome was my tormentor that I lay paralyzed 'neath my blankets, hoping without hope that I might the next day evade my nemesis. Desperate hours I spent mapping devious alternate routes from school to store while still knowing well that however mazy the streets I took, they would in the end but deliver me unto Boy. And many times I sensed that he had glided into our yard and stood smoking beneath our tree, staring red-eyed at my unlighted window. Other times, I heard him open our back door and float through the kitchen to hover motionless outside my door. What good now was my intellectual and spiritual superiority to Boy Teuteburg? Of what use my yearnings? Ice-cold fear was all I knew. Mornings, I dragged myself from bed, quaking, opened my door to find Boy of course nowhere in sight, fed my ice-cold stomach a slice of bread and a glass of water, and dragged myself to school, hopeless as the junkman's nag. Had I but known of the thousand eyes upon me...

Why does Ethel Carroway report to her window on the fourth floor of the Oliphant Hotel at the full of the moon? Guilt? Grief? Remorse?

In life, this was a thoughtless girl, vibrant but shallow, the epitome of a Visible, who felt no more of guilt than does a cast-iron pump. For months, Ethel had gone about her duties in loose overblouses to conceal her condition, of which even her slatternly friends were ignorant. The infant signified no more than a threat to her employment. She never gave it a name or fantasized about it or thought of it with aught but distaste. Captain Starbuck had departed the day following conception, in any case a hasty, rather *scuffling* matter, no doubt to sow his seed in foreign ports. Delivery took place behind the locked door of Ethel's basement room and lasted approximately twelve hours, during which she had twice to shout from her bed that she was violently ill and could not work. During the process, she consumed much of a bottle of bourbon whiskey given her by another priapic guest of the Oliphant. When at last the child bullied its way out between her legs, Ethel bit the umbilicus in two and observed that she had delivered a boy. Its swollen purple genitals were a vivid reminder of Captain Starbuck. Then she passed out. An hour later, consciousness returned on a tide of pain. Despite all, Ethel felt a curious new pride in herself—in what she had done. Her baby lay on her chest, uttering little kittenish mewls. It resembled a monkey, or a bald old man. She found herself regretting that she had to dispose of this creature who had brought her so much pain. They had shared an experience that now seemed almost hallucinatory in its intensity. She wished the baby were the kitten it sounded like, that she might keep it. She and the baby were companions of a sort. And she realized that it was hers—she had made this little being.

Yet her unanticipated affection for the infant did not alter the facts. Ethel needed her job, and that was that. The baby had to die. She moved her legs to the side of the bed, and a fresh wave of pain made her gasp. Her legs, her middle, the bed, all were soaked in blood. The baby mewed again, and more to comfort herself than it, she slid the squeaking child upward toward her right breast and bumped the nipple against his lips until he opened his mouth and tried to suck. Like Ethel, the baby was covered with blood, as well as with something that resembled grease. At that moment she wanted more than anything else to wash herself off—she wanted to wash the baby, too. At least he could die clean. She transferred him to her other breast, which gave no more milk than the first. When she stroked his body, some of the blood and grease came off on her hand, and she wiped his back with a clean part of the sheet.

Some time later, Ethel swung her feet off the bed, ignored the bolts of pain, and stood up with the baby clamped to her bosom. Grimacing, she limped to the sink and filled it with tepid water. Then she lowered the baby into the sink. As soon as his skin met the water, his eyes flew open and appeared to search her face. For the first time, she noticed that their color was a violent purple-blue, like no other eyes she had ever seen. The infant was frowning magisterially. His legs contracted under him like a frog's. His violent eyes glowered up at her, as if he knew what she was ultimately going to do, did not at all like what she was going to do, but accepted it. As she swabbed him with the washcloth, he kept frowning up at her, scanning her face with his astonishing eyes.

Ethel considered drowning him, but if she did so, she would have to carry his body out of the hotel, and she didn't even have a suitcase. Besides, she did not enjoy the idea of holding him under the water while he looked up at her with that funny old-king frown. She let the water drain from the sink, wrapped the baby in a towel, and gave herself a rudimentary sponge bath. When she picked the baby off the floor, his eyes flew open again, then closed as his mouth gaped in an enormous yawn. She limped back to bed, tore the sheets off one-handed, cast a blanket over the mattress, and fell asleep with the baby limp on her chest.

It was still dark when Ethel awakened, but the quality of the darkness told her that it would soon be morning. The baby stirred.

Its arms, which had worked free of the towel, jerked upward, paused in the air, and drifted down again. This was the hour when the hotel was still, but for the furnaceman. The hallways were empty; a single sleepy clerk manned the desk. In another hour, the bootboys would be setting out the night's polished shoes, and a few early-bird guests would be calling down their room-service orders. In two hours, a uniformed Ethel Carroway was supposed to report for duty. She intended to do this. When it became noticed that she was in pain, she would be allowed another day's sick leave, but report she must. She had approximately forty-five minutes in which to determine what to do with the baby and then to do it.

A flawless plan came to her. If she carried the baby to the service stairs, she would avoid the furnaceman's realm, and once on the service stairs, she could go anywhere without being seen. The hallways would remain empty. She could reach one of the upper floors, open a window, and—let the baby fall. Her part in his death would be over in an instant, and the death itself would be a matter of a second, less than a second, a moment too brief for pain. Afterward, no one would be able to connect Ethel Carroway with the little corpse on the Erie Street pavement. It would seem as though a guest had dropped the baby, or as though an outsider had entered the hotel to rid herself of an unwanted child. It would be a mystery: a baby from nowhere, fallen from the Oliphant Hotel. Police Are Baffled.

She pulled on a nightdress and wrapped herself in an old hotel bathrobe. Then she swaddled her child in the towel and silently left her room. On the other side of the basement, the furnaceman snored on his pallet. Gritting her teeth, Ethel limped to the stairs.

The second floor was too low, and the third seemed uncertain. To be safe, she would have to get to the fourth floor. Her legs trembled, and spears of pain shot through the center of her body. She was weeping and groaning when she reached the third floor, but for the sake of the baby forced herself to keep mounting the stairs. At the fourth floor, she opened the door to the empty, gas-lit hallway and leaned panting against the frame. Sweat stung her eyes. Ethel staggered into the corridor and moved past numbered doors until she reached the elevator alcove. Opposite the closed bronze doors, two large casement windows looked out onto Erie Street. She hugged the baby to her chest, struggled with a catch, and pushed the window open.

Cold air streamed in, and the baby tugged his brows together and scowled. Impulsively, Ethel kissed the top of his lolling head, then settled her waist against the ridge at the bottom of the casement. She gripped the baby beneath his armpits, and the towel dropped onto her feet. The baby drew up his legs and kicked, as if rejecting the cold. A bright, mottled pink covered his face like a rash. His mouth was a tiny red beak. One of his eyes squeezed shut. The other slid sideways in a gaze of unfocused reproach.

Gripping his sides, Ethel extended her arms and moved his kicking body through the casement. She could feel the ribs beneath his skin. The bottom of the frame dug into her belly. Ethel took a sharp inhalation and prepared to let go by loosening her grip. Instantly, unexpectedly, he slipped through her hands and dropped into the darkness. For a moment briefer than a second, she leaned forward, open-mouthed.

What happened to her in the moment she watched her baby fall away toward the Erie Street sidewalk is the reason Ethel Carroway returns to the window on the fourth floor of the Oliphant Hotel.

A doorman found the dead infant half an hour later. By the start of the morning shift, the entire staff knew that someone had thrown a baby from an upper window. Policemen went from room to room and in a maid's basement chamber came upon an exhausted young woman stuffing bloody sheets into a pillowcase. Despite her denials of having recently given birth, she was arrested and given a medical examination. At her trial, she was condemned to death, and in April 1893, Ethel Carroway departed from her earthly state at the end of a hangman's rope. During the next two decades, several fourth-floor guests at the Oliphant remarked a peculiar atmosphere in the area of the elevators: some found it unpleasantly chilly even in the dog days, others said it was overheated in winter, and Nelly Tetrazelli, the "Golden Thrush," an Italian mezzo-soprano touring the northern states with a program of songs related to faerie legend, complained that a "nasty, nasty porridge" in the elevator alcove had constricted her voice. In 1916, the Oliphant went out of business. For three years, the hotel steadily deteriorated, until new owners took it over; they ran it until 1930, when they went broke and sold the building for use as a boarding school for young women. The first sightings of a ghostly figure on the fourth floor were made by students of the Erie Academy for Girls; by 1948, when the academy closed its doors, local lore had supplied the name of the spectral figure, and a year later, when the Oliphant opened yet again, Ethel Carroway began putting in regular appearances, not unlike Nelly Tetrazelli, the "Golden Thrush." Over the decades, Ethel acquired a modest notoriety. The Oliphant devotes a long paragraph of its brochure to the legend, an undoubtedly idealized portrait of the revenant hangs above the lobby fireplace, and a bronze plaque memorializes the site of the crime. Guests with amateur or professional interests in the paranormal have often spent weeks in residence, hoping for a glimpse, a blurry photograph, a sonic, tape-recorded rustle. (None have ever been granted their wish.)

Ethel Carroway does not reappear before her window to increase her fame. She does it for another reason altogether. She's hungry.

I have told you of bad Boy and the thousand eyes fixed upon the Shining Boy, and alluded to a secret. In the same forthright manner with which I introduced myself, I shall now introduce the matter of the wondrous secret, by laying it out upon the methaporical table. All throughout my life I possessed a crystalline but painful awareness of my superiority to the common man. To put it squarely: I understood that I was better than the others. Just about *all* the others.

A fool may say this and be ridiculed. A madman may say it and be bedlamized. What befalls the ordinary-seeming mortal whose great gifts, not displayed by any outward show, he dares proclaim? He risks the disbelief and growing ire of his peers—in humbler words, spitballs, furtive kicks and knocks, whispered obscenities, and shoves into muddy ditches, that's what. Yet—and this must be allowed—*that the mortal in question is superior has already aroused ire and even hatred amongst those who have so perceived him.* Why was I the focus of Boy Teuteburg's psychopathic rage? And why did my fellow kidlings not defend me from our common enemy? *What inflamed our enemy, Boy, chilled them.* It would have been the same had I never generously taken pains to illuminate their little errors, had I never pressed home the point by adding, *and I know this because I'm a lot smarter than you are.* They already knew the deal. They had observed my struggle to suppress my smiles as I instructed our teachers in their numerous errors, and surely they had likewise noted the inner soul-light within the precocious classmate.

Now I know better than to speak of these matters (save in privileged conditions such as these). In my mid-twenties I gave all of that up, recognizing that my life had become a catastrophe, and that the gifts which so elevated me above the run of mankind (as the protagonists of the great *Poe* know themselves raised up) had not as it were elevated my outward circumstances accordingly. The inward soul-light had dimmed and guttered, would no longer draw the attacks of the envious. Life had circled 'round and stolen what was most essentially mine.

Not all ghosts are dead, but only the dead can be counted on for twenty-twenty vision. You only get to see what's in front of your nose when it's too late to do you any good.

At that point, enter hunger.

My life had already lost its luster before I understood that the process of diminishment had begun. Grade school went by in the manner described. My high school career, which should have been a four-year span of ever-increasing glories culminating in a 4.0 average and a full scholarship to a Harvard or even a College of William and Mary, ground into a weary pattern of C's and D's hurled at me by fools incapable of distinguishing the creative spirit from the glib, mendacious copycat. In his freshman year, young Frank Wardwell submitted to the school literary magazine under the pen name Orion three meritorious poems, all of which were summarily rejected on the grounds that several of their nobler phrases had been copied down from poets of the Romantic movement. Did the poets own these phrases, then? And would then a young chap like Frank Wardwell be forbidden to so much as *utter* these phrases in the course of literary conversations such as he never had, due to the absence of like-minded souls? Yes, one gathers, to the editors of a high school literary magazine.

I turned to the creation of a private journal in which to inscribe my exalted thoughts and far-flung imaginings. But the poison had already begun its deadly work. Brutal surroundings and moral isolation had robbed my pen of freshness, and much of what I committed to the page was mere lamentation for my misunderstood and friendless state. In coming from the depths to reach expression, the gleaming heroes with cascading blond hair of my high-arching thoughts met the stultifying ignorance about me and promptly shriveled into gat-toothed dwarves. The tales with which I had vowed to storm this world's castles and four-star hotels refused to take wing. I blush to remember how, when stalled in the midst of what was to be a furious vision of awe and terror, my talent turned not to Great Imagination for its forms but to popular serials broadcast at the time over the radio waves. *The Green Hornet* and *Jack Armstrong, the All-American Boy*, my personal favorites among these, supplied many of my plots and even, I grant, some of my less pungent dialogue.

A young person suffering the gradual erosion of his spirit cannot be fully aware of the ongoing damage to his being. Some vestige of the inborn wonder will beat its wings and hope for flight, and I saw with weary regularity the evidence that I was as far superior to my fellow students at Edna Ferber High as I had been at Daniel Webster State Graded School. As before, my well-intentioned exposures of intellectual errors earned me no gratitude. (Did you really imagine, Tubby Shanks, you of the quill-like red hair and carbuncled neck who sat before me in sophomore English, that Joyce Kilmer, immortal author of "Trees," was necessarily of the female gender for the sole reason that your mother and sister shared his Christian name? My rapierlike witticism that Irish scribe James Joyce must then be a sideshow morphadite did not deserve the blow you addressed to my sternum, nor the wad of phlegm deposited atop my desk at close of day.) True, I had no more to fear the raids of Boy Teuteburg, who had metamorphosed into a sleek ratty fellow in a tight black overcoat and pearl gray snapbrim hat and who, by reason of constant appointments in pool halls, the back rooms of taverns, and the basements of garages, had no time for childish pursuits. Dare I say I almost missed the attentions of Boy Teuteburg? Almost longed for the old terror he had aroused in me? That his indifference, what might even have been his lack of recognition, awakened nameless but unhappy emotions on the few occasions when we ancient enemies caught sight of one another, me, sorry, I mean I, dragging through our native byways at the end of another hopeless day at Edna Ferber, he emerging from an Erie Street establishment known as Jerry's *Hotcha!* Lounge, his narrow still-red eye falling on mine but failing to blaze (though the old terror did leap within me, that time), then my immemorial foe sliding past without a word or gesture to mark the momentous event? At such times even the dull being I had become felt the passing of a never-to-be-recovered soul-state. Then, I had known of my preeminence and nurtured myself upon it; now, knowing of it still, I knew it did not make an ounce of difference. Boy Teuteburg had become a more consequential person than Francis T. Wardwell. I had seen the shades of the prison house lowered 'til nearly all the light was blocked.

Soon after the unmarked momentousness, two other such yanked them all the way down.

After an unfortunate incident at school, admittedly not the first of its kind, involving the loss of a petty sum on the order of six or seven dollars from a handbag left hanging on a lunchroom chair, the meaningless coincidence of my having been seated adjacent to the chair from which hung the forgotten reticule somehow led to the accusation that I was the culprit. It was supposed, quite falsely and with no verification whatsoever, that I had also been responsible for the earlier incidents. I defended myself as any innocent party does, by declining to respond to the offensive accusations. I did possess a small, secret store of money, and when ordered to repay the careless slattern who had been the real source of the crime, I withdrew the wretched seven dollars from this source.

Humiliated, I chose to avoid the hostile stares and cruel taunts surely to greet me in our school's halls, so for some days I wandered the streets, squandering far too many quarters from my precious cache in diners and movie theaters when supposed to be in class, then reporting as ever to Dockweder's Hardware, where, having passed down my broom to a shifty urchin of unclean habits, I was entrusted with the stocking of shelves, the fetching of merchandise to the counter, and, during the generally inactive hour between 4:30 P.M. and 5:30 P.M., the manipulation of the cash register. After the fifth day of my self-imposed suspension from academe, Mr. Dockweder kept me after work as he ostentatiously balanced the day's receipts, the first time I had ever seen him do so, found the *awesome*, the *majestic* sum of $1.65 missing from the cash tray, and immediately charged me with the theft. Not the boyish mistake of returning a surplus of change to an impatient customer or hitting a wrong button when ringing up a sale, but the theft. I protested, I denied, alas in vain. Then look to the boy, I advised, I believe he steals from the stockroom, too, fire him and the pilfering will cease. As if he had forgotten my seven years of unstinting service, Mr. Dockweder informed me that sums of varying amounts had been missing from the register many nights during the period when I had been entrusted with its manipulation between the hours of 4:30 P.M. and 5:30 P.M. He demanded I turn out my pockets. When I did so, he smoothed out one of the three bills in my possession and indicated on its face the check mark he had placed upon each bill in the register before entrusting it to my charge.

In all honesty, check marks are entered upon dollar bills hundreds of times a day, and for hundreds of reasons. I have seen every possible sort of symbol used to deface our nation's currency. Mr. Dockweder, however, would accept none of my sensible explanations. He insisted on bringing me home, and gripped my shoulder in an iron clamp as we took to the streets. Within our shabby dwelling, he denounced me. My denials went unheard. In fact, I was trembling and sweating and undergoing a thousand torments, for once or twice I had dipped into the register and extracted a quarter, a dime, a penny or two, coins I assumed would never be missed and with which I could sustain myself through the long day. I even *confessed* these paltry lapses, thinking to improve the situation with a show of honest remorse, but this fearless candor did nothing of the kind. After remunerating Dockweder from his own skimpy reserve of cash, my father announced that I personally would make good the (inflated) sum and learn the ways of the real world. He was sick of my airs and highfalutin' manners, sick of my books, sick of the way I talked—sick of me. From that day forth I should work. As a dumb beast works (my father, an alcoholic welder, being a prime example of the species), without hope, without education, without letup, without meaning, and with no reward save an inadequate weekly pay packet.

Reeling from the depth and swiftness of my fall, that evening after the welder and his weeping spouse had retired I let myself out of our hovel and staggered through the darkness. What I had been, I scarcely knew; what I now was, I could not bear to contemplate; what I was to become, I could not imagine. On all sides life's prison house rose up about me. In that prison house lay a grave, and within that grave lay I. The streets took me, where I knew or cared not. At intervals I looked up to behold a dirty wall, a urine stain belt-high beneath a broken warehouse window, a mound of tires in a vacant lot. These things were *emblems*. Once I glimpsed a leering moon; once I heard the shuffle of feet close by and stopped in terror, sensing mortal danger, and looked all 'round at empty Erie Street.

Bitterly, childhood's stillborn fantasies returned to me, their former glow now corpse gray. Never would I kneel in meadows and woods 'midst bird's-foot trefoil, daisy fleabane, devil's pulpit, Johnny-jump-up, jewelweed, the foxglove, and the small sundrop. Never would I bend an enchanted ear to the lowing of the kine, the tolling of bells in a country rectory, the distant call of the shepherd, the chant of the lark. Mountain lakes and mountain streams would never enfold me in their chill, breath-giving embrace. The things I was to know were but *emblems* of the death-in-life ranged 'round me now.

I lifted my all-but-unseeing eyes to the facade, six stories high, of the Oliphant Hotel, dark dark dark. Above the lobby, dimly visible through the great glass doors, the ranks of windows hung dark and empty in the darker brick. Behind those windows slept men and women endowed with college degrees and commercial or artistic skills, owners of property, sojourners in foreign lands, men and women on the inside of life. They would never know my name, nor would I ever be one of their Visible number. Radiantly Visible themselves, they would no more take note of me by daylight than at present—and if they happened to look my way, would see nothing!

A figure moved past an upper window, moved back and then reappeared behind the window. Dark dark dark. A guest, I imagined, wandering sleepless in the halls, and thought to turn away for my long journey home. Some small awareness held me, looking up. High above behind a casement window hovered a figure in black garb, that figure, I now observed, unmistakably a woman's. What was she doing, why was she there? Some trouble had sent one of the gilded travelers roaming the Oliphant, and on that trouble she brooded now, pausing at the window. Recognizing a fellow being in misery akin to my own, I brazenly stepped forward and stared up, silently demanding this woman to acknowledge that, despite all that separated and divided us, we were essentially the same. White hands twisted within her black garment. We were the same, our world the same, being dark dark dark. Perhaps the woman would beckon to me, that we each could soothe the shame of the other. For streaming from her vague figure was shame—so I thought. An oval face emerged from shadow or from beneath a hood and neared the glass.

You shall see me, you shall, I vowed, and stepped forward once again. The alabaster face gazed at a point some five feet nearer the hotel than myself. I moved to meet her gaze, and just before doing so experienced a hopeless terror far worse than anything Boy Teuteburg had ever raised in me. Yet my body had begun to move and would not stop when the mind could not command it. Two mental events had birthed this sick dread: I had seen enough of the alabaster face to know that what I had sensed streaming out was something far, far worse than shame; and I had suddenly remembered what the first sight of this figure at this window of this hotel would have recalled had I been in my normal mind—the legend of the ghost in the Oliphant. Ethel Carroway's eyes locked on mine and scorched my innards. I could not cry out, I could not weep, with throat constricted and eyes singed. For a tremendous moment I could not move at all, but stood where her infant had fallen to the pavement and met her ravishing, her *self-*

ravishing gaze. When it was over—when she released me—I turned and ran like a dog whom wanton boys had set on fire.

The following day my father commanded me to go to McNair's Fine Clothing and Draperies and inquire after a full-time position. He had recently done some work for Mr. Harold McNair, who had spoken of an opening available to an eager lad. Now that my circumstances had changed, I must try to claim this position and be grateful for the opportunity, if offered. I obeyed the paternal orders. Mr. Harold McNair indeed had a position available, the position that of assistant stockboy, hours 7:30 A.M.–6:00 P.M., Monday–Saturday, wages @ $0.45/hr., meals not supplied. He had thought the welder's boy might be responsive to his magnanimity, and the welder's boy, all that remained of me, was responsive, yes sir, Mr. McNair, sir. And so my endless drudgery began.

At first I worked to purchase, at the employee rate, the shirts and trousers with which an assistant stockboy must be outfitted; and for the next twenty-nine years I spun long hours into dress shirts and cravats and worsted suits, as Rumpelstiltskin spun straw into gold, for a McNair's representative must advertise by wearing the very same articles of clothing offered its beloved customers. I had no friends. The only company I knew was that of my fellow employees, a half-brained lot devoted to sexual innuendo, sporting events, and the moving pictures featuring Miss Jean Harlow. Later on, Wallace Beery and James Cagney were a big hit. Even later, one heard entirely too much of John Wayne. This, not forgetting the pages of our Sunday newspaper wasted upon the "funnies," was their culture, and it formed the whole of their conversation. Of course I held myself apart. It was the old story repeated once again, as all stories are repeated again and again, eternally, just look around you. You are myself, and I myself am you. What we did last week, last year, what we did in our infancy, shall we do again tomorrow. I could take no delight in the gulf dividing my intellect from theirs, nor could my fellow workers. Doubtless all of them, male and female alike, secretly shared the opinion expressed during our Christmas party in 1955 by Austin Hartlepoole, an accounting junior who had imbibed too freely of the fish-house punch: "Mr. Wardwell, have you always been a stuck-up jerk?"

"No," I might have said, "once I was a Shining Boy." (What I did say is of no consequence.)

By then I was Mr. Wardwell, note. The superior qualities that condemned me to social and intellectual isolation had seen me through a series of promotions from assistant stockboy to stockboy, then head stockboy, thence laterally to the shipping department, then upward again to counter staff, Shirts and Neckwear, followed by a promotion literally upstairs to second floor, counter staff, Better Shirts and Neckwear, then assistant manager, Menswear, in time manager, Menswear, and ultimately, in 1955, the year soon-to-be-sacked Hartlepoole called me a stuck-up jerk, vice president and buyer, Clothing Divisions. The welder's boy had triumphed. Just outside of town, I maintained a large residence, never seen by my co-workers, for myself and a companion who shall remain nameless. I dressed in excellent clothing, as was to be expected. A gray Bentley, which I pretended to have obtained at a "price," represented my single visible indulgence. Accompanied by Nameless Companion, I regularly visited the Caribbean on my annual two-week vacation to occupy comfortable quarters in the same luxurious "resort" hotel. By the middle of the nineteen fifties, my salary had risen to thirty thousand dollars a year, and in my regular banking and savings accounts I had accumulated the respectable sum of forty-two thousand dollars. In another, secret account, I had amassed the even more respectable sum of three hundred and sixty-eight thousand dollars, every cent of it winkled away a little at a time from one of the worst people, in fact by a considerable margin actually the worst person, it has ever been my misfortune to know, my employer, Mr. Harold McNair.

All was well until my transfer to Better Shirts and Neckwear, my "ascension," we called it, into the vaulted splendors of the second floor, where affluent customers were spared contamination by the commoners examining cheaper goods below, and where Mr. McNair, my jailer-benefactor of years ago, was wont to appear from the depths of his walnut-paneled office, wandering between the counters, adjusting the displays, remarking upon the quality of a freshly purchased tweed jacket or fox stole (Ladies' was sited across the floor), taking in the state of his minions' fingernails and shoes. Mr. McNair, a smallish, weaselish, darkish, baldish figure in a navy suit, his solid red tie anchored to his white shirt with a visible metal bar, demanded courteous smiles, upright postures, hygienic habits. Scuffed shoes earned an errant clerk a sharply worded rebuke, unclean nails an immediate trip to the employee washroom. The dead thing I was did not object to these simple, well-intentioned codes. Neither did I object to my employer—he was but a fixed point in the universe, like his own God enthroned in His heavens. I did not take him *personally*. Not until my "ascension," when we each fell under the other's gaze.

Living Visibles like Harold McNair do not expect merely to be seen. Though they be discreetly attired, quietly spoken, and well-mannered, within they starve, they slaver for attention and exact it however they must. In Mr. McNair's case, this took the form of divisiveness, capriciousness, sanctimoniousness and, for lack of a better word, tyranny. He would favor one counter clerk, then another, thereby creating enmity and rivalry and an ardent wish in two hearts to comprehend his own heart. He would select an obscure minion for weeks of special treatment, jokes, confidences, consultations, then without explanation drop the chosen one back into obscurity, to be pecked to death by his peers. He drew certain employees aside and whispered subtle criticisms of their dearest friends. Throughout, he searched for his true, secret favorites, those whose contempt for themselves, masked behind a smooth retailer's manner, matched his own for them, masked behind the same. In time I began to think of Harold McNair as a vast architectural structure something like his great store, a building charmingly appointed with fine though not ostentatious things, where a smiling but observant guide leads you ever deeper in, deciding room by room if you have earned the right to behold the next, by stages conducting you into chambers growing successively smaller, uglier, eventually even odorous, then through foul, reeking sties, and at last opens the final door to the central, the inmost room, the room at the heart of the structure, the most terrible of all, and admits you to—the real Mr. Harold McNair.

He knew I was his the first time he saw me behind the Better Shirts counter on the second floor. He may have known it on the day he hired me, long years before. In fact, he might even have regarded the alcoholic welder laboring in his basement and seen that this man's son, if he had one, would be his as if by Natural Law. His in the sense of easily flattered, thus easily dominated. Ready to be picked up by a kind word and downcast by a harsh one. Capable of attentive silences during the Great Man's monologues. Liable to be supine before power, abject before insult. A thorough and spineless subordinate. A kind of slave. Or, a slave. Long before my final promotion, I had been shown into the final room and met the true Harold McNair. I knew what he was and what I was. In many ways, I had fallen under the sway of a smoother, more corrupt Boy Teuteburg, a Boy who thought himself a noble being and wore the mask of a dignified, successful man of business.

I accepted this. But I had determined to be paid well for the role.

My thefts began with an impulsive act of revenge. I had just departed Mr. McNair's office after a session in which the whip lashed out more forcefully than was customary from within the velvet bag, both before and after my employer had expressed his apocalyptic disgust for womankind, those sly scented obscenities, those temples of lust, et cetera, et cetera. Making my way granite-faced through Better Gowns, I observed an elderly temple of lust depositing her alligator bag upon the counter as she turned to scrutinize a bottle-green Better Gown with Regency sleeves. A wallet protruded slightly from the unclasped bag. Customer and saleslady conferred in re the wisdom of Regency sleeves. My legs took me past the counter, my hand closed on the wallet, the wallet flew into my pocket, and I was gone.

Heart athud, I betook myself to a stall in the male employees' washroom, opened the wallet, and discovered there sixty-eight dollars, now mine. I had been rash, I knew, but to what an electric, unharnessed surge of life force! All I regretted was that the money had been the temple's, not Mr. McNair's. I left the stall and by reflex stepped up to the sinks and mirrors. Washing my spotless hands, I caught my face in the mirror and froze—a vibrant roguish Visible a decade younger than I looked back with blazing eyes, my own.

Anyone in a business that receives and disburses large amounts of cash will eventually devise a method for deflecting a portion of the moolah from its normal course. Some few will test their method, and most of those will be found out. A primitive snatch and grab like mine, unobserved, is as good as any. During my tenure in the store, many employees located the imperfections in their schemes only as the handcuffs closed around their wrists. (Mr. McNair never showed mercy or granted a second chance, ever.) From the moment I met my living eyes in the washroom mirror, I was withdrawing from the cash available an amount appropriate to my degradation, or *stealing my real salary*. All that remained was to work out a method that would pass undetected.

Many such methods exist, and I will not burden you with the details of mine, save to reveal that it involved a secret set of books. It proved successful for better than two decades and yielded a sum nearly compensatory to my endless humiliation. Mr. McNair knew that significant quantities of money were escaping his miserly grasp but, despite feverish plotting and the construction of elaborate rat-traps, could not discover how or where. The traps snapped down upon the necks of minor-league peculators, till tappers, shortchange artists, bill padders, invoice forgers, but never upon his greatest enemy's.

On the night I placed my hundred thousandth unofficial dollar in my secret account, I celebrated with a lobster dinner and a superior bottle of champagne in our finest seafood restaurant (alone, this being prior to the Nameless Friend era) and, when filled with alcohol and rich food, remembered that the moon was full, remembered also my night of misery so long ago, and resolved to return to the Oliphant Hotel. Then, I had been a corpse within a grave within a prison; now, I was achieved, a walking secret on the inside of life, an invisible Visible. I would stand before Ethel Carroway and be witnessed—what had been written on her face now lay within me.

I walked (in those pre-Bentley days) to Erie Street and posted myself against a wall to await the appearance of the shade. By showing herself again to me, she would acknowledge that the intensity of my needs had raised me, as she was raised, above the common run. Mine was the confidence of a lover who, knowing this the night his beloved shall yield, savors each blissful, anticipated pleasure. Each moment she did not appear was made delicious by its being the moment before the moment when she would. When my neck began to ache, I lowered my chin to regard through enormous glass portals the Oliphant's lobby, once a place of unattainable luxury. Now I could take a fourth-floor suite, if I liked, and present myself to Ethel Carroway on home ground. Yet it was right to stand where I had before, the better to mark the distance I had come. An hour I waited, then another, growing cold and thirsty. My head throbbed with the champagne I had taken, and my feet complained. My faith wavered—another trial in a test more demanding with every passing minute. Determined not to fail, I turned up the collar of my coat, thrust my hands in my pockets, and kept my eyes upon the dark window.

At times I heard movement around me but saw nothing when I looked toward the sound. Mysterious footfalls came teasingly out of the darkness of Erie Street, as if Ethel Carroway had descended to present herself before me, but these footfalls were many and varied, and no pale figure in black appeared to meet my consummating gaze.

I had not understood—I knew nothing of Visibles and those not, and what I took for confidence was but its misshapen nephew, arrogance. The cynosure and focus of myriad pairs of unseen eyes, I surrendered at last after 3:00 A.M. and wandered sore-footed home through an invisible crowd that understood exactly what had happened there and why. In the morn, I rose from the rumpled bed to steal again.

Understanding, ephemeral as a transcendent insight granted in a dream, ephemeral as *dew*, came only with exposure, which is to say with loss of fortune and handsome residence, loss of Nameless Companion, of super-duper Bentley, of elegant sobersides garb, of gay Caribbean holidays on the American Plan, loss of reputation, occupation (both occupations, retailer and thief), privacy, freedom, many constitutionally guaranteed civil rights, and, ultimately, of life. As with all of you, I would have chosen these forfeited possessions, persons, states, and conditions over any mere act of understanding, yet I cannot deny the sudden startling consciousness of a certain piquant, indeterminate pleasure-state, unforeseen in the grunting violence of my last act as a free man, which surfaced hand in hand with my brief illumination. This sense of a deep but mysterious pleasure linked to my odd flash of comprehension often occupied my thoughts during the long months of trial and incarceration.

I had long since ceased to fear exposure, and the incarnadine (see *Shakespeare*) excess of exposure's aftermath would have seemed a nightmarish impossibility to the managerial Mr. Wardwell, stoutly serious and seriously stout, of 1960. Weekly, a gratifying sum wafted from Mr. McNair's gnarled, liver-spotted grip into my welcoming hands, and upon retirement some ten stony years hence I expected at last to float free in possession of approximately one and a quarter million dollars, maybe a million and a half. My employer's rat-traps continued to snap down on employees of the anathema stripe, of late less frequently due to widespread awareness of the Byzantinely complex modes of surveillance which universally "kicked in" at the stage beneath the introduction of my invented figures, on account of their having been set in place by the very anathema they were designed to entrap. Had not the odious McNair decided upon a storewide renovation to mark the new decade, I should after twenty, with luck twenty-five, years of pampered existence in some tropic clime and sustained experience of every luxury from the highestly refined to basestly, piggishestly sensual, have attained upon death from corrupt old age an entire understanding of my frustrated vigil before the Oliphant, of the walkers and shufflers I had heard but were not there, also of Ethel Carroway and her refusal to recognize one who wrongly supposed himself her spiritual equal. But McNair proceeded upon his dubious inspiration, and I induced a premature understanding by smashing the fellow's brains into porridge—"nasty, nasty porridge"—with a workman's conveniently disposed ballpeen hammer.

The actual circumstances of my undoing were banal. Perhaps they always are. A groom neglects to shoe a horse, and a king is killed. A stranger hears a whisper in an ale-house, and—a king is killed. That sort of thing. In my case, coincidence of an otherwise harmless sort played a crucial role. The dread renovation had reached the rear of the second floor, lapping day by day nearer the accounts room, the art department, and the offices, one mine, one Mr. McNair's. The tide of workers, ladders, dropcloths, yardsticks, plumb lines, sawhorses, and so forth inevitably reached our doors and then swept in. As my employer lived above the store in a velvet lair only he and his courtiers had seen, he had directed that the repaneling and recarpeting, the virtual *regilding*, of his office be done during normal working hours, he then enduring only the minor inconvenience of descending one flight to be about his normal business of oozing from customer to customer, sniffing, adjusting, prying, flattering. As I owned no such convenient bower and could not be permitted access to his, not even to one corner for business purposes, my own office received its less dramatic facelift during the hour between the closing of the store, 6:00 P.M., and the beginning of overtime, 7:00 P.M. A task that should have taken two days thus filled ten, at the close of every one of which, concurrent with my official duties, I had to manage the unofficial duties centered on the fictive set of books and the disposition of the day's harvest of cash. All this under the indifferent eyes of laborers setting up their instruments of torture.

Callous, adamantine men shifted my desk from port to starboard, from bow to stern, and on the night of my downfall informed me I had to jump ship posthaste that they might finish, our boss having lost patience with this stage of affairs. I jumped ship and bade farewells to departing employees from a position near the front doors. At 6:55 P.M. I made my way through the familiar aisles to my office door, through which I observed Harold McNair, on a busybody's journey from the sultan's quarters above, standing alone before my exposed desk and contemplating the evidence of my various anathematic peculations.

The artisans should have been packing up but had finished early and departed unseen by the rear doors; McNair should have been consulting his genius for depravity in the velvet lair but had slithered down to ensure their obedience. We were alone in the building. As Mr. McNair whirled to confront me, a combination of joy and rage distorted his unpleasant features into a demonic mask. I could not save myself—he knew exactly what he had seen. He advanced toward me, spitting incoherent obscenities.

Mr. McNair arrived at a point a foot from my person and continued to berate me, jabbing a knobby forefinger at my chest as he did so. Unevenly, his face turned a dangerous shade of pink, hot pink I believe it is called. The forefinger hooked my lapel, and he tugged me deskward. His color heightened as he ranted on. Finally he hurled at my bowed head a series of questions, perhaps one question repeated many times, I don't know, I could not distinguish the words. My being quailed before the onslaught; I was transported back to Dockweder's. Here again were a marked bill, an irate merchant, a shamed Frank Wardwell—the wretched boy blazed forth within the ample, settled, secretive man.

And it came to the wretched boy that the ranter before him resembled two old tormentors, Missus Barksdale and Boy Teuteburg, especially the latter, not the sleek rodent in a pearl gray hat but the red-eyed bane of childhood who came hurtling out of doorways to pummel head and body with sharp, accurate, knifelike fists. I experienced a moment of pure psychic sensation so foreign I could not at first affix a name to it. I knew only that an explosion had taken place. Then I recognized that what I felt was pain, everlasting, eternal pain long self-concealed. It was as though I had stepped outside my body. Or *into* it.

Before me on my oaken chair lay a ballpeen hammer forgotten by its owner. The instant I beheld this utilitarian object, humiliation blossomed into gleeful revenge. My hand found the hammer, the hammer found Mr. McNair's head. Startled, amazed even, but not yet terrified, Mr. McNair jumped back, clamoring. I moved in. He reached for the weapon, and I captured his wizened arm in my hand. The head of the hammer tapped his tough little skull, twice. A wondrous, bright red feeling bloomed in me, and the name of that wondrous feeling was Great Anger. Mr. McNair wobbled to his knees. I rapped his forehead and set him on his back. He squirmed and shouted, and I tattooed his bonce another half-dozen times. Blood began to drizzle from his ears, also from the abrasions to his knotty head. I struck him well and truly above the right eye. At that, his frame twitched and jittered, and I leaned into my work and now delivered blow after blow while the head became a shapeless, bloody, brain-spattered... *mess*. As the blows landed, it seemed that each released a new explosion of blessed pain and anger within Frank Wardwell; it seemed too that these blessings took place in a realm, once known but long forgotten, in which emotion stood forth as a separate entity, neither without nor within, observable, breathtaking, utterly alive, like Frank Wardwell, this entranced former servant swinging a dripping hammer at the corpse of his detested and worshiped enemy. And there arose in an unsuspected chamber of my mind the remembered face of Ethel Carroway gazing down at but in fact not seeing the disgraced boy—me on Erie Street, and, like a reward, there arrived my brief, exalted moment of comprehension, with it that uprising of inexplicable, almost intellectual pleasure on which I chewed so often in the months ahead. Ethel Carroway, I thought, had known this—this shock—this *gasp*—

Into the office in search of a forgotten hammer came a burly tough in a donkey jacket and a flat cap, accompanied by an even burlier same, and whatever I had comprehended blew away in the brief cyclone that followed. Fourteen months later, approximately dogging Ethel Carroway's footsteps, I moved like a wondering cloud out of a sizzling, still-jerking body strapped into our state's electric chair.

The first thing I noticed, apart from a sudden cessation of pain and a generalized sensation of lightness that seemed more the product of a new relationship to gravity than actual weight loss, was the presence in the viewing room of many more people than I remembered in attendance at the great event. Surely there had been no more than a dozen witnesses, surely all of them male and journalists by profession, save two? During the interesting period between the assumption of the greasy hood and the emergence of the wondering cloud, thirty or forty onlookers, many of them female, had somehow crowded into the sober little room. Despite the miraculous nature of my exit from my corporeal self, these new arrivals paid me no mind at all. Unlike the original twelve, they did not face the large, oblong window looking in upon the even smaller, infinitely grimmer chamber where all the action was going on.

I mean, although the obvious focus of the original twelve, one nervously caressing a shabby Bible, one locking his hands over a ponderous gabardine-swathed gut, the rest scratching "observations" into their notebooks with chewed-looking pencils, was the hooded, enthroned corpse of the fiend Francis T. Wardwell, from which rose numerous curls and twists of white smoke as well as the mingled odors of urine and burned meat, these new people were staring at *them*—the Bible-stroker and the warden and the scribbling reporters, really *staring* at them, I mean, lapping up these unremarkable people with their eyes, *devouring* them.

The second thing I noticed was that except for the thirty or forty male and female shades who, it had just come to me, shared my new state, everything in the two sober chambers, including the green paint unevenly applied to the walls, including the calibrated dials and the giant switch, including the blackened leather straps and the vanishing twists of smoke, including even the bitten pencils of the scribes, but most of all including those twelve mortal beings who had gathered to witness the execution of the fiend Francis T. Wardwell, mortal beings of deep, that is to say, radiant ordinariness, expansive overflowing heartbreaking throat-catching light-shedding meaning-steeped—

The second thing I noticed was that everything—

At that moment, hunger slammed into me, stronger, more forceful, and far more enduring than the river of volts that had separated me from my former self. As avid as the others, as raptly appreciative of all you still living could not see, I moved to the glass and fastened my ravenous gaze upon the nearest mortal man.

Posted beside the blazing azalea bush on Boy Teuteburg's front lawn, I observe, mild word, what is disposed so generously to be observed. After all that has been said, there is no need to describe, as I had intended at the beginning of our journey, all I see before me. Tulip Lane is thronged with my fellow Invisibles, wandering this way and that on their self-appointed rounds; some six or seven fellow Invisibles are at this moment stretched out upon Boy Teuteburg's high-grade lawn of imported Kentucky bluegrass, enjoying the particularly lambent skies we have at this time of year while awaiting the all-important, significance-drenched arrival of a sweet human being, Tulip Lane resident or service personage. These waiting ones, myself included, resemble those eager ticket buyers who, returning to a favorite play for the umpty-umpth time, clutch their handbags or opera glasses in the dark and lean forward as the curtain rises, breath suspended, eyes wide, hearts already trilling, as the actors begin to assemble in their accustomed places, their dear, familiar words to be spoken, the old dilemmas faced once again, and the plot to spin, this time perhaps toward a conclusion equal to the intensity of our attention. Will they get it right, this time?

Will they *see?* No, of course not, they will never see, but we lean forward in passionate concentration as their aching voices lift again and enthrall us with everything they do not know

Boy is an old Boy now in his eighties I believe, though it may be his nineties—distinctions of this sort no longer compel—and, wonderfully, an honored personage. He ascended, needless to say without my vote, into public life around the time of my own "ascension" to the second floor, and continued to rise until a convenient majority elected him mayor shortly before my demise, and upon that plateau he resided through four terms, or sixteen years, after which ill health (emphysema) restrained him from further elevation. His mansion on Tulip Lane contains, I am told, many rooms—seventeen, not counting two kitchens and six bathrooms. I do not bring myself here to admire the mansion of my old adversary, now confined, I gather, to an upper floor and dependent on a wheelchair and an uninterrupted flow of oxygen. I certainly do not report to Tulip Lane at this time of the day to gloat. (Even Boy Teuteburg is a splendid presence now, a figure who plants his feet on the stage and raises his brave and frail voice.) I come here to witness a certain moment.

A little girl opens the door of the room beyond the window next to the azalea. She is Boy Teuteburg's youngest grandchild, the only offspring of the failed second marriage of his youngest child, Sherrie-Lynn, daughter of his own failed second and final marriage. Her name is Amber, Jasmine, Opal, something like that—Tiffany! Her name is Tiffany! Tiffany is five or six, a solemn, dark-haired little personage generally attired in a practical one-piece denim garment with bib and shoulder straps, like a farmer's overalls but white, and printed with a tiny, repeated pattern, flower, puppy, or kitten. Food stains, small explosions of ketchup and the like, provide a secondary layer of decoration. Beneath this winning garment Tiffany most often wears a long-sleeved cotton turtleneck, blue or white, or a white cotton T-shirt, as appropriate to the season; on her feet are clumsy but informal shoes of a sort that first appeared about a decade or two ago, somewhat resembling space boots, somewhat resembling basketball sneakers; in Tiffany's case, the sides of these swollen-looking objects sport pink check marks. Tiffany is a sallow, almost olive-skinned child in whom almost none of her grandfather's genetic inheritance is visible. Whitish-gray streaks of dust (housekeeping has slacked off considerably since Mayor Teuteburg's retirement to the upper floor) can often be observed on her round, inward-looking little face, as well as upon the wrinkled sleeves of her turtleneck and the ironic pastoral of the white overalls.

Smudgy of eye; streaky with white-gray dust; sallow of skin; dark hair depending in wisps and floaters from where it had been carelessly gathered at the back, and her wispy bangs unevenly cut; each pudgy hand dirt-crusted in a different fashion, one likely to be trailing a single footlong blond hair, formerly her mother's; introspective without notable intelligence, thus liable to fits of selfishness and brooding; round of face, arm, wrist, hand, and belly, thus liable for obesity in adulthood; yet withal surpassingly charming; yet gloriously, wholly beautiful.

This little miracle enters the room at the usual hour, marches directly to the television set located beneath our window, tucks her lower lip beneath her teeth—pearly white, straight as a Roman road—and snaps the set on. It is time for the adventures of Tom and Jerry. By now, most of those Invisibles who had been sprawled on the Kentucky blue have joined me at the window, and as matters proceed, some of those who have found themselves on Tulip Lane will wander up, too. Tiffany backpedals to a point on the floor well in advance of the nearest chair. The chairs have been positioned for adults, who do not understand television as Tiffany does and in any case do not ever watch in wondering awe the multiform adventures of Tom and Jerry. She slumps over her crossed ankles, back bent, clumsy shoes with pink check marks nearly in her lap, hands at her sides, round face beneath uneven bangs dowsing the screen. Tiffany does not laugh and only rarely smiles. She is engaged in serious business.

Generally, her none-too-clean hands flop all anyhow on her flowered denim knees, on her pink-checked feet, or in the little well between the feet and the rest of her body. At other times, Tiffany's hands go exploring unregarded on the floor about her. These forays deposit another fine, mouse-gray layer of dust or grime on whatever sectors of the probing hands come in contact with the hardwood floor.

During the forays, the small person's face maintains a soft immobility, the soft unconscious composure of a deep-diving rapture; and the conjunction of softness and immobility renders each inner delight, each moment of identification or elation, each collusion between drama and witness—in short, you people, each emotion that would cause another child to roll giggling on the floor or draw her smeary fists up to her face, each emotion is rendered *instantly visible*—written in subtle but powerful runes on the blank page that is Tiffany's face. As the eerie tube-light washes over this enchanted child's features, her lips tighten or loosen; an adult frown redraws her forehead; mysterious pouches 'neath her eyes swell with horror or with tears; a hidden smile tucks the corners of her mouth; joy leaps candlelike into her eyes; the whole face irradiates with soul-pleasure. I have not even mentioned the dreamy play brought over the wide cheeks and the area beneath the eyes by thousands of tiny muscle movements, each invoking the separate character, character as in fictional character, of a piquant, momentary shadow.

And from time to time, a probing hand returns to base and alights on a knee, a space shoe, wanders for a second through the dangling wisps, hesitates, and then, with excruciating patience, approaches the opening mouth and, finger by finger, enters to be sucked, tongued, warmed, above all cleaned of its layers of debris. Tiffany is eating. She will eat anything she finds, anything she picks up. It all goes into her mouth and is absorbed into Tiffany. Cookie crumbs; dust; loose threads from who knows what fabric; now and then a button or a coin. When she is through with her fingers, she might graze over the palm. More often, she will extend a newly washed forefinger and push it into a nostril, there to rummage until a glistening morsel is extracted, this morsel unhesitatingly to be brought to the portals of the mouth and slipped within, then munched until it too has been absorbed into the Tiffany from whence it came.

We watch so intently, we crowd so close, thrusting into the azalea, that sometimes, having heard a dim version of what twice I heard on Erie Street, she yanks her eyes from the screen and glances upward. She sees but a window, a bush. Instantly, she returns to the screen and her ceaseless meal. I have given you Ethel Carroway letting fall her child, and I have given you myself, Frank Wardwell, battering in a tyrant's brains; but no riper spectacle have I summoned to the boards than Tiffany. She embraces and encompasses living Ethel and living Frank, and exactly so, my dear ones, does Tiffany embrace and encompass you.

"The Fooly" copyright © 2008 by Terry Dowling. First published in *Dreaming Again*, edited by Jack Dann (Harper Voyager: New York). Reprinted by permission of the author.

"The Toll" copyright © 2000 by Paul Walther. First published in *New Genre #1*, Spring 2000. Reprinted by permission of the author.

"The Pennine Tower Restaurant" copyright © 2010 by Simon Kurt Unsworth. First published in *Lost Places* (Ash-Tree Press: British Columbia, Canada). Reprinted by permission of the author.

"Distress Call" copyright © 1991 by Connie Willis. First published in *The Berkley Showcase: New Writings in Science Fiction and Fantasy, Vol. 4*, edited by John Silbersack and Victoria Schochet (Berkley: New York). Reprinted by permission of the author.

"The Horn" copyright © 1989 by Stephen Gallagher. First published in *Arrows of Eros*, edited by Alex Stewart (New English Library: London, England). Reprinted by permission of the author.

"Everybody Goes" copyright © 1999 by Michael Marshall Smith. First published in *The Third Alternative 19*. Reprinted by permission of the author.

"Transfigured Night" copyright © 1995 by Richard Bowes. First published in *Tomorrow Speculative Fiction*, April 1995. Reprinted by permission of the author.

"Hula Ville" copyright © 2004 by James P. Blaylock. First published in *SCIFICTION*, November 3, 2004. Reprinted by permission of the author.

"The Bedroom Light" copyright © 2007 by Jeffrey Ford. First published in *Inferno*, edited by Ellen Datlow (Tor Books: New York). Reprinted by permission of the author.

"Spectral Evidence" copyright © 2007 by Gemma Files. First published in *The Chiaroscuro e-zine 31*. Reprinted by permission of the author.

"Two Houses" copyright © 2012 by Kelly Link. First published in *Shadow Show: All New Stories in Celebration of Ray Bradbury*, edited by Mort Castle and Sam Weller (Gauntlet/Borderlands, Harper Perennial: New York). Reprinted by permission of the author.

"Where Angels Come In" copyright © 2005 by Adam L. G. Nevill. First published in *Poe's Progeny*, edited by Gary Fry (Gray Friar Press: West Yorkshire, England). Reprinted by permission of the author.

"Hunger, An Introduction" copyright © 1995 by Peter Straub. First published in *Peter Straub's Ghosts*, edited by Peter Straub (Pocket Star Books: New York). Reprinted by permission of the author.